# Sagebrush Sojourn

## by

## Maeve Kim

Cover Art by *Teddi Black*

The Wild Rose Press, Inc.
PO Box 708
Adams Basin, NY 14410-0708
Visit us at www.thewildrosepress.com

Publishing History
First Edition, 2026
Trade Paperback Print ISBN 978-1-5092-6439-1
Digital ISBN 978-1-5092-6440-7

Published in the United States of America

# Dedication

With thanks to the warm and welcoming people of central Montana.

Chapter One

The station master looked like a ferret. He sat inside his little cage with the metal bars, hunched over the money he was counting, his sharp nose twitching and his little ferret hands stained with ink and dirt. He held up one bony finger to indicate that Caleb should wait. And after far too many minutes, the ferret lifted small black eyes.

"Whatchawant?"

"I'm here to pick up a T.E. Barrington. He came on the last stage."

The beady little eyes shifted to the clock on the wall over the door.

"Stage come 'most an hour ago."

"I realize that. I was delayed. Please direct me to T.E. Barrington."

"Bench outside. South side."

Caleb turned on his heel. Two long-legged strides carried him across the tiny station, but he wasn't fast enough to miss the ferret's parting shot.

"Was there last I knows, anyways. But that was 'most an hour ago."

Caleb shoved the door open, made his way around the side of the station, and stopped dead. Only one person was on the bench, and it was a woman. A girl. She was sitting upright, her back stiff, her head turned away from him. There were two good-sized leather Gladstone bags and a trunk at her feet, and a smaller valise next to her.

****

Back home in Boston, the temperature might reach the seventies on a late May afternoon. Women, if they were outside at all, would be carrying parasols or waving intricately painted fans. Some would have on sheer lawn dresses, although it was more proper to keep those in storage for another month. Others would have gowns of dimity or dotted Swiss or one of the flowered calico fabrics that were beginning to gain popularity. But here in Montana, where Teddy was to spend the next several months, she had on a high-necked and long-sleeved traveling dress of heavy brown cotton, with a full-length checkered duster to protect her dress during the long days on train and stagecoach. A wool shawl was wrapped tightly around her shoulders and, of course, she had on dark gloves and a traveling bonnet with a full veil. And under it all her travel corset, a bit less constricting than most, and chemise, pantalets, and two petticoats—and she could still feel the biting wind.

Corset, she thought, trying to get a deep breath of the prairie air that smelled so different from city air. Back home in Boston, she would have to wear a corset all summer, no matter how hot and humid the day. Here on the frontier, she promised herself that the uncomfortable garments were going into her trunk as soon as the weather warmed up. She had work to do, and working women shouldn't be trussed up like a country ham.

She had more than four months ahead of her, four months in this vast open land, four months without the smells and the sounds of the city. No wheels rattling over cobblestones. No street urchins begging for coins. No paper boys bawling out the headlines from every corner. No dramatic temples of worship with their bells pealing out every hour, a cacophony she found delightful at times and irksome at others. Hours and hours when there might be no noise at all save the wind and the birds. Four months doing work she had trained for, work she loved.

Four months in that vast open prairie that started just beyond the town. She shivered with delight and anticipation, so lost in gazing at the emptiness that she didn't hear the man approaching.

"Miss?"

She started, turned, and found herself looking at filthy work pants and a large brass belt buckle. She jerked her head up, past broad shoulders to a weathered face that looked as if it hadn't known anything like a smile in the last decade. The man lifted his broad-brimmed hat, revealing wavy hair the sooty brown color of black walnut dye.

"Yes?"

"I am looking for a gentleman who's waiting to be picked up."

"Oh! Yes!" She stood up in a flurry of skirts and travel dust. "My grandfather, no doubt. He will be back within a few minutes. He walked down the street to get a newspaper, and maybe something to eat and drink."

His stony expression didn't change, so Teddy tried a tentative version of her best smile. "We haven't had a mid-day meal, you see. And it's getting quite late."

Caleb did not like where his thoughts were going. He did not like it one bit. The famous ornithologist would not have brought a girl with him all the way from Boston. That was impossible. A girl would be nothing but a nuisance. Not one of the five men on the ranch

3

would have time or energy to watch over a girl, leastwise not a city girl with her fancy hat and gloves and little boots with white pearl buttons.

His already tight lips tightened still more under a neatly trimmed mustache.

"T.E. Barrington? Is that your grandfather?"

"Theodore Barrington. Yes. And I am Theo*dora* Barrington. I'm usually called Teddy. Are you here to take us to Long Butte Ranch?"

Caleb briefly closed his eyes. The day had just finished its dismal progression from too busy to frustrating, to irritating, to infuriating.

Teddy looked up at the man's closed face and felt a twinge of pity. He seemed slow to understand her words. Perhaps he was dull-witted. Perhaps the owner of the ranch sent this man into town to pick up the visitors and kept his more capable workers back with him. She noticed now that he was filthy, his tight pants covered with mud, blotches of mud on his frayed flannel shirt, even some on the bottom of his chin.

"My grandfather and I. We are the ornithologists?" She was appalled to hear herself making a question of what should have been a statement. She had not come all this way west, to the frontier, to behave like one of the weak and simpering lasses she despised back home. "We are the ornithologists that have contracted with Long Butte Ranch. And you are?"

The man grunted. Actually grunted. Then his eyes shifted to over her head, and Teddy turned with relief to see her grandfather approaching with a newspaper under his arm, a cardboard box wrapped in twine in one hand and a canning jar in the other.

"Mr. Barrington?"

"Professor Barrington. And you are—?"

"Caleb Asher. Wagon's this way." The man hefted their trunk and one of the big Gladstone bags as if they weighed nothing and stalked off.

Teddy could not believe her ears. The taciturn and filthy cowboy could not possibly be the forward-thinking rancher who had contracted with the famed Boston Birding Alliance to have the most prominent ornithologist in the country stay at his ranch all summer and do a comprehensive census of birds of grasslands and mountains.

She met her grandfather's eyes. "I thought he might be half-witted," she murmured. "I now believe he is merely surly."

"Well, Teddy my dear, we do not need him to be charming. We will be fine if Rancher Asher provides us with temporary lodging and meals, as agreed, and a means of getting out into the countryside to do our work."

He picked up the other bag, she picked up her valise, and they followed the rancher across the rutted road. By the time they caught up with him, their heavier luggage was stowed in the back of a large, red-painted buckboard, and the man was waiting, scowling and impatient.

"You ready?"

"Pardon?"

Before Teddy realized what he was about to do, the rancher had both hands on her waist and had deposited her unceremoniously in the buckboard's bed.

Her skirts and petticoats flew up, giving him a close-up view of long legs clad in dark stockings, and all the way up to the lace on her white, uh, underthings. Caleb wanted to hit something, hard. He wanted to howl. This morning, hours and hours and frustrating hours ago, he left home before dawn so he would have plenty of time for the Choteau house with the orange paint. It had been three weeks now, and he needed the kind of relief and intense pleasure he knew awaited him in that house. He thought about it all along the dirt road from the ranch. He was so deep in the anticipation of delight that he didn't notice the mud until it was too late. It took him three hours to get the rig unstuck. Three hours when he could have been with that new brown-haired girl, or that older woman who knew so many ways to make a man moan.

He needed that. He did not need to feel curves under his hands when he lifted the professor's granddaughter, and he definitely did not need to see under her skirts. He was furious at fate, furious at the mud, furious at the girl, and furious at his own enthusiastically-responding body.

He jumped up into the wagon bed beside her and roughly hauled her to her feet. Then he stomped forward, opened two wooden storage boxes and emptied them onto the floor. One of the piles looked like old clothes and fur. The other appeared to be a fishing net like those Teddy saw on the Boston docks.

"Sit between the boxes. Some blankets under, some on top."

He was moving so quickly, with such tight-lipped determination, that she felt a similar sense of haste. She hurriedly folded two blankets, laid them on the floor, and plopped down with her back against the front board and her legs straight out before her. The fishing net was now stretched across the wagon from side to side. She wanted to say something to show she wasn't just an unthinking and unwanted piece of luggage, to show she understood the net was to keep things from sliding off the back, but the man had already jumped down and was heading for the high driver's seat.

"Up here with me, sir—Er—Professor. You need help?"

"I can manage."

The buckboard lurched as the two men climbed up and lurched again as the horses started moving.

"You might want to hold onto the seat, sir—Er—Professor. We'll be moving fast if we want to get to the ranch before supper."

He made chirping noises to the horses. As the wagon picked up speed, Teddy was grateful for the securely fastened boxes on either side of her. She pulled blankets around her and then reached out and added the motley fur. It looked like a variety of animal skins loosely sewn together: glossy black, dull black, brown, gray-brown, tan. Two sections were untanned leather, looking very much like... No. Surely they wouldn't use horses for leather...

On the other hand, maybe nothing got wasted out here.

She wiggled around and peered under the high seat to look at the animals pulling the buckboard. They were much bigger than carriage horses back in Boston, gigantic glossy black animals with long tails and manes. In Boston, only the wealthiest young women rode horses in the parks. But here in Montana, she would get to touch the huge beasts. Yes! What a wonderful idea! Before the summer ended, Teddy vowed that she would sit up there on that high seat and she would direct a team of horses! And she would not be wearing a corset while she did so!

She felt a gentle tap on the top of her head.

"Teddy? I was able to obtain three small pasties with meat inside. Reach a hand up and I will give you one."

The pie was about the same size as her palm, still warm, with a golden crust.

"Thank you, Grund."

"There are three pies and three of us. This one, I do believe, is destined for our driver."

"Not necessary."

"You will be feeding us for weeks, Mr. Asher. It is only right that we feed you something now."

"You are paying me to feed you."

"To be accurate, the Boston Birding Alliance is paying you. That is, however, beside the point. We have three pies, there are three of us. Therefore, this pie is yours."

There was a pause during which Teddy wondered if the surly rancher was going to refuse yet again. Then, a growled *Thank you.*

"Teddy, my dear, we also have a jar of cider. Let me know when you would like some."

She had never in her life shared a glass of water or a cup of tea with anyone else. Now both her grandfather and a stranger would put their mouths where she would place hers. She wondered if Rancher Asher chewed tobacco or smoked cigars or had rotting teeth, or possessed any other disgusting characteristic that she might be able to taste in the cider. But she was no longer in Boston. She would drink the cider and maybe taste a stranger and count it as one of the many new experiences she could never have back home.

She settled back, wedging herself in more tightly. A warm pie in her hand, cider available to wash it down, and all around her vast open space. No houses, no streets, no sidewalk signs advertising pubs and cure-alls and ladies' clothing. No noise but the sounds of the horses' hooves, the occasional creaking of the animals' harnesses, and the wind.

"May I ask a few questions about Long Butte Ranch?" Professor Barrington must have taken the rancher's grunt as a yes, for he continued. "Has the ranch been in your family for long?"

"The original homesteader was my father. My brother and I ranched it with him when we got old enough."

"Does your brother still run the ranch with you?"

"He has a ranch of his own now. Colorado."

"And your parents?"

"My mother left when my brother and I were young." He made a quiet noise in his throat and the horses picked up speed. "My father's dead. Nine years now."

"I am sorry to hear of your loss, Mr. Asher."

Another grunt, and a few minutes of quiet. Alone in the back of the wagon, Teddy knew that her grandfather would not let much time pass before he asked for additional information.

"What is the distance between your ranch and the town of Choteau?"

Teddy turned her head slightly to hear the answer.

"Under ten miles. But we can't go the most direct way. Mud."

"Ah. I presume you had trouble with mud earlier today."

There was a harsh sound that could have been a laugh. "You presume correctly, sir—Professor. We had a wet spring. The wagon got bogged down. Took me almost three hours to free it."

Oh. That explained why he was late picking them up.

"I take it that a wet spring is not exactly the norm here?"

"There is no norm here, s—Professor. Not in Montana. Tomorrow might feel like spring. Two days later, three feet of snow."

"Your letter warned us, and I believe we have made adequate preparations."

Another grunt.

"How far out of the way must you go to avoid the muddy section?"

"We'll be going a little over eight miles by road, three more cross-country."

"I see."

Teddy leaned her head against the board below the two men, her eyes and mind full of the immensity of the landscape. They were traveling in a broad valley with ridges on either side, rocky and bare of trees and so unlike the hills and mountains back east that she wanted to hug herself and send loud hosannas into the crystalline air. Several prominences were capped by sheer vertical walls that looked like medieval parapets. She'd have to ask Grund if the walls were volcanic in origin. But now she wanted to look around her and feel the wind and smell—What was that smell? She sat up straighter. The sides of the hills were gray-green with foliage. Sage! She was sure of it!

Back in Boston, sage was added to stuffing at Thanksgiving. Here in Montana, it was growing all around them, knee-high and filling the air with aroma. It would not matter one whit if their host were surly. He could glare at her. He could grunt and growl. He could answer every one of her questions in single syllables for the whole four and a half months. She didn't care. She was here, in Montana, and she could smell wild sage all around her.

Interesting man, though. He apparently ran a large ranch and cared enough about the wildlife to contract for an ornithological study. He was quite good-looking, in a rugged sort of way, of average height but broad-shouldered and strong. She tried in vain to imagine him in the black wool trousers, narrow black suspenders and brocade vests that men were wearing this year back in Boston.

Those muddy pants he had on were probably jeans. Even people in Boston knew about jeans. She'd seen advertisements for them, the brand name proudly displayed over a sketch of two horses trying to pull apart a pair of pants. Jeans were made of stiff material called denim, with double-sewn seams and metal rivets. They were advertised for working men. *Men.* But Teddy vowed that she would get herself a pair of jeans even if she had to wear them only in the privacy of her room.

The rancher's jeans were not only muddy. They were tight. No one in Boston would wear pants that tight. Not even the sailors. Not even the low life that hung out near the bars, the coarse men her grandfather warned her about. He always referred to tight clothing, on men or women, as *leaving nothing to the imagination.*

Well, that might be true for a married woman. She had been given an eyeful of the man's masculine parts when he was standing in the buckboard, above her, but she had no experience on which to build an accurate mental picture of that part of a man's body. She remembered seeing a drawing of a statue somewhere in Greece, but the smooth little marble protrusion on the statue's front would not have made a bulge like that in the front of the rancher's jeans.

A private and mischievous smile tipped up one corner of her mouth. Another goal for her months in Montana: Find an occasion that would let her get a better look at a man's body. At fourteen months short of twenty, she was too old to be ignorant.

Chapter Two

A crow-sized bird flew across the dirt track behind the buckboard, a bird with an absurdly long down-curved bill. Teddy sat up straighter. A long-billed curlew! Her first Montana bird! There were no long-billed curlews in New England, but Teddy recognized it immediately and she whispered a thank you to Abigail Brooks, the fellow member of the Boston Birding Alliance who worked at the Harvard Library and had unearthed a decade-old list of birds in central Montana.

And now there were more birds in the distance, scores of birds dappling a long flat lake that gleamed like molten silver in the slanted light.

"Freezout Lake." Her grandfather half-turned and gently shook her shoulder. "We should plan to spend at least five or six days there, my dear. A few during spring migration and several more in July and August, for shorebirds."

"Ducks, grebes, and shorebirds. I can't wait."

The sun was low in the sky, and the wind was increasing. Teddy felt deliciously snug in her nest of blankets and furs, but the two men on the high seat in front were at the mercy of the elements. Her grandfather had his heavy canvas overcoat. Did the rancher have anything but damp and muddy jeans and a flannel shirt? Maybe he was wearing long johns. She remembered seeing something off-white in the open neck of his shirt.

Proper lady Bostonians did not speculate about a man's underclothing. But maybe out here in Montana, women could speculate on anything that caught their fancy. She was smiling when she felt another touch on her shoulder.

"Teddy, my dear. Turn around, so you can enjoy your first view of Long Butte Ranch."

They were passing under a wooden arch with the ranch name carved deeply into thick logs. The sun, now low in the sky to their left, lit the wide valley and cluster of buildings, making every line and edge stand out sharp and clean against the distant forested ridge. At first glance, the entire homestead looked small, huddled together in all that space, under all that sky. But as the buckboard drew closer, Teddy saw that the two red barns, surrounded by paddocks and log fences, were bigger than any she had seen from the train or the stagecoach. A long flat building and several sheds lay between the house and the barns, all painted the same dark red. At each end of the cluster of buildings was a small log cabin. The main house, in the middle, was two stories tall, foursquare, glossy white and unadorned. She couldn't remember what her grandfather said about where they would be staying, and she wasn't at all sure she would enjoy sharing that grim white house with the grim rancher.

A half dozen horses in one of the paddocks lifted their heads to watch the wagon approach. Teddy didn't see any sign of humans until a loud clanging noise came from the direction of the main buildings, like the bells on Boston fire trucks. Then she noticed a man coming out of the flat building and another emerging from one of the barns.

"First supper bell," the rancher said. "Next bell, food's on the table."

He had the net out of the way and their luggage inside the larger of the two log cabins before Teddy finished struggling out of her sheltered nest and had the blankets folded and returned to the box. She sat on the edge of the wagon and jumped down before he could come back and lift her again.

"You two are in here. Two bedrooms. Work space. Stove's for heat, not cooking. Eat in the main house with the crew. There's stacked wood out back—" He glanced at Teddy. "Beside the outhouse."

She thought Mr. Asher expected a proper East Coast ladylike reaction. Eek. Oh no. An outhouse. Sniff. We don't have outhouses in Boston. We have indoor plumbing. Of gold and ivory. And decorated with precious gems.

When she didn't respond, he went on. "There's another privy in back of the main house, and another for the cabin on the far side. That's Ku-Long's. Inside the main building are two bath tubs and a wash tub. You don't have to carry hot water. Arthur rigged it so water heats next to the cook stoves and goes through pipes into the wash rooms."

"Indoor plumbing," Teddy murmured.

He scowled. "Of a sort. You can use the baths and wash tub any time. All the doors have latches."

"Excellent, Mr. Asher. This will do us very well. Everything is precisely as described in your letter. My dear," he turned to Teddy, "why don't you investigate the bedrooms and choose one?"

"I'm going to take care of the horses." Caleb backed out of the doorway and glanced up at the setting sun.

"Ku-Long'll be ringing the second bell soon. Use the side door, the one you can see from here." He started toward the buckboard. "Don't be late."

\*\*\*\*

Well, Caleb thought. This ought to be interesting.

He was drying his hands at one of the washstands in the mudroom when the two newcomers pushed open the side door. The three hired men were already seated, their hands and faces clean, their hair wet and combed back. The cook turned from the two huge black stoves, holding a cast-iron Dutch oven with both gloved hands, and froze.

It was never completely silent at mealtimes, except right now. Every man's eyes were fixed on the first woman ever to set foot in that kitchen. Caleb took a step closer to their guests.

"This here's Professor Barrington and his daughter. I told all of you the professor would be bringing an assistant. I had not realized at the time *he* would be a *she*. I expect all of us to treat Miss Barrington with the same care and respect as we do the mayor's wife, or the schoolmarm in town. Understood?"

Two of the seated men nodded and murmured something. The third, a wizened monkey of a man with blindingly white hair, just nodded.

"Good." Caleb lightly touched the shoulder of a beefy man with close-cropped yellow curls. "This here's my foreman, Hank. If you two ever have a question and can't find me, Hank's the man to go to." He nodded across the table to the dried-up little man. "That there's Arthur. He doesn't talk. Arthur's our handyman. He can fix anything and make anything. He also raises the chickens, ducks, and geese. And this youngster—" He laid his hand on the third man's shoulder. "This is Bucky. Looks like a kid but he's our horse expert and damn fine at it. Ku-Long over there is our cook. Many folks, me included, believe he's the best cook in the Montana Territory."

Ku-Long nodded gravely. He was dressed like the other men, in blue jeans and a flannel shirt, but he wore his sleek black hair in a braid that reached almost to his waist.

Teddy was surprised when the rancher pulled out a chair for her. "You sit here, with your grandfather next to you."

She sat down primly, a dimple in her right cheek. She would not have guessed that the surly rancher could be mannerly.

The silence continued as the cook set down the cast-iron pot and then huge ceramic bowls and large serving spoons. He opened one of the ovens, got out three loaves of dark bread and put them on a wooden cutting board, sliced all three loaves with a knife almost as long as his arm, and plopped the cutting board down in the middle of the table. He added pitchers of water and a blue-and-white coffeepot that stood almost two feet tall. With a last look at the table, the cook stood by the empty chair to Teddy's left.

The rancher looked at the laden table and the people sitting around it. He cleared his throat. Teddy waited to hear and be impressed by her first-ever cowboy prayer of grace.

"Bless this food."

And he plopped into a chair.

There was immediate noise and movement. The cook ladled stew and handed plates around the table.

Bowls of corn, coleslaw, and rice made the rounds, along with a large blue glass jar filled with clear liquid with chunks of something white and flecks of bright red. The men helped themselves to bread and mugs of steaming coffee.

Her grandfather took a forkful of stew, raised his eyebrows, and leaned closer to Teddy. "As good as any Boeuf Bourguignon in France." He took another bite. "I was inaccurate. This is superior to any I have ever tasted." He inclined his head toward the cook. "I salute you, sir. This is the best stew I have ever had the pleasure to savor. What is the wine you used?"

"Brandy. Some."

The kitchen was filled with the clink of cutlery against crockery, and food began disappearing from plates, serving bowls, and the cast-iron pot with impressive speed. Teddy noticed that only Hank, Caleb, and Ku-Long took anything from the blue glass jar standing tall in the middle of the table.

"Well," her grandfather muttered, "when in Rome..." He picked up the blue jar and forked out what looked like a pickled parsnip. One of the men sucked in his breath, and a hush fell over the room. The professor lifted the fork to his nose, sniffed, and took a tentative bite. He chewed. He swallowed. His eyes started to water. Then he saluted Ku-Long with what remained on his fork.

"This, sir, is a prodigious pickle." His usually deep and mellifluous voice was a breathless croak. "We have a hot condiment called horseradish back home in Boston. This puts horseradish to shame." He finished the pickle and put a second on his plate. "I may not be able to talk normally for the next hour, but I have to say that you have introduced me to a wonderful taste sensation. What is it called?"

"Is big head pickle. Hot spicy."

"Hot spicy indeed. Did you say Big Head?"

"Big head pickle. Yes."

Caleb tapped a long finger against the blue jar. "I understand that big head pickle in China is almost always made with long white radishes. Ku-Long sent a letter to China and one of his relatives sent some seeds, but he also pickles turnips, beets, and parsnips. At the end of every gardening season, Ku-Long pickles whatever we still have a lot of. Nothing gets wasted."

Aha, thought Teddy. So maybe that patch of leather on the coach blanket *was* from one of their horses. It might be wise to avoid questioning any unfamiliar food items. But she leaned closer and peered into the jar. "Hot red peppers?"

"Hot, yes." The cook fanned his mouth with one hand. "Salt too. Cider vinegar."

"Summers aren't long enough for peppers to ripen outdoors so Ku-Long and Arthur devised a glass house for hot red peppers and tomatoes." It was obvious from the warmth on the rancher's lean face that he both respected and liked the Chinese cook. "Those of us lucky enough to live on Long Butte Ranch eat better than anyone in the county."

There was a murmur of agreement around the table, and Ku-Long solemnly bent his head in acceptance.

"When we finish up here, professor, I will give you a map of the ranch. While I'm doing that, Ku-Long, would you show Miss Barrington where the lunch box is?" He met her eyes, and once again she thought he looked defensive, as if he anticipated a disparaging reaction. "There is no general mid-day meal. We are all too busy. You and your grandfather will do what everyone else does and take something with you each day."

"Of course," she murmured.

**\*\*\*\***

"This root cellar." Ku-Long pointed to deep shelves behind wire mesh. "This lunch box." He knelt and opened a cube made of rough slabs of wood, with LUNCH BOX painted on the top in barn red. "Always closed. Mice."

"Of course."

Inside the box were loaves of bread wrapped in brown paper, jars of jam, dried apples, and two tins of what looked and smelled like ginger snaps. There was also something that Teddy decided to think of as beef jerky.

"Get food here. Jars upstairs for water. Cider later in year."

"This will be excellent. Thank you, Ku-Long." Teddy looked around at the wooden shelves lining three walls of the cellar. "You do an astonishing amount of canning."

"Yes. Canning. Hungry men."

She ran her fingers over the raised lettering on a jar similar to the big head pickle jar at supper. "I have used this kind at home. Millville Atmospheric. I often have better luck with Victory jars, though."

"Victory. Good jars. Victory for applesauce, Meelveel for pickles."

"I will remember that."

Teddy had wondered many times about novel experiences she might have in Montana—but not once had chatting about pickles and fruit jars with a braid-wearing Chinaman even occurred to her.

****

"Well, my dear, we will most assuredly not starve out here in the wilds. That meal was as good as any I've had in Boston."

"As good as any, and more plentiful. I am astounded at how much those men ate, and how quickly."

"They work hard, my dear."

"Of course. And the air here in Montana must be conducive to a hearty appetite. I think I ate more than I ever eat at one meal."

They walked in comfortable silence toward their little log cabin.

"Montana is a long way from China, Grund."

"It is, my dear. It is. But Ku-Long is not alone here. Remember those copies of *The Choteau Montanian* we read before we left? That estimable publication estimated that one out of every ten people in the Montana Territory right now is Chinese."

"My goodness. I am astonished. What made them come so very far?"

"If memory serves me, large areas of China have been unsafe since the middle of the century. There have been Opium Wars, rebellions, droughts, even invasions. When gold was discovered in Montana, back in the sixties, hundreds of Chinese men came here and stayed on. I believe there is an entire town west of here that is almost exclusively Chinese, with their own neighborhoods, stores, and even temples."

"So men came here to search for gold. Did women come also?"

Even in the fading light, Teddy could see her

grandfather's bushy eyebrows come together in a frown.

"Ah. Women. When I left you at the station to look for some food, I saw a—a house."

"There were many houses in Choteau."

"I am of the opinion that one is a house of ill repute. There is a large window in the front, and two women were sitting behind it, dressed in—Well, I shall simply say they were not dressed like decent women."

"Oh."

"They were, I believe, Chinese. So, to answer your question, some women came here from mainland China, yes. And I believe many became, uh, women of the night."

"I see." She pushed open the door to their cabin. "Well, I am glad for Ku-Long that there are other people from his homeland here in Montana. But it must still be lonely for him living on an isolated ranch, in a foreign country, without a wife or family."

****

Teddy lay, wide awake, on what was to be her bed for the next four and a half months. She should have been exhausted but she couldn't fall asleep. There was nothing but silence. Silence for the first time since she and Grund left Boston. She thought her ears would never be free of the creak of leather, the sound of horses' hooves, the endless thunk-thunk-thunk of train wheels, the shrill cries of whistles. She could still feel the rocking of the train as they traveled from Boston to Helena. She could feel the stagecoach lurching, endlessly lurching. The Huntley Stage and Express Line was a ridiculously fancy name for anything so miserably uncomfortable. She would have bruises on her hip bones and elbows for weeks from the countless times she was thrown against the coach doors.

But it would take only one or two more meals on Long Butte Ranch before she put the endless series of tasteless meals behind her. Every single one of those meals had cost her grandfather a dollar for him and a dollar for her, first on the train and then at the coach stations that appeared out of the Montana wilderness every ten or fifteen miles. And now, for the next almost five months, they would have Ku-Long's delicious and filling meals every single day, for free.

Not free, she reminded herself. The meals were part of their payment. She and her grandfather had a job to do. A job she had studied for since her early teens when she began accompanying Grund to meetings of the Boston Birding Alliance, the only female there under forty-five. She had traveled with him to the Maine coast and to the White Mountains in New Hampshire to find and watch and enjoy birds they couldn't see in Boston. She had sat for hours in the Harvard Library as they read through the list of Montana birds prepared by Vermont naturalist Frank Hall Knowlton, making occasional comments as they took copious notes. She had studied those notes again and again, as had her grandfather, in the days before their journey and as they traveled westward.

And now she had an important job to do, at least for now. And after these Montana months, she hoped with all her soul to find another job, to continue using her learning to catalogue other birds and to continue making worthwhile contributions to science. Perhaps Frank Hall Knowlton himself would read her name on a scholarly paper someday. Perhaps he would contact her with a question or a comment, one ornithologist to another.

An owl hooted in the distance, the hollow stuttering sound of a great horned owl. It was answered, or challenged, by a long series of hoots that she thought might be a short-eared owl.

Or maybe not. They might make noise only during the day. She would have to ask Grund. She...

And she was asleep.

Chapter Three

"You have a map of the ranch now, Professor. Let me know each morning where you and your granddaughter will be working."

"Of course. For our first day, possibly the first two or three days, we plan to leave the ranch and head back along the road to that alkaline lake with the strange name."

"Freezout Lake." Teddy's interjection was somewhat distracted. She was watching with a mixture of veiled amazement and amusement as the beefy foreman Hank grabbed an empty bowl, covered the bottom with rice and then fried potatoes, crumbled bacon into it, added a thick layer of scrambled eggs, topped it all off with cabbage pickles that smelled as ferocious as the previous evening's offering—and then picked up a huge wooden spoon and dug in.

"Ah. Yes. Thank you, my dear. Freezout Lake is the only sizeable body of water nearby, and it will give us a chance to document birds that don't occur within the boundaries of Long Butte Ranch."

"Fine, as long as I know where you'll be. I have made a small wagon and a horse available to you, as agreed in our correspondence." The rancher nodded across the breakfast table at his oldest worker. "Arthur here will harness up."

"There is no need for him to ready the wagon and

horse for us. After today, I will go out to the barn before breakfast and prepare so we can leave as soon as we eat."

"Today you will go out to the barn with Arthur. He will be there to assist or give advice."

Teddy and her grandfather both understood the message. Before trusting them with the ranch's horse and wagon, Rancher Asher would make sure that at least one of them knew what to do.

****

"So, Grund? Did he talk?"

"What's that, my dear?"

"Did Arthur say anything this morning? Mr. Asher told us he never talks."

One corner of her grandfather's mouth lifted in an amused smile. "He did not talk. The enigmatic Arthur leaned against a stall and watched me like a hawk and made nary a sound." He looked at her out of the corner of his eye. "I should be at least marginally embarrassed to admit, my dear, that I did my best to try the man's patience. You would not believe how carefully I examined every single piece of tack. How long and hard I cogitated over which bits I wanted to use. How I moved at a veritable snail's pace from tack room to wagon. How I stared at the traces as if I might have seen something like them several decades ago, but I was not quite sure. I moved, my dear, slower than molasses in a Boston winter."

Teddy's eyes twinkled. "Just to see if he would say anything?"

"Exactly, my dear. I wanted to discover for myself at what point the silent man with the snow-white hair would not be able to stand another moment of silence."

"Grund. You are a wicked, wicked man."

"I am indeed. But Arthur outlasted me."

"Do you think he's actually mute?"

"I have no idea. But I am fascinated. The only mutes I have encountered have also been deaf, and it appears that Arthur hears very well. Ah! Here's the turn-off Mr. Asher mentioned."

**\*\*\*\***

"Oh you are a true beauty, you are." The pinto nudged her hand with its soft nose. "Your black is so very black, and your white is so perfectly white, and your overall pattern looks random but is absolutely perfect. I don't have any treats for you today, but I promise I will bring something tomorrow."

While Teddy made the pony's acquaintance, her grandfather reached into the back of the wagon and pulled out two folding chairs and what looked like a bundle of long sticks wrapped in mottled cotton.

"Come help me, my dear, and we can get this blind set up in no time."

It took considerably longer than either of them would have predicted, but at last they had the four long corner poles pushed deep into the soil, the cotton fabric unrolled, and the chairs set up where each of them could peer through a rectangular slit.

"We will get faster with experience, my dear. Of that, I am sure." He got his binoculars and one of the new cameras from the duffle bag at his feet. "Several waterfowl swam away while we were struggling with the blind, but they will return if there is no additional activity on our part."

"Yes." Teddy was speaking as quietly as he was. "Oh! Look straight out. What is that gray and white bird?"

"On the water?"

"No. It's—Yes. It's a marsh hawk! A male marsh hawk. How odd that our first Freezout Lake bird should be one we have seen in Massachusetts! Do you see it?"

"No."

"It's drifting about ten feet above the grasses. No, not drifting. It is floating. Floating and tilting right along the edge of the lake straight out from—"

"I've got it. Good eyes, my dear! Good eyes indeed. We probably won't see one on Long Butte Ranch so it is fortunate we can document one here."

Teddy leaned back a bit and opened her sketchbook.

"Ahh! Green-winged teal to our right, my dear," he whispered. "And both redheads and canvasbacks. Excellent! We shall be able to compare the two and document their similarities and their differences." He held the camera to the slit and clicked the shutter. "I would get better photographs if I stepped outside the blind, but I want us to document what's here before we scare anything away."

"This whole lake is—" She put her face against the fabric and peered in both directions. "This whole lake is a nursery, Grund! A duck and grebe nursery! Oh look! Shovelers! Just look at those bills! Aren't they extraordinary?"

"Teddy, my dear, we might add more than twenty species to our census while sitting right here."

For over two hours, the two ornithologists huddled in their canvas blind, both of them taking notes and Teddy making page after page of sketches. She crouched over her sketchpad, waiting patiently as three species of mergansers disappeared for minutes at a time and then came up with small fish and crayfish. She fell in love with baldpates, compact little ducks with brilliant green on the sides of their heads and blinding white on the tops. She could hardly wait to be back in their cabin with her colored pastels, decorating the sketches, showing the baldpate's green head patch and warm chestnut breast and the black on the tail, and the white bill with the dark little dot at the very end. She would carry her colors with her from now on, every day.

When a cinnamon teal drake lingered only yards from the blind, the professor could not resist. He cautiously stood up, cautiously stepped out of the blind, and took photo after photo as the teal fed on marsh grasses and occasionally plucked a long-legged water boatman insect off the surface. When he finally ducked back into the blind, he was grinning from ear to ear while at the same time rebuking himself for wasting precious film.

"Two photos of the teal would have been sufficient. Three would have been luxurious. But like a fool, I kept right on pressing that beguiling little button."

"At least you can be fairly certain of ending up with one or two good photos. Oh look, Grund! Those birds are walking on water! No! They are dancing on water!"

A pair of good-sized white birds dashed along the edge of the lake, both upright and facing in the same direction, their necks curved, their wings held up and back, their bills pointed skyward, their feet pattering in unison.

"Grebes. Western grebes, I am quite sure. Although Clark's grebes do the same kind of dance." The professor held up his binoculars, his chagrin over the egregious overuse of film temporarily forgotten. "Ah. Western grebes. Yes. The black cap extends down to enclose the eye."

The two birds simultaneously plopped down into the water, turned to face each other and took turns jerking their heads before rising up and doing the complex running ballet again.

"Grund," Teddy whispered. "The ducks are wonderful but these dancing grebes make the whole day perfect."

"Ahh! I do believe that's a Holboell's grebe only about two yards past the courting pair of Westerns. Yes. A little smaller, and just beginning to show its beautiful red-necked breeding plumage." The bird with the long russet neck made a loud whinny, answered almost immediately by a second. "Holboell's grebe. Yes. And in the far distance, is it... Yes, it is! One lone Clark's grebe. He'll be seeking a mate soon too."

"There's a smaller grebe closer to us, Grund. To our right. I think it's a pied-billed. Oh yes. What an adorable bird. It's cuddly!" Her hand flew over the sketchpad. "I know that's not a scientific description, but it is true. Oh! And is that a horned grebe? Just emerging from the vegetation to our left? Yes! Look at those blazing orangey-yellow tufts! What a handsome, handsome little bird!"

"If we were poker players, Teddy my dear, we could say we have been dealt a full house of grebes."

Another hour of watching and note-taking and sketching and occasional camera work, then Teddy sighed. "I hate to stop, Grund, but my fingers are getting too cold for any more drawings. Let's not eat our packed lunch here. Let's head back and eat in our cozy little cabin, next to our own woodstove."

"That is a magnificent idea, my dear. I am getting

chilled also. The sun is warm but that wind saps the body of heat." He stood up and stretched, and Teddy could hear a variety of creaks from his older joints. "I am happily anticipating a quick lunch by a hot stove, followed by a hot soak in one of those two bathing tubs, and then a short nap and one of Ku-Long's excellent suppers."

Teddy realized with a pang that her grandfather looked tired. Grund was never tired. Not ever. When they went birding along the coast of Maine, he outlasted men half his age. His thick hair had been white when she was very young, and it was still thick and white. She had believed, until that very moment, that he never looked any older, not in all the years she had known him, that he was miraculously standing still at the exact age he was when she was a child. But now he looked chilled, tired, and old. Next to this Montana lake, surrounded by waterfowl they could never have seen at home in Boston, Teddy realized for the first time that her grandfather was an elderly man, and she felt afraid.

****

She was restless. She didn't feel like a nap. They had eaten their lunch, along with hot cups of her grandfather's favorite English tea. Her frozen toes and fingers had thawed out, and the air here on the ranch was considerably warmer than back at Freezout Lake.

"Grund, I'll meet you at supper. I'm going to wander around a bit."

"You'll stay inside the log fence, won't you?"

"Of course." Her grandfather was sitting by the woodstove wrapped in a thick brocade robe that looked remarkably out of place here in the wilds of Montana. "As we drove in, I saw that young hand working with a horse in one of the paddocks. Bucky, that's his name. I would like to watch him for a while. And then I think I'll visit Ku-Long's garden and the glass house Mr. Asher mentioned. Maybe I can help by doing some weeding."

As Teddy walked toward the paddock, she could hear a horse's loud and agitated neighing, and under that noise a continuous low murmur. The animal looked wild, tossing its head, stamping its hooves, running to the far side of the paddock and then back, running right at the young man who looked so calm and who was talking to it in a constant stream of words.

"May I watch?"

"Sure, from there. Don't come no closer. Better if you sit on that rock." The young cowboy answered her in the same low, even murmur that he'd been using with the horse, as if his voice were part of the Montana wind and the Montana dust and was absolutely nothing for the skittish horse to fret about.

Teddy stopped a few yards from the paddock and sat. She made her voice as quiet as his. "Is this the unbroken dun mare you and Mr. Asher mentioned at breakfast?"

"Yes'm. Ain't she a beauty?"

"She is." The mare wasn't entirely the color that Teddy now knew was called dun. Her legs, mane, and tail were almost black, and there were reddish-brown dapples on her rump. She was considerably smaller than the huge horses that pulled the buckboard, and more delicately made.

"She's gonna be my beauty, boss said so, if'n I break her to saddle. And I'm gonna, acorse. She's pretendin' to be all tough and wild, ain'tcha, you beauty? But I knew first time I saw her she was gonna be a great saddle horse. I think she knew me, too. She knew the two of us'd be a team. Didn'tcha, beauty?" He looked over at Teddy. "I betcha I'll have a saddle on her by the middle of next week. And she'll be my own horse. My first own horse."

"Right now she seems a bit skeptical."

The horse again ran to the far corner of the paddock and then turned and charged back. Teddy gasped, but the young man stood his ground and the horse veered off at the last minute and stood, breathing hard, her eyes wild and wide.

"Sure she is. Everything's new, ya see. Scary. And she's all alone." He moved a few steps, not toward the skittish horse but to the side. "See, mustangs are herd animals. They're happy in a herd. Downright miserable without one. Lost, ya might say. See her afollowin' me with her eyes? This mare done lost her herd. But, see, I can be her herd. I can be a safe place for her. She don't know it yet, but she's gonna."

He moved three steps in the other direction. The mare backed up two steps and kept her eyes on him. "Not gonna crowd her. She's jest beginnin' to know that." Bucky took four steps backward. The mare fidgeted, snorted, tossed her head, and then moved a yard closer. "Been workin' with her six days now. First two days I kept shooing her away, not nasty-like, but just shooin'. Like, yes ma'am this is a herd but you cain't join it. Sorry, but that's just the way it is. Third day, shooed her some more but she started walkin' closer whenever I turned my back to her. Fourth day, had carrots in my pocket. She done smelled 'em and she come a little closer. And I let her. See, I was tellin' her she might have a chance to join my herd after all. Maybe so, maybe no.

I put a carrot down on the ground and she come closer and got it. She liked it, didn'tcha, you beauty?"

He reached into his side pocket, and the mare's ears pricked up.

"She's smart. She's lookin' right at my pocket. She liked the next day's carrot too. Came right up close so I coulda touched her with my hands. But I didn't. Not yet. I jest dropped the carrot in front of her and stood there like a fence post." He bent and picked up a short riding crop. "Yestuhday and today I been touchin' her with this whip. Ain't gonna whip her, not never ever. Jest usin' it as sumfin to touch her with. She might not be ready for a person's hands yet. But the whip's just a bit a cowhide." He stroked the handle of the crop along the mare's neck, barely touching. "See, she don't mind. She's thinkin' it feels sorta good, sorta like havin' another horse rest its head on her neck."

He turned his back on the horse and walked a few steps, and the mare followed.

"See, she's not just lookin' for carrots, though that's fer sure part of it. She's lookin' for some sign she has a herd again, she's not alone, see. But I'm the boss of this herd, not her. So now and tomorrow and the next few days we gonna dance. Ain't we, beauty? I'm gonna turn and walk away and she's gonna foller. I gonna touch her side and she gonna turn in that drecshun. I gonna walk toward her and she gonna walk backward. And then, after she done danced with me, then I gonna put this carrot that she's smelling on the ground and gonna stand real close and she'll consider for a while and then she'll snuffle up that carrot. And we be a step closer, won't we? We be a step closer to being a team."

Teddy sat, fascinated, wrapping her wool shawl

around her and watching the young man and the young mare. She lost track of the number of the times that Bucky approached and backed up, and the number of times the horse approached and danced sideways and got closer and backed up and then got closer again.

"'Course, I can't go riding her for a few months anyway. Acause she's carrying a foal. Don't look it yet but she's gonna get all round and barrel-bellied pretty soon. Fulla the wild stallion's git." He ran the handle of the crop along the mare's neck again. "See, her eyes don't look all wild no more, do they? She thinking oh yes I do like jest a bit of petting. You ready for a carrot, are you? I got two today. One right now and one a few minutes more. And mebbe I'll touch you with my hand before you get that one. Just mebbe. You almost ready, ain'tcha?"

The mare's eyes followed his hand as he slowly reached into his pocket, slowly brought out the carrot, and slowly bent and laid it on the ground. She looked twice at the man and twice at the carrot, and then she stretched out her neck as far as it would go and used her lips to bring the carrot closer so she could pick it up with her big teeth.

"That's right. Ain't gonna trick you with a carrot and then grab you, not ever ever. Safe with me, you are, you beauty."

Teddy thought that almost any wild animal would respond to Bucky's smooth, nonstop murmuring. And many humans would too.

"Tastes real good, don't it?" He angled just a bit so Teddy would know he was talking to her now, but he kept using the same velvety voice. "Useta think it'd be grand if we could bring in the stallion and get him to

35

accept a saddle. But now I seen him, out there where he belongs, I gotta agree with the boss. Leave him out there." He took two steps closer to the fence, and the mare followed. "He'll keep herd on his mares and he'll keep on breedin' foals that's got his lines and his spunk. And we'll keep on bringin' in some of those foals and making riding horses outa 'em. But not him. Not that wild stallion."

The sun was much warmer than it had been that morning, and both man and horse were coated in sweat. But the soft, even voice kept right on, unchanged, and the man was just as focused on the mare as the animal was on him.

"I was watchin' when that stallion mounted you, wasn't I, beauty? You didn't like it, not one itty bit. You tried to run but he caughtcha. Acourse he did. It ain't no wonder he got so many mares and those mares got so many foals. Just like that foal that's in yer belly right this very minute."

The difference between the mare now and the mare when Teddy first sat down was astonishing. The horse's ears were pricked forward. No white showed in her eyes. She was only a foot or two from the man but she looked more interested than panicked. And every single time Bucky turned and walked away, she followed, her nose almost touching his shoulder.

"Gonna stop this time. Gonna see what she does. Ah. I thought so. She wants to be part of my herd and this time, my beauty, I jest think I'll let you."

Teddy was surprised to find herself getting teary as the so-recently-wild animal nudged the man with her nose and snuffled around near his pocket. Bucky reached down without turning and ran his fingers along the side of the mare's face. Then he pulled out the second carrot and slowly, slowly, he turned to face his horse.

"As smart as your papa, ain'tcha? Here, you beauty. You earned this carrot, you truly did. And then I'll let you go and I'll fill your water trough and tomorrow we'll do some more dancing. And maybe I'll bring a fistful of oats. You gonna like that."

He reached out and laid his hand on the mare's neck.

"Smart as that stallion. And just as feisty. Little one's gonna be smart and feisty too." Bucky's hand was stroking the mare's neck while she placidly crunched the carrot. "Didn't you scream bloody murder when that stallion put that baby in you?" He moved his hand up toward her ears and she bent her head. "And no wonder 'cause that stud's got a thing long as my arm and just as thick. Musta hurt like the dickens, specially the first time and—"

Bucky suddenly stopped talking. He whirled to look at Teddy, and the startled mare wheeled and ran to the far side of the corral.

"Oh darn, oh darn, oh shucky darn! I weren't thinking, miss. I weren't thinking atall. I was concentratin' on her and I forgot you was here and I said things I shoulda never said and I'm so sorry. Oh gosh all Friday, the boss'll fire me fer sure."

"It's all right, Bucky. I understand. You were focused on doing your job." She stood up. "There's nothing to worry about. Really."

"You ain't gonna tell the boss?"

Teddy had a sudden mental picture of facing the dour rancher and telling him what she had learned that day about the size of the stallion's *thing*.

"I am, Bucky. I am going to tell your boss that you

gave me an impressive demonstration of gentle and effective mustang taming. And that he is as fortunate to have you as you all are to have Ku-Long."

The young man turned scarlet and apparently lost all power of speech, and Teddy grinned all the way to the gardens.

**\*\*\*\***

Grund was sitting on the bench in front of the cabin when Teddy got back from looking at the young vegetables and herbs.

"I saw you watching that young man and the mare."

"I was awed, Grund. I still am. That horse went from wild to almost tame in under an hour."

"I…" Her grandfather looked uncomfortable. "I have to admit, my dear, that I had not thought ahead to the possible complications of bringing you to a ranch."

"Complications?"

"You have had a most isolated upbringing, without the social interactions enjoyed by most young women your age."

Teddy sat down next to him. "I had a very happy upbringing, Grund."

"I believe you did, and I appreciate your saying so. But I would hate for you to… to overreact to your first exposures to young men."

"Grund!"

"I have no doubt at all that every man here has noticed that you are a most attractive young lady. I believe you have a level head on your shoulders, my dear. I do. But it is human nature for young women, even those with level heads, to have their heads turned by young men who admire them. I would mourn, my dear, if you were to be successfully wooed by an uneducated horse trainer or ranch foreman and waste your education being nothing but a ranch wife."

She patted his hand.

"Grund, there is no danger at all of my falling for the horse trainer. Bucky is a child. And as for the foreman Hank, huge beefy men do not attract me. Now the rancher—"

She watched with amusement as her grandfather turned with a scowl.

"Mmmm, yes. Rancher Asher," she cooed. "Now there is a man who just might turn my head. Handsome. Capable. And possessed of a personality we can only call enchanting."

The professor lifted her hand to his lips.

"It is not kind to tease an old man, my dear."

"I am sure you are right. But it is indeed enjoyable."

****

The rancher. Teddy could see him in her mind's eye as she got ready for bed. He was indeed pleasing to look at. Much more so than any man she met back in Boston.

But a ranch wife. Not likely!

Chapter Four

Caleb stopped his horse near the edge of the ridge and looked down into what he had named Lively Valley. The stream there was rarely more than a few yards wide and a few inches deep, but it ran year-round. In spring, summer, and fall, the cottonwoods and dogwood and willows hummed and hopped with insects and birds too many to count. Clean-flowing water and lush undergrowth attracted mule deer, big horned sheep, pronghorns, foxes, coyotes, skunks, rabbits, and hares, as well as the occasional badger, bobcat, and cougar. Caleb could not think of a better name for the valley than Lively.

Until today, he had avoided the parts of his sprawling ranch where the two Easterners were working. The fact that the two of them were there, in his kitchen, every breakfast and every evening meal was enough; he did not need to see them during the day as well. But he wasn't going to ignore a chore that had to be done just because he might catch sight of Miss Barrington and her professorial granddad. He had cattle to check on, and they were on the far side of Lively Valley.

The cart horse had been unharnessed and was hobbled in a patch of grass under the shade of a giant cottonwood. Good. One of them knew how to treat a ranch horse. Probably the professor. But what were the two of them doing? Caleb expected to see them walking around with binoculars, staring up into trees and down into the shrubs and grasses. Instead, they had set up the folding table that the professor shipped out before they arrived, and they were seated in folding chairs on either side of the table. The professor's gray head was bent, looking down at something he held in his cupped hands. The girl was looking down also, huddled into her heavy wool shawl, her red-brown hair almost hidden under what looked like her grandfather's fur hat.

Going on a month already. Almost a month with a female on the ranch. She hadn't caused any trouble. She was unfailingly sunny and pleasant and polite. She never chattered during meals and she always thanked Ku-Long before leaving the table. She had no complaints about their log cabin or the privy or the cold Montana spring weather or the never-ending wind.

But her presence was felt, every day, all day, by every man on the ranch. It was as if the very air around the ranch buildings swirled with invisible female particles that danced before the men's eyes and landed on their faces and were breathed into their lungs. Hank and Bucky had been to the orange house in Choteau every Friday, same as usual, but they'd also been every Tuesday, and even old Arthur went with them once.

Caleb wasn't comfortable leaving the ranch, not with a young woman staying there, so he was left with his imagination and his right hand, on those rare nights when he wasn't so tired that he fell asleep as soon as he hit the sheets. And every single time he could hear his mother telling him that the Bible strictly forbade that behavior, and he could see his father catch his eye and wink at him and his older brother Ike.

"If you two boys live out your lives *not* doing all the

things those men who wrote the Bible said you shouldn't be doing, and *doing* everything all those men said you *should* be doing, you would end up doing nothing but praying. Praying and planting a few date trees."

And, of course, their mother huffed and tightened her lips. *All those men* did not write the Bible. God did. Directly. Himself. Well, maybe He used men to write down the words but they were His words, not the words of mere humans.

And Caleb's dad would wink, again.

No doubt about it. Miss Barrington's presence on the ranch was felt every day, all day, and would probably be felt until the very moment she and her grandfather left.

He had no idea what the two ornithologists were doing down there. He hadn't heard any shots, so it seemed unlikely they had any birds in front of them to study. Caleb frowned and leaned forward on his patient horse. He scanned the area around the two visitors. Nothing in the wagon bed. Nothing on the ground that he could see. Suddenly furious, he touched his heels to his horse and cantered down the slope.

The girl looked up and beamed. "Good morning, Rancher Asher! And a glorious morning it is!"

"I told you both not to be out here without being armed."

"So you did." She straightened her shoulders, and one hand moved to the pocket in her skirt.

"And you decided to ignore me?"

She turned toward her grandfather. "Did we, Grund? Did we decide to ignore our kind and always genial host?"

Caleb shifted his gaze and found himself staring

down the muzzle of a shiny new Remington six gun.

"Would you like to see my gun also?" Miss Barrington asked sweetly. "Colt .31 caliber. Some folks call it a pocket Colt. I understand that it's not good for distance. But if a man were to get close to us, as close as you are, for instance, it could do quite a lot of damage." She pulled the little gun out of the top of her pocket and let her gaze drift down from Caleb's face to his midriff. "Quite a lot of damage indeed."

Caleb shifted uncomfortably in his saddle.

"I can shoot right through my skirt, so a man with nefarious intent wouldn't even see the gun until it was too late."

"I…" Caleb looked from one shining pistol to the other. "I am gratified that you are both so well-protected. I stand corrected."

"Actually, sir, you sit corrected."

He swung his leg over and dismounted.

"I stand corrected."

She dimpled at him and withdrew her hand from her skirt pocket. "You're just in time to see us release a rather irritated wood-pewee."

"Release? I understood ornithologists shot birds to study them."

"Most do. You are right. But there isn't a lot known about avian wildlife in your area. We don't want to risk killing a bird that might be part of a very small population. So we've been putting nets where birds are likely to be. We wait, and then we take the birds out of the nets and Grund does various measurements while I work on drawings."

Caleb walked closer and looked down at the pad in her lap. She had made a detailed pencil sketch labeled

*Western Wood-Pewee*, along with close-ups of the bird's head, an extended wing, and the tail. In one corner, there were numbers and words in a neat precise script.

"That looks very professional."

"Professorial, I am hoping. The Boston Birding Alliance has contracted with Harvard University Press to publish our findings. There will be particularly close scrutiny given to any publication that has a female co-author."

"I would have thought people on the East Coast were more enlightened."

"Hah." That near-snort would have been considered most unladylike back home in Boston. She was astonished that she'd made the noise so calmly. Perhaps she was becoming a true Montana woman. "There is one earlier listing of birds of central Montana, a draft of a paper due to be published this year. That one was compiled from anecdotal evidence and some dead bird specimens. Ours will be the first scientific census." She favored him with another glowing smile. "So you see, for several reasons, it is vitally important that all our data and all my drawings be as accurate as possible."

"Do you have the measurements for this pewee, my dear?"

"I do indeed, Grund."

"And we agreed to label the plumage colors medium gray, olive, and light gray?"

"I think that's the most accurate, yes. With an off-white belly and throat and white wing bars." She looked down at her notes. "Oh, and yellowy-orange lower mandible. And a little not-quite crest."

"Would you like a closer look before I release the little fellow?"

Caleb stepped closer to the table and looked down at a bright-eyed little head poking up between two of the professor's fingers. The tiny beak was slightly open, nipping at the hand that held it.

"He won't do any damage with that beak, but he wants me to understand that he is not particularly happy." The professor stood up. "And it is time to let him return to his daily activities." He walked a few steps away and opened his fist. The pewee hesitated and then, in less than a second, it was high above them.

"Pewee. Named for the call?"

Teddy beamed like a teacher taking delight in a particularly bright young lad. "Yes! Well, sort of. The variety of wood-pewees we have back east clearly say *Peee-uh-WEEE, PEE-eeeee*. The western variety sings a somewhat truncated version."

"Why didn't your grandfather release the bird right where he was, sitting down?"

Her dimple appeared for an instant before she made her face serious. "Well. Um. The bird might not have been the only thing released."

"Wh—Oh. Understood."

"We have no desire to have our equipment splattered with avian excrement."

"I'm heading back to the net, my dear." A frown appeared between his brows as the older man looked down at his granddaughter's bent head and at the rancher standing so close to her chair. He took a deep breath, retrieved his pistol from the table, and turned away. "I shall be back in just a few minutes."

Teddy didn't look up, busy choosing pastels from the box in front of her. Caleb moved to a large rock and sat down, content for the moment to sit and watch the young scientist at work. She was quite pretty, actually, with that mass of red-brown curls and those hazel eyes and the little band of light-colored freckles across the tops of her cheeks. It was unusual for a woman her age to be single, especially a fairly attractive one. Maybe her grandfather was overly protective. Maybe he hadn't let her meet any eligible young men.

"I've been meaning to ask you. What's that word you call the professor?"

"Oh. Well. I call him Grund."

"That's what I thought you were saying. Is that some sort of babytalk?"

"In a way. My mother was from Quebec. When I started talking, I was taught to say grandpère." She smiled. "With French pronunciation, the first syllable sounded more like 'grah' or 'gruh' than *grand*. Over time, my name for my grandfather evolved into Grund."

He watched her in silence for a few moments. "How did you parents feel when you headed off into the untamed frontier with your, uh, grund?"

"My parents died of diphtheria when I was three."

"Sorry to hear that."

"My grandmother, Grund's wife, fell ill before I was born, and she died when I was two. My parents were fairly penniless schoolteachers, so they agreed to move in with my father's father. Grund." The dimple showed again, briefly. "Also known as Theodore Barrington. He has a giant house. My parents and I had one wing and I think Grund often forgot we were there, except at mealtimes."

Caleb watched the dimple fade and tiny frown lines appear on her forehead.

"There was an east coast diphtheria epidemic back

in the early 1700s. Thousands of people died. But by the mid-1800s, many believed the disease was a threat only to the poor. That it stalked people who lived in stinking tenements and had no proper place for sewage and ate off filthy plates and drank contaminated water. My parents were scrupulously clean. And Grund had money so we always had the best and freshest food." Now her eyes were full of remembered pain. "It took Grund completely by surprise when his son and daughter-in-law fell ill. And died."

"And he was left with a toddling child."

"Well, at first his housekeeper Mary bore most of the burden. She was my substitute mother until she left to get married when I was six." Her smile was back. "She hugged me and promised she would come and visit. Her new husband was a lobsterman at heart. He had come to the city because he'd heard he could make good money on the docks, but he pined for the coast of Maine. I knew even at age six that they wouldn't get back to Boston very often."

She lifted her sketch pad and tilted it into the sunlight.

"Did you ever see Mary again?"

"Only once, a year after she left." The dimple was back. "And wasn't she scandalized! Grund had hired a cook/housekeeper, but my rearing was entirely his. He bought my clothes, he supervised my chores and my meals, and he had started daily lessons with him as my personal tutor. I was being raised by an old man."

"Horrors."

She grinned. "Exactly. But Mary had to admit that I was clean, well-fed, and happy."

"And Mary? Was she clean, well-fed and happy

too?"

Now the girl's smile positively glowed. "She was! She loved her lobsterman dearly, and they were expecting their first baby. She said she loved breathing fresh air, all around her, every single day." She looked around and gestured at the rocky ridges and the sage and the dry sandy soil and the vast blue sky. "And now I can so deeply understand what she meant, now that I am experiencing your Montana!"

"Two this time." The professor returned carrying a small wiggling cloth bag in each hand. "Both eager to be sketched, measured, and released."

He sat back down, put one of the bags into a small box by his feet and reached into the other. The little bird this time had a mostly yellow body with a dark gray hood and small bright white marks, one above and one below each eye.

"Ah! McGillivray's, I do believe!" The professor held the bird up. "I first thought it might be a mourning warbler but of course this is the wrong location. And that species has that black mourning band across the chest, hence the name."

"I hoped we would see one! What a beauty!"

"What's a magilla-whatever?"

Miss Barrington looked up at the rancher. "It's a kind of warbler. Warblers are insect-eaters so they must keep active to find enough tiny caterpillars and other insects to keep them alive. The males are often showy, like this little gent."

"You know it's a gent?"

"Definitely." She was already sketching, her hand moving rapidly over a clean piece of paper, the little bird already taking shape. "There is a visible difference between males and females in many species of birds. Not all species, to be sure. But it is clear in most New World warblers."

"What do you record if you can't tell?"

"We can almost always tell. Or at least Grund can, if he can get the bird in hand." She answered absently, her gaze darting back and forth between the bird and her drawing. "Almost all birds have reproductive organs called cloacas. Males have protuberant ones, females sort of concave. Grund blows on the feathers and notes which kind of cloaca the bird has."

"I see."

"I'm ready with measurements, my dear."

Caleb didn't listen to the series of numbers and unfamiliar words. Primary. Secondary. Coverts. Something that sounded like retricks. And super-silly-um?

"Let me see the front, Grund. Ah. Perfect."

"Ready to have me release him?"

"Ready."

The second bird was a little larger than the warbler, mostly gray with a bit of sky blue in the wings and tail.

"Ah. A female."

"A female what?"

"Mountain bluebird. Her mate will be almost all blue."

"Now that is a logical name. Unlike the magilli-whatever."

"I believe the famous John James Audubon himself named McGillivray's warbler, to honor a fellow naturalist and friend of his." Her sudden fierce scowl was like clouds appearing from nowhere and covering blue sky and sun. "Of course, every New World bird already had a name, often many names, given to them by native peoples who were here way before the Europeans. Sadly, those names are pretty much lost."

"Along with a great deal of wisdom about healing plants, the weather, and such."

"Yes. That is true."

Caleb had work to do. Too much work, as always. But he wasn't ready to leave. He sat back on the rock and watched as the professor measured and Miss Barrington sketched and the shadows began lengthening on the ridges. He sat there as the bluebird was released and the professor went once more to the net and Miss Barrington leaned back and stretched and then bent again over her sketch pad.

"My father used to say that bluebirds are signs of good luck."

"I don't know about that, but it is certainly a treat to see one. While Grund is gone, I'm going to sketch a male bluebird too, just to get the shape. I'll have to see one, though, to know exactly where to put the color." Her hand was again moving quickly over the paper. "Did your father build the main house?"

"No. There was a sod hut first. Then your log cabin. My brother and I built the current building several years ago." Caleb's mouth twisted. "Your cabin was one of the many things my mother didn't like about the ranch."

"On the wagon ride that first day, you mentioned that she left when you and your brother were young."

"She didn't go far. She got a bed-sitting room in Choteau, in an establishment for gentlewomen." He looked at her under his eyebrows. "That's how the owner and residents described it. An establishment for gentlewomen. She paid for her room and board by

cooking five suppers a week and doing all the baking."
He was staring into the distance now, his dark blue eyes
troubled and his forehead creased in a frown. "Dad went
into town and brought her out to the ranch a few days
every month. Sometimes a bit longer in good weather.
So she was still part of our lives. Dad was always happy
when she was there." He heaved a big breath. "But not
every woman is suited for ranch life."

"What was it she liked so much about Choteau?"

"She could walk to church. That was very important
to her. And she could walk less than a block and get sugar
if she ran out, instead of sending Hank or Arthur miles
and miles to the closest neighbor. She could go to
quilting bees and socials without having to ask Dad to
hitch up a wagon and drive her into town and then wait
for her and drive her back home. And I think she just
liked having other women around, talking with them,
playing cards, doing jigsaw puzzles with them on winter
evenings."

Miss Barrington's blue eyes were wide and
sympathetic. "How confusing for you and your brother."

"I was barely three when she moved to town, so it
was the norm for me. It was worse for Ike."

"He's older?"

"Four years older, yes."

"But he didn't get the family ranch when your father
died?" She grimaced. "Good gracious. I am being nosy.
You don't have to answer."

Caleb stretched his long legs out in front of him.
"Yes, you are being nosy. But I don't mind answering.
When Ike was sixteen or seventeen, he went down to
Texas with some other local ranchers to bring a herd of
longhorns up north. The drive took them through

Colorado, and I guess Ike saw his promised land. Couple years later, he headed back down, spent a few years working for others, and then bought his own ranch. Then he met a woman who can tolerate ranch life. Not just tolerate it. His wife Becky loves it."

"It sounds like your brother's life is good, then."

"I think his life is pretty close to paradise." His head jerked up. "Looks like he wants to be captured all over again. That macgilly warbler."

The gray, black, and yellow bird was almost directly over the girl's head, on a little sapling.

"How very odd. One would think getting tangled in a net and held by human hands would make any wild creature want to get far away and *stay* far away. Maybe this is a different male."

"Will your net capture larger birds? Hawks and the like?"

"Oh heavens no. They would rip the net to shreds. The beaks and sharp talons would do some real damage to us too."

"So how will you document them?"

"Well, we've already been close enough to herons, ducks, and grebes so Grund could estimate dimensions and take notes, and I could make sketches." She grinned. "Many, many sketches of each species. And before we headed out here, my grandfather ordered three of the brand-new Eastman cameras. No, that's not right. I think the inventor is Eastman, but the cameras are called Kodaks. Yes, that sounds right."

Caleb watched her tongue peek out the corner of her mouth as she concentrated on mixing the right color of blue.

"Anyway, the new cameras are much more

manageable than any previous ones. They're lightweight, they don't have to be stabilized on a tripod, and they're more affordable than the older huge ones." She twinkled up at him. "Anyway, Grund has boatloads of money."

"What did he do? For a living?"

"He started out as a teacher but he was a banker most of his life."

"I see."

"Each of the new cameras allows the user to take a hundred photos, so we'll have at least three hundred pictures of Montana birds. More if Grund decides to order extra film. We'll include some photos in the book. They won't show colors, of course, so we'll have to take good notes and I will add color to my sketches." Her voice was quieter as she focused on putting the finishing touches on her drawing. "The cameras will allow us to document species like hawks and eagles and vultures, birds we probably can't get close to. Unfortunately, we have to mail the cameras back to the Eastman company, the Eastman-Kodak company, and we might not get the results for several weeks. There! I'm pleased with this one."

"You should be."

"Why, thank you, Mr. Asher."

"How many drawings have you done already? Here in Montana?"

"This sketchbook has twenty-five pages. It's almost full, and we've sent five completed books back to Boston twice now, when Hank went into Choteau. And there are two other full ones in our cabin, so that's almost three hundred sketches so far."

"You aren't worried about their being lost between

here and Boston?"

"The very thought scares me to death, Mr. Asher. I always make copies, in the afternoon or after supper, and we keep the copies in our metal trunk, for backup."

"That's a lot of work, for you."

"It is. That's why I am getting such an extravagant salary."

For a moment he thought she was serious, but then he noticed that the little dimple was back.

"Oh. What I told you about cloacas, that's mostly songbirds. And shore birds. And raptors. And I believe herons and the like. Ducks are different, though. They are built more like mammals and they copulate similarly."

Perhaps Miss Barrington's unmarried state wasn't so surprising after all. In the space of twenty minutes, the proper young Bostonian had mentioned bird excrement and copulation. Even here in the untamed Montana territory, most young ladies, when talking with a man, pretended they had no knowledge of what went on between bull and cow, ram and ewe, boar and sow. Man and woman.

Caleb stood up abruptly. "I have to check on some cattle. That's why I came out here."

Teddy watched with a puzzled frown as he vaulted into his saddle, dug his heels into the horse's sides, and was gone.

"I see our host has left."

"He raced out of here as if he'd been stung by a wasp. Odd man."

The professor watched the rancher's disappearing cloud of dust. He opened his mouth, looked down at his granddaughter's head, thought better of what he was going to say, and just nodded.

"Perhaps."

\*\*\*\*

Teddy was unusually quiet during the wagon ride back to their cabin. Those few minutes with the rancher were the first extended conversation she'd ever had with a man other than her grandfather. She felt that it should mean something, that it had import, but she wasn't sure what the import was.

Once, she remembered, she and Grund went to a fund-raising event for the Boston Birding Alliance and a young man singled her out and brought her a cup of punch. He introduced himself and asked about her connection to the Alliance, and he appeared to be interested in her initial answers. But as they continued talking, his eyes repeatedly strayed to her decolletage and his tone became teasing. She had little experience of teasing, but she knew that it made her uncomfortable. And as it continued, she realized he was mocking her breadth of knowledge and her willingness to share that knowledge, exactly like someone who is amused by a precocious toddler.

But Mr. Asher appeared truly interested. He asked thoughtful questions and listened intently to the responses. And he hadn't scowled or grunted, not once. And he *was* an attractive man. She liked the looks of his legs in tight blue denim, and the look of his muscular forearms below the rolled-up sleeves of his cambric shirt. He wasn't as tall as Grund, but then not many people were. He was, she thought, four or five inches taller than she was, and that height might be perfect for dancing together.

Silly. Where would she ever have a chance to go dancing, here on a ranch?

Chapter Five

For the next two weeks and two days, Caleb avoided the parts of his ranch where the two Barringtons might be working, and he kept his eyes on his plate and his coffee mug during breakfasts and suppers. He was angry with himself for having spent over an hour sitting on a hard rock, watching the young ornithologist sketch and listening to her blather on about her nanny and her baby nickname for her grandfather. He was disgusted by how well he remembered wisps of red-gold hair peeking out from under that ridiculous fur hat, and how the girl's cheeks turned cherry blossom pink in the brisk wind. He was angry with her for talking about cloakies or whatever that word was, those body parts birds use for mating. And he was furious at his own body for reacting the way it did. It could not be normal for a full-grown adult to respond like that.

He had a ranch to run. He had a thousand Hereford and Angus cattle spread over the open range for miles, plus a couple hundred longhorns and they were just plain dumb. They were Texas cows, only a few generations removed from the first of their kind to arrive in Montana thirty years ago, and they hadn't been around long enough to develop Montana smarts. They didn't know that land that was bone dry most years could turn to a sucking quagmire after a rainy spring, and the dumb animals were always finding every bit of swampy land on the ranch and getting stuck and spending the whole day bellowing. Give him Herefords or Angus any day.

But he wanted to try crossbreeding. He wanted to develop a new strain of cattle that would be as large as Texas longhorns and as smart as black Angus. He wanted Long Butte Ranch to be known all over the west for its unique breed of cattle.

****

"I'll let you off here, my dear. I want to tell Arthur about that frayed place on the pinto's bridle."

Teddy got down from the wagon, stretched, and looked around. This yard, these buildings, those fences, the smells of animals and sage and dust, the wind, the hot afternoon sun on her head and shoulders, the dry ground at her feet, the bare rock ridges in the background and the butte that gave the ranch its name—All of it felt like home, already. Much more like home than Boston ever was.

Ku-Long came out of the kitchen door. Back in May, when she and her grandfather first came to the ranch, the Chinese cook dressed like one of the ranch hands in blue jeans and flannel shirts over long-sleeved undershirts. Now, with the start of summer weather, he wore a sleeveless singlet with cotton draw-string pants and sandals made of rope. Teddy couldn't remember ever seeing a single adult foot but her own.

She waved, but Ku-Long was heading for the garden, carrying one of his harvesting baskets. Probably gathering herbs to add to whatever he's making for supper, she thought. Or maybe fresh asparagus. Her stomach growled in anticipation.

Teddy turned as a man's voice yelled something behind her. One of the long-horned range cows bolted through the half-closed gate of the corral, scattering broken bits of wood behind it, with Hank and Bucky in full pursuit. Teddy felt droplets of sweat and spit as the wild-eyed animal thundered past her, udder flapping from side to side. Ku-Long also whirled around, waving his basket in front of him and yelling. Later, the ranch hands said it was those Chinese curses that confuddled the cow and made it veer off before trampling the cook. Montana range cows spoke only Montana cowboy English, they explained, not Chinese. The cow changed course, but the tip of one horn caught Ku-Long's forearm.

Teddy reached him before the two ranch hands did. His arm and hand, his singlet and pants, even the ground around his feet were already glistening with blood. When he bent over, she feared he was fainting, but he grabbed a kitchen towel from the basket at his feet and straightened up with the towel tight against his arm.

"Good! That's good. Push hard!" She reached up, tugged the scarf from around her hat and wound it around and around Ku-Long's upper arm, pulling as tight as she could.

"Harder. More." Ku-Long's teeth were gritted. "Tighter."

The rancher was suddenly beside them, pushing her hands out of the way and taking over the job of tightening the makeshift tourniquet. "Will he need stitching?"

"Yes."

"Can you do it?"

"I—Yes. But it's book knowledge for me. Grund has experience." She looked around. "Where is he?"

"No idea. But we can't wait."

"No. Ku-Long, come with me into the kitchen."

"You two. Get a rope around that dadblamed cow. And fix the fence before they all get out."

Later, Teddy remembered no time at all between being outdoors in the dust and blood, and standing in the cool kitchen, in front of the sink, watching as Ku-Long lifted the soaked towel and fighting to keep her face calm as she saw the wound that ran from just above his wrist to his elbow.

"Is that hot water on the stove?"

The rancher added hot water to the cold in the bucket by the sink and she washed her hands and Ku-Long's arm over and over and over before leading him to a chair.

"Rest your arm on this towel. On the table." Teddy glanced up at the rancher, her voice curt. "You. Loosen the tourniquet for a half minute or so and then tighten it again. Do that over and over again. Make sure blood keeps flowing to his fingers and hand."

Caleb handed Teddy a metal box and put a bottle of whiskey on the table.

"No, boss. No hooch."

"Ku-Long. You're going to need it. Believe me. I've had stitches."

"No."

Teddy rummaged in the box and held up an almost empty bottle. "Is this all the iodine you have?"

"Not possible. That bottle was full last time I looked."

"No. That all." Ku-Long pushed the whiskey bottle toward her. "Use. Pour."

"This will sting even worse than iodine."

"Use. Now."

Spreading the sides of the long gash with her

fingers, Teddy poured the alcohol until it splashed on the floor, mingling thin amber liquid with deep red blood. The cook sucked in his breath but didn't make any other sound. The rancher handed her a curved needle and a small vial containing oil and silk thread. There was no time to pray that her grandfather would arrive in time to do the stitching. Teddy took a deep breath, dipped the needle in iodine, threaded it, got a firm hold of Ku-Long's arm, and poked the needle through the skin on one side of the gash. She heard another sharp intake of breath but she didn't look up. His clenched hand and the shaking leg against her side told her how much he was hurting.

Through the skin on the other edge of the cut. Pull tight. Tie. Cut. Another stitch. And another. And another.

She realized her grandfather had come into the kitchen. She felt his warm hand on her shoulder, and then he pulled out a chair and sat across the table.

Now she was at the deepest part of the wound. Teddy glanced up at Ku-Long's face. His teeth were clenched and sweat stood out in perfectly round drops on his forehead. The rancher put his strong arms around him from behind to hold him still.

"Just a few more minutes," she murmured. "It's almost done."

As Teddy tied off and cut the last stitch, a roll of gauze bandage was pressed into her hand.

"Iodine first." She cut off a small part of the bandage and used it to paint the injured arm, using all the bacteria-killing tincture left in bottle. "Just enough."

"Confounds me how little of the stuff was left."

The cook jerked his head up and met Caleb's eyes. "I use. You know."

"I—Oh. Of course. I'll get more next time I'm in town."

Teddy finished wrapping Ku-Long's arm and moved her chair back so he could stand. The injured man's breath was uneven, but he was steady on his feet.

"You stir stew. Bread in oven. Punch. Make four. Cook."

"My granddaughter and I know how to make bread." The professor stood also. "We will manage supper, and tomorrow's breakfast as well. Teddy, you will probably want to check Ku-Long's arm in the morning."

"Yes. And change the bandage."

"Good. After that, we can decide how to proceed. Your main job, Ku-Long, is to heal."

"Thank. I thank, both. Thank." He took a step toward the door and then turned his head. "Beans. You know beans? Water all the night? Cook in morning?"

"Boston is famous for baked beans. We will put beans in water this evening, boil them tomorrow morning, and then bake them."

"Water for ham. All the night."

"We shall soak a ham also. Beans and ham for tomorrow's supper. It will be fine, Ku-Long. Stop worrying. Go with Rancher Asher now, and get some rest."

Caleb took the cook's good arm, but before they reached the door he turned back and jerked his head at Teddy. "You there. Come."

She purely hated being ordered around. But she remembered with chagrin that she had barked an order to the rancher only minutes ago. And Ku-Long was her patient, so she followed the two men out the door. The trio was silent until they were almost at the smaller log cabin. Then the rancher turned to Teddy with a fierce scowl.

"Listen up. There's a girl in Ku-Long's cabin. Metis. You are not to mention her to anyone. Not even to the ranch hands. Not to anyone who might stop by. Absolutely no one. If you have to tell your grandfather, do so only inside your cabin with the door and windows closed."

"I don't understand."

"You don't have to understand. Just do as I say."

Teddy set her jaw and stared straight ahead. Fine. There was a girl in the cook's cabin and she was named Metty or Matties or something, and she was a secret.

Ku-Long touched her arm. "Her name Isabelle. She scared."

"I... Oh."

The smaller log cabin had only one room, with a woodstove, a table, two kitchen chairs, and a bed. The girl was standing against the back wall, her right arm in a sling, her left hand clutching a short but lethal-looking knife. She was wearing a man's Union suit, incongruously fastened around her waist with a multicolored and intricately beaded belt. One side of her face was puffy and almost black, the eye swollen closed. Her lip was split and beginning to scab. There was a raw spot on the side of her head, as if some of her hair had been yanked out. A horizontal slash marked her left cheek from just below the ear almost to her mouth.

A red-orange slash.

Ah. The missing iodine. Ku-Long had used the iodine for her injuries.

The girl's slight body quivered with a mix of terror and defiance. She looked wildly from Caleb to Teddy, but she moaned when her eyes dropped to the bandage on Ku-Long's arm and the blood on his white clothes. She set the knife on the windowsill, pulled back the quilt on the only bed, and held out one hand.

"No. I rest there." Ku-Long turned toward a pallet on the floor by the table.

"Not right now you don't." The rancher's voice was firm, even harsh. "It'd hurt like hell to get down and up from there with that arm. The girl's getting better now. She can sleep on the floor for a few nights."

There was a brief silent struggle as Ku-Long again tried to move toward the pallet and Caleb relentlessly pushed him toward the bed. The cook was solidly-built and muscular, but he was no match for the determined rancher.

"Tonight, then. I sleep here tonight."

"You sleep here as many nights as you need. Or I'll tie you up and take you over to the main house. I am not joking, Ku-Long."

Another silent contest of wills.

"Take off blood clothes. No dirt bed."

The rancher grunted and held out his hand. To Teddy's astonishment, the girl reached for her knife and laid it in his palm. A few quick slices, and the cook's blood-smeared singlet fell to the floor.

"Look away."

"What?"

The rancher grabbed Teddy's shoulders and turned her around, but not before Ku-Long undid the drawstring on his pants and let them drop to the floor. She stared at the cabin door, struggling with a wholly inappropriate desire to giggle. One of her goals for her sojourn in the wilderness was to know what a man looked like without clothes on. Now she knew. And the drawing of the Grecian statue she saw long ago in a library book was highly inaccurate.

"Water."

Teddy darted to the table, filled a basin and carried it to the bed, scrupulously keeping her eyes downcast. She felt the rancher's warm fingers take the basin from her, and she listened to the liquid noises, the bed springs creaking, a groan from the injured man, and a whispered comment from the girl.

"I will bring over some supper later for you, Ku-Long. And for, for Isabelle. I will be back in the morning with breakfast, and to check your wound. Now you must try to sleep. And you must keep drinking water, whenever you are awake. Will you do that?"

"Water. Yes. Sleep, water." For a startled moment, Teddy caught what looked like humor in the somber cook's eyes, and she realized he knew very well how to care for wounds. He had been nursing Isabelle, and her injuries appeared far worse than his.

"That's good then. Good."

****

Teddy stood stock still outside the cabin, her head tilted to the sky, breathing in the sweet sage-scented air. It was fortunate for Ku-Long that her hands had been steadier a half hour ago than they were now. She was shaking all over and felt bruised from head to toe. In a moment she would help her grandfather with bread and supper, but first she needed a few moments of solitude.

"Are you all right?"

She jumped.

"What? Yes. Of course I am all right." She straightened her shoulders. "I believe, Mr. Asher, that it is not uncommon for a person to need a little time to herself after a… a stressful event."

"I've stitched wounds before. I know it's as upsetting for the stitcher as well as for the wounded."

"You have stitched wounds before."

"Of course."

"Then why did you ask me to do it?"

In the late afternoon light, the rancher's blue eyes looked almost black, and wary. "I reasoned that a woman's touch would be gentler."

"When someone is poking a needle through you, and that someone is drawing thread through the newly opened holes in your bleeding skin, it cannot possibly matter whether the person wielding that needle is male or female. It was *your* responsibility to tend to your cook, Mr. Asher. Not mine." She turned away and made her wobbly legs carry her toward the kitchen. "I am going to help with supper."

My goodness, Teddy thought. First, she ordered the rancher around, then, she snapped at him, and then she slammed his own kitchen door in his face.

Her grandfather was standing at the table, jacket off and shirt sleeves rolled up, and a large mass of dough in front of him, cut into four. One of his pant legs was dusted with flour, and he was whistling under his breath. Teddy stood and cherished the sight of him, feeling her first smile in over an hour begin to spread over her face.

"Our cooking duties are likely to have some effect on the bird census, Grund."

"Not as badly as you might think, my dear." He smacked a ball of dough down onto the counter. "The afternoons are getting hot. Hawks of course are active but we would struggle to find songbirds. We will have plenty of time for our original job and our new job both."

Teddy lowered herself into the nearest chair, her legs still shaky.

"Breakfasts are relatively easy, my dear. Ku-Long already has tonight's supper started, and beans and ham are planned for tomorrow. We can add something to both meals from the store of canned vegetables in the root cellar, and we'll think of something for dessert."

"What about apple cake? If I make a triple batch, it might do for both suppers."

"An excellent idea. Would you get that started while I finish this task?"

"In just a minute."

He turned and looked sharply at her. "That was hard on you, my dear. I regret that I wasn't there from the start."

"I do too."

"You did an excellent job."

"Thank you. Thank you." She leaned back and closed her eyes. "Grund, there's a girl in Ku-Long's cabin. Rancher Asher said she is mettees. Or mattize. He said something like that. I thought it was her name but it isn't. What did he mean?"

"Ah. Yes. M-E-T-I-S. There are many Metis in Montana. They are indigenous but not precisely a tribe. They are more accurately a cultural group, descendants of native indigenous women and European fur traders, mostly French or Scottish or Irish." He leaned down on the dough with both fists and his breath became uneven as he lifted and pushed and lifted again.

"That bread smells wonderful and it's not even cooked yet."

"Sourdough. Yes." He shaped one loaf, dusted the

counter with more flour, and plopped down a second ball of dough. "Metis are quite fascinating. Many were taught by, or at least have had contact with, French-Canadian nuns. And many are named for Catholic saints. They are often Catholics but it is a variety of folk Catholicism, blended with pre-existing native spiritual beliefs."

She opened her eyes. "The girl is called Isabelle. I was expecting a name like Lone Willow or Woman Who Carries Water or something similarly exotic."

"It is delightful, isn't it, how the world around us constantly shakes up our expectations?" The second loaf was shaped, and he reached for another ball of dough.

"Now what else have I read about the Metis people? Oh, yes. Music! I truly hope, my dear, that we have the opportunity to hear Metis music while we are here in Montana. I understand they make violins and percussion instruments like those used in Europe, and their music sounds Celtic, or like dances or ballads from Cape Breton."

"And there are Metis around here?"

"I am sure there are, yes. I saw two men with beaded belts in Choteau, and I believe Metis are sometimes called the Flower Beadwork People."

"Yes! The girl had an extraordinary beaded sash, or belt. I got just a quick look but I think the design was birds, though, rather than flowers."

Grund chuckled. "Artists all over the world are characterized by individuality and individual creativity. It would not surprise me one bit to learn that while most Metis make flower designs in their beadwork, others choose to incorporate bird designs. Curious. I wonder how that particular Metis beadworker ended up in the cabin of a Chinese cook."

"Ku-Long is protecting her, Grund. I think she was severely beaten, and maybe cut up too. I think she is terrified that the person who beat her might find her. That's why the rancher and Ku-Long are keeping her secret."

"And that speaks well of both men! Of course they should protect her!" His bushy eyebrows almost met over the bridge of his nose as he frowned fiercely. "You and I shall be on the lookout too, for any strangers. We shall now be her defenders, along with Rancher Asher and Ku-Long."

Teddy stood up, leaned across the table and kissed his forehead.

"Yes we should. And we will. Now I shall make apple cake. Oh! And coffee! Is there any left in that pot? But I suppose I should clean up first. Do I have time?"

He pulled out his pocket watch.

"If you get the apple cake into the oven an hour from now, we will be fine. I shall send hot water heading your way immediately. Go, my dear. Go. You will feel better once you have washed and changed your clothes."

****

Holding her duffel bag of clean garments, Teddy entered one of the two small rooms with cast iron tubs. Her stockings and shoes were the only things she wore that didn't have blood on them. She ran cold water over everything else, squeezed out as much as she could, and then put everything in clean cold water to soak overnight, this time with shavings of lye soap.

She didn't like the idea of sitting in bloody water, so she stood in the bathtub and poured a cupful of warm water at a time, soaping that one section of her body and then using another cup of water to rinse off. The water was deliciously hot, tipped out of the huge vat on one of the kitchen stoves into a small sink that led to pipes rigged by the ingenious Arthur to flow directly into the wash rooms. By the time Teddy was finished bathing, she felt clean and competent and increasingly hungry.

She also felt guilty. Rancher Asher had been specific. She was not to mention the Metis girl except in the log cabin, with her grandfather, and with doors and windows closed. But she had talked about Isabelle in the kitchen, where the ranch hands could have walked in at any minute.

****

"Supper went very well, my dear. Ku-Long's stew is always excellent, and your cake was much appreciated."

"And Bucky offered to help with the dishes!"

"I must admit that I was startled and touched."

"I was too. I think all of them are deeply concerned about Ku-Long. He is not only the cook but their friend."

Her grandfather nodded. "There are Chinese in Boston but they keep to themselves. And the Irish keep to the Irish, and the Italians to the Italians. It is a hopeful omen for humanity that here on America's frontier, there can be true friendship across racial and cultural differences."

"Oh! I have a thought!" She plopped down beside him at the table and opened her sketchbook. "I want to show the girl, Isabelle, that I am a friend. One of the birds on her belt looked like a kingfisher. We saw one... Ah, here it is. We saw one that first day at Freezout Lake. Maybe if I make her a copy of my kingfisher sketch and bring it to her when I check on Ku-Long's arm tomorrow morning, it will give her the message that I am a friend,

70

and a protector."

"An exemplary idea, my dear. Exemplary."

"Drat. I did it again." She met his eyes, her face a study in chagrin and worry and a bit of humor. "The girl must be kept a secret, Grund. Even from Hank and Bucky and Arthur. Please, please, don't mention her. The rancher warned me, and I have forgotten twice now. He is apt to exile me from the ranch if others find out about her and he discovers it was due to my big mouth."

****

Once again, Teddy expected to fall asleep the instant her head touched her mattress. Her body craved the solace of deep sleep after the long and traumatic day, but she lay staring out the window long after her grandfather's snores had settled into a low even rumble.

She thought she had done the best she could with Ku-Long's arm. But had she cleaned the wound completely? Would his arm become infected? She wasn't a doctor or a nurse. She should have insisted that Rancher Asher take the cook into Choteau to be seen by a medical professional.

No. The wound needed immediate attention. She had to stop worrying. She did what she could and she would see her patient in just a few hours. And maybe the Metis girl knew some healing herbs, or roots, or some such. People got injured all the time out here in the west, and they didn't *all* die.

But many did.

Ku-Long would not die. She would see to it if she had to go with him on the Huntley stage all the way to Great Falls. Great Falls was a city, or what counted as a city out here on the frontier, so there must be a hospital or a clinic there.

She shouldn't have snapped at the rancher. But it galled her to come so far, to central Montana, where there were women running ranches and driving teams of horses, and women in Choteau with their own businesses, and end up listening to some *man* spouting the same nonsense she heard back in Boston ever since she was old enough to understand. To hear the same convictions that women were not to be allowed near higher education, or business. Heavens no! But by some bizarre alchemy women were perfect for tending gaping bloody wounds.

Maybe she should behave like a proper young lady from Boston and make a polite and ladylike apology. Maybe after she did that, she might dare to ask a question or two at mealtimes, or make a comment, and be confident that she would receive a civil response. Rancher Asher had barely looked in her direction since the day he had watched the two ornithologists netting, measuring, sketching, and releasing birds.

Teddy suddenly sat bolt upright. Coyotes! She knew Montana had coyotes but she hadn't seen or heard one yet. Now the night was full of yips and whines, squeals and long wavering howls, barking and noises that sounded uncannily like laughter. There had to be a good-sized pack of coyotes up on the ridge behind the ranch. Were they a threat to the horses? Were Arthur's chickens safe in their night roost?

She would never get to sleep now. She couldn't see how *anyone* could sleep through all that, but she was still hearing Grund's even snores through the wall. She lay back down, her arms wrapped around herself, listening and grinning and feeling the wild excitement of the coyotes filling her whole body.

No, she decided abruptly. She would not apologize to Rancher Asher. Nothing would ever change if women occasionally dared to correct the ignorant beliefs of the men around them and then turned right around and asked for forgiveness from those same thoughtless and prejudiced men.

The coyote cacophony got quieter, farther away, and finally faded to nothing. Teddy turned on her side and curled up with one hand under her cheek. Just as she fell asleep, she felt the brush of the rancher's fingers as he pushed her hand out of the way and tightened the tourniquet, and again as he took the basin of water from her in Ku-Long's cabin. He had long fingers, and they felt warm and firm and....

## Chapter Six

"Excellent meal, Professor. Excellent!" The rancher's eyes flicked to Teddy and then back to her grandfather. "It can't have been easy to equal Ku-Long's high standards."

Teddy had avoided speaking up at meals ever since all four ranch men greeted her few early comments with as much surprise and discomfort as if one of the chairs had interrupted their manly conversations. But now she answered immediately, before her grandfather could. "Why, thank you so much, Mr. Asher." She looked around at the almost-empty serving dishes and the plates piled with second and third helpings of ham and baked beans and coleslaw and bread. "It is gratifying indeed to know that my efforts were appreciated."

"Your efforts and your grandfather's. Isn't that what you mean?"

The professor didn't look up, apparently absorbed in mopping his plate with a piece of bread.

"Grund spent the day at the wooded area where we were yesterday, so he could get photos of the roosting owls." She looked into the rancher's eyes and smiled sweetly. "I stayed here and made supper and baked more bread. Eight loaves, a double batch, since Ku-Long will need several days before he can use that arm for kneading dough." She nodded toward the counter. "I am afraid I did not make the dried apple pie he was planning for dessert. I am not particularly adept with pie crust. But there is apple cake left over from yesterday, and I made two large pans of my special gingerbread, and we have applesauce."

"I stand corrected. No. I sit corrected."

Was that a bit of humor from the always serious, sometimes surly, ranch owner? Teddy peered closely at his face. His mustache prevented her from seeing even a small smile, but the sun wrinkles beside his eyes were tilting up.

"Your meal was delicious, Miss Barrington. We greatly appreciate the double batch of bread. And your gingerbread looks and smells delicious." He shifted his gaze to her mute grandfather. "And you, professor, did you see any owls?"

Grund caught Teddy's eye with a quick wink before turning to the rancher. "That little copse is a daytime roost for several different species. I saw one long-eared owl, a Rocky Mountain screech owl, no fewer than three great horned owls, and I believe one pygmy owl. It was shady in that area, however, so I will have to wait until the photographs are developed to be sure. We have heard great horned and one screech, but not a pygmy yet. Is that correct, my dear?"

"I haven't heard one, no."

"But I have a question for you, Mr. Asher, about a different kind of bird. Yesterday morning my granddaughter and I saw three turkey vultures on the ridge east of where we've been working. This morning, the number had increased to at least a dozen, the most we have seen since we've been in Montana."

"I believe people out here call them buzzards, Grund," Teddy put in, still heady with the success of her recent foray into verbal assertiveness.

"Oh, yes, of course, my dear. Buzzards. There must be something large up there to attract that number of scavengers. If the birds are still feeding tomorrow, I believe we could get both photos and sketches. Is there a trail or a path to that location?"

The rancher swallowed a mouthful of beans and shook his head. "The only way is on horseback. I'll ride up to the ridge and check out what's attracting the birds. If it's one of our cattle, I'd sure like to know what it's doing up there dead."

\*\*\*\*

Damn.

Not a range cow.

Not a mule deer either.

A cloud of black birds took to the air as Caleb dismounted, their naked red heads gleaming with what they'd just been eating. Two ravens, bolder, merely walked a few steps sideways and croaked their displeasure.

"Damn and damn and damn."

There was almost nothing left of the man's face. The legs were still in blue jeans and boots, but the birds or perhaps coyotes had opened the belly and pulled out the intestines. Above the glistening pile was a belt with intricate beadwork.

"Damn again."

\*\*\*\*

Someday, Teddy vowed, she was going to invent a device that would allow women to relieve themselves from a standing position. Her grandfather left the blind and ducked behind a tree whenever he had to go, and now that they were back at the ranch he was free to go directly to their cabin and start working on notes while everything was fresh in his mind. But she had to squirm uncomfortably for hours and then make a beeline for the privy the instant they got back to the ranch. Just because she was a woman. Yes. She would design something and it would be welcomed by every woman anywhere who enjoyed spending time outdoors. It would require an opening in the skirt, like the buttoned placket in men's pants. And perhaps some sort of funnel. Maybe she could design an entire line of women's outdoor clothing. That would be an excellent project for her when the bird census was completed and she was back in Boston.

Back in Boston. Teddy was dismayed by how unenthusiastic she felt about that.

She closed the privy door behind her and stopped in the midst of descending the steps. A small wagon was pulling up in front of Ku-Long's cabin, with Rancher Asher driving. His passenger had long white hair and was dressed in light-colored leather pants and a vest covered with bright floral designs.

Metis. Teddy was sure. Perhaps he was the girl's father. Or grandfather. Perhaps he had come to take her back to the village. Proper young ladies in Boston were never nosy, at least not obviously, but this was Montana and Teddy very much wanted to know what was going on. She considered sneaking along the dry stream bed behind the ranch buildings, but that was quite a distance. No. She had to use the direct route. She waited until the two men were inside the cabin, glanced around, saw no one, picked up her skirts and ran, passing the back of the main house and racing toward Ku-Long's cabin. She was fairly confident the rising wind would hide any noise she might make, but just to be sure she slowed down and crept stealthily along the back wall and then the far wall, bending double to duck down under the cabin's only window. No one could see her there, but she could hear perfectly.

Oh no. The Metis girl was crying. She was repeating the same few sounds over and over, almost drowning out the raspy voice of the old man.

"Dadblame it!" That was the rancher. "She isn't listening to a single word you say. Show her this!"

There was sudden complete silence.

"Now tell her, quick, while she's quiet. Tell her the man who beat on her is dead. Tell her I saw him and he is food for buzzards and coyotes. I took this belt off his dead body. Tell her she is safe. She can go back to the village."

The elder said several sentences, and then the girl's voice came again, spitting out individual words as if they were hard evil-tasting rocks.

"She say she happy he dead. She say she hope he suffer. Suffer much."

"Then she'll go back with you? Back to the Metis village?"

The elder said only a few words before the girl's wailing began again.

"What the hell?" The rancher sounded baffled and irate. "She gets to go home. The man is dead. What's the matter now?"

Teddy lifted her head a few inches, listening intently as the girl's story slowly emerged, first in a fountain of words, a river held back for days, a torrent of fear and loneliness and aching sorrow, every sentence retold in the old man's halting translation. She wished she had one of her notebooks with her, so she could write down what she heard.

The halting voice of the Metis elder was saying, "She say she live with mother. Father gone, many years. She say her mother don't live in village. Village made her leave. Oh yes. That true fact, what she say. I know her now. Her mother left village long time ago. Her mother say village not like her. Take baby and go."

Teddy closed her eyes to listen more intently, promising herself that she would write the girl's story down the minute she got back to their cabin. Maybe someday she would put it in a book. *Lives of Montana's Metis*. She would tell it straight, though, without the elder's hesitations and difficult English. She could almost see it on the page, with the title *Isabelle's Story*.

****

Isabelle had a good life with her mother. They rarely saw other people. They had a little garden, and her mother was often successful at hunting and fishing. Some days they were hungry, especially in the winter, but they laughed together and her mother taught her songs and stories. She told Isabelle about Wisahkecahk, who could change his shape so he could play tricks on people. She taught her daughter to pray to Kitchi-Manitou or *Bon Dieu*, the name used by the French nuns. Isabelle said it was not true what they said in the village, that her mother didn't know the Great Spirit. Her mother was a holy woman. A believing woman.

In the summer when Isabelle was fifteen, a man came to their hut and Isabelle had to sleep outdoors. There was more food when the man was there but she did not like him or trust him. She asked her mother to send him away, but her mother answered that she wasn't as strong as she used to be and they would need his help to get food for the winter.

And then, in the spring, when the snow started melting, Isabelle's mother got sick. She was coughing, sometimes so much that she could barely breathe, and she was burning hot to the touch. The man went away because he was afraid to be near her, afraid he would get sick also.

Isabelle's mother died just as the first buds appeared on the cottonwood trees. The girl held her dead body all night long, and the next day she took her mother's gardening shovel and hoe to a spot many yards from the cabin. She dug for hours until she had a proper grave. Her mother had told her that Metis buried their dead in boxes painted blue and white, but Isabelle didn't know how to make a box so she wrapped her mother in a blue and white blanket and then tugged her on more blankets from their cabin to the grave. Isabelle jumped down into the grave and pulled her mother in after her, holding her mother in her arms and then laying her down and rearranging the blue and white blanket around her. She asked for forgiveness because she had to stand on her mother's legs as she clambered out of the grave. She used the shovel to bury her mother and pushed and rolled stones until they covered the fresh dirt, protecting her mother's body from the sharp teeth and sharp claws of animals. It was almost night when she finished, and she stood in the dark beside her mother's grave and said prayers and wept and danced and wept again.

Three nights later, the man came again. He said she must lie with him now that the mother was gone, and he hit her when she said no. He knocked her down and fell on top of her. He yelled and hit her face with his fists. Maybe he would kill her and she would be with her mother, but she would not make it easy for him. She fought and he pulled her hair and he had a knife in his hand and he cut her face. She drew back her head and brought it forward, fast and hard, into his jaw and mouth and teeth. When he yelled and dropped the knife, she grabbed it and used it to cut his side and his leg and his side again. Then she was crawling out the doorway and she was standing up outdoors and she was running, running.

She heard the man yelling, following her, chasing her. She knew she must keep running all night, as long and as far as she could.

Isabelle's mother always called the moon Pale Sister. Now Pale Sister Moon came out from behind clouds to light the trail up toward the ridges. The girl ran, jumping over rocks, pushing through brush, tearing her clothes and her skin on sharp thorns. She fell many times and she hurt her leg and her arm, but Sister Moon made sure she didn't lose the trail. When it was almost day, Isabelle knew she might be seen if she kept running. She needed to find water but she was afraid to look for some, afraid the man might be on the ridge too, so she hid behind a rock and fell asleep.

When she opened her eyes, a man was standing over her. She grabbed for her knife but then she saw that it wasn't the same man. This man spoke gently to her. He brought water. He washed the blood away from her cheek and mouth. He helped her stand up, and slowly, so slowly, he helped her walk down off the ridge to a log cabin. The man had black hair like her people but he wasn't Metis. She thought his words were like the words of the white people near the big town, even though he didn't look like them. She didn't understand what he said, but his voice was gentle and soft. When they got to his cabin, he gave her clothes and put soothing paste on her face. He made willow tea for her. He held sticks against her arm and wrapped it so it didn't hurt as much. He gave her a piece of a tree to lean on so she could move around inside the cabin without using the leg that was so painful.

But she knew she could not go outside the cabin, not ever. She knew the other man, the bad man, would be out there looking for her.

****

The rancher's voice broke in at that point in the story. "But she *is* safe. She *can* go outside now. Tell her again. She can go anyplace she wants. The man is dead. Tell her."

The girl's voice was now ragged with tears and emotion. Teddy remembered, later, that the Metis elder's voice also sounded ragged, emotional, as he translated.

*Other men out there, other men don't care about girls except for to use. She young. She have no family. She like small rabbit with coyotes all around. Never go back. Stay here. Stay in this little house. Or big house. Or build small cabin for herself. Anything. She work in garden. Help with cooking. Wash clothes. She no trouble. She safe here. She stay.*

Teddy crossed her fingers. Let her stay. If she stayed, Teddy would spend time with her. Isabelle would be happier if she had another girl to talk to, on this ranch with so many men.

The silence inside the cabin was broken by the rancher's deep voice.

"Ku-Long. It is up to you if she stays here, not me."

Another silence.

"Yes. She stay. She safe here. She feel safe."

"It doesn't have to be forever, Ku-Long. Just until we can figure out something more permanent. Perhaps in time she will be more comfortable about returning to the Metis village."

"Yes. Tell her."

The old man spoke again. This time Isabelle's response was calmer, but there were still several more back-and-forths before the old man sighed and said the girl would stay where she was, at least for now.

"Good. Then I will drive this gentleman back to the Metis village."

Teddy realized with a start how vulnerable her position was. The minute the rancher and the elder left the cabin, they might see her crouched down along the side wall. There was nothing to do but brazen it out. She bent over and ran several yards straight back, away from the tiny log cabin. Then she took a deep breath, straightened up, brushed the dust off her skirts, and walked with quick and confident steps at an angle that would take her right by the front of Ku-Long's cabin.

"Oh! Hello!" She stopped abruptly, arranging her face in what she hoped was an expression of startled surprise.

"I thought you and the professor were gone for the day."

"Grund called it quits around lunchtime. It was getting very hot, and the wind was playing havoc with our papers. Also," she dimpled, "I think he wanted to take an afternoon nap." She smiled at the older man. "I am sorry for butting in. I am Theodora Barrington. My grandfather and I are studying birds on Mr. Asher's ranch."

The elderly man inclined his head solemnly. "I Joseph Doney."

"Mr. Doney is an elder in the Metis settlement near Choteau."

"I am pleased to meet you, Mr. Doney." Teddy turned back to the rancher. "I am fairly sure I just saw a sage hen, there, in the streambed. We never expected to find one this close to the ranch buildings!"

Mr. Doney nodded. "Sage hen good to eat. Eat sage, makes them taste."

"In the east, where I come from, we use sage for stuffing turkeys."

"Turkey?"

"They are large birds, bigger than grouse."

"Ah." He climbed laboriously up into the wagon. "Turkey."

Teddy turned her smile on the rancher. "I must get my sketchbook quickly. The grouse flew, but I think I can remember enough to make a good drawing. Maybe Grund and I will haunt the streambed for the next couple of afternoons."

He stood for a few seconds more, studying her with an expression that Teddy thought looked skeptical, before he rounded the wagon and climbed in.

****

Ku-Long was back in the kitchen on the fourth afternoon after having his arm ripped open by the sharp horn of the range cow. He couldn't use his left arm for chopping or kneading, but together he and Teddy roasted three chickens and made enough chicken and dumpling stew for two suppers. And the day after the crew finished eating the stew, one of the cows stepped into a gopher hole and broke its leg. Hank and Bucky killed and slaughtered the animal out on the range, so coyotes wouldn't be drawn closer to the ranch by the blood smell, and then they rode into the ranch with over two hundred pounds of beef.

"You help?"

"Of course I will help, Ku-Long. This is a truly vast amount of meat."

First, steaks went into a deep crockery jar in the cellar, and Ku-Long covered them with a lot of water, a little vinegar, some sugar and black pepper, and a great deal of garlic. Then he separated out a large pile of the remaining meat to be made into jerky. Teddy cut it into thin slices, and Bucky carried it outside and put it on the metal barn roof to dry.

"Don't you worry none about crows 'n ravens 'n buzzards, Miss B," he said earnestly. "Gonna lay metal fencing atop it, some one way and some t'other so the birds can't get through. And rocks to hold it down. They won't get none."

After that, Ku-Long and Teddy chopped up the many pounds that were left, fried the meat slowly with onion and garlic, packed it in canning jars with a bit of salt and vinegar, and put the jars in the largest two kettles to boil for a few hours.

"For sauce. Stew." The cook fixed her with a stern look. "Use all by end of spring. Not later. Make sick."

"I will remember that. Thank you."

But Teddy wouldn't be there long enough to worry about the beef going bad. And she doubted she would ever have to can beef back home in Boston. She and her grandfather ate seafood, pork, and fowl. The only beef they ever tasted was tough stew beef from an Angus farm a few hundred miles away in northern New Hampshire.

"Steaks special. Three, four suppers. Everybody like."

Everybody like indeed. Those first meals after the beef bonanza were a revelation to Teddy. Ku-Long had her dice a basket full of onions and cook them in bacon fat while he used his good hand to smack the steaks with a hammer. After the beef was cooked with the onions, it was more tender than any meat she had ever tasted and it had a sweet and spicy flavor that became more pronounced with each passing night, as the meat spent more time in the marinade.

"Ku-Long, you have introduced me to a truly wonderful taste sensation. Grund has tasted fine steaks before, of course, but I never have. Thank you! And thank you, Hank and Bucky, for finding the injured cow before all this wonderful beef spoiled or was eaten up by scavengers."

She looked up, smiling, and then wiped her chin with one of the dish towels she had cut up to use as napkins.

Chapter Seven

"I am of the opinion, my dear, that these additions to our rig are testimony to the creativity of Silent Arthur."

A wide roof of burlap bags now shaded the wagon's seat, and a tattered old tarp fastened over the back of the wagon shielded lunch basket and water pails. The pinto looked dapper in a floppy straw hat that kept the sun off eyes and tender nose, and an unmatched pair of wool socks protecting his ears.

Teddy gazed up at the unbroken blue sky. "I believe it is the quality of the sun in Montana, not the temperature alone, that has made these last few days uncomfortable. We had hot summer days in the east, occasionally, but there was always something to break the sun's effects: tall leafy trees, large houses, taller buildings downtown, big puffy clouds drifting by from time to time. There are trees up on that ridge, but down here there is relentless sun from dawn 'til dusk."

"We would bake inside the blind today, my dear, so my plan is to stay in the wagon, now shielded by Arthur's creative canopy, and circumnavigate Freezout Lake. We and the pinto should be fine if we keep hydrated. We can even wade into the lake and wet our clothes if need be." He glanced sideways at her. "And speaking of clothes, I do believe that's a new garment."

"Oh, dear. I hoped no one would notice that the

proper Miss Barrington is not properly dressed in proper leg-hobbling apparel." She looked down at her voluminous trousers. "I couldn't get the blood out of one of my lightweight summer dresses, from Ku-Long's injury. So I cut out the stained parts and made what was left into wide-legged pants!" She did a little twirl. "I would prefer a pair of jeans, but at least I can move more easily in this than in skirts and petticoats."

The professor looked at her thoughtfully, his head to one side. "Unless you vault over a fence, my dear, or turn cartwheels, the men will assume your garment is less full today because of the heat."

"I hope so." She climbed into the wagon and settled herself. "This is sheer fabric, so I used the stained parts of the dress as lining. I would not want to scandalize anyone by showing the shadow of—gasp—a leg!"

"We'll be off ranch property in just a few minutes, and the road is smooth and straight. I think it's time for you to learn to drive."

"Thank you! Here in Montana, widows and spinsters drive their own rigs, and I *am* getting to the age when I count as the latter."

"You are not a spinster yet! You are not even nineteen, a lovely young woman with a lot of life to live, both before and after marriage." He gathered up the reins and chirped to the pony. "I'll stop up ahead and we can change places."

"Can't I drive from where I am, from the right side of the seat?"

"Ah. Interesting. It might not make any difference. However, I have been led to believe that horses are creatures of habit, rather than creatures of flexibility and intellect. Let us not confuse our loyal pinto."

\*\*\*\*

"Remember, my dear. You are not actually turning the animal with the reins. That would be an impossibility. You are using the reins to communicate, to signal what you want the animal to do. If a horse is well trained, as I believe all of Rancher Asher's horses are, it will need only a twitch of the reins. There's a right-angle turn ahead. Take it calmly and slowly… Beautiful, beautiful! Teddy, I believe you are a natural-born horsewoman!"

"This is exciting, Grund! I feel, I feel—Independent! Yes! That is exactly the word!"

She heard a low rumbling chuckle from the seat next to her. "My dear, you have been independent since the first time you climbed out of your crib and toddled around the house."

\*\*\*\*

Before the pinto's leisurely pace had taken them halfway along the eastern shore of the lake, the professor had almost three dozen photos and several pages of notes, and Teddy had completed twenty quick drawings.

"At this rate, Grund, I will finish this sketchbook and start another before noon."

"Remind me what we've seen that was close enough to photograph or sketch."

"Well, the cowbirds of course. We'd already seen them at the ranch. And the kingbird on that little snag. And the Carolina rail in the short grass between this path and the lake"—she flipped the pages of her sketchbook—"and the willets so amazingly close. The trumpeter swans. They weren't close, but they are big enough to see well from a distance, and draw and photograph."

"Indeed, my dear."

"The sandhill cranes, of course! I shall never forget the tall, alert, gray parents with their crimson caps, and the two fluffy orange youngsters. I took good notes so I can work more on coloring this evening."

"Someday, my dear, Mr. Eastman will invent camera film that records the true shades and hues of everything around us."

"That will be amazing. Oh!"

A brown bird with unusually large eyes in an unusually small head darted out of the grass beside the path.

"Stop the pony, Teddy. That is, I do believe, an upland plover. Yes!"

A second bird darted out of the grasses, followed by four miniature replicas of the first two, scurrying along on little stick legs. The whole family began running down the center of the track, the adults repeatedly looking back toward the wagon and making little fluttering noises.

"The parents are agitated," Teddy whispered. "Why don't they just duck into the brush on one side of the track or the other?"

"They have very tiny heads, my dear. Perhaps they also have very tiny brains."

Teddy giggled. "This is like a parade."

The parade continued—six plovers, one pony, and two humans—until they reached the northern corner of the lake. Then Teddy turned the wagon left along the dirt track, and the birds dove into the grasses straight ahead.

"That was a treat, Grund!"

"Look straight ahead and up for another treat. Stop the pony."

"What is—Oh my gracious! Is that a prairie falcon?"

"It is indeed." The professor lifted his camera, imploring the falcon to remain visible for just one more minute. But the famously speedy bird was already above their heads, hidden from sight by the canopy so thoughtfully provided by Arthur.

"Judas Priest!" He lowered his camera. "I apologize, my dear. You know I eschew cursing at any time. But that might have been our only chance for a photo of a falcon."

"If that bird is hunting in this area, we might see it again." Teddy's head was bent over her sketch pad, trying to get at least a fleeting impression of the falcon.

"True. True." The professor sighed. "The sun is turning me into a lunatic, my dear. I will take a few deep breaths and drink some water and try to calm down."

Teddy glanced over at her companion. "You look very heated, Grund. Here I am, quite comfortable in the shade, oblivious to the fact that the sun has been beating in on your side of the cart ever since we got to the lake. It should be better now we've changed direction."

"It is, it is. I will be far more comfortable with the slanting sun behind us."

The next half hour was slow and relatively unexciting. Teddy stopped once to give their patient pony some water, and she made a few sketches of a pair of shovelers to supplement the drawings from their first visit to the lake.

"Aha! *This* makes up for the lost falcon!"

Teddy didn't need to be told to stop the wagon, not when her grandfather had the camera up to his chest and was lining up the two v-shaped lines on the top with a quartet of elegant birds that were methodically sweeping their bills from side to side in the shallow water.

"Avocets! Apricot-colored avocets, as I live and breathe!"

Two of the long-legged birds had delicate orange fronts, with black and white wings. The others were completely black and white. All four had long upturned bills.

"Apricot-colored isn't part of the name, is it?"

"What? Oh. No. I was waxing poetic, as I am wont to do." He clicked two photos. "I don't have much film left so I shall have to exercise self-discipline. But I would enjoy making a whole album of avocet photos. I had been hoping we would get at least one good close look, and now we can sit here and enjoy them at our leisure."

"That's the most unusual beak we've seen yet."

"The Latin name for the species is *Recurvirostra americana*, the first part referring to the recurved bill. I believe no other species have been found in North America with bills like these." He snapped two more pictures and then put the camera in his lap. "Teddy my dear, the draft of Knowlton's birds of this area lists just under two hundred species, if I remember correctly. We have been in Montana only six weeks and have seen and documented over a hundred and fifty. Our book is going to make history!"

"Oh dear! What is the matter with that grebe? The one closest to the little island. It has lost several feathers on the back. And is it bleeding?" She leaned forward, her hands on the wagon's curved front. "Oh, how amazing! It's not blood! It's a young grebe, tucked between the adult's wings. The red splotches on the little one's head made me think I was seeing blood." She looked up and then down at her sketchbook and then up again, wanting to capture every nuance of the young bird's multicolored plumage. "Let's stay here until I get a good sketch and you take at least one photo. I wish you had one of those color cameras now!"

There was silence as Teddy sketched and her grandfather took notes.

"Won't those bright colors make the young perilously visible to flying predators?"

"Hmmm. I haven't seen any studies about this, my dear, but it occurs to me that a broken pattern of light and dark like that on the young grebe's head might provide excellent camouflage."

"I'm not familiar with that word."

"I heard it only recently. I believe it comes from a French word meaning disguise, or trick. The varied colors trick predators into overlooking the youngster."

"How crafty nature is! The camouflage worked with me. I didn't see that little grebe at all at first. Only the unusual pattern."

**** 

"My dear, the heat is bothering me more than usual. I am feeling a tad dizzy. I believe I should lie down in the back while you get us home."

Teddy had been too entranced with birds, and too dedicated to getting every sighting down in a rough sketch, to notice her grandfather's increasingly red face and rapid breathing.

"You do look far too hot, Grund. Why don't you drink some more water?"

"I believe that even water might result in nausea." He gave her a weak shadow of his usual warm smiles. "Lying down is the best thing for me, I do believe."

"Yes. That's a good idea. You will feel better soon.

I know you will."

He climbed out of the wagon without help, but he reached out and held onto the railing as he made his way toward the back. Teddy watched as he pulled himself up into the wagon's bed and pushed the lunch basket and water pails to one side. Then he slid under the canvas tarp, angling his body so his long legs didn't hang off the end.

"I will open one of the bottles in our lunch basket and pour the water over my shirt, and let evaporation provide a bit of cooling. Ahhhh."

"That sounds like a fine and scientific thing to do, Grund. You rest, and I'll head back. Maybe Ku-Long knows a remedy for too much heat."

"Don't fret, my dear. I will be fine. I've lived most of my life in New England, and my old body isn't accustomed to this kind of sun."

The track around the rest of the lake felt infinitely long to Teddy.

"Grund?"

"Yes, my dear?"

"I—I just wondered if you had fallen asleep."

His quiet chuckle was one of the most welcome sounds she had ever heard.

"Sleep is highly unlikely, my dear. I am lying on a hard surface and being rocked none too gently every time the wagon wheels go over a rut."

"I remember well from our trip from Choteau in the buckboard. I would have been thrown about wildly had Rancher Asher not instructed me to sit between two sturdy boxes fastened to the wagon bed." Teddy continued to talk with her grandfather, needing to hear his voice and feel assured that he was all right. "We're back on the road now."

"Excellent."

"You know, Grund, I haven't properly thanked you for allowing me to be part of this adventure. And for training me so I could be an active partner."

"It has been a delight sharing this with you, my dear."

"For me, this is an adventure of a lifetime."

"Surely not! You are an independent and adventurous young woman, and you will be financially comfortable. There is no end to what you can accomplish."

"I would like to believe that. But there are still many limitations for women in this country."

"That will change, my dear. That will change."

"I hope so. But no matter what I do later in life, this trip with you will always be a treasured memory. I have come to love this part of the country, and I love working together on a project that is so important to you."

"It is indeed, my dear." His voice was sounding stronger now, and his breathing less noticeable. "I was a success as a teacher, I believe, and then as a banker. Both teaching and helping others manage their finances are valuable services." He reached up under the seat and touched her leg. "Your father was a wonderful man and a wonderful human being. I am proud to have sired him. I am even prouder of you, Teddy, because I had a greater hand in your upbringing than I did with your father. I *should* be satisfied with what I have done with my life. But I am greedy. I want this book. I want to see it, with our two names on it. I want to know that two generations of Barringtons have contributed to science. I want to know that bird lovers in libraries all over the country will open the pages of our book and learn what we have learned. That will be my legacy."

The road ahead blurred as Teddy blinked back tears. She realized, at that moment, that her grandfather feared he might not have time for further achievements after their book, and that he had come to terms with his advancing age. But she had not.

She stopped the wagon after another half hour to get the pail of water out of the back and give their pony a chance to dip his muzzle and drink.

"Would you like me to wet your silly hat, you wonderful beast? Does that feel good? I think I shall wet my face and neck too." She looked around. "No one will see if I splash a little water on my legs also. Ahhhhh. Much cooler!"

She climbed back onto the seat and picked up the reins.

"Grund," she murmured.

"Yes, my dear?"

"There are half a dozen small birds in the road ahead of us. Pipits, perhaps."

"Take your time, my dear, and get some good sketches."

"At least a dozen! Eating grass seeds, I believe."

"And possibly picking up grit. It helps them with digestion."

"I had forgotten that." She was already drawing, her hand moving rapidly over the paper. "Are you sure you are all right with the delay?"

"Absolutely. The shade and the damp shirt have done wonders. Look closely, my dear. I believe pipits are often found in mixed flocks with other small birds."

"Oh! Oh, yes! Several of the birds have little raised

horns. How delightful! The faces are black and bright yellow, and they have little black horns."

"Horned larks. Pallid horned larks, to be exact. Excellent!"

"Oh, I wish I had three or four hands so I could make that many sketches at once!" Her voice trailed off into quiet muttering, telling herself what she was seeing, what colors, what patterns of darker and lighter. "One bird looks different. Blunter bill. Sparrow bill. Little white rings around the eyes. Oh! White outer tail feathers! Western vesper sparrow?"

"Another for our list! I would love to see them, but I am afraid my getting out of the wagon would spook the whole flock."

Teddy had just turned to the ninth new page of her sketchbook when all the small birds suddenly took flight.

"Phew! That was an intense and exciting few minutes! And now…" She clucked to the pony and the wagon started moving. "Back to the ranch."

\*\*\*\*

"Damnation. What has that Easterner female done now?"

Caleb reined in his big appaloosa and glared down at the pony and wagon passing under the Long Butte Ranch sign. Miss Barrington was in the driver's seat, but there was no sign of the professor.

The pinto tossed its head and neighed a welcome as the rancher galloped down the ridge and reined in beside her in a cloud of dust.

"What happened? Where is your grandfather?"

"I am here. I am invisible," the professor called out.

The rancher glanced toward the back of the wagon and then back at the driver.

"Why?"

"Your Montana sun was a bit too much for him."

What in Hades was the woman wearing? He had seen more decently dressed women in the orange house. He jerked his head up and glared at the pony's hat.

"Managing a cart is another of your many skills?"

"It is now," she said cheerfully. "It is quite remarkable what women can do when the need arises."

Caleb grunted. He knew his voice would be harsh, his words impolite, but he had to get away from her. The image of her thighs outlined in thin damp fabric would stay with him for days. And the possibility that he might have detected a faint darker triangle in her lap was not going to help one bit.

"Take the wagon directly to your cabin and go inside with your grandfather. Leave the rig to me."

Her stubborn little chin lifted. "We took the cart out. It is our responsibility to unharness the pony and put the tack away."

As far as he knew, the professor did all the harnessing and unharnessing while the girl stood by, chattering like a magpie. But Caleb was sure she would try it on her own even if it took her the rest of the day. She would stand right there in the barn, in *his* barn, wearing flimsy wet clothing that showed every curve and every softness.

"Taking care of the pony and wagon would usually be your duty, Miss Barrington. But the ranch is my responsibility. I will not allow you to walk around my ranch in transparent clothing."

He watched her neck and cheeks flood with scarlet. Finally. He had discomfited the infuriating young lady.

"Oh! I—I spilled water on my dress when—When I

was getting the pail for the pony. I—Of course I have no intention of walking around like this! I will…"

He could not stay for another second, only a yard away from clear outlines of knees and thighs. And chests. He slapped the reins on his horse's neck and headed for the safety of his ranch.

\*\*\*\*

She knows I'm waiting. No doubt she is enjoying making me wait.

Caleb wondered what she would do after she stopped the wagon. He hadn't seen anything with her that she could use to cover herself. Maybe the extra half hour had dried her clothes, but maybe not. Would she brazenly climb down and flaunt herself in front of him? He *could* be a gentleman and offer her the shirt off his back. But he had been working in that shirt for two days in the blistering sun, and it would no doubt offend her proper Bostonian nose.

She pulled up, finally, glanced in his direction, took a deep breath that made him wish he had been looking elsewhere, and climbed down with her chin held high.

The professor's legs appeared from under the wagon cover. "I don't require assistance, my dear. You go ahead in."

"Very well."

The older man clambered down. He walked into the cabin under his own steam, but Caleb followed until he was safely seated.

"Professor. This may sound illogical given all the sun you have soaked up today, but you are apt to feel chilled. I'll light a fire in your stove. If you wrap up, and drink hot liquids, you should be back to normal by morning."

"Thank you. Ahhh. It feels good to be sitting on something that isn't bouncing around."

"You are fortunate you were able to get under cover. People can die from heatstroke or sunstroke."

"After this morning's experience, I well believe that. Why Teddy, my dear! You look like a sweet-faced mummy."

At least she was decent. The curve of her arms was still visible under damp fabric, but the rest of her was swathed in a tightly wrapped bedsheet.

"I need to get my sketchbooks from the wagon seat." She pushed by Caleb and out the door. "And I wish a private moment with you, Mr. Asher."

"Professor, the fire should catch nicely now. I'll be in shortly to check."

She started talking the moment the door closed behind him, her face pinched and anxious. "I had no idea that becoming overheated could be fatal. Is that true? Or were you trying to frighten us?"

"I know of two ranch hands in the Choteau area who succumbed to sunstroke."

"How can that be? Is it—" She flapped one hand and then quickly grabbed the sheet and held it more tightly. "Does a person dry out so much that blood no longer runs through the veins? Can drinking water prevent that?"

"Drinking is a good idea. But I understand that too much summer sun can cause something to break, burst, inside the brain."

"I had no idea." She glanced toward the closed cabin door and shuddered. "Could that have happened to Grund? Could he have something broken in his head right now? Is there anything I should look for, over the next few hours?"

Caleb had seen her proud, caring, defiant, angry, entranced, delighted, intent. He had never seen her vulnerable.

"Was your grandfather dizzy? Did he lose consciousness?"

"He said he felt dizzy, but he didn't pass out. He was red-faced and breathing hard when he first lay down, but after a few minutes his voice was strong and steady."

"Did he, uh, empty his stomach?"

"No. But he said a drink of water might nauseate him."

"Well, Miss Barrington. I believe you and your grandfather dealt with his symptoms sensibly. His color is good now, he's not panting or gasping, and he didn't need help walking from the wagon to the cabin. He should be fine."

Her whole body relaxed.

"Thank you." She looked toward the cabin door. "Thank you. Grund has been the most important person in my life since I was very small."

"How old is he?"

"I don't know." She looked up at him, her eyes wide. "I really don't. How odd. We never celebrated birthdays. Well, we might have when my parents were alive. I have a vague recollection of a cake with candles on it. But Grund always says it makes more sense to celebrate an accomplishment instead of just another three-sixty-five or three-sixty-six days." The dimple in her cheek made a brief appearance. "We had a four-layer cake with cherries when I mastered the times tables." She frowned. "He must be over eighty, given my father's age and mine."

"He walks and talks like a much younger man."

"He does. It is difficult for me to accept that he is—That he is getting old. I suppose I have always thought of him as static. As if he stopped at the age he was when I was six or ten or thirteen." She grimaced. "That sounds idiotic."

"Not at all. It sounds like you love him."

Her eyes were wide and startled. "I do. Thank you for understanding. I didn't expect that." She was appalled when she heard herself make the waspish comment. "I am so sorry! That was unforgivably rude. And foolish! I saw you with Ku-Long when he was hurt, and with the Metis girl. I have ample reason not to judge you so harshly. I am rattled right now. Please forgive me."

Caleb lost both voice and the power to think when he felt her fingers, smooth and gentle, on the inside of his wrist.

"I should get back inside, Mr. Asher. Would you mind getting the lunch basket out of the back of the wagon?" She reached up and lifted her two sketchbooks from the wagon seat, keeping a tight grasp on the sheet with the other hand. "Thank you. For your help today and your empathy and your calm advice. I needed someone calm around me."

"I am sure, Miss Barrington, that you would have continued to handle things competently on your own."

"Oh. Thank you. Again."

As Teddy walked into the cabin, as she changed out of her damp garments and dressed in dry things, as she fixed a pot of tea for her grandfather, as she felt his forehead and built up the fire, as she told him briefly what the rancher said about sunstroke, she was haunted by the memory of Rancher Asher's arm under her fingers. Most of her life had been spent around men like her grandfather and father, teachers and bankers and librarians, men whose starched and ironed shirt sleeves were always securely fastened with cufflinks, men who would never show their naked arms to a decent woman. But she liked the rancher's naked arms. She liked the muscles and the dark hairs on his tanned forearms, and the smooth hairless skin on the inside of his wrist.

****

Caleb was haunted also, all the time he put his horse Spike and the pinto pony in their stalls, gave both animals food and water, brushed them down and checked their hooves, and pulled the pony cart to its designated spot. It would be a very long time before he could forget pale, taut, womanly legs outlined by a wet skirt. And what she looked like when she took a deep breath. Her breasts were what he'd call middling. Not huge by any means, but not tiny either. He wanted very much to run his hands up under those middling breasts, and lift them, and feel their soft weight.

There were two kinds of females in Montana's ranch country. There were the girls and women in Choteau's orange house. And there were ranch wives and a few businesswomen, all of them strong, capable, weathered women who were good partners for their husbands. Miss Theodora Barrington was neither.

And Miss Theodora Barrington was not the kind of female who would let him touch her breasts. But if she did... If she did, she would also let him do other things. She would let him take her down onto the hay in the barn, or to his bed upstairs in the big house. And she would reach for him with her arms, and she would lift her long legs around him, and she would...

And then he would be trapped. She would wheedle and cajole and harass him until he gave up the ranch and moved into town, because proper young women from eastern cities like Boston preferred towns.

Big Hank would look at him with pity and humor in his all-knowing eyes. Hank would say that Miss Barrington's behavior today was just like a woman. He would say she let Caleb see her in carefully dampened clothing to arouse his manly desires. And her sweet smiles and gentle thanks, after he had leered at her like a drunken lecher, were calculated to put him at a disadvantage. Make him feel guilty and uncouth. Make him indebted.

Hank would tell his boss there was nothing wrong with feminine wiles, so long as a man didn't take them seriously. Sure, he would tell Caleb, enjoy looking at the girl while she's here. Then forget her.

But Caleb couldn't believe that Miss Barrington was sly or devious. He believed, he wanted to believe, that she was honest as the day was long. And she had apologized for insulting him. He appreciated anyone who would apologize, man or woman.

Chapter Eight

"Grund, I would like to stay on the ranch tomorrow morning and do laundry. We're both running out of clean clothing, and tomorrow should be excellent for drying."

"That is most fortuitous, my dear. Rancher Asher offered to show me a golden eagle nest. That particular pair of birds has already fledged three fine youngsters, so we should be able to get close enough to photograph the nest without being attacked. I understand it will require climbing that would be difficult or even impossible while wearing women's clothing. He and I can go tomorrow morning and I will come back for you at mid-day."

She reached out and touched her grandfather's sleeve. "Grund? Maybe you could give your camera to Mr. Asher and let him climb up and get the pictures. Then you could stay on level ground."

"I appreciate your concern, my dear. But if I understand correctly where the eagle's nest is located, I am quite confident I can scale it without undue effort, even with my advanced years."

Teddy watched him as he strolled away, whistling under his breath, looking forward to the morning's adventure.

"He is confident that he can scale ridges at his age," she muttered. "He and I are both confident that I cannot do the same, even though I am more than sixty years younger. And why not? Because of what I have to wear! I hope with all my heart that outdoor clothing for women becomes a reality before I reach his age!"

****

No one else was around, so Teddy allowed herself a fair amount of grumbling as she bent over the wash tubs. She wanted to be where her grandfather and the rancher were. She wanted to see the golden eagle nest. She might have been able to climb up there with them if she had worn the loose pants made from her ruined summer dress. As long as she didn't get wet, there was little chance of scandalizing the rancher again. But the wash needed to be done. At last, she was able to head outdoors on a sunny and hot and windy day, a perfect day for drying what she had just scrubbed. She lugged the big basket out to the lines strung up behind the main building.

"Lovely," she murmured, "just lovely. Everything will smell so good!"

"Miss?"

She whirled around. A stranger was standing only a few yards away, a large soft-looking man with a black handlebar mustache. He was incongruously dressed in a formal cutaway coat, brocade vest, black trousers, shiny black shoes with white spats, and a black top hat.

He swept the hat off and bowed. "Sure didn't mean to startle you, miss. Is your beloved spouse around?"

"He—He will be back within minutes. You may wait for him in the front yard."

"I think, instead, that I shall wait right here. Yes'm. I would prefer that."

Teddy frowned and lowered the laundry basket to the ground. "In that case, I will head over to the barn and find someone who can help you."

The man sidestepped, blocking her way with his bulk. "No need for that, miss. I am confident that you can help me." His toothy grin increased Teddy's feeling of discomfort. "To say the truth, and I always do, I am convinced that you can help me easily and effortlessly, and it will not take but a few minutes of your time." His left hand moved to the buttons in the front of his wool pants. "I will just take it out and you won't even have to touch it. All you have to do, miss, is open up three—no, *four* buttons on that pretty blouse so I can get a look at your bubbies."

"Sir! I am asking you to leave this yard. Now!"

He shook his head sadly. "Oh, dear. Dear me. I do not think that's going to happen. I really do not. You are here, fresh and pretty as a spring dawn, and I am here in need of just a few short minutes of that freshness and beauty. I am not asking much of you. A lot of pleasure for me, and so easy for you to give me that pleasure." He had now unfastened the buttons and his trousers gaped open. "I will just take it out and it will be quite wondrously happy. But you do have to show me your bubbies, you know."

Teddy clenched both arms across her breasts. She kept her eyes on the man's face, willing herself not to glance over his shoulder, willing herself not to let him know that Ku-Long had come through the kitchen door and was silently moving across the yard, holding a cast-iron skillet by the handle and slowly bringing it up to shoulder height.

"I am afraid that I don't understand you, sir. I ask again. Please wait for my husband at the front of the house."

"'Fraid not. Cannot do that, miss. Just can't."

Fast as a snake, he reached out and grabbed her wrist and yanked her toward him. At that same moment Ku-Long lifted the skillet in both hands and smacked it hard against the side of the stranger's head. The man dropped into a boneless heap, his legs twisted under him, his torso to one side, his cheek against the dirt.

"Ku-Long," Teddy gasped. "Any baseball team back home in Boston would pay good money to have you join them. That hit would have been a home run for sure."

"You are all right?"

"I'm—" She took a deep breath. "I am fine, Ku-Long. And I am very, very glad that you came along!"

\*\*\*\*

Caleb slowed the buggy as they neared the ranch house. There was a neat brightly-painted wagon in the shade between the house and barn, with a small white horse lazily flicking its tail against the flies.

"That looks like the Tobin sisters' rig. Would you mind taking care of the horse and wagon, Professor? I'd like to find out what the neighbors might want of us."

"Of course." Professor Barrington took the reins as Caleb jumped down. "I thank you again for a morning that was both productive and adventurous."

\*\*\*\*

But it wasn't the Tobin sisters Caleb saw as he crossed the yard. Instead, he saw Ku-Long and Miss Barrington, and a man crumpled up on the ground between them like a giant doll.

"Is he ill?"

Both Teddy and Ku-Long jumped.

"This… He…"

Teddy touched the cook's arm and interrupted. "This man thought I was alone here. He tried to take advantage of that fact. Ku-Long and his skillet saved me."

"I see." Caleb looked from Teddy to Ku-Long and then to the man on the ground. Then he put one hand on the cook's shoulder and squeezed. "It looks like you and your skillet did some good work today, my friend." He knelt, touched the stranger's forehead, lifted one eyelid and put his fingers to the man's throat. Then he stood up very slowly, his solemn eyes on Ku-Long's face. "That was a powerful blow. He's dead."

The cook took a step backward. "They hang Chinaman."

Caleb looked down again at the body at his feet. After a long moment, he shook his head and squared his shoulders with determination. "Not this Chinaman. Grab his shoulders, haul him up, turn him to face me." He nudged Teddy with his elbow. "Out of my way."

Ku-Long lifted the inert body, flipped it over, and pulled it up in front of him so the stranger's head rested against the cook's chest. Teddy made an involuntary sound as Caleb smacked his big fist into the dead man's face, splitting the lips, knocking out at least one tooth, and flattening the nose.

Ku-Long laid the dead man back down on the ground, face up, and both men stared down.

"Not enough blood."

The cook nodded. He dug in his pocket for his knife, flipped it open, pushed up his sleeve, and gritted his teeth. Teddy realized what he planned to do a split second too late to stop him. Before her horrified eyes, Ku-Long scraped the knife over part of the long healing scab on his left arm. Then he leaned over the dead man and let his own blood drop onto the nose, into the open mouth, over the chin, onto the neck and the bright white shirtfront.

Teddy turned away, feeling queasy.

"Horses are coming. More than one. Ku-Long, get back in the house. Take the skillet with you. Get ready to shoot someone out of his saddle if it comes to that, but otherwise stay inside and stay hidden."

The cook whirled and headed for the house. Teddy called out, "And clean and bandage that arm!" just as he reached the kitchen door.

"Why do you think there might be shooting?"

The rancher looked at her as if she were imbecilic. "Do you know who those riders are? I sure don't. We already had one stranger here this morning, and he was not a friend. There could be more like him coming."

"Oh. Yes." She looked toward the main house. "I don't understand why Ku-Long cut himself. Why?"

"Dead men don't bleed much. Now it looks like the guy was alive when I hit him."

"But what difference—?"

The rancher grabbed her shoulders. "Stop asking questions and listen up. This is what happened. A stranger surprised you. He…" Caleb abruptly pulled at her crossed arms and then took a fistful of her blouse and yanked. Two buttons popped open and the thin fabric ripped apart from the buttonholes to one sleeve. "He put his filthy hands on you. You screamed. I heard you and I came and I punched him. He fell down and died. You do not even mention Ku-Long. Got it?"

Two riders had left the main road and were heading for the ranch yard.

"Yes. I—Of course. You killed the man." She frowned. "Would Ku-Long—Would he be hanged?"

"Probably. A Chinaman killing a white man. There's a lot of anti-Chinese feeling in town, much more than there used to be."

"And if you say you killed him, you might be hanged?"

"Not likely." He looked at her and Teddy saw what looked like a slight smile on his face. "I will be a hero, Miss Barrington. I have saved a fair maiden from a fate worse than death."

She didn't smile back. She had just seen a man die. She knew the approaching horses represented some new danger but she didn't understand what. She looked down at her front and quickly crossed her arms over the gaping blouse.

"You can keep your story straight?"

"Of course. I am—" She stood up straighter, glaring at him. "I may be shaking all over, but I am neither a child nor an idiot."

"Shaking is good. You were assaulted. Shaking is expected." He took a few steps from her, getting between her and the approaching men, his right hand on the pistol in his holster. But his shoulders relaxed when the two men got close enough for him to see their faces.

"These are not strangers. They are vigilantes."

"But vigilantes—"

"Hush." He moved closer to the riders. "Mr. Hawkins. Mr. Truchot. You two out for a pleasant ride in the country?"

Both men rode their horses to within a few feet of Caleb, two sets of eyes taking in the white-faced girl with the ripped blouse, and the bloody stranger laid out on the ground. The taller of the two men dismounted and walked over to stare down at the dead man.

"Goldarn. Miracles do happen. You know who you got here?"

"I know nothing about this gentleman. Only that he assaulted Miss Barrington. I was out in the barn and I heard her scream." He pushed at the body with his boot. "I pulled him away from her and punched him."

"As any decent man would. Any decent man would." The tall vigilante turned to Teddy. "Are you all right, miss?"

Teddy raised her chin, her hands still clenched across her breasts. "I am shaken but perfectly fine. Mr. Asher's intervention came at a most opportune moment."

"So you came running, you saw what was going on, and you punched him. That right?"

"One punch. Yes. But I do believe the man is dead."

The vigilante's bushy eyebrows disappeared under the brim of his hat. "Quite some punch. Quite a punch indeed. Well, sir, you have saved us a great deal of time and trouble. A great deal." He turned toward Teddy. "And you, miss, you were lucky. Lucky indeed. This man in the dust, unless I am very much mistaken, is none other than Gentleman Charlie Chase. He has assaulted four fine Montana women in the last week alone. He is a wanted man here and in Wisconsin and Ohio. A wanted man." He stared down again. "Yup. The mustache. The heavy build. The fancy vest and fancy coat. The spats. Did he have a top hat?"

"He did…" Teddy looked around, baffled, and then took two quick steps and reached down behind the laundry basket. "It must have fallen when he—when he grabbed for me."

"That clinches it then. That's his hat. Gentleman Charlie Chase." He nodded at Caleb. "Your mighty punch, sir, saved us from having to hang him. You may not believe this, but hanging a person takes it out of a man. Takes it out of his immortal soul, you might say, no matter how evil the outlaw might have been while he was alive. Every one of us vigilantes knows that to be the case. Every man jack of us."

"I'm sure that's true. And people around here are grateful for what you do."

"That his rig out to the side of the house?"

"It looks like the gig and pony belonging to the Tobin sisters."

"Is that so? Well, now, that is mighty worrisome. Mighty worrisome indeed. We will want to check on those two fine ladies immediately. Judson, I believe we should take our leave posthaste."

The vigilante who was still mounted gathered up his reins.

"Mr. Asher sir, will you give me a hand carrying the deceased to that cheerful little wagon? Judson, you drive it and I'll lead your horse and we'll check on the Tobin sisters on our way back to town."

The other rider spoke for the first time. "Hope yall'll be praying along with us two, that them ladies is all right."

"Yes indeed. Yes indeed. After we leave their place, we'll bring the body to old Justice Knowles. You might want to check in at his office next time you're in Choteau, Mr. Asher. He might have a few questions for you."

"Of course. I will. And thank you, again."

The quieter man tipped his hat toward Teddy. "Nice speaking atcha."

Teddy stood mute, still clutching her clothing across her chest, watching as the body was carried across the yard and loaded into the back of the brightly painted wagon, watching as the two men and the makeshift hearse left the yard, watching as the rancher strode back toward her.

"I don't understand. I thought vigilantes were no better than criminals. Lawless. Taking the law into their own hands."

"Do you have police back home in Boston?"

"Of course. We—"

"Sheriffs?"

"Yes, but—"

"Let me give you a bit of history, Miss Barrington. Western *facts* to replace eastern prejudices." His words were clipped and his face grim. "Montana Territory has never had effective law enforcement. Not since white people got here anyway. The mining communities in particular are havens for the lawless, and the mining courts are informal and largely toothless. When the Vigilance Committees were first formed, they were the only law enforcement in the whole region."

He looked down at his hand, winced, and blew on the scraped and abraded knuckles.

"About twenty-five years ago, some politician lawyer declared that vigilante groups were criminal. But the politicians and the city lawyers didn't come up with any alternatives. No surprise there. So then came Committees of Safety, and Stockman's Associations, and civic protection commissions. Same thing, different names." He looked directly at her, his deep blue eyes stern. "How did you get to Choteau?"

"What?" Teddy was still shaky, and she was nonplussed by the abrupt change of topic. "We—We took the train from Boston to Great Forks. And the stagecoach from there."

"Well, before the Choteau vigilante group was up and running, the very group that includes those two men who were just here, that coach had a damn good chance of being held up. Robbed. The company hired armed guards, but one guard sitting up with the driver was no match for five or ten robbers. They'd just shoot the driver and the guard both and then they'd order everybody off the coach while they emptied the valises and trunks and took whatever caught their fancy. From women passengers, they often took something more precious than jewelry or money." He turned and looked out over the range to the cloud of disappearing dust. "So you are right, Miss Barrington. Vigilantes like Mr. Hawkins and Mr. Truchot take the law into their own hands. But theirs are the only hands holding onto any semblance of law and order. Some folks think the vigilantes might have hanged a few innocent people, and I can't say that might not be the case. But I have no doubt at all that they have taken out of circulation a great number of men who should *not* be running around free. Men like Gentleman Charlie Chase of your recent acquaintance."

"I—I see. Thank you. Thank you for that very thorough explanation. You were right. I didn't understand the reality out here." Teddy turned and bent down to pick up the laundry basket. "And now I have wash to hang up. I will fix my blouse later. Will you check Ku-Long's arm for me?"

"I will." He started toward the main house but then

turned back. "I apologize for ripping your clothing."

"It was probably necessary."

"I thought so at the time. But I am sorry anyway."

"Please forget about it."

**\*\*\*\***

He wouldn't forget about it. If he closed his eyes, he could still see the softly rounded top of her breast above the thin chemise.

And he could hear his big brother Ike, just as clear as if he stood beside him.

*You sure you had to do that, Caleb? You sure the young lady needed a ripped blouse so those men would believe her story? You sure you didn't have another motive, your own motive? You know that men get their blood up when they've lived through violence. Are you sure you didn't want, didn't need, to see that young lady's breast, immediately, right then, while your blood was still running hot?*

Caleb wasn't sure. And being not sure made him embarrassed and angry. Miss Barrington was a guest on his ranch. He was responsible for her. He did not at all enjoy the possibility that he might belong in the same category as the dead man. A lecherous, unprincipled man taking advantage of an innocent young woman.

And now, when Caleb came back out of the ranch house, he was faced with the laundry flapping on the line. The professor's underthings, shirts, and socks. And women's drawers. Women's fancy undershirts. Long stockings still holding the shape of a woman's legs.

And three upside-down dresses, held on the line with wooden pins along the bottom, the skirts dancing and billowing with every breath of wind.

Chapter Nine

"Oh, Mr. Asher," caroled a female voice. "Yoo-hoo! Mr. Asher!"

Caleb reined in his horse and looked around. The little rig belonging to the two Tobin sisters was pulling up under the sign for Long Butte Ranch, and both women were energetically waving their gloved hands at him.

"How fortunate we are to run into you, Mr. Asher! We feared we might have to search all over your vast holdings before we found you!"

"What can I do for you ladies?"

"It is what you have already done that brings us out here today."

"What I have…"

The sister who always did the driving leaned across and wagged her finger at him.

"Now don't you go all modest on us! Pretending you have forgotten! My stars! If you hadn't killed that dreadful Gentleman Charlie person, we would never have seen our beloved little pony again."

"But it was Misters Hawkins and Truchot who returned your rig."

"We have already thanked those two men. Thanked them handsomely, I must say." The closer sister lifted a cardboard box from the seat between them, a box wound about with many lengths of yarn and fastened with an impressive array of knots. "And for you, we baked a

German chocolate cake with dark chocolate frosting, using our dear mother's favorite recipe."

As he reached out to take the box, he was engulfed in a mouthwatering aroma.

"This is a mighty wonderful surprise. Thank you both!"

"Now you have to promise to eat this entire cake yourself. Don't you go sharing it with your crew!"

"Mrs. Tobin, I honestly don't believe there will be a crumb left to share by the time I get back to the ranch house."

Damn. Maybe that was Miss Tobin. One sister was widowed and the other was a spinster, and he was never sure which was which. One was a bit taller, a bit thinner, and had more gray in her hair, but apart from that they could have been twins with their soft brown weathered faces and their sharp blue eyes and their deceptively childlike smiles.

Caleb hoisted the cake box to a safer position, inhaling another blast of chocolate and feeling his mouth start to water.

"Your cake smells better than an entire bakery."

"Our mother was a fine cook, that is a true fact."

"And you two have clearly inherited her skill along with her recipes, judging by how fast your pies and cakes go at the annual Choteau auction and craft fair."

As one, the Tobin sisters put their hands to their mouths and tittered.

"Tell me, ladies. How did Gentleman Charlie manage to steal your rig?"

The change in the sisters was immediate and startling. Both of them sat up straighter, their lips tightened, their blue eyes narrowed, their gloved hands

118

clenched into fists, and their delicate blushes deepened into twin circles of red high on their powdered cheeks.

"It was bold, downright bold. Sophy and I were in the house the whole time—"

"Putting up some dilly beans—"

"And that always takes concentration—"

"Or they turn out mushy."

"And then we might as well just toss them out—"

"The whole batch!"

"All that time wasted!"

"So you two were indoors," Caleb prompted, trying to get back to Gentleman Charlie and the pony.

"Yes! And when we finally finished up with the beans—"

"And it was a big crop this year."

"Elsie went outdoors to see if there might be a cucumber for lunch—"

"And there was a wretched sway-backed nag—"

"Right in the middle of our front yard!"

"I looked around for the owner, and I called out—"

"And she never even guessed that our own pony was gone out of the barn!"

"Didn't guess for a minute—"

"Not until those two men brought her back for us!"

"Well, ladies, I believe you were very fortunate. The man who stole your rig had assaulted women here in Montana and was wanted in two other states besides."

One of the sisters gave a delicate shudder. "Father always told his girls to keep the door locked whenever he wasn't home. That's what he called Mother and us. His girls."

"I do believe your father was looking down on you that day, and he saved you from a great deal of unpleasantness."

Now the sisters shuddered in unison.

"Do you think that dreadful man might have tried the door? Our very door—"

"Before heading out to our barn?"

"We will never know."

"Scares me just about to death—"

"To think about it!"

"And to think of that awful man in our barn—"

"Putting his filthy hands on our fine little pony!"

"It fair makes my blood boil!"

"Well, Miss and Mrs. Tobin. I have work to do. Thank you again for the cake." Caleb gathered up the reins, but then turned back toward the sisters. "What happened with Gentleman Charlie's old nag?"

"You will never believe—"

"The good fortune! You know the Whitcombs—"

"That family that lives just east of us—"

"With all the children? Well!"

"The parents have been looking for a project to help their children learn responsibility. They have dogs—"

"But the dogs are hunters and the father tends to them."

"And the mother looks after the milk cow and the chickens because they need the butter and eggs and meat to sell—"

"So they took the horse for their children!"

"And now it's the children's job to turn it out to pasture in the morning and bring it in every evening—"

"And groom it and exercise it and feed and water. So it was—"

"Just simply perfect!"

He intervened, trying to leave the conversation.

"That old horse must think he died and went to heaven. Well. Thank you again for the chocolate treat, ladies. I have to get back to work."

"One more thing, Mr. Asher."

Caleb turned back once again.

"We understand you have a young woman living with you."

Hell and damnation. Hank or Bucky wouldn't have said anything in town. And no one had been out to the ranch except... Oh. The vigilantes. Damn.

"There is a woman here for a few weeks, but she is not living with me. She is the assistant to the ornithologist from Boston, the expert who is doing a census of birds in the area. Professor Barrington and his granddaughter are spending the summer in one of the ranch's log cabins. They were hired by an eastern organization called the Boston Birding Alliance."

"Oh! We misunderstood then. We shall have to explain to the Circle." The nearer sister leaned forward with an earnest expression on her face. "No doubt you have heard of the Choteau Area Women's Sewing Circle."

"I can't say I have."

"How very surprising. We were of the opinion that every citizen for miles around knows about our group."

Both sisters tut-tutted. They had tittered just a few minutes ago. Caleb had never heard any female younger than fifty make either of those sounds. He couldn't imagine Miss Barrington, for example, pursing up her lips and tut-tutting, or covering her mouth with her fingers and tittering.

"It seems that you have not spent much time talking with women in Choteau then." Now both sisters were gazing at him with a combination of censure and pity. "Decent women, that is. We do understand that you have had interactions with the females in the orange house."

Caleb could feel his neck and ears reddening. "I have had many conversations, Miss Tobin, with Mrs. Williamson at the mercantile. And Mrs. McNamara at the pie shop."

"We are delighted to hear that. However." The driver gave a brisk nod. "To the point of this particular conversation. The Women's Sewing Circle has a long-standing tradition of holding our monthly meeting in the home of any woman who is a new resident in the area. We introduce ourselves and we help her with specialty items such as hand towels and pillowcases—"

"And curtains."

"Yes, Sophy. And curtains. Several of our members suggested that we hold our July meeting at Long Butte Ranch, now that a woman is living there. The main house surely has sufficient room for eight or ten busy seamstresses."

The other Tobin frowned. "But surely, Elsie, this young woman isn't actually putting down roots, is she?"

"No," Caleb said firmly. "She is not."

The sisters sighed, in unison.

"Well then, there is no point in helping with her household sewing."

"No point at all."

"Ah well. We will take our leave then—"

"And thank you again for your courageous actions last week!"

****

"That was too damn close, Spike," Caleb muttered to his horse. "One female sets foot on the ranch two

122

months ago, and now those two sisters drive out here from town and start talking about eight or ten females in the ranch kitchen all at the same time. They are like mice, Spike. You see one and the next minute you got hundreds."

The cake was a kind and generous thought, though. It rightly belonged to Ku-Long, and the ranch cook should get it before it melted in the heat. Damn. At this rate, it would be mid-day before the rancher got around to what he set out to do that morning.

But he couldn't resist a few minutes just sitting on his horse and contemplating his land. His land. Grassland and wetland and prairie and forested ridges and stony ridges, the original homestead of just under seven hundred acres and now almost five thousand acres of grazing land. He wished his father were alive to sit here with him and look out over all those acres, to see the fat and healthy cattle wearing the Long Butte brand, and the sturdy and prosperous barns and the bunkhouse and the fenced-in paddocks and the spirited horses. To walk into the main house that was so much grander than the sod-and-slat shack and the later log cabin. To see what Caleb and his brother, and then Caleb alone, had made of the ranch.

He sighed and looked down to his right, past the little wooded hill where the visiting ornithologists had seen the roosting owls, down to a flat open area where, in wet years, a stream leaped and splashed down the ridge and created a soggy spot several acres in size. An unexpected blotch of tan caught his eye. The bird-watching blind! What with meeting up with the Tobin sisters and listening to their sweet voices chirping about a women's sewing circle meeting in his kitchen, he plumb forgot that the Barringtons planned to spend the morning studying bird activity along the stream and in the muddy wetlands and among the willows, aspens, and cottonwoods.

He could see two people in the process of easing out of the blind, moving so slowly and cautiously that he was sure there was an unusual bird nearby. Even at a distance, and even from the back, Miss Barrington was easy to identify. The other person was a surprise: the Long Butte Ranch cook, his long black braid neatly dividing the back of his white shirt in half.

"We just got ourselves a lucky break, Spike. I can hand over the cake on the way to check on that well and we won't have to go all the way back to the ranch house."

By the time he and Spike emerged from the little woods, Miss Barrington was no longer visible and the professor had joined Ku-Long. The ranch cook looked quite professional as he held the older man's camera to his chest and aimed it, the long scar from the range cow's horn bright pink in the morning sun.

"Huh. It is entirely possible, Spike, that your rider has taken leave of his senses." Caleb would have sworn the cook was wearing a white shirt with long sleeves, only a few minutes ago, but now he had on one of his white singlets. "Those Tobin sisters discombobulated my brain, Spike. That is the only plausible explanation."

He tightened his fingers through the yarn on the cake box, dismounted a good distance from the blind, and walked quietly over the damp sandy earth.

"You got it, Ku-Long!" The professor clapped the younger man on his shoulder. "That is *your* flycatcher! You saw it when we didn't, you kept your sharp eye on it, and you photographed it. Henceforth it should be referred to as Ku-Long's flycatcher, not Wright's flycatcher."

The cook's mobile mouth twisted up at the corners, and his eyes crinkled. "Ver' exciting, Mr. B. Ver' please."

"Very pleasing for us too. This is the ideal habitat for that species but we've been here several times already with no success. Teddy my dear! Did you get a good sketch?"

"I did!" She pushed aside the cloth side of the blind. "I am so glad it stayed around long enough for me to get a good look and for you two to get some photographs."

She glanced up and grinned. "Rancher Asher! We didn't hear you coming! You can join us in a quiet celebration of a species that has been maddeningly elusive."

He held out the box. "And I brought a celebratory cake."

"How very fortunate. And unexpected!"

"Ku-Long, the cake is for you, to share or hoard as you wish. The Tobin sisters baked a German chocolate cake as a thank-you for killing the man who stole their horse and buggy. They don't know it was you, but we all do."

"Share, yes. Good time for break." His eyes crinkled again. "Cake break. We go in tent."

Teddy snickered. "That would be a tight fit. Why don't you go in, and cut the cake and hand pieces out to us?"

"Yes. Good. Have knife."

The professor held open the flap on the canvas blind. "I have an extra scratch pad in my bag. We can use the paper as plates."

\*\*\*\*

"Ladies first, my dear." Grund handed her a slice of chocolate cake with chocolate frosting, and then turned back toward the blind. "And you, of course. Our other lady."

Caleb blinked. Ku-Long came out. Another Ku-Long, with his white clothing and his long dark braid. And a lateral scar across her cheek.

"Isabelle!"

The Metis girl smiled and murmured, "I Ku-Long too."

"I see that." Caleb glanced at the others. "I thought Ku-Long Two here was staying inside the cabin."

"She was, for too many days." Teddy moved to stand next to the other girl. "Isabelle has been outdoors her whole life. She needed to be in the fresh air. I decided that if she dressed like Ku-Long, and if only one of them were visible at any one time, then she could go outside and no one who saw her from a distance would guess the truth. She has spent time sitting behind the cabin for several days now, and this morning I asked if she would like to join us."

Caleb frowned. "How did she get here? Anyone who saw the wagon would surely notice two Ku-Longs."

"Not at all. Isabelle was in the back of the cart, under the canvas, just like Grund that day we came back from Freezout Lake."

"I see. And this was your idea."

"It was." She dimpled at him. "It has turned out to be a smart and crafty plan."

Isabelle had been watching their faces as they talked, and now she reached out and touched Teddy's arm.

"Need air. Sky. Dearth."

"Dirt, Isabelle. Or earth. But not dearth."

"Dirt. Thank."

"How long has she been able to speak English?"

"We have been teaching each other." Teddy grimaced. "But one of us is an unusually quick learner, and the other is a numskull. Isabelle knows scores of English words already, and I have learned fewer than a dozen words in mih-chiff. Mischief. Did I say that right?"

"Michif. Is right."

"And that is one of the few words I know. Mischief is the name of the Metis language." She sighed. "Do you remember, Grund, when you tried to teach me French?"

He handed Caleb a thick slab of cake. "My dear, I shall never forget. It was, I do believe, the single most frustrating experience of my life."

"I was so vastly relieved when you finally admitted defeat!"

He patted her shoulder. "Language learning is an unusually specific ability, my dear, and it is not evenly distributed among the human population."

"I suppose that should make me feel a bit less stupid." She broke off a bit of the cake with her fingers and put it in her mouth. "Oh my goodness. This is extraordinary!"

"The Misses Tobin are known to be excellent cooks, and this was their mother's favorite recipe."

"I can see why. Oh my goodness goodness goodness."

Ku-Long joined them with his own piece of cake. "Is more. More for everybody."

"So what was the good bird?"

"Every bird is a good bird. You should know that by now, Mr. Asher." Teddy spoke primly but her dimple betrayed her. "Today we saw many species of good birds. We watched a flock of at least eight magpies, and then two or three white-crowned sparrows, and our first little grasshopper sparrow."

"Named because of the size?"

"Because they catch and eat grasshoppers, among other insects."

"Ah. So you saw sparrows and magpies and a grasshopper-eater. But what was Ku-Long's very exciting and very pleasing bird?"

The professor answered this time, and Caleb had the passing thought that he looked younger than when he first arrived, with color in his cheeks and his eyes twinkling with excitement under the bushy brows.

"A Wright's flycatcher! They are in the Empidonax genus, a group notoriously difficult to distinguish one from another. We would not have been able to identify that bird with any confidence had it not stayed in the area for many minutes, allowing all four of us to get a good look at the round gray head and olive back."

"And the little white teardrop shape behind the eye."

"And the teardrop, my dear. Other options for this habitat were alder flycatcher and possibly a least flycatcher or even a Hammond's, but the three-part whistle clinched it. The rising *prrrrt*, then the husky *prrrrt*, and then the clear high-pitched *seeeee*. Once we heard that, and we heard it no fewer than four times, there was no doubt at all. It was a Wright's! But it took Ku-Long's sharp eyes to find it the first time, and Ku-Long's persistence in finding it again and again so he could point it out to us."

"Congratulations to you all." The rancher gave them all a little bow. "Now I have a well to check on."

Teddy watched him walk back uphill to his horse, allowing herself just a minute to enjoy his long legs and firm behind and broad shoulders. He looked, she thought, exactly like a Montana cowboy should look, from his scarred and dusty boots to his wide-brimmed hat. She turned away, smiling to herself.

This day had given her another Montana experience that she could not possibly have predicted, another one she would remember the rest of her life. Standing under a brilliant blue western sky, under a hot western sun, eating German chocolate cake that was a thank-you for the killing of an outlaw who was wanted in three states, all the while discussing confusing Empidonax species with a rancher, a Chinese cook, a Metis maiden, and one of the country's most eminent ornithologists.

****

"Today has been a very productive day, my dear. We now have drawings and measurements of a red-naped sapsucker, yellow-headed blackbirds, and two black-headed jays. And, of course, photos and drawings of the Wright's flycatcher."

"And drawings of a male rufous hummingbird."

"We were fortunate to see that hummer. I believe we are at the far eastern part of their range. I wish I could have taken a photograph, but he was moving much too quickly."

"He stuck around long enough for me to do a series of sketches."

"Excellent."

"What other birds did you capture with your camera, Grund?"

"The Rocky Mountain hairy woodpeckers, both male and female. The ever-present magpies. And Rocky Mountain jays, male and female of that species also."

"I am becoming very fond of jays. I love their big startled-looking crests, and the way they hop so boldly on their long legs. All varieties of jays are so gregarious and talkative that it makes me feel as if we are joining their groups rather than just sitting and watching."

"That was thoughtful of Rancher Asher to deliver the cake to Ku-Long."

"It was. He is always busy, so that was very kind."

"My dear?"

"Yes?"

"I want you to, I want to…"

Teddy was astonished. Her grandfather was rarely at a loss for words.

"Rancher Asher is a most attractive man, my dear. From what I can tell, he has no attachments. And I imagine he, like most men his age, would someday like a wife and children. You are a lovely young woman, and I am sure he has noticed that fact. However, as I believe I mentioned to you earlier, you have lived a sheltered life and have had very few encounters with men your age."

Teddy dimpled. "There was that young Harvard student who kept his eyes firmly focused on my chest while I was trying to interest him in diving sea birds."

"You have just made my point exactly, my dear. You have had little experience with men. I want you to be aware that there might develop feelings between you and the rancher, and I want you to assess any feelings you might have very carefully. There can be great appeal in novelty."

She took one of her grandfather's big hands in both

of hers.

"Thank you, Grund. I know you want to protect me. And I know I might someday feel attracted to the rancher, or he to me. I have warned myself, and now I will carry your warning close to my heart."

"That is good then, my dear. That is good."

## Chapter Ten

"My dear, I believe today is the ideal day for transporting the blind, table, chairs, and nets to the remote section of Long Butte Ranch where Mr. Asher has seen a nutcracker. A Clark's nutcracker, to be exact. *Nucifraga columbiana.*" The professor turned from packing up his notebooks and camera, his eyes gleaming with anticipation. "The day promises to be sunny but not unpleasantly hot, with light wind and almost no chance of rain."

"I'll go fill water bottles and raid the Lunch Box."

"We should bring more than usual today. We probably won't get back until mid-afternoon. Not only a nutcracker awaits us, my dear. We have a good chance of completing the section of the book dealing with woodpeckers and sapsuckers." He closed his satchel with a decisive snap. "You have become an accomplished wagon master, my dear. Nevertheless, I believe I should drive today. I understand from the men that wild mustangs can gallop straight up the slopes where we are heading, but the pony and cart will have to zigzag to avoid damp areas that could mire us down, and to avoid what Bucky called a big much of rocks big enough to tip the cart over."

"I am happy to be a passenger, Grund."

\*\*\*\*

"We have seen magpies so often that I'm starting to

think of them not as birds to be tallied and sketched and photographed, but as familiar companions. Friends."

"Yes indeed, my dear. They are familiar. But that sparrow is not."

"Oh! Goodness! What an unusually fancy head for a sparrow! It looks like Harlequin, like that trickster in the Italian play you took me to."

He chuckled as he raised his camera. "It does, it does. We are seeing our first lark sparrow. And you are a delight, my dear. We are out here in the wilds of Montana, and you compare a sparrow in the dust to a character in *commedia dell'arte*. That is a connection not every ornithologist would think of making."

"Stand still, bird. We want to immortalize your head."

****

By the time they headed up the ridge in the farthest corner of Long Butte Ranch, Teddy was delighted that she wasn't driving. Their route was rutted and grassy, littered with good-sized stones and small seeps. Brave little patches of ticklegrass, needle and thread grass, and even a few twinflower plants tried to survive on soil that wasn't much more than fine gravel.

"Ah, finally. Good-sized stands of conifers ahead, Grund. I am sure a nutcracker awaits, as soon as you and our loyal pinto safely negotiate the next bend."

"We might have to go a little higher up, where there are fewer spruce and more whitebark pines. I understand that whitebark seeds are the nutcracker's preferred food. They use their sturdy bills to open the cones and then shell the seeds and either eat them at once or store them. It is thought that a single nutcracker can carry over a hundred seeds under its tongue and might travel more than ten miles before caching them for the winter."

"That has to be an extraordinary expense of energy, Grund. Why don't they store the seeds closer to where they found them?"

"That is one of the myriad natural mysteries that scientists coming after us will no doubt figure out. Perhaps the birds want to ensure that one marauding competitor or one hungry mammal cannot eliminate an entire winter food supply."

"That makes sense. Oh! What was that? A flash of yellow and red to our left!"

The professor immediately brought the cart to a stop and raised his binoculars to his eyes.

"I do believe… Yes, my dear! Your flash is a male western tanager."

"Oh my goodness! It looks like a flame! But a quiet, orderly flame. Look at how business-like it is, as it gleans from branch to branch. Oh! Lower on that same tree! Another bird is moving, and that one is much more frenetic. A warbler! Yellow with a black little cap."

"Another first for us, my dear! That is a pileolated warbler. I assume it was given the name because of the little cap. The Latin word for a brimless cap was *pileus*." His deep voice sounded distracted as he focused the camera on the larger and less active tanager. "Roman slaves wore *pilei* of different colors, to show either their exact station or their job, or possibly to identify their owners."

"How well-organized nature is, Grund, with the tanager remaining in his part of the tree, eating insects there, and the warbler staying on the lower branches and eating the insects there."

"I am often confounded and delighted by order in

nature, my dear."

****

"Teddy my dear, I believe you should drive us home."

Teddy looked sharply at her grandfather. His face was pale and his forehead was covered with small beads of sweat.

"Are you feeling the sun again, Grund? We should have been more aware of the sun, even if the temperature is pleasant today."

"No. Not that." He turned away, looking around him. "Bring the wagon around and stop near that outcropping."

"What?"

He walked unsteadily toward a large flat rock. "It will serve as a step."

Teddy's grandfather always climbed into the wagon as quickly and effortlessly as a man half his age. But now his knuckles were white as he grabbed the seat and the front of the cart, awkwardly pulled himself up, and flopped heavily onto the seat.

Teddy handed him a bottle of water. "I will get us home as quickly as possible, Grund. You need to be lying down."

"No haste, my dear. Safety. Safety." His breath was uneven, almost gasping. "Won't do us any good if the cart tips over." He gave a faint chuckle and closed his eyes. "Our poor patient pony would not be happy harnessed to something without functional wheels."

Teddy chirped to the pinto, and they began the long, long trip down the endless switchbacks. She felt an icy fear, much worse than what she experienced on that hot ride back from Freezout Lake weeks ago. Her grandfather's breathing was still uneven, and he was still clutching the edge of the seat as if he needed to hold himself in place.

"Teddy my dear. You will find a large manila envelope in the top drawer of the dresser in the bedroom I have been using this summer."

"No talking now. You can tell me later."

"Now. Important." He pulled a bandana from his pocket and wiped his forehead. "Manila envelope. Information you may need in the days to come." He stopped to straighten his shoulders and take a deeper breath. "The deed to the Boston house. How to access my savings. The estimated worth of the furnishings in the house."

His breathing was a little easier now. "I believe you know the name and address of my lawyer and the accountant at the bank. There is also information in that envelope about a second lawyer and a second accountant, two men I hired to keep an eye on the first two." He almost smiled and she heard, for that instant, an echo of his usual strong self. "I have no doubt, no doubt at all, that the first two are honest men. But money corrupts, my dear. Money corrupts. So twice a year, the second two sit down with the first two and go over all my accounts. I have always joined them, of course, until this summer. If they followed the plan, they should have met last week without me."

"You are a wise businessman, Grund. You have always been wise."

"Hmmm." He mopped his sweating forehead again. "It is possible that I was not wise about this trip." He opened his eyes and glanced over at her. "I followed my heart, and my heart may be stubborn but it is no longer strong."

She opened her mouth but he put his hand on her arm. "No. Let me talk. I had an earlier episode, ten months ago. Similar to now. Remember? I told you I had the flu? My doctor sent me to a specialist and he sent me to a second specialist. Experts, every one of them." He took a deeper breath. "They all agreed. There was nothing they could do. No miracle cure. No magic elixir. I am, simply put, wearing out. The second specialist advised me, in his words, to start treating myself like a man of my advanced years. Stop climbing hills that would challenge a mountain goat. Stop tramping around in the woods. I should sit in my front room, in my comfortable chair, and wait for death."

"Grund! Please don't talk about death. Please."

"I must, my dear." He took another deep breath and looked around him at the green conifers above them and the dusty tan prairie below. "I wanted this trip." He gave a short chuckle. "I wanted it with all my poor failing heart. I wanted to see this part of our country, this extraordinary landscape, and I wanted to see it with you."

"You will be fine! I know you will! I will get us back to the cabin, or I'll drive us straight past the ranch and into Choteau where you can see a doctor. Just keep breathing. Oh!"

One of the rear wheels bumped against a good-sized rock and rode up over it, tipping the little wagon wildly from side to side before the wheel was back on level ground.

"Sorry," she gasped. "Sorry."

They were both quiet as she negotiated the rest of the steep hill and was able to urge the pony to a bit more speed.

"We're on our way now, Grund. Just keep breathing." She glanced over at him. His face was gray, his jaw was set, and the tendons on his neck were standing out. "I need you, Grund. You are my best friend. My whole family. You are the dearest person in my universe."

He patted her leg. "And you, my dear. You are immeasurably dear to me. I cannot regret for an instant being here with you."

She thought his voice was weaker than before.

"Montana has been good for you, Teddy. You are blooming. I see your health and happiness every single day..... I.... Oh." He grabbed his left arm, gasping now.

"Grund!"

"Forgot to mention. Inside the manila envelope. Letter addressed to you." His fingers were white around his arm. "And purse... Purse with gold coins... under the mattress. More... inner pocket... black overcoat."

"Please stop talking. I beg you! You must save your breath. Everything will be all right, Grund."

"I am sorry, my dear. I am—" He slumped heavily against her.

Teddy stopped the cart and turned to put her arms around him. She couldn't tell if he was breathing. She couldn't hear anything but her own panicky panting. He felt very heavy and she had to straighten her back and push against his weight to hold them both upright on the seat.

"No! Grund, no! Please not! Please! Oh Grund. Please breathe. Please say something. Please nod or move your hand or—Oh please let me hear your voice again. Please. Please!"

\*\*\*\*

Caleb and his foreman were sharing a foul mood. They spent the entire morning combing through woody groves and wet areas for five of their longhorns, including the magnificent bull that Caleb bought as the start of his new herd of longhorn-Angus crossbreeds. There were only two possibilities left. The missing cattle fell into a gulch full of the greasy mud called gumbo, stuff that was hard as concrete when it was dry but nigh unto impossible to traverse in a wet season. If the damn brainless longhorns had wandered into gumbo, they would be there until hell froze over. Or the animals were stolen. The last couple of cattle rustlers in the area had died at the end of a vigilante's rope, but maybe some other fools figured rustling was an easy way to make a living.

"That don't look right, boss."

Caleb tightened his knees and Spike moved up to join the other horse and rider. "I agree, Hank. It surely doesn't."

Below them, about a half mile away, the little pony cart was at an angle across the track, the pinto leisurely grazing in a patch of sedge. Miss Barrington was in the driver's seat, turned sideways, her arms around her grandfather's broad shoulders. The professor lay still, twisted awkwardly, feet and legs out to the side and his head buried against her neck.

"I have a bad feeling about this."

They spurred their horses toward the cart, welcomed by the pinto's loud neighing. The girl lifted her head in slow motion, her eyes gradually focusing on the rancher's face.

"Is there anything to be done, miss?"

"No." She rubbed her cheek against her grandfather's white hair. "He is gone. He was right here, talking to me, and the next instant he was gone. His voice, his breath. His thoughts. All his knowledge. His hopes for the book. Gone. Just like that."

"I am truly sorry, Miss Barrington."

"I don't know what to do next. What to do now."

"Well. First, Hank and I will move him to the back of the cart." It would be much easier to lift the body out before the professor stiffened where he was. "Then I will drive the cart back to the ranch. You can ride up front or in back with your grandfather, whichever you prefer."

He and Hank awkwardly unfolded the old man's body, lifted him down and slid him under the canvas covering of the wagon bed. Caleb glanced up at the girl and then unfastened some of the tarp so there was room for her to sit up beside the body. When he turned to help her, she was already scrambling over the seat.

\*\*\*\*

"Sorry to disturb you, Miss Barrington."

She looked pale and very lonely, standing by the window in her bedroom. Both hands were crossed over her breast, and Caleb could see a piece of paper against the fabric of her shirtwaist.

"We took your granddad into the barn. Arthur is making him a coffin."

"Yes. I... Yes."

"Here." He held out his hand and Teddy saw Grund's pocket watch, with the gold chain and the two small fobs, one a tiny gold bird and the other his wife's wedding ring.

"Oh. Yes. Thank you."

"There are decisions to be made, and they should be

made almost immediately. If you wish to have your grandfather buried back in Boston, we will have to take him to Choteau for—uh—embalming."

"Oh. No." She uncrossed her hands and held out the paper. "He—He left a letter. He thought..." She straightened her shoulders. "It is clear that Grund expected to die out here in Montana. He left written instructions to be buried here." She looked down at the letter, and he was surprised to see a little smile. "Quote. With bare rock and tall trees that have stood since the beginning of time. With fresh air and the smell of sage. Not among the stuffed shirts and self-conscious gentry in a Boston cemetery. Unquote."

Her eyes were red-rimmed but she was calm as she looked up. "He would like to be buried on the ridge behind the ranch buildings, half way up, so he can look down at this wide valley. If you will permit it."

"Of course. No question."

"Good. That's good then."

"Do you want your grandfather buried in the clothes he has on?"

"I—I guess so. Yes."

Caleb turned to go.

"No!" The word came out louder than she intended. "No. What was I thinking? Grund abhorred waste! Surely one of the men on the ranch can use his boots. I'm sure they were expensive, and they have more than a few years left in them. And maybe his jacket. And vest and shirt." She was talking faster now. "I will take his trousers. At least for now. I think I can alter them so I can wear them under my skirts in the winter. For warmth." She looked around her. "I will sort out the rest over the next few days. If no one here can use Grund's clothing, I am sure there's a church in Choteau where they might take it and—and distribute it."

"I can help with that."

"Thank you."

"I'll tell Arthur. He's just about finished. We should have the burial soon."

"I understand."

****

The sun was just setting as they stood around the new grave, Teddy and the rancher and the cook and the three ranch hands.

Hank cleared his throat. "The Lord is my—"

"Oh please don't! Please don't pray!" She looked at the foreman, aghast but determined. "I don't mean to insult anyone's beliefs. But I want this to be about Grund, about my grandfather. I don't know if he believed in a god at all, but I know that he referred to organized religions as, um, shared self-selected brainlessness." She couldn't tell from the men's faces what they were thinking. "And if there is a god, then there is no need for us to intervene on Grund's behalf. Any god would know exactly how good a man he was." Her voice wavered but then steadied. "But Grund deeply loved music, even church music."

Arthur wordlessly dug into his pants pocket and pulled out a harmonica.

And they all stood and listened to the familiar strains of *Amazing Grace*.

****

Teddy again stood by the window in her bedroom. The moon was almost full and its cool white light shone on the ridge where her grandfather's body was buried. She could almost make out the rocks the men had placed

142

on top, to keep off predators.

What would she do now? What *could* she do? There was nothing for her back in Boston. Her home had always been with Grund, in his house, surrounded by his belongings, learning from him and delighting in him. He had been her home.

She realized with a small jolt that she had decided already. The decision had been made for her, without conscious thought. She would stay in Montana, at least until she finished the bird census and made a good start on the book. There was, really, no other choice.

Something white was near the new grave. Teddy opened the window wide and peered out. Yes. A person was up there, a person dressed all in white, moving rhythmically in one direction and then the other. Teddy suddenly knew, without being able to see it in the dark, that there was a wide belt with beaded birds around the figure's slim waist. Now she could hear a low murmur, a chanting. Teddy's eyes filled with tears as she stood and watched the Metis girl dance and sing for her grandfather.

## Chapter Eleven

"I have harnessed the pony and cart. I am going into town."

The men looked up from their breakfast. Miss Barrington was standing in the doorway to the kitchen, wearing the dark brown traveling dress she wore on her first day at Long Butte Ranch, with the little veiled hat and gloves.

"One of us can take you—"

"No!" Teddy didn't notice Bucky's little gasp or Arthur's raised eyebrows. They had never heard anyone speak sharply to the boss. And the young lady from Boston was always so polite.

"I have several errands to run. I prefer to go alone." She turned to leave. "I will be back before supper."

Ku-Long moved from the stove. "Eat. No supper before. No breakfast now."

Teddy stared at him blankly. She had everything planned. She had pulled the cart out into the yard and harnessed the pinto. She had told the men she was taking the cart. She was going to drive into Choteau, mail her letters and find the telegraph office. That was the sum total of what she had to do today. Her plan didn't include eating, and certainly didn't include conversation. She felt completely befuddled by the unexpected deviation from her plan.

"I can't eat, Ku-Long. Not now."

He picked up a clean towel, dumped the last two biscuits into it, and added three pieces of bacon.

"Bacon rolls. Good."

Teddy's face softened. "They are, Ku-Long. I will take them, with thanks."

He opened a tin box, took out a handful of ginger snaps, and added them to the small pile of food before closing the towel around it. Then he handed her the bundle and a jar of water.

"Thank you." She felt tears prickling her throat and nose again, and she quickly turned toward the door. "Thank you."

**\*\*\*\***

Teddy didn't know she was hungry until she had driven out under the ranch gate and was well on her way to town, and she realized she was smelling bacon and ginger. She opened Ku-Long's bundle with one hand and took out a cookie. Then another. Then she stopped the pony right in the middle of the dirt track and gobbled the biscuits and the thick salty bacon and washed them down with water. She finished the meal with another cookie and took a deep breath.

"I feel much better, little pinto. Now I can do my tasks and not alarm any of the fine residents of Choteau by fainting dead away in their streets." She twitched the reins and the obedient pony started moving again.

She would find the telegraph office and send six telegrams, and then she would mail the six letters she wrote during the long and sleepless night. The telegrams would inform the secretary of the Boston Birding Alliance, the bank manager, the two lawyers and the two accountants that Professor Barrington had died, and would alert them all that a detailed letter was following.

She told the five men that she planned to purchase a smaller home if and when she returned to Boston and that she wanted to begin the process of putting her grandfather's big house up for sale, with the stipulation that all the belongings would be left as they were for at least five months until she could decide what to do with them. The last telegram, to the secretary of the Boston Birding Alliance, assured the group that she would complete the bird census and the book.

****

Teddy was so focused on mailing the letters and then sending the telegrams that she could not make sense of what the postmistress was saying.

"Oh lawdy, miss. Telegraph lines ain't extended to Choteau, not quite yet. No worry though. If you write out your messages real neat, I'll make sure a rider carries them out within the hour. He'll take 'em over to…"

Teddy stopped listening. She didn't care where the nearest telegraph line was. She didn't care who the rider was or how he was related to the postmistress. She didn't care about the cost. She just wanted to know her messages were on their way. She handed over what she had written in the night, added what would normally have seemed like an astonishing sum of money, and walked back out into the Montana sun.

It was going to take energy to get into the wagon and drive back to the ranch. She looked across the street at the imposing hotel. What would they think if she asked for a room for just a few hours so she could get some sleep? No. That was idiocy. No doubt her body needed more fuel, that was all. She followed her nose to a small bakery down one of the side streets, drank two cups of hot chocolate, ate two sticky rolls, bought a half dozen chocolate-covered nut squares and a box of chocolate cremes, and she didn't care if they were all gone before she got back to Long Butte Ranch.

**\*\*\*\***

"Mr. Asher?"

Supper had been a silent and solemn meal during which no one said a word except for muttered requests for more bread or coffee.

"May I speak to you as soon as you finish eating?"

"Of course, Miss Barrington."

Teddy had never been in the private part of the main house. Now the rancher led her through a bare and dusty sitting room into a good-sized office lined with shelves, with a big window looking out toward the barns and bunkhouse. He held a wooden chair until she sat down, and then he lowered himself into the high leather seat behind the desk.

"I have been giving thought to my circumstances. And to my immediate future."

"I assume you will be heading back east."

"No. At least not yet. You hired the Boston Birding Alliance to have a bird census done on your ranch. I am a member of that Alliance. I intend to honor that obligation. I also want to—To honor my grandfather in that way."

"I see."

Teddy gazed out at the sweet evening light. "And I cannot imagine leaving yet. Leaving Montana. These last months were the best in my life, and I believe they were among the best in my grandfather's life." She could smell sage coming in the open window. "I have become accustomed to your, your openness, Mr. Asher, here in Montana. The space you have all around you. I would find it difficult to live in a city again. At least not for the immediate future."

"Is there nothing waiting for you back in Boston?"

"No." She looked back at him. "Well, yes. Corsets. Afternoon tea with the ladies. Polite conversation about absolutely nothing. Proper behavior."

He didn't smile. "Staying here, with several men, now that your granddad is no longer here to serve as a chaperone—That could give you a reputation you neither want nor deserve."

"I thought, I hoped, that I had left nosy and busybody Puritanism back in Boston."

"Choteau is a small town. Small towns are nosy. It goes with the territory."

"I see. Well, Mr. Asher, I am not uncomfortable, not in the least, about being alone here at your ranch. But if you prefer not to have me here, I can seek other accommodations. I would have to find something nearby so I can continue with my work." She leaned forward. "However, I had a lot of time for thought as I drove back from town today, and I have a suggestion that might allow me to stay while relieving you and, um, the Puritans as well." She was irritated when her voice quavered a little. She knew the next few minutes would be important. "No one knows about Isabelle except you and Ku-Long and me. Is that correct?"

"As far as I know."

"And she is still trying to be invisible?"

"Yes."

"Why, exactly?"

"Partly because she is still afraid of other wandering Metis, like the man who attacked her." He frowned. "Also because—How can I say this? Women are in short supply around here, Miss Barrington. And there is a lot of anti-Chinese feeling in town and on the surrounding ranches. There is the possibility of an ugly reaction if it became common knowledge that Long Butte's Chinese cook has a woman living with him, a woman who isn't, er, available to others."

"Oh. I see." She looked out the window again, reluctant to watch his face as she told him her idea. "That being the case, my suggestion might solve more than just my dilemma. I propose, Mr. Asher, that I ask Isabelle to move into Grund's room for the remainder of the summer. And September. We can let the ranch hands, and other people, know she is here. We can introduce her as my companion. She will be able to be outdoors whenever she wants, without having to hide or dress herself up like a second Ku-Long. She can accompany me every day and eat with all of us every morning and evening."

Caleb felt his ears getting warm. "I am not entirely sure that either she nor Ku-Long would be happy with that arrangement."

"Oh?"

"I am not sure that they have not, are not—That they are not now sharing the same bed."

"Oh! I had not thought of that. Well…" She took a deep breath. "I shall ask her, and she can say no if she wants."

"True."

"If she says yes, will you allow me to stay on the ranch for the next month and a half, with Isabelle as companion and chaperone?"

He hesitated so long that Teddy felt the beginnings of despair.

Then—"Yes."

"Thank you." She stood up. "Thank you."

\*\*\*\*

She could hear a clatter of pots and pans, and maybe the slam of an oven door. Ku-Long must have been working on supper already. She hurried across the yard to the smaller log cabin and knocked quietly.

"Isabelle? It's Teddy."

She ducked inside when the Metis girl opened the door, and her eyes went immediately to the sleeping pallet still on the floor near the table. Maybe Rancher Asher was wrong. Maybe Ku-Long would be pleased to regain his privacy, to move back into his own bed. Maybe Isabelle would be delighted to join Teddy in the other cabin, to move out into the open and stop hiding.

She took the girl's hands. "First of all, Isabelle, most of all, I want to thank you. For dancing for my grandfather last night. For singing for him. I am sure—" Her voice broke and her eyes filled with tears. "I am absolutely sure he knew you were there."

"Your grund good man."

"He was." Teddy withdrew her hands and stepped back. If she started sobbing, she would not stop for a very long time. "I will miss him every day of my life."

"Miss? Same ache?"

"Ache. Yes."

How on earth did anyone learn another language? How could the same four letters mean an unmarried girl, and also the pain a person felt when a loved one died? Just yesterday morning Bucky said something about a scrap and Teddy wondered why he was talking about a bit of fabric, but he was telling the other men about a scuffle, a quick fight, in the main street of Choteau.

Just yesterday morning. Before her whole life changed.

Isabelle was nodding. "Miss. Ache. Miss the mother."

Teddy's eyes flooded again. "I know." She took a deep breath. "I have something important to ask you."

"I help you."

"I am not going back east, Isabelle. Not now, anyway. I am going to stay here in Montana until I finish my grandfather's bird census and spend time on the book." She wasn't sure the girl knew the word "census" but she kept going. "I want to ask if you will be my companion. My…" She searched for a synonym. "I would like to ask you to move into Grund's bedroom and go out with me every day in the wagon. I would tell people that I met you in Choteau this morning and asked you to stay with me until autumn. You would not have to hide anymore. Everyone on the ranch would know about you. You could eat with everyone. With all of us. And you could go outdoors whenever you wanted."

At first, Teddy couldn't read the girl's expression. She had become very still, almost as if she was holding her breath. But then there was a flood of relief.

"I live over there? Grund's room?"

"Yes."

"Ku-Long know?"

"No. We have to go tell him."

"He be happy. For me."

"I think so too, Isabelle. He knows how hard it is for you to stay indoors."

"Go. Now." The girl looked around almost wildly as her fingers plucked at her white shirt and pants. "No. Ku-Long's. Not look Metis."

151

"Oh. No. Good thinking. If I just met you this morning—I will run and get a dress for you."

"I fix."

Isabelle turned, dropped to her knees by the bed, and pulled out a rolled-up bundle. Teddy jerked her head away when the girl yanked the cord on her pants and let them drop. First Ku-Long and now Isabelle. People in Montana might be comfortable with partial nudity, but Teddy was not. She had never seen another woman's body, not once in her almost nineteen years of life.

"I fast." Isabelle's voice was muffled. "I almost. Yes. I ready."

Teddy turned around. Now the girl was wearing pale-colored leather pants and a long leather shirt. The shirt was marred by an irregular stain on the front, the leather stiff and wrinkled from repeated scrubbing, and Teddy had a sudden recollection of the girl's beaten and bloody face and bandaged arm.

"Belt." She tied the brightly beaded belt around her waist and looked up into Teddy's face. "Now I proper Metis girl."

"Perfect. Let's go see Ku-Long."

**\*\*\*\***

The rancher caught up with them as they left the main house after supper.

"You did a fine job of lying in there, Miss Barrington."

"Thank you. I think."

"How unusually fortuitous that you happened to overhear a homeless Metis maiden asking the postmistress if she knew of any place to stay. What are you going to do if Hank brings up that imaginary conversation the next time he's in the post office?"

"You go ahead, Isabelle. I will be right along... Thank you for your concern, Mr. Asher. I don't believe it is likely that Hank will stop to chat. But if he does, he will have to assume the postmistress has more to do than remember specific conversations from days earlier."

"You hope."

"Oh! A great horned owl, calling from out near the barn."

"Grain draws mice. Mice draw owls. I didn't know her last name was Norquay."

"Nor did I. Until I asked."

"Norquay is a well-known Metis name. A man by that name is chief or premier or president of the Metis up in Manitoba. In Canada. Not sure what term they use is."

"Perhaps he is a relative of hers."

"Perhaps."

They walked in silence for a few steps.

"It's fortunate that Bucky is currently besotted with Mr. Truchot's middle daughter."

"Why is that?"

"Bucky is at a most susceptible age, Miss Barrington. And Isabelle is a fetching young woman."

"Oh. Yes, she is."

"If Bucky made advances, I believe Ku-Long might object. I would not want to choose between the ranch's excellent cook and the ranch's talented young horse trainer."

"Oh. No." She lifted her skirts and started walking faster. "Good night, Mr. Archer."

**\*\*\*\***

Her grandfather's letter was still lying on her bed. Teddy picked it up and held it in shaking hands. She had already read it twice, and she knew she would read it again and again. Because Grund had written these words. Grund had held his favorite pen in his strong hands. He had formed these letters. His hand had rested on the paper. His fingers had folded the letter and put it in the envelope. She held the paper to her cheek for a long moment, and then moved closer to the lantern.

*Teddy, my dear—You know that you have been the shining center of my life since you were very small. I have cherished every second of the time we have had together.*

*But this letter is not about the past. It is about your future.*

*You will inherit my wealth, as you know. However, in many parts of this country, everything you inherit will become your husband's property immediately upon your marriage. And I imagine that you will marry, my dear, in due time. You are lovely and charming. You are also intelligent, independent, and educated. I would hate for you to be dependent on anyone, me or anyone else, ever. I would hate even more to see you unhappy in a marriage but unable to escape for want of funds.*

*Therefore, I have taken steps to ensure that you alone will have access to some of your inheritance. Immediately upon my demise, the house in Boston will be yours, along with my savings account at my bank. These assets are easily traceable and will likely become your husband's. I hope you will find a man who will use my money wisely, in a manner that enhances both of your lives and the lives of your offspring.*

*But there are now four other savings accounts, in four different banks, under different names, each with either your birthdate or that of your father. Only two lists of those accounts exist. One is in a safety deposit box under your name in the Great Falls First Avenue Bank. The other is in the bedroom you are using this summer, sharing a frame with your parents, between your photo of them and the stiff backing. You, and only you, can access any of those accounts.*

*What I have done might not be entirely legal in some states. A determined and greedy man might seek legal help to gain possession of your additional money, were he to know about it. I urge you, no matter how in love you may be, to keep the secret accounts secret. You know that I do not believe in an afterlife. But if I am wrong, if I awaken in some other place and can watch you from there, my old heart will rejoice if I know you are protected.*

*With love, admiration and caring, Theodore Barrington (Grund)*

\*\*\*\*

She wanted to lie flat on her grandfather's grave and sob until all her misery was gone. And she wanted to apologize to him again and again, apologize ahead of time. She wanted to tell him how afraid she was that she might ruin the census, that she might misidentify a bird and leave the book, his book, open to professional ridicule. She wanted to tell him the project should not be in her hands alone, that she was too young, too inexperienced, too scared.

She wanted to tell him that he had to be alive again.

Teddy's whole body knew it was past the time when she should be asleep, even though the sun wouldn't set for another full hour. But she was once again staring out the window at the ridge where her grandfather's body lay. She had never been birding by herself, not once. She always had her grandfather at her side, to confirm or correct every identification she made. Now everything depended on her memory of what she was taught, on her ability to sort through what she knew and come to conclusions and then have the audacity to record those conclusions and know they would be read by amateurs and experts alike.

And it was not only identifying birds. It was the professor's notes, the notes that were going to be such an important part of the book. One appendix would list the native foods preferred by various species. Another would describe behaviors they had witnessed. Grund had planned for the extra chapters by drawing up a chart with a row for every species they had seen and check marks or tiny barely legible notes in columns headed *habitat, plants, number in flock, behavior, time of day, birds nearby*, and two more headings she hadn't deciphered yet. There was a staggering amount of work to be done on the book, and he should have been there to do it.

She stiffened as something white and circular appeared in the air above the grave.

"Oh. Silly me. That is not a spirit or a phantom. It is an owl. Not the great horned, of course, with that white face. A short-eared owl or possibly a long-eared owl. Grund said they look very similar in flight."

The owl hovered near the grave, its wings raised and its white face turned toward the cabin, dark eye patches clearly visible.

"But it's still light out and long-eared owls are strictly nocturnal. I think. I wish I could remember. No. I wish Grund were here so I could ask him." She shook her head. "That is just lazy, Theodora B. You know this. Long-eared owls are nocturnal, and short-eared owls are crepuscular. No. Not quite. They do hunt at dusk and dawn but they might also hunt anytime, day or night. Ah! And short-eared owls have pale faces with their eyes sunk in dark, that's what Grund said. Long-eared owls don't have that black around the eyes. So this one is short-eared."

The owl made another low loop over the ridge and then flew downhill, heading straight at the cabin. Teddy automatically backed away when it looked like the bird would come right in the open window, but it banked suddenly and disappeared.

"All right, Grund. I will keep trying."

Chapter Twelve

Teddy stood stock still in the ranch yard, staring down at the sheet of paper in her hand. The polite little smile she had dredged up for the postal rider began changing into a real smile, her first real smile in almost a month.

"Yes!" she whispered. She flipped the letter over and quickly read the back. "Yes!" she said aloud. "Oh yes yes yes!"

She looked around for someone, anyone, who might agree with her how utterly, perfectly, perfect it was. But Hank and Rancher Asher were out on the range, Bucky was working with another recently caught mustang, and Isabelle was helping Ku-Long make strawberry jam and elderberry jelly, a process that Teddy understood should not be interrupted except in a dire emergency.

Her eye was caught by movement in the doorway of one of the big barns and a saddle came into view, apparently walking by itself on skinny bow legs and dusty cowboy boots.

"Arthur!"

Back in May, Teddy had said "pleased to meet you" and Arthur had nodded. More recently she had thanked him for making the casket, and he had nodded again. That was the sum total of her interactions with the wizened little man. But he was there, and no one else was, and she *had* to tell someone.

"Arthur!"

He effortlessly hoisted the heavy saddle onto a fence rail and turned around.

"I want to tell someone about this letter!" The weathered little monkey face looked somewhat alarmed as she fetched up in front of him, breathless. "You know that your boss hired the Boston Birding Alliance to do the bird survey, right?"

Arthur bent his head once.

"And Grund and I belong, belonged, he belonged and I still belong, to the BBA." She sucked in air. "Well! A while ago I wrote the BBA telling them that I would be staying here in Montana to finish the census, and that I would not want Grund's house if and when I ever returned to Boston."

He arched one bushy white eyebrow.

"It is a very big house, Arthur. Bigger than any buildings I saw in Choteau, except maybe the bank. It is..." She held up both fists in front of her. "When I was little, my parents and I lived in one wing—" She flung out her right fist, with the piece of paper crumpled in it. "And Grund and my grandmother, his wife, my grandmother, lived in another wing—" She backhanded the air in front of her, causing the little man's eyes to widen when she almost hit him in the chest. "And the housekeeper-cook and her gardener husband lived there too—" She flung wide her left arm. "And we never even saw each other except at mealtimes. Wouldn't you agree that is too much house for me alone?"

Again, Arthur nodded solemnly.

"So I told Grund's banker and accountant that I will be selling it. The house. Once I am sure what things I want out of it. But now!" She waved the paper under his

159

nose. "Now the BBA, the birding group, wants to buy it! They want to buy Grund's house and whatever furnishings I don't want! It is perfect, Arthur! The BBA has never had a *place*, a *home*. Now they will have a meeting place and a museum and a library. And I won't have to worry that thoughtless people might tear down walls, or rip out the woodwork my grandfather put in, or do something with the windows that wouldn't be right for that historical period."

Arthur's puzzled frown suggested that he was not a man to share a proper Bostonian's concern about historical accuracy in architecture. But then, Teddy thought, most Montana residents were focused on surviving in a hard land. And none but the Native Americans had much history in the area anyway.

"Grund would approve, I know he would, of the BBA making the kitchen and pantry and dining room downstairs and two bedrooms and bathroom upstairs into a rental apartment. That's what they are planning, to help defray the cost. It even looks possible that our friend Abigail Brooks might live there, in that apartment, because part of her house keeps getting flooded every spring. Abigail was the woman who found so much helpful information for us, for Grund and me, about Montana." She felt her smile widening, tickling the corners of her mouth. "Abigail living there! Can you imagine how perfect that is, Arthur?"

The little man shook his head slowly from side to side.

"The museum will have Grund's handwritten notes and some of my drawings and the collections of feathers and eggs and nests and stuffed birds that the BBA has been storing in members' houses for years and years.

Arthur, I am almost beside myself!" She reached out and touched his sleeve. "It has been good talking with you. I should run indoors and write a reply so it gets in the post tomorrow."

Teddy turned and raced toward the cabin.

Talking with him, she thought as she ran. Talking *at* him was more accurate.

****

"I didn't realize she knew how to drive a wagon."

Teddy whirled around so quickly that she stumbled, and the rancher's big hand grabbed her elbow.

"Didn't mean to startle you, Miss Barrington. I guess you were lost in thought."

"Oh. No. No thoughts, Mr. Asher. More like lost in lethargy." She freed her arm. "Yes, Isabelle knows how to manage the wagon and she is going to unharness the pony. I was standing here trying to work up the energy to go inside and get back to work."

The afternoon sun revealed changes in the young woman that weren't noticeable in the big, shadowed kitchen. Her face was still tan from sun and wind, but her skin no longer glowed with health and there were deep lavender circles under her eyes.

"You and the Metis girl leave every morning right after breakfast, and I have seen a light in your cabin late at night. You can't expect to do all that you and the professor were doing together, before."

"I am working exactly as much as I have to." Her voice was quiet and flat, her eyes absently following a distant hawk. "Swainson's."

"What?"

"A Swainson's hawk. They are quite common around here, and quite beautiful."

161

She turned to go, but he reached out and touched her sleeve.

"How are you doing, in truth?"

For a split second, her eyes flashed with anger. "Doing? I am doing what I have to be doing. I am getting through every day."

"And at night?"

"At night, sometimes I sleep." She looked away. "Surely you recognize that this is normal, Mr. Asher. I am grieving. I will no doubt continue grieving for many more months. But, with Isabelle's help, I am getting done what I have to get done."

"It's working out well, then. The Metis girl as your companion."

"Yes. It is. Isabelle is a fast learner." Now her voice held just a little of her old enthusiasm. "I am beginning to suspect there is nothing she can't learn, and learn more quickly than most other people. She took over the driving after the first week and that frees me up to spend every minute looking for birds. I added fifteen species to the census in two days, most of them yesterday when we made what will probably be the last trip to Freezout Lake, for late migrating shorebirds."

Caleb had work to do. He always had work to do. But he wanted to keep Miss Barrington talking about anything that kept that little bit of brightness in her eyes.

"Migrating from where?"

"Oh. Many shorebirds nest way up on the Canadian tundra. There is a very short season of warmth up there, and they are done raising young by late July or early August. Then they have a leisurely southward migration, very different from their mad springtime rush north to the breeding grounds. At this time of year, whenever they find a place with lots of good food and not many predators, they stay for several days. Weeks sometimes. They are—"

Ah. Just a hint of the dimple.

"—on vacation, with nothing to do but eat and fly and eat and fly and then spend the winter months, Montana's winter months that is, in the warmth of the southern hemisphere."

"You are very knowledgeable."

"I am not nearly as knowledgeable as my grandfather."

"Does Isabelle help you with whatever you do in the afternoons and evenings?"

"Oh, no. She spends the afternoons in the garden and greenhouse, or helping Ku-Long with baking and cooking. It is better for me to have the cabin to myself while I work on the duplicate sketches and package the originals to mail back to Boston, and while I try to make notes to match the—" Her mouth twisted in a wry little smile. "The scientific wonders of Grund's notes. I have been working hard on the text for the book, which is not at all as enjoyable as watching birds." She looked over his shoulder. "Oh. There are two riders approaching."

Caleb recognized the man on the left by his hat. The vigilante named Richard Hawkins was the only person in the area who kept the wide brim of his hat almost perfectly flat. Hank said the man owned four books and never read a single one. Every night before bed, according to Hank, Mr. Hawkins laid those four huge and heavy books around the brim of his hat to keep it flat.

The other man was unfamiliar. From the way he sat his horse, Caleb figured that neither he nor the animal was having a particularly enjoyable afternoon.

"Mr. Hawkins," he murmured. "And a stranger."

Teddy considered going inside and letting the rancher attend to his business. But it took so much less energy to stay where she was, to put off the work she knew had to be done. Besides, the cabin was always chilly on overcast days, and she was always cold now. She recognized the vigilante also, but the stranger was decidedly odd-looking. His narrow face was pale and he was so thin that he was almost skeletal, with narrow shoulders and long skinny arms. A beard only one inch wide started in the precise middle of his chin and tapered to a sharp point many inches below his jaw. His black pants and black cutaway coat were no different from what many city dwellers wore, but the silk vest of orange and yellow squares was unusually gaudy.

"Is that a sunbonnet?" she murmured.

Caleb made a sound low in his throat. The visitor's hat did indeed look like a woman's sunbonnet, tied down over a fancy black bowler.

The visitors dismounted, the stranger sliding awkwardly from his horse and landing with a grunt. He removed his headgear, peeled off the bonnet, and slapped the bowler back on his head.

"Wife's grandma's sunbonnet," he rasped. "Sun this morning. Burn something awful, I do."

"Good afternoon. It's a pleasure to see you again, Mr. Hawkins. How can I help you two gentlemen?"

"Well, Mr. Asher, we do not have any outlaws for you to lay out upon the ground with one mighty punch. Today it is more a matter of us helping you. Yes indeed. Us helping you." He turned toward his companion. "Mr. Wylie, I am proud, proud indeed, to introduce Mr. Caleb Asher, the man who felled Gentleman Charlie Chase with one mighty blow. And the young lady, if I recollect rightly, is Miss Barrington from Boston. She is here for the summer with her grandfather, a well-known East Coast ornithologist. New word for me. Means a person who studies bird life. Well-known ornithologist indeed. Mr. Asher, Miss Barrington, this here is Mr. Wylie, from the great little city of Great Falls, Montana. Great little city indeed."

If the rancher wasn't going to mention that Grund had died, Teddy wouldn't either. She made a little curtsy. "You have had quite a long ride, Mr. Wylie."

"Took the coach to Choteau, miss. Not up fer riding a horse sixty miles. Usually leave horse riding for other men."

"Mr. Wylie is here as a representative of the Great Falls Civic Safety Committee. I got that title right, Mr. Wylie?"

"Civic Safety, yes."

"And he has been in touch with similar organizations in the great state of Wisconsin. And in Ohio. Dunno if you remember," the vigilante looked from the rancher to Teddy and back, "but that fancy-dressed scallywag—pardon my language, miss—he was a wanted man in those two states. And just like Great Falls and Choteau, the responsible and civic-minded members of the populace in those states wanted him caught and punished. Or dead. Or dead. So, unbeknownst to each other, civic associations put together reward purses. And once the sheriff certified that Gentleman Charlie was indeed deceased, Mr. Wylie here contacted those other citizen groups and they sent post riders to Great Falls and Mr. Wylie here combined their offerings with what he gathered up." He reached into a pocket and drew out a soft leather pouch. "And then he personally escorted the reward purse up to Choteau. A civic-minded man indeed."

He held the purse out to Caleb. "On behalf of the grateful citizens of three states, three different states I might add, Mr. Wylie and I are proud, proud indeed, to hand over this reward money to you, Mr. Asher."

The rancher took a step backward and, for a dreadful moment, Teddy thought he was going to say it was Ku-Long who killed Gentleman Charlie. But he shook his head and cleared his throat and then shook his head again.

"I am pleased that the man is dead. That goes without saying. But it was just a lucky punch."

"Don't matter, Mr. Asher. It was your lucky punch. And it might of saved who knows how many decent women from that man's unwanted and unlawful attentions."

The stranger lifted one hand, apparently to signal that he had something to say.

"One of—It was—My own—Mrs. Wylie."

"Mr. Wylie's wife was one of Gentleman Charlie's victims."

The skeletal man nodded so energetically that his bowler hat tipped forward and he caught it and tapped it smartly back into place. "Accosted. Accosted! Traumatic! You understand, Miss Bovington." The man's anxious eyes were fixed on Teddy's face. "Nervous hanging out wash now. Nervous walking the sidewalk. Safe sidewalks in Great Falls, Miss Barningham. But nervous nonetheless."

"Mr. Wylie traveled from Great Falls not just to hand over the purse, Miss Barrington. He wanted to meet you."

This time the man took his bowler off and swept it down in a somewhat awkward flourish. "Want to tell Mrs. Wylie I met another victim. Want to know how you are doing."

"I am feeling quite safe now. Unlike your wife, however, I saw Gentleman Charlie dead on the ground. That might have helped."

"Yes. Yes, exactly." He tipped his head to one side and eyed her hopefully. "Too much to ask. Return with me? Sit with Mrs. Wylie? Tell her how that man looked, dead."

Too much to ask indeed. Teddy was not about to give up a bit of the time she had at Long Butte Ranch traveling to Great Falls and back.

"I am most sorry for your wife, sir. But—I know!" She lifted the leather strap off her shoulder and handed the satchel to the rancher. "Hold this, would you please?"

Teddy undid the clasp and pulled out one of her sketchpads and then a pencil. "If you have a few minutes, Mr. Wylie and Mr. Hawkins, I will make a sketch. You can show your wife…"

The men watched in silence as Teddy's hand flew over the paper and the picture began to take shape. The legs flat on the ground. The fancy boots and spats and dark pants. The arms spread out to the sides.

"Did he have a belt, Mr. Asher? I can't remember."

"He was wearing a belt with a gold buckle. And what looked like a diamond in the middle of it."

"Was a diamond," the vigilante put in. "Men like Gentleman Charlie don't deserve to get buried like decent folk. They just get dumped in a pauper's grave, after the sheriff strips 'em and sells the clothes and all.

Money goes to the Settlement House over by the courthouse. That there diamond fetched a pretty penny. One of them rich bankers bought it. Pretty penny for sure."

Teddy caught her lower lip in her teeth as the pudgy torso appeared on the paper, with belt and buckle and fancy brocade vest. Then the face, with dark blood on his chin and in his mouth, and a gap where Caleb had knocked out his teeth. She thought for a brief moment and then erased a bit and changed the drawing so the pants were unbuttoned and gaping. Then she sketched the top hat lying in the dust. A few tufts of grass, some scuff marks in the dirt, and the drawing was done.

"Here. Do you think this might help your wife?"

The man's hand shook as he took the paper. "Might. Might." He looked at the other two men. "Thankee, Miss Beaumont." He looked at the others. "And mebbe if you two write a line. What you did, Mr. Asher sir, and what you saw, Mr. Hawkins. 'Nother way to show her the man is dead. Relieve her soul, so to speak."

\*\*\*\*

"Drawing that sketch was a fine idea, Miss Barrington." Caleb grinned. "Miss Beaumont. Miss Bovington."

"I believe he is just as anxious as he says his wife is."

"Indeed. And saddle sore."

"Oh?"

"I doubt that man has spent ten uninterrupted minutes in the saddle in his life."

"Oh dear."

"It says a lot about his devotion to his wife that he rode out here today." The rancher turned toward the main building. "And now I have a purse to deliver to the rightful recipient."

**** 

"Boss? Two minutes? Talk?"

"You can have all the time you want, Ku-Long." Caleb leaned back in his office chair and patted his full belly. "Especially after a meal like that one."

"Letter. Cousin." The cook pulled a folded paper from his pocket. "New York City. Chinatown, he say. He have—" Ku-Long frowned and studied the letter. "Not sure English word."

"Maybe I can help." Caleb held out his hand.

Humor lit the cook's dark eyes as he handed the letter across the desk.

"Sure thing, boss."

"Oh." Caleb looked down at the unintelligible symbols. "I guess I can't."

"Chinese word can-ting. Eating place. People come."

"Restaurant?"

"Ah. Thank. Cousin own rest-ow-rayunt. Family *restowrayunt*. Own building." Ku-Long made a horizontal movement with his hand. "*Restowrayunt* by street." He made another movement a bit higher. "Cousin and wife. Two children." A third movement, higher still. "For me, he say."

Caleb had a sinking feeling where the conversation was going.

"All go mountains—" The cook again looked down the letter. "Cat-Kill?"

"Catskills. North of New York City."

"Cat-skills. Summer. People leave New York City summer. Hot. Go mountains. Eat Chinese food there.

He—" The cook lifted his head and met Caleb's eyes. "He want me cook mountains in summer. Cook Chinatown other times. He say many Chinamen. He say safe."

"Ku-Long. I hate like hell to say anything that might end up with you leaving. But your cousin is right. There are hundreds of people from China in New York's Chinatown. It's an accepted part of the city. I read that rich young people go there in fancy carriages to have supper and watch dragon parades and shop in Chinese stores."

"Safe."

"Yes."

"Not safe Montana."

Caleb's eyes were bleak as he contemplated the man he had hired off the train almost ten years ago, a man who had become a trusted friend. "I wish I could argue with you, Ku-Long. But I can't. There's an ugly feeling in Choteau these last few years. Mostly a few loudmouth troublemakers, but all it takes is one fool with a gun."

"I go, boss. Use reward money for coach. For train."

"Well. Then. Would you be willing to wait until after fall round-up?"

"Wait. Yes."

"Thank you. Very much." He stood up. "When you leave, Ku-Long, I will ride with you through Choteau and take the stage with you to Great Falls and see you get on the train."

Ku-Long's mouth quirked up. "With guns?"

"Several."

"Good. Safe. Safe Isabelle too."

"Isabelle."

"Metis girl. Isabelle."

"I know who Isabelle is."

"She help with garden. Meals. Canning."

"I know."

"We talk."

"I assumed that you do."

"We talk marry."

Caleb's eyebrows shot up. "Married!"

"She wonderful woman, boss."

"I know that. She is."

"She say I wonderful man."

Caleb's mustache twitched. "You are, Ku-Long. You are indeed. Well. Married and moving to New York City. Congratulations. But I will hate to see you go. You are more than the best ranch cook in the state. You are a good friend, Ku-Long. To me, to Hank and Arthur, to young Bucky. And since May, to the Barringtons as well."

"You friend to me." The cook stood up also and held out his hand. "Good friend."

## Chapter Thirteen

"I would like a few minutes of your time, Miss Barrington. While you finish up your spuds."

Teddy looked up. There was no one left at the breakfast table, and she hadn't even noticed the men leaving.

"Oh. Of course, Mr. Asher."

"Would you like more coffee while we talk? Or more hash?"

Her mouth immediately started watering. She loved Ku-Long's hash. The ranch cook made it with canned beef and onions and potatoes and red beets and then fried it until the beets caramelized and it was crispy on the outside and mouth-melting inside. She looked down at her plate. There was an empty spot next to a few cold fried potatoes and a smidgen of egg. Hash. They must have had hash that morning, and she must have eaten it without tasting a bite, without even noticing what was on her plate.

"Hash. Yes. That would be good. And coffee."

Ku-Long was already reaching out with a spatula of hot crispy hash. Then he refilled their mugs and headed down to the root cellar.

"You have no doubt heard that fall round-up will be starting soon."

She hesitated. "I think I heard something about it. Yes."

His mouth quirked. "Once it starts, you'll know about it for sure. We're going to move more than a thousand head of cattle through here in just a few days. Every one of the men will be working straight out and I've got three more hands coming from Choteau, kids who hope to be ranchers someday. Spring and fall round-up are organized chaos."

"I see." She took a forkful of hash and wanted to close her eyes as the tastes exploded in her mouth. How could she not have noticed before? She knew she was not sleeping well, and she knew she was overly focused on birding and sketching and working on the book, but she could not believe she had chewed and swallowed mouthful after mouthful of this incredible food and remained completely oblivious. "Are there places Isabelle and I shouldn't go, then?"

The rancher took a big swig of coffee and leaned against the back of his chair with a sigh. "It's more complicated than that. The whole ranch shuts down during round-up. Ku-Long goes with the men out onto the range and cooks from a wagon. There are usually no meals here at the house during round-up." He plunked the mug down on the table. "Arthur used to do the cooking during roundup. But now, after all these years of Ku-Long's food, I would have a rebellion on my hands if Arthur came out with us and cooked for the men while Ku-Long stayed here to cook for you two women." He shot her a look out of the corner of his eyes. "And you do not want Arthur cooking for you here at the ranch. He does fine with bacon and eggs, and that's about it."

Teddy blinked. "Oh. I see. Well, that should be no problem. If I have yours and Ku-Long's permission to use his kitchen, Isabelle and I will be fine."

"Good. That's good." He hesitated. "But I have a favor to ask you."

She scraped the last bit of hash up onto her fork and looked up. "All right."

"Men might be coming through the ranch yard any time of the day, for the whole five days of round-up. They'll be bringing cattle in wherever and whenever they find them. They'll want to change horses and they might do some doctoring and some branding, if we find any calves we missed in the spring. They can make coffee out in the bunkhouse, and the Lunch Box is full, but if you and Isabelle will be here, and the kitchen stoves will be hot…"

Finally, *finally*, Teddy felt as if she was waking up and paying attention. "I see. When they come in, they might appreciate hot food."

"It's not necessary, but I know they would welcome something substantial in their bellies before they head back out. They used to do for themselves, here in the kitchen, but after a near-disaster two years ago Ku-Long would rather not have various people working his stoves when he's not around. You and—" He stopped himself before adding *your grandfather*. "You know your way around the kitchen, and Isabelle has been helping Ku-Long for weeks. It would be much appreciated if you two would keep something ready. Soup, chili, baked beans, stew. Things that can be kept hot on the stove all day."

"All day."

"I realize that this will cut into your time in the field."

"Eliminate it."

"Well, yes. For five days. But many parts of the ranch will be nothing but dust as we drive the herds through. You might not mind being here rather than outside."

"I see." She looked out the window, frowning. "I have many sketches to copy and a great deal of editing and writing to do. I can finish Grund's introduction and work on his descriptions of individual species. I will bring my work over here and keep the kitchen going, with Isabelle's help."

He stood up and briefly laid his hand on her shoulder. "I said this before, Miss Barrington, but I didn't say it strongly enough. I believed you would be a burden, here on the ranch. I was wrong. You have been a real asset all along."

Teddy felt herself tearing up and quickly looked down. "Is there any more hash?"

She heard him chuckle as he walked the few steps to the stove.

"Here. Finish it up."

\*\*\*\*

"Men eat lot."

"They do indeed." Teddy took the stack of dirty dishes from Isabelle and slid them into the hot water. "I am thinking of making chili. If we use four or even five jars of canned meat and a pound of dried beans, perhaps it will last three days, depending on how many of the men come through today and tomorrow."

"Rice too."

"Good idea. We'll make a big pot of rice and it will stretch the chili. Then maybe we can take two of Arthur's older hens and make chicken pie."

"Long time pluck."

"Oh. True. And I guess I would be nervous about taking Arthur's hens without him here to ask."

175

"Me. Nerve too."

"I know what we can do. There's quite a lot of salted fish downstairs. We can soak it overnight and make fish pie with some of the canned peas."

"I go garden. Dig potatoes for fish pie. Get cabbage and carrots, mix with vinegar."

"Salad. Good. And we'll make mountains of cookies today, and bread." She turned around and dried her hands. "It is very good having you here, Isabelle. It makes all this cooking and baking not only easier, but very enjoyable."

"Thank. Me too."

"And it is a true delight to look at you now! You are a very different person than you were when I first saw you."

"Happy now. Yes." The girl plopped down in one of the chairs. "Ted-Dee? I talk to you?"

"I listen to you."

"I go soon. With Ku-Long. Go New York City."

"New York City!" Teddy sat down too. "My goodness! Why?"

"Not safe for Chinaman no more. Ku-Long stay ranch all time. Hide when riders come. Is safe in New York City. Many Chinamen. Ku-Long cousin want him work in food place. Have rooms for him to stay."

"And you want to go with him?"

A blush spread up the girl's neck to her cheeks. "We marry. I with him."

"My goodness again, Isabelle! Do you love each other?"

"Yes. Love. Very."

"Oh, Isabelle." Teddy took the other girl's hands in hers. "I will be so, so sad to see both of you leave. You are such a big part of my life here. But I am so, so happy for you at the same time."

"You leave ranch too. Soon."

"I know." She stood up. "Rancher Asher will have a very different home after we all leave."

"Is true."

"When will you and Ku-Long be going?"

"In three days. After round-up over. Marry here. Ranch. Caleb say he ask judge to come out. Then Caleb go with us." She frowned. "With guns. Choteau. Stagecoach. Train. We safe then, and Caleb go back ranch." Her eyes were sparkling again. "Ku-Long and me, go to new life."

****

"Once Isabelle goes, Grund, I will probably have to leave also. Rancher Asher has made it patently clear that staying on the ranch without a chaperone will do irrevocable harm to my reputation." She frowned. "Although I am not at all sure why I should care one whit about my reputation here in Montana if I am going to leave anyway."

Teddy was again sitting by her grandfather's grave, talking to him, aching to have him alive and listening, feeling with her whole being the need to hear his deep gravelly voice and see his beloved face.

"I purely hate the thought of leaving, Grund. I want at least several more weeks. I want to be here, birding, for most or all of fall migration. I want to be sure the census is truly complete. And I want to finish the book, our book, in our cabin, here on the ranch where it's so quiet and I can smell sage and hear distant owls."

She reached out and ran her hand over a smooth rock. "So I have decided to tell Rancher Asher that I want to stay at least through the first week of October." She leaned closer to the grave. "I am prepared to resort to genteel bribery, Grund. Well, not exactly bribery. But I will remind him that he has asked favors of me and I have done them. I stitched Ku-Long when Mr. Asher could easily have done it himself. And Isabelle and I stayed on the ranch these last several days so there is hot food and coffee when the men come in from the round-up. I believe I am within my rights to ask a favor in return. I shall mention fair play. And western values. I shall grind his nose in guilt, if that is required."

She shifted her position on the hard ground. "Because I want very much to stay. My reputation be damned! I want to go out every day in the wagon, just me and our faithful pinto. I want to get data on what birds stay here until the first snow falls. What birds might migrate through from Canada. But don't worry, Grund. I shall carry my little pocket gun and your bigger gun as well. I will tell Rancher Asher exactly where I will be each day, and I will always be back by early afternoon."

She lifted her head, hearing soft chirps overhead.

"Western nighthawks! I thought they made sharp booming noises. Oh, of course, that's during courtship, not migration. Oh, look at them!"

There were at least six streamlined shapes above her, flapping like giant bats, white wing stripes vivid against the darkening sky.

"Fill up on all those yummy little insects! You need lots of fat on your bones. According to my grandfather, you might migrate all the way to Brazil."

She watched, mesmerized, as the long-winged birds looped and glided above her, the whole flock making soft noises that she began to hear as *cheer, cheer, cheer*. Then one bird stopped feeding and flew up and over the ridge. Then another. And more, until there was only one.

"Hurry, you. Hurry! The rest have already left."

At last, the straggler was gone also. Teddy turned back to the grave. "I am being very silly, Grund. I saw that short-eared owl as a sign from you, just after you died, and I just had the thought that those nighthawks might be a sign also. I assure you, you as a scientist, that I am not turning into one of those addlepated women who read wisdom in tea leaves and believe the clouds are talking to them. Remember that odd person we met at the Cape? Wearing a dozen floaty scarves and two dozen necklaces and telling us that she was in tune with the Greater Consciousness?" She pushed herself to her feet. "I soaked up too much of your scientific teaching to turn into that woman, Grund. Don't worry. And now I am stiff and cold and I'm heading downhill and to bed. Tomorrow I will talk to the rancher."

****

"Yes already? But I barely started. I have a fairly lengthy speech prepared."

The rancher's mustache twitched. "I am sorry you didn't get to give your speech, Miss Barrington. But I have done a lot of thinking also, about your eventual departure."

He pulled out his usual chair at the end of the big kitchen table. "Sit. Please sit. You can finish up with our supper in a few minutes." The rancher looked uncomfortable, perhaps even embarrassed. "Tomorrow, on the way back after seeing Ku-Long and Isabelle safely on the train, I will leave an advertisement at the office of *The Choteau Montanian*. For cook and housekeeper. But it is likely to take weeks, perhaps even months, before anyone responds. It's not easy to find someone willing to work as hard as Ku-Long worked, especially on such an isolated ranch. " He looked away from her, staring out the window at the distant hills. "If you were to agree not to leave yet, not quite yet—If you were to agree to continue baking bread and cooking suppers, then Arthur can do coffee and bacon and eggs and porridge for breakfast. You could leave early each morning and have several hours for field work and writing. That arrangement should allow you to finish the census and would, at the same time, make life much easier for me."

"I could stay in the cabin, alone. Without a chaperone."

"Yes."

"I could go out in the wagon, alone."

"If you continue to carry your gun. Yes."

"I find it most interesting, Mr. Asher, that your howls about the unavoidable and horrific damage to my maidenly reputation are silenced when it is in your interest to have me here." She shook her head abruptly. "Please forget I said that. It was rude and unnecessarily harsh. And it was also foolish. You just suggested exactly what I was going to ask. So, yes. I will stay on and do the cooking, and I will plan on not leaving before October, at the earliest. Preferably even later."

He cleared his throat. "I also gave some thought to another alternative. While I was out on the range. I thought about you not leaving at all. Staying on."

"Goodness. I would truly love to see the birds that are here during the winter. It would add greatly to the book. But then I would be truly living here, at the ranch."

"That would not raise eyebrows..." He looked directly at her for an instant before staring fixedly at the stoves. "It wouldn't raise eyebrows if you were my wife."

"What?"

"My wife."

Her eyes widened. "Why, Mr. Asher, is that a declaration of undying love?"

"It is not," he snapped. "I am making a logical suggestion to a young woman who considers herself a scientist. I expect you to react with logic and common sense."

"I plan to marry for love, Mr. Asher. And I believe that is *very* sensible."

He was scowling at her now, his jaw tight, his hands in fists on the table. "All over the world, Miss Barrington, all throughout history, people have married for practical reasons. To cement family or clan ties. To merge fortunes, or to make it possible to eke out a living with no fortune at all. Out here in Montana, people marry so they can run a ranch together, farm together, run a store together. Raise children together. Surely you believe those are worthwhile things to do with one's life."

"Worthwhile things to do with *one's* life perhaps, but not with *my* life. I have seen examples of married love that bring great happiness to all involved. My parents. My nanny Mary and her husband. Grund and his wife. I believe Isabelle and Ku-Long will be another example. I wish to find that for myself."

"And I have seen examples of successful marriages that began without your so-called love. I know of at least four couples where the bride was mail-ordered. Brought from the east on a bride train. She and her husband never saw each other until the day she arrived, and that was the same day they got married." He leaned forward, earnest now, reaching out with one hand until he almost touched her arm. "What you call love killed my father, Miss Barrington, just as surely as a bullet to the heart. When my mother moved into Choteau, it just about broke him. But he kept going because he relished, he *loved*, every minute she spent out here on the ranch. Then when she died, he did break. He was a powerful man. A strong man. But loving that woman wasted him. He lived another two years, but he was never the same. My brother and I believe he was eager for death, maybe even courted death."

She jumped when he brought one closed fist down hard on the table. "If my father hadn't been in 'love', Miss Barrington, he would have mourned for a while and then found a local widow and started living again. He might be around today to see what has become of his ranch. Love is not an essential part of a successful marriage, and it might even be a dangerous part."

She looked down at the table, at the huge cabbage and cutting board and sharp knife. "I should make this coleslaw, or supper won't be ready when the men start coming in."

Caleb rose and moved around the table, leaning against the wall, filling her peripheral vision. "Most young women don't have a choice, Miss Barrington."

"I am aware of how fortunate I am." She pulled the cutting board closer. "Most women have to choose marriage, or servitude, or a convent." One hard whack split the cabbage in two. "Or an orange house. Or working twelve hours a day in a factory with no air, no light, no heat, and dying before they are thirty. That's back East, not here, but wait a few years." She looked up at him. "In Boston, I was made keenly aware that I was a commodity, a potential possession. I was of value because my female body was a possible source of carnal pleasure and a possible source of heirs. And I was of value because of my grandfather's wealth. Not a single one of the few gentlemen who showed interest cared one whit for my thoughts, my educational attainments, or my skills."

He opened his mouth but she kept talking.

"You are going to say that my skills are useful here, on the ranch. My skills in, in stitching wounds and cooking meals." She swept an arm toward the stove. "I am pleased to have those skills, Mr. Asher. But I have other skills, thanks to my grandfather, and I intend to use them. I am going to finish the book, our book, and I have already thought of additional books with the Barrington name on them. I am fortunate indeed to have money because, unlike most women my age, I don't have to get married just to stay alive."

She hadn't realized that she would copy his gesture and pound her fist on the table until after she did it.

"And if and when I do, I will *know* my husband. We will have shared what we believe, our hopes and wishes. He will know me not only as a female body, and not only as one more worker on his ranch or in his store, but as a person. And we will love each other, Mr. Asher!"

\*\*\*\*

Teddy didn't notice Arthur until she headed back into the kitchen after throwing the dirty dishwater outside. He must have been in one of the wash rooms, or in the living room. Now he was standing by the stoves, pouring water into a large pot.

Wonderful, she thought. Breakfast will be the

oatmeal that everyone but Arthur finds almost inedible.

"Marry him."

She stopped dead.

"What?"

"Marry him."

"I thought you couldn't talk."

"Can." He lifted one shoulder in a half-shrug. "Don't."

She was briefly torn between curiosity—why did Arthur never speak, if he was capable of doing so?—and anger. Then the anger became dominant. How dare this odd little man listen in on a private conversation? How dare he pretend he couldn't talk and then decide to tell her what she should do with her life?

"My private life is mine, Arthur. Mine."

Chapter Fourteen

"Hank? May I ask you a question? Before the others come in?"

The ranch's big foreman was early for supper, as usual, lumbering in as soon as he heard the first bell, pulling out his chair, and sitting with his ham-sized hands folded in front of him, waiting.

"You kin ask, Miss. S'long as I have the right not to answer."

"Of course. You might not want to answer. It might be private, for Rancher Asher. Or you might not know. But I am curious about his parents, how they died."

He sat and stared at her for so long that she began to worry the others would start coming through the door before he said a word.

"Might be good fer you to know." He heaved a sigh that lifted the napkins closest to him. "Boss's mom lived mostly in Choteau."

"I know."

The man's curly blond eyebrows shot up until they almost touched the curly blond mop on his head. "Well now, that fairly surprises me. It fairly does. Boss don't never talk about that. All right then. Makes me easier about telling you the rest." He leaned back till his chair creaked, stretched his arms out, interlaced his fingers, and cracked his knuckles. "She lived in Choteau. Came out here a weekend a month, most months. After couple years—no, it were more like a half dozen years—she caught some sorta fever in town. Died four days later. Wouldna caught it out here on the ranch."

"You can't be sure of that."

"Sure can. Stands to reason. Lotsa people in Choteau died. Not one of us out here was sick."

"Oh."

"Never saw a man hit harder. Didn't get to see her, neither, on account of the quarantine."

"Did he get sick also?"

"No he did not."

"So how did he die?"

"Well, now, miss, I have to say that man died from a bad case a careless."

Teddy pulled out a chair and sat opposite him.

"Sod house was first, way back when boss's ma and pa moved here. Then the log cabin you're using now. Then the boys and their dad started building the big house. This house. Well one day, the boss's dad had the thought to use a coupla big timbers that was holding up the sod roof. He built that thing, miss. He knew 'zactly what was where and how it all held together. But he just went right in and yanked on the fust timber his eyes lit on."

Teddy gasped.

"You guessed it. Whole thing collapsed. His boys Ike and Caleb found him when they got in from the range, but it were too late. Prob'ly too late right from the start. Buried under hunnerds and hunnerds a pounds of logs and dirt."

From outside, they could hear Bucky's laughter. Teddy stood up.

"Thank you, Hank. That was very kind of you."

He leaned his massive elbows on the table and looked into her face. "Boss got no experience talking to females. But seeing as how he told you about his mom living in Choteau, could be he'll talk to you some more. Do him good."

**** 

"Mr. Asher?"

He closed his ledger and leaned back in his leather chair. Miss Barrington was hovering in the doorway to his office.

"I would like to speak with you about leaving."

"You leaving, I assume. Not me." He hoped she might smile, but she didn't.

"Oh. Yes. Me."

"You have been here longer than you expected."

"Yes. I have. And I thank you again for allowing me to stay on."

"Your suppers have been much appreciated. Yours, and before that yours and Isabelle's."

"Thank you."

"You are no doubt eager to return to Boston."

"In truth, I am not." She looked over his head, out the window. "Before Grund died, I felt deep happiness here every single day, a happiness I never felt in Boston. Bubbling-up-inside happiness, with all the wild and open space around me and the smell of sage in the air." She frowned, trying to puzzle out what she wanted to say. "Boston was where Grund worked, where he made a home with his wife and their child. But I lived for those times when the two of us left the city. When we went to Plum Island to watch shorebirds, or the coast of Maine to look for gannets and diving ducks. Or down to Cape Cod. I never enjoyed the traveling part, but I was always happy away from the city." She looked back at him. "Have you ever been in Boston?"

"Never been east of Great Falls."

"Well, even in the nicest parts of Boston, we never smelled anything as clean and wonderful as sage. Down by the docks one can sometimes smell the ocean but usually it's fish guts, or rotting crabmeat. The parks smell like horse manure and the poorer neighborhoods reek of sewage."

She perched herself on the very edge of the wooden chair.

"I am rambling. What I want to say is this. I am considering finding a house to buy, in Choteau."

He jerked, pushing his shoulders against the high back of his chair.

"The birding alliance hasn't raised all the money for Grund's house yet, but I have access to his savings. I would like to find a place on the outskirts of town, with open space around. If I can't find something suitable, I will rent for a year or so and have a house built. A small house."

"I'm—I'm astounded, Miss Barrington."

"I was too, astounded, when I first had the idea. But now I know it is the perfect thing for me to do." She leaned forward, knotting her hands together on her knees. "I have already sent a telegram into Choteau with Hank, asking the birding alliance to pack up everything in my bedroom, back in Grund's house, and ship it out here. I want to live here, Mr. Asher. In Montana."

"You have certainly—You have adapted very well."

"I think so. I think I have. Grund said he could see that being here was good for me." She had not yet moved past the catch in her throat, the prickling in her nose, whenever she thought about her grandfather. She blinked several times and changed the subject. "Oh! Goodness! I forgot to ask. Have you found a cook?"

"Not yet. But I have been thinking about a suggestion I made a while back."

"Yes?"

"You stay here. Live here. As my wife. Wait! Hear me out! I will make sure you have time each day for your work. I will make sure you have a horse and buggy whenever you need them. I will help you with the nets and the bird blind during spring migration, even if it means hiring another ranch hand. We can write those promises into our vows." He lowered his brows and glared at her. "I am not being romantic, Miss Barrington. I am not talking about love. I am talking common sense. You want to complete the bird census, and you need to be on my ranch to do so. You want to stay in Montana. You need a house. I have a house. I need a cook, and you are a very good cook."

"So I would get to finish my grandfather's work and my own work as well. And I would get help doing it. You and the ranch hands would continue getting hot meals. Is there—Is there anything other than hot meals that you would get out of such an arrangement?"

She was startled to see the tips of his ears redden.

"Of course. I would much prefer to satisfy my, er, my normal male needs here at home, in my own bed, instead of heading into Choteau every week or so."

"Ah. More convenient then."

Caleb leaned back in his chair, pleased that the stubborn young woman from Boston had so quickly come around to his way of thinking.

Then she stood up and he got a good look at her

eyes.

"I see no reason to continue with this conversation, Mr. Asher. I would like to return to what I was saying. I have not been eager to return to Boston. I have decided to remain in Montana. I will go into town and look at houses to buy."

"I see."

"You know that I love Montana. And the ranch. I do not, however, love you. And you cannot say you love me either."

"No. I can't. However—" His deep blue eyes looked frustrated and baffled and determined. "I admire you. I have enjoyed the few conversations we have had together. I respect your abilities and your learning. I like looking at you. Isn't that enough?"

"No. It is not." Now she looked as baffled as he did. "I—I admire you also, Mr. Asher. I admire how you treat the other men. Your behavior with Isabelle and Ku-Long. When you protected your cook, after he killed that man."

He noticed that she didn't include liking to look at him. He blew out a long breath. "Will you, at least, give some consideration to my suggestion?"

"Your proposal."

"Yes. My marriage proposal."

"I am sure I will think of it, Mr. Asher. With continued disbelief."

"I see."

She hovered in the doorway, looking down at him, her mouth in an unhappy curve. "What if—Can we agree that things will go on as they are for another month? I will do what I have been doing and you won't mention marriage again?"

"And then what? After that one month?"

"Then I will either leave the ranch—" She took a deep breath. "Or I will have decided to stay here as your wife."

"I see. Well then. Yes. You have an agreement."

He watched her leave, her back straight and her chin high. Then he sat and stared at the doorway for several minutes. That had gone better than the first time he suggested marriage. At least she would think about it. And he had been clear. He had told her exactly what he expected from marriage. He had, for the second time, dissuaded her from expecting that love would be part of the relationship.

Yes, he thought. That hadn't gone badly at all.

\*\*\*\*

"No!" Teddy reined in the pony and reached for her grandfather's binoculars. A jay-sized gray bird had just flown across the track, the wings dense black with white trailing edges. "This is unfair, bird! You should have shown yourself back in mid-summer when Grund was alive to see you."

The nutcracker landed in a nearby ponderosa pine and gazed at the human and the pony with mild curiosity.

"Oh please stay right there." Teddy laid the binoculars on the seat and picked up Grund's camera. "Let me get one photo. No. Two. All right. Three, then." She exchanged the camera for her sketchpad. "Oh you handsome thing. Grund hoped we would be able to add you to the census. Now we can."

The bird fluttered to another branch and applied its sharp bill to a cone.

"I thought Clark's nutcrackers stayed in the higher elevations, but now I think they move down in the fall.

Yes," she murmured. "I remember now. You spent the summer hiding thousands of seeds all over the place. By now you've cleaned out the trees higher up, and you'll spend the winter flying to your food caches or finding seeds down here. Aren't you crafty, you handsome nutcracker?"

Teddy had three pages of sketches by the time the bird finished removing the seeds from the opened cone and holding them, one at a time, between its feet to hammer them open and eat them. After it flew away, Teddy closed her eyes and sat for several minutes, feeling her grandfather's presence around her, loving him as much as she always did, wanting him to be alive, wanting him to be with her sharing every little adventure, sharing ten minutes with a nutcracker.

****

There was no activity in the ranch yard when Teddy got back that afternoon. She left the big barn after caring for the pony and tugging the cart into its designated spot, hearing only the quiet movements of horses in the paddock and the softer sounds of Arthur's chickens scratching around their coop.

Bucky was standing at the door to her cabin. It was unusual to have anyone seek her out during the day, so she quickened her steps.

"Oh, miss! Thought you was gone too. You willin' to help with my mare?"

"Where is everybody?"

"They all went to town. Be back for supper, don't you worry."

As Teddy followed the young man into the smaller barn, in her mind's eye she saw an orange house, saw Rancher Asher following a scantily-clad woman through a doorway, his hands already unfastening his belt and opening his jeans and then…

"Is her foal coming?"

"Think so."

She took off her coat and draped it over the side of the stall. Their little pinto pony was one thing. The mare was much bigger and she was agitated. Her eyes were showing white, there was foam around her mouth and nose, she kept thrashing her long legs, and her whole body was heaving and shaking.

Well, Teddy, she thought. You wanted to get close to horses this summer. Helping a mare give birth is about as close as you can get.

"Bucky. You have been with mares in labor before, haven't you?"

"Acorse. Lotsa times. But it'll be easier with two of us in here. Watch out she don't knock you with her hoofs. Don't be askeert though. She won't hurt you."

"I will pretend to be calm, Bucky. That is the best I can do."

"Good 'nuf."

"Tell me what to expect."

"You stay by her head. She'll jest lay there and we'll see her sides go—There! Jest like that!"

The mare snorted as a contraction pulled in the sides of her barrel belly.

"Them'll come more and more. And faster. An' then I'll see the legs."

"Is it always the legs first?"

"Unless sumpin's gone cadywompus."

"Cadywompus?"

"Wrong, miss. Twisted. That'd be not good."

"Well then. We shall pray that nothing goes

cadywompus." Teddy knelt by the horse's head. "How long will it take?"

"Dunno. Prob'ly she dunno neither." He looked up with a crooked grin. "Mebbe the little one knows."

"Will you let me touch you, Beauty?" Teddy laid her hand tentatively on the lathered neck. The mare's wild eyes rolled, but she didn't resist or try to bite.

"I thought most horses gave birth out on the range, by themselves."

"Lots do, miss. But there be a chance o' coyotes gettin' the little one. Mebbe wolves. If'n we want to keep the foal, we try and get the mare into the barn."

"That makes sense." She stroked the mare's mane. "You've got friends here, Beauty. Bucky is your best friend in the whole world. And you may not believe it right now, but your body knows what to do. Mares have given birth since the very first horses ever on earth." She glanced up at Bucky. "See? I learned from you. Keep your voice at the same even level whether you're talking to a nervous horse or a nearby human."

He didn't answer, watching as another contraction rippled through the mare's body. When it was over, the mare blew out air and leaned her head against the girl's leg.

"Oh yes, you beauty. You know I am a friend. I will stay right here, right next to you, and I will keep on talking and touching you. What's happening, Beauty, is your very own youngster ready to be born. You protected it and fed it for months and months, and now it's ready to come out of you and stand on its spindly little legs and butt you with its head and drink some of the rich and nourishing milk your body is making."

"Good, miss. She's trustin' you."

Teddy lost track of how much time and how many contractions. She kept stroking the mare's head and neck as the animal's eyes no longer showed white and became dulled with pain and exhaustion.

Then Bucky knelt upright, breathing almost as fast as the mare.

"Think I kin see the sac."

"What?"

"The sac 'round the foal. If'n I was to see red it'd be bad. But this is sorta blue and sorta white, and that's good."

"What happens next?"

"Well, in a minute I'll see one o' the feet. Whoa." He stopped for another contraction. "Jest finished one and here's 'nother."

"Is that good?"

"Depends."

"On what?"

"If foal be in the right position."

"Oh."

"Yup. Foot. 'Nother foot. Yes! Here's the nose. Now I kin take the feet and I kin pull, real gentle like, right when she's a tryin' to push. Come on, little one. Come on out and say howdydoo. Come on."

Now Teddy could see the foal's head lying on its long forelegs. And then, in an instant, the whole baby animal was lying on the straw.

"Ain't she a pretty little filly though?"

Teddy said nothing. The foal looked like a slimy mess of blood and mucus with a head that was much too large. But Bucky picked it up in both his arms and cooed over it and then waddled forward on his knees.

"Gotta let Beauty smell it. Clean it."

The mare lifted her head, her eyes losing their dullness as she snuffled over her baby. Then she began washing the tiny animal with her tongue.

"Good, Beauty. Yer doin' jest fine. Yer doin' 'zactly whatchu should be doin'."

The filly was looking a bit less disgusting by the time Beauty stopped cleaning and lurched onto her knees.

"She's a tryin' to stand so's she can nurse. Here. Hold this little one for a sec so her mama don't step on her." He dumped the foal into Teddy's lap. "Push yerself back inta that corner. Give her lotsa room. That's right, Beauty. You stand right up. Yer tired, I know, but you got another 'portant job to do. That's it, my beauty."

Teddy looked down at the tiny animal. The filly was darker than the dun mare, with lighter dapples on the rump and across the shoulders and a tiny white blotch high on the forehead.

"It's shaped like a leaf."

"Eh?"

"This little bit of white. It is shaped like a cottonwood leaf."

Bucky bent over and stared. "So 'tis. Jest look at that! Mebbe this little lady jest got her name."

"Leaf?"

"Yer funnin' me! Cotton, acorse. Cotton Beauty. But we'll mostly call her Cotton."

"Cotton Beauty is perfect, Bucky. Here."

Bucky took the filly from her and set it on its shaky legs.

\*\*\*\*

"Ya hear that?" Hank paused in unsaddling his horse and cocked his head.

All three men could hear two murmuring voices coming from the other barn, one male and one female.

"What d'ya think, boss? Bucky's got Mr. Truchot's daughter out here?"

Caleb scowled. "If that young man has got that girl out to the ranch, and if they're alone in the barn when it's getting dark, they better both be planning a wedding. Soon."

They heard Bucky say something, and then a husky feminine chuckle.

"That don't sound like Miss Truchot. That girl's laugh sounds like a puma got its tail caught between a coupla porcupines. Must be some other gal." Hank waggled his curly eyebrows and grinned. "Young Buck's gettin' to be quite a stud."

There was something familiar about that soft female chuckle.

No, thought Caleb. It was not possible. He could not imagine Miss Barrington rolling around in the hay with the ranch's young horse trainer.

But it certainly sounded like her.

And it was. There they were, together in the barn, down in the straw, the educated lady ornithologist from Boston and the rough young Montana mustang trainer. They were sitting side by side with their backs against the side of the stall, watching a slate gray filly guzzle from the dun mare's swollen udder. They both looked up when the three men walked in, and their faces wore almost identical expressions of wonder, amusement, and delight.

"Mr. Asher! Hank! Arthur! Meet the newest resident of Long Butte Ranch! Meet Cotton Beauty!"

"Well now. Look at that. Your mare birthed a fine

filly, Bucky."

"She done it, didn't she?" The young man stood up and leaned against the stall next to his boss. "This little one's gonna be jest like her ma. Jest as pretty and jest as strong and jest as wunnerful." He held out a hand to help Teddy up. "And this here Easterner lady is a durned fine rancher. She is!"

Caleb studied the disheveled girl. Her dress was almost as smeared as Bucky's shirt and pants. Her hands were red and looked cold, and even her red-brown hair had birthing muck in it. But she was smiling, smiling like she hadn't smiled since before the professor's death.

"She is, is she?"

"I am, Mr. Asher! I do believe I am! That was magical! I would love to have this exact same experience again and again and again. I held—I held new life! I watched this little one being born." Teddy knew she was getting teary and she didn't care. "I want to laugh and cry and do some, I don't know, some loud hooting or something."

"You go right ahead, Miss Barrington. You go right out into the ranch yard and throw back your head and hoot all you want. You earned it!"

She laughed at him, her eyes glistening with tears. "No. I don't want to scare Arthur's chickens. And you men must be ravenous. I just realized I am too! Utterly ravenous! I'll go inside right now, clean up a bit, and get supper on the table. You all come in as soon as you hear the first bell. Don't wait for a second."

She turned and headed outside, her cheeks still wet and her smile still wide. Just as she got to the door, she heard Hank's always loud voice.

"Hey, Buck. Arthur here got that little Bonnie, the

one you like. He musta give her quite a ride. That little gal looked plumb tuckered out when we was ready to leave!"

Better add another bowl of greens and bacon, Teddy thought dryly. And make even more biscuits than usual. Those three men probably worked up an appetite in that orange house.

## Chapter Fifteen

Aspens were turning yellow in the higher elevations. There had been two snowfalls already, melting before noon to make glittery icy-cold ribbons down the sides of every ridge and mesa. The sun was setting earlier and the evenings were chilly. Now when Teddy sat next to her grandfather's grave, she wore her own traveling coat under her grandfather's canvas overcoat, with her hands shoved deep into the pockets.

"Rancher Asher has mentioned marriage twice now, Grund. He doesn't love me, and he doesn't want to love me, not ever. I don't love him, I don't think, but perhaps that would come in time." She pulled the two coats closer. "You are a scientist, Grund. Let me lay out the problem scientifically for you, step by step. First. You and I have seen him looking humorless and grouchy. But we also saw him with Ku-Long and Isabelle. He is fair and even-tempered with the other men. And he is gentle with animals. I am fairly confident that he won't turn into one of those husbands who beats his wife."

She squinted into the setting sun without really seeing it.

"Second. He is hard-working. No one could doubt that. Third, and I will admit this to you, Grund, and to myself, but to no one else. I like the way he looks. I like the wrinkles at the sides of his eyes. I like the way his dark brown mustache twitches when he is almost smiling. I liked his legs in muddy jeans that first day, and his forearms. And his shoulders are broad." She stifled a giggle. "But not as broad as that man we saw at that one coach stop. Remember? That man looked like a triangle uneasily balanced on its point."

She picked up a handful of sandy earth and dribbled it over the grave.

"Fourth. I never wanted to touch a man before. I realize that I didn't spend time with many young men, but there were a few unattached young men on some of our birding expeditions. And I sat on a blanket and shared a picnic with that lad whose name I always forget. But I never wanted to reach out and touch a man's hands. I do, with Rancher Asher." She sighed. "But then I think I might be reacting to the loss of you in my life. You patting me on the shoulder. Me kissing your cheek goodnight. I am without any kind of touch now. I am without a family. Without my dear beloved Grund. Perhaps I am foolishly thinking of the rancher as some sort of replacement." She blew out an exasperated breath, ruffling the hair that always fell over her forehead. "It is his fault, Grund, that I am so confused. I am not the one who brought up marriage!"

She leaned back on stiff arms, lifting her face to the star-spangled sky. "I love this part of the world so much. I love the emptiness, the sky, the ridges and the desert, the smell and—Well, everything. And I have come up with ideas for several more Montana-based books. One will be about native bird lore, using the stories Isabelle told me. I wish you had heard her, Grund! She could recall a story from her mother for almost every species we saw, and I wrote almost all of them in my bird notebooks. If I gather them into a book, think how popular it would be back east! How fascinated people would be! Perhaps I could also write a book about the Metis people themselves. If I sat down with the elder who came out to the ranch that day, I could fill a whole notebook with facts and stories about their history and their religion and culture. And their music, of course." She stretched out her stiff legs and wiggled frozen toes. "I honestly don't believe I could write those books anywhere but here, in Montana. And you heard what Bucky said, and the rancher agreed with him. I am becoming a real ranch woman."

"Of course, there are other ranches, and other ranchers." She got to her feet. "I'm going to walk around a bit, Grund, and bring my legs back to life. And while I am doing that, I shall bring my mind back to scientific thoughts."

She stamped and walked in one direction and another, and then she stood for a few minutes, looking down at the ranch buildings. There was light in the main building, probably the lantern in the rancher's office, and in the bunkhouse, and of course the light she left burning in her cabin.

"I think I was up to number five, Grund." She coiled herself back down on the cold rock by the grave. "So here it is. Fifth. This is foolish, I have no doubt, but I can imagine my children running around in that very yard. Boys and girls alike dressed in sensible play clothes that will let them run and skip and climb trees and ride their ponies. And while their father is out on the range, the children and I will enlarge Ku-Long's garden because we are sure to need more strawberry jam and more canned vegetables for the growing family, and for the additional ranch hands that will be needed once Mr. Asher increases his herd. And—"

She shook herself impatiently.

"Do you remember a girl back in Boston, Grund, a little older than I am, named Cordelia? Or maybe Claudine? She married a man whom everyone described as foolish and simpering and blindingly boring, and all the gossips said she chose him only because he had inherited a large house in one of the wealthiest parts of Boston. I don't want to be like her. I don't want to marry a man to get a, a *place*. That wouldn't be fair to him or me. Or to the children I just imagined into existence."

She sat, scowling down at the ranch until she couldn't feel her toes at all. "Drat. To quote Bucky, shucky darn. Here is number six, Grund. And the last for now. I am confused. I want to stay here. I want to live here. I think I might come to love him, but I don't think he would ever come to love me. I wish you were alive. And I guess that's it. Scientifically speaking."

**\*\*\*\***

"Mr. Asher?"

She was standing in the doorway to his office, her hands knotted in front of her like a little girl, wearing an expression of determination.

"Yes, Miss Barrington?"

"I have been here several months. I know how hard you men work every day, but I don't know what it is you do, exactly. Therefore, I would like to ride along with you."

He leaned back in his big chair. "Have you ever been on a horse?"

"When I was five or six years old, I went to a birthday party and there was a Shetland pony. But I assume that doesn't count."

There, she thought. There were the upward slanting wrinkles beside his eyes, and the twitch at one side of his mustache, the signs that he was almost smiling.

"No. I don't think it does."

"Would it work if I drive the cart and you ride your horse?"

"Spike."

"Pardon?"

"My range horse is Spike."

"What a perfect name. Tough and western."

"He's called that because he has a silly-looking tuft, a cowlick I suppose you could call it, between his ears. Sticks straight up like a pointed spike."

"You could have named him Unicorn."

"Now that I think about it, yes."

She watched his face and waited.

"No, Miss Barrington. I think Spike will have the day off. Hank and I will juggle chores so you and I can use the cart. We'll head to areas that don't require being on horseback."

"Oh! That would be very kind of you! Thank you." The tension in her body relaxed, and she unknotted her hands. "What kind of chores will you be doing?"

"Mostly checking cows. Noting which ones will calve this fall. Then I should check a couple of the wells. By then it will be mid-afternoon and I will probably want to head back in and work in the office."

"What exactly do you do in here? In your office?"

He plopped a long-fingered hand down on the ledger in front of him. "This one's for cattle. Were they purchased or were they bred here? Information about offspring."

"My goodness. You can keep track of specific

204

animals?"

"Not always, no. All of them are wearing the Long Butte brand, of course. But many are individually identifiable. Like this one." He followed a line of writing with his finger, reading aloud. "Longhorn Hereford cross, red topknot, two plus two, marshes. That means she's a good breeder, with a set of twins and two single calves so far." He looked up. "Twins are rare with cattle, healthy twins even more so."

"What does the 'marshes' mean?"

"This particular cow is bound and determined to get herself stuck in the most remote wet areas she can find."

"What happens when she does?"

"Then, if we're lucky, and we have been so far, one of us sees her and gets a rope on her and drags her out."

"And do you cuss at her?"

"Always, Miss Barrington. Always." He looked down again. "Or this bull. One of the biggest Texas longhorns I've ever seen. I bought him as the start of a new herd of Angus-longhorn mixes. But the creature has wanderlust. I do believe Hank and I rode two thousand miles this summer just hunting for that bull."

"Goodness. I am surprised it didn't end up in Ku-Long's stew pot." She moved to stand in front of the bookcase. "Are these ledgers from other years?"

"Some are my father's, some my brother's, some mine. This one…" He reached over and pulled down one of the leatherbound books, his arm brushing her skirt as he did so. "This is for horses. Which mares we believe were bred by the wild stallion, which ones we know were bred to stallions owned by other ranchers. Each mare's colts and fillies. When each was broke to saddle. And so on. And there's a third ledger where I keep track of income. When there is any."

"Is your only income from selling the steers each fall?"

"Most years, yes. We've sold a few mustangs after Bucky tamed them, and he's getting a name for himself so we'll probably sell more in the future. And one year we had a surprise windfall."

Teddy thought the rancher's sudden grin made him look no older than Bucky.

"Hank and Bucky take scythes to the high grasses along the creeks to store for winter feed. Well, one spring we had extra and other ranchers didn't, so I sold it. For a pretty penny too. That might happen again in the future. I know of one rancher east of Choteau who makes more money cutting and selling forage than he does selling beef."

"I hadn't even thought about what cattle eat during the winter." She moved toward the door. "I will learn a great deal tomorrow, Mr. Asher. I can be ready immediately after breakfast."

"The pinto and I will meet you in front. Bring your sketchpads and pencils and all. And the professor's camera. Just in case we come across some bird species you haven't documented yet."

"Oh. Yes."

Yes indeed, Teddy thought as she walked through the barren living room. Tomorrow will be my chance to get to know Rancher Asher, just the two of us together, without interruptions. And that might be even more important than understanding what he and the other men do all day long.

\*\*\*\*

It was still dark when Teddy headed over to the main

building for breakfast. Forty minutes later, she stepped out into a perfect October day, with a high pale blue sky, a few wispy clouds, light breeze and warming sun. She stood still for a moment, pulling on her traveling gloves and breathing the air.

The rancher was already in the wagon, seated on the passenger's side.

"I figured you should drive so I can keep my eyes out for cows."

She pushed her bulging satchel under the tarp in the back of the wagon, handed up the camera, and hoisted herself into the driver's seat. The wagon felt crowded in a way it never had before, even though Rancher Asher wasn't as tall as her grandfather and was a good deal less bulky. She thought he was sitting closer than Grund used to, and she was sure she could feel heat coming from his thigh and his arm and his shoulder.

"Where to first?"

"Head past your cabin and the paddocks and keep following that trail."

\*\*\*\*

"Stop." The rancher dropped to the ground near a sizeable group of cows and began moving among them, talking in a low and even tone.

So much for getting to know the man, Teddy thought. They had been gone a half hour and hadn't said fifteen words to each other.

"All right, Theodora," she scolded herself. "It's up to you to come up with a whole raft of scintillating conversational topics, one by one, until you get that man to answer with at least one whole sentence. His cows might be the perfect place to start."

She sat quietly, studying the huge animals milling

around the rancher and marveling at how close he got to the wickedly pointed horns. After several minutes, he patted the last one on the rump and headed back to the cart.

"So will there be calves?"

"Every one of those cows is carrying. They don't show early on, but this late you can see their rounded bellies and bigger udders. They'll start dropping their calves in just a few weeks." He pulled himself up into the cart. "Our wandering bull has been doing exactly what I bought him for."

"How do you know that same bull sired all the calves? I am sure I have seen many animals out here that aren't cows."

"Before the round-up. Not today. Right?"

"Yes, but—"

"You saw steers. Steers aren't exactly famous for their breeding capabilities."

"Why... Oh. Of course." She knew she was blushing, but at least he was looking right at her, and the wrinkles beside his deep blue eyes were slanting upwards. "I must admit I was baffled at first when Hank mentioned snipping. I couldn't understand why he wanted to cut their hair."

For the first time, she heard an actual laugh from the solemn rancher. It was short, to be true, but it was a laugh.

"Tell me which kinds of cattle are which."

"The red ones with white faces are Herefords. The black beasts are Angus. I am particularly fond of Angus. All the ones with different colors are longhorns. They can be gray, like that one on the right, or rust-colored, or almost palomino, with the possibility of splotches of any of those colors. All of them have long horns, cows and bulls alike." He slanted an amused look in her direction. "Steers too. The great-great-granddaddies and great-great-grandmamas of those cows came over from Spain with Christopher Columbus himself. But the breed is relatively new here in Montana, brought up from Texas a couple decades ago."

"And your elder brother was one of the people who brought them here."

He raised his eyebrows. "You have a good memory, Miss Barrington. Yes, Ike went on one of the drives, but that was several years after the first ones." He looked into the distance. "More cows up ahead."

And now it was easy. Rancher Asher talked about cows. He pointed out individuals and told her what made them unique. He told her what plants his cattle ate that were good for them and what plants they insisted on eating even though the animals ended up sick. He described his dad's first small herd. He talked with pride about his brother's ranch in Colorado. He talked about his plans for his own future herd. And she drove the wagon and murmured a few words now and then, enjoying his deep voice, learning and memorizing and feeling very proud of herself.

****

Teddy pulled sharply on the reins, reaching for her sketchpad even before the wagon came to a stop. Something large had just whizzed over their heads and dropped to the ground, followed instantly by the agonized scream of a rabbit.

"Goshawk, I think," she muttered, leaning forward. "Yes!"

The raptor was mantling its prey, facing them with

fierce red eyes, daring the pony to come closer, daring the humans to try and take the fine meal it just caught. The unfortunate rabbit thrashed its back legs, desperate to get free of almost four pounds of muscle and hunger pressing it into the ground, desperate to escape the razor-tipped talons digging into its sides.

"The hawk won't start feasting," she murmured, "until the rabbit stops struggling. So I have time to draw. Why don't you use the camera?"

The goshawk lifted its proud head and screamed, *ki-ki-ki-ki, ki-ki-ki-ki*. Teddy wished she had some way of letting the bird know it was safe, that the two humans and one pony would not challenge it, that all she wanted to do was document its beauty and ferocity and grandeur.

"I'm not sure how to use this."

"Oh. Sorry." She glanced over at him. "I should have explained. Lift the camera to your chest and line up what you want to photograph with the two v-shaped lines. Then pull the string to take a picture. Turn the key and pull the string again for a second photograph."

"Ahhh."

"Grund usually tried to ration film. But this is an extraordinary sight, Mr. Asher. It's worth several shots."

She turned to a clean page, now drawing only the hawk's head, its slate gray face and white eyebrow, the hooked bill, the barred gray front. She had started a third sketch when the rabbit finally stopped moving. The goshawk glared at the wagon for a full minute before loosening the grip of its talons and lowering its head to begin feeding. Many more minutes passed while the hawk opened the rabbit and consumed much of the insides, never once relaxing its ferocious glare at the humans, the pony, and the wagon. At last, it dug its talons into what was left and lifted into the air, the rabbit's remains dangling limply below.

"That was a true adventure."

"It didn't bother you to watch an animal meet its death?"

"It's not pretty, no. But goshawks are magnificent birds, and they hunt to live."

"Would you have minded more if the hawk took a grouse? Or some other bird?"

She looked up from her last drawing, a sketch of the hawk in the air.

"Why? Nature is nature, Mr. Asher. All living things eat, and not all of us limit ourselves to grasses, nuts, and seeds." She looked back down, itching to finish the last sketch before the picture faded from her mind. "Goshawks do eat grouse, as well as other good-sized birds. Jays, crows, woodpeckers. And of course they prey on squirrels and rabbits. There." She held up her sketchpad. "Does that look fairly accurate?"

"It looks extremely accurate."

"And we'll have your photos as additional documentation."

He made a noise like a grunt and then asked, "Are there many female ornithologists?"

She looked up, startled. "Quite a few. Why?"

"It seems like a somewhat blood-thirsty hobby for ladies."

"For ladies, yes. But you asked about females."

He hadn't seen that little dimple in many weeks.

"One time the BBA led a spring migration bird walk at a local cemetery and a covey of *ladies* showed up. Real ladies, with dainty white shoes, dainty lacy parasols, little white gloves. We would get close to a feeding songbird and those silly ladies would scare it off by twirling their parasols and giggling. One of the ladies started out pouting and ended up weeping because she got a spot of dirt on her shoe." She looked down at herself. "They were ladies, Mr. Asher. *Female* ornithologists look like me."

He half-turned and surveyed her attire. She was wearing her grandfather's disreputable field jacket with the many pockets, his canvas overcoat that was much too big for her, and something odd on her legs.

"Are those the professor's trousers?"

"They are. Two pairs at once." She glanced over at him. "Isabelle's invention. Grund brought four pairs of pants with him to Montana. Isabelle needed clothes, so we cut one pair of trousers along the outside seam—"

When she ran one hand along her side from knee to waist, her elbow jostled his thigh, and they both stiffened and leaned apart.

"And then we took off the waistband and made the top of the pants smaller to fit her and then we cut up another pair of trousers and used the legs to add width so the finished garment would look somewhat like a skirt, and then we did the same thing with the other two pairs of trousers and that's what I'm wearing. A two-pant skirt."

"Isabelle looked quite fancy the day they left. Was that your doing?"

"Ours. She's a much better seamstress than I am. We made two blouses for her, using Grund's expensive nightshirts, and I gave her one of my skirts."

"You two became good friends."

"We did. I miss her."

"I'm sorry."

\*\*\*\*

"Giving thought to lunch. How about you?"

"Oh. Yes. That would be good."

He turned and lifted a bag from the back.

"Hank stopped at the Whitcomb place on the way back from Choteau yesterday and bought butter. We never have butter around in hot weather, but it sure tastes a treat as soon as it gets cool enough to keep it in the pantry. So here's bread and butter, bacon, cookies and apples. And water, of course. Why are you laughing?"

Teddy reached around, pulled her satchel into her lap, opened it, moved her sketchbooks aside, and pulled out a brown paper package.

"Bread and butter, some with honey and some with jam. Bacon. Cookies and apples and water."

"Miss Barrington, we are going to feast."

"Indeed we are, Mr. Asher."

"Stop just ahead, by that little woods. It'll be chilly in the shade but we can sit on the sunny bank."

"That sounds ideal." And also, Teddy thought, those trees are large enough to hide me when I duck behind one. And I promise myself. Within the next year, if not sooner, I *am* going to invent a convenient way for a woman to relieve herself outdoors that doesn't involve baring her behind and squatting! I truly am!

Once the wagon was stopped, and the pinto had been given a pail of water and was enthusiastically ripping up grasses, the two humans walked to two different parts of the copse. Teddy was surprised at how comfortable she felt, knowing that each of them knew what the other was doing.

The rancher was sitting on the grass when she returned, with the contents of their two lunches spread out on a faded and frayed woolen blanket. He waited until she was seated, and then he picked up two of the water bottles, handed her one, and clinked his against it.

"To a picnic lunch."

"Cheers, Mr. Asher."

They were both hungry enough to eat without talking for several minutes.

"This is an odd combination, but tasty."

She held up a sandwich and he leaned closer to stare at it.

"Honey, butter, and bacon?"

"Sweet honey, salty bacon. I think I might serve this to the men tomorrow."

He watched intently as she licked honey from her mouth, leaving her lips moist and pink in the sun.

"When you and your grandfather first arrived on the ranch, Miss Barrington, I wondered why an attractive young woman such as yourself wasn't married."

"Oh. Thank you." She licked honey off the side of a finger. "And you, Mr. Asher, are an attractive man. However, I have not wondered why you are single."

"That hurts. Is it my personality?"

She grinned at him. "It's because Grund said there are many more men than women out here in Montana."

"There are indeed."

"Do you want any more?"

For a blank instant, he had no idea what she was talking about. He didn't particularly want more women in Montana. But he suddenly and powerfully wanted the young woman sitting across the blanket from him, the two of them alone in the vast sweet emptiness of a Montana morning.

"More lunch. No. I'm fine. Let's get going."

\*\*\*\*

"It's me again, Grund. Still awash in conundrums. I would be better off with only one or two choices! Having money for many possibilities makes coming to a decision exceedingly difficult." The sound of rapid wingbeats made her lean back, look up, and gasp. She sat absolutely still while a pair of swans passed overhead, the nearer one almost skimming the rocky ridge with its tremendous wing, and she watched until they disappeared into the darkening sky. "Trumpeter swans, Grund! We saw them at Freezout Lake that day you got too much Montana sun, but this pair was only a yard or so above me. They are magnificent! And I like knowing they stick with their mates for years, perhaps for their whole adult lives."

She put her arms around her knees and pulled them in tighter to her body.

"Back to choices. Possibilities. I know I don't want to go back to Boston. I don't want to live in any city anywhere. I know I can afford travel, and it would be exciting to see birds in South America or Africa or even the Far East. But I wouldn't enjoy getting to any of those places. Not at all. I found even our short trips to Plum Island long and boring and uncomfortable." She sighed. "I think I wouldn't mind having my own house in Choteau, except I would be sized up just as I was in Boston. I wouldn't be *me*, a person with education and knowledge and aspirations. I would be a—a potential housekeeper and cook with female organs. And buying a house would make it worse because it would announce that I have money and that would attract even more bachelors who wouldn't be looking for a human person but rather an asset."

She tilted her head to the darkening sky.

"I think I want to be a ranch wife, Grund. I'm unhappy because you said you didn't want that for me. But I enjoy planning and cooking for the men. I enjoy organizing the root cellar and the pantry. I loved helping Bucky's mare give birth. I can't see any logic in leaving Long Butte Ranch in the hope that I might find another man as decent as Rancher Asher. Rancher Asher has promised that I can finish our book, Grund, and write more books, and I believe him. And, thanks to you, I have enough money stashed away to simply leave if he hasn't been truthful. Oh! Geese flying right across the moon. How exciting!"

She sighed again.

"I recognize that I might be relying more on emotions or maybe even, um, biological urges, than on scientific reasoning. But biological urges have their basis in science, so I shouldn't make that distinction. I am an animal, just like all other humans. And I want to reproduce, just like other animals." She stifled a giggle.

"I would never have said that to you while you were alive, Grund. At least I don't think so. But if I had, you would have understood, and you would have empathized and supported. And that, Grund, brings me back to my decision. After thinking and thinking and thinking, I believe I would be wise to stay right here. To bear Mr. Asher's children and raise them with him here on this ranch. So. Here's my decision. I am going to wait another week or so, just in case something happens to change my mind, and then if nothing does... If nothing happens, I am going to say yes."

Chapter Sixteen

"Mr. Asher? May I interrupt you?"

Miss Barrington was once again standing in the doorway to his office, stiff and upright and ladylike, her hands knotted in front of her.

The month wasn't up yet. She must have decided to say no. Caleb leaned back, put both hands flat on the ledger in front of him, and braced himself.

"Come in."

"Thank you." She took her customary perch on the edge of the hard wooden chair. "I believe I have arrived at a decision."

Her expression didn't give him any clues about what she was about to say.

"Go on."

"I would like to stay here. On Long Butte Ranch. As your wife."

There was a moment, maybe several moments, of complete stillness. No movements from either of them, no sounds.

"I am—I am surprised, Miss Barrington. Considerably surprised."

"Are you—Do you—Are you still interested in doing so? Getting married?"

"Yes. Of course. I am delighted. I was just startled. I thought..." He stopped talking, flooded with the realization of what she had just said. The young woman sitting so primly in his office was going to share his bed. She would dress and undress in front of him. He would see the legs he had glimpsed that day when her clothes were wet. He would see her belly, her breasts. She was going to allow him to lift her nightgown and spread her legs and push his aching throbbing hardness into her, not just once but night after night.

It was fortunate that he was sitting down, with the desk in front of him.

"When?"

"I hadn't thought of a date. What do you think?"

"Soon."

"Oh. Yes. That is probably sensible."

"Where?"

"Pardon?"

He cleared his throat. "In a church? No. Probably not if you didn't want prayers at the professor's burial. But maybe for a wedding—"

"I have never been to a church service in my life. I don't see any reason to start now. Unless—Is that very important to you?"

"Me? No, not at all."

"Can we—" She looked around as if she expected to see rows of chairs and flower arrangements suddenly appear in his crowded office. "Can we have the ceremony here at the ranch? With a, a justice of the peace? Or what about the judge that married Ku-Long and Isabelle?"

"Judge Peterson was a friend of my father's. He would be pleased to marry me. Us, I mean. Marry us."

"Judge Peterson then. Here at the ranch?"

"That might work. But only if the wedding takes place within the week. After that, it's likely to be winter, and there just isn't enough room inside for a crowd."

"We would have a crowd?"

"Miss Barrington, a wedding brings out every rancher for miles around. Their wives and children. Spinster aunts. Hired hands. A hundred people at the least."

"Oh my goodness." She frowned. "Feeding them all might be a challenge."

"Food is never a problem. Long Butte Ranch will roast a side of beef and everyone else will bring covered dishes. Chances are we end up with more food than we need."

"Goodness." She stood up. "It's settled, then. Will you contact the judge?"

"I will. I'd like to tell the men at supper."

"Tonight?"

"Tonight. Yes."

"Oh. Then yes. All right."

****

"Hold off for just a minute before you start serving. Please."

She turned and stood still at the head of the table, a serving ladle in one hand. Caleb marveled again, looking at her blue eyes and pink lips and the red-gold curls piled haphazardly atop her head. At her curves under the big apron. His wife, in just a few days.

He cleared his throat.

"I have—We have an announcement."

Caleb looked around at huge and hairy Hank, young Bucky, and wiry old Arthur. These men weren't just his employees. They were his only friends since his brother Ike moved to Colorado.

"I have, uh—I have asked Miss Barrington to be my

219

wife. And she has accepted."

There was a moment of silence, and then Hank's loud "Good fer you two! Good fer you!" competed with Bucky's "That's jest plain sweet news! Jest plain sweet!" Arthur looked somberly from Caleb to Teddy and made a thumbs-up sign.

"We are planning on Saturday or Sunday afternoon, depending on Judge Peterson. Right here at Long Butte."

"This very next weekend?"

"This very next weekend. We'll need a pit for roasting, and we'll have to slaughter a cow and give it a few days to age."

"You got a treat comin', Miss B. Ain't nothin' like slow-cooked beef. Nothin!"

"Bucky, I find it hard to believe any meat could be better than those steaks Ku-Long marinated and we fried with onions. My mouth is watering already!"

They all jumped when Hank groaned loudly, like a man suffering sudden and violent stomach cramps.

"Men," he said, his voice even deeper than normal, scowling at them all from under his curly brows. "I purely hate to tell you. But I gotta. We gotta prepare ourselves for frillacious doodads. And *doilies*!"

"Gentlemen." Teddy tipped her head to one side and pursed her lips. "I have never been overly fond of doilies. But what woman wouldn't thrill to frillacious doodads? And embroidered seat cushions! Yes! With little flowers and butterflies, and lace around the edges!"

Now three of the four men groaned loudly.

"I am joking. I'm not sure about the rest of the house, but this kitchen is a joy to work in, just the way it is. Ku-Long arranged things so he could work efficiently and neatly, and I don't want to change a thing." She looked out the window. "Well. Maybe lacy curtains."

More groans.

"And now I would like to serve this chili before it gets cold."

****

She'll do, thought Caleb. She's got a sense of humor and the men like her. And her chili is just as good as Ku-Long's.

When she filled bowls and bent forward to pass them around the table, he thought he could see the shape of high firm breasts under her blouse. He hoped he couldn't because if he could, the other men could too.

There was no point in talking about chores, not when every head was down and every hand was busy shoveling in chili and cabbage salad and lifting hot biscuits to waiting mouths. He applied himself to his own supper and didn't speak again until everyone was almost finished with seconds.

"We've got a lot of work to do before snow flies. The big job's going to be moving the cows that are way out on the southwest grazing land, but that's going to have to wait until after the wedding. Hank and Bucky, will you knock together some long tables for food? Arthur, would you get some fence posts and wire and make an enclosure from the corner of the big barn to the bunkhouse to the little barn and back again? If push comes to shove, we could use that as an extra pen for cow-calf pairs. They'll be sheltered from the wind there, at least a bit, and the coyotes won't be happy coming close to the house."

He got only brief nods.

"My job for the next few days is to look for any early calves. There might not be any, not yet, but if I find some, I'll put calves and cows into the big barn. We might get lucky and have another week or two of good weather but I don't want to risk having newborn calves out there if we get a repeat of last fall."

Hank stopped scraping the bottom of his bowl long enough to growl, "Five feet", and Bucky leaned forward to answer Teddy's unspoken question.

"Five feet a snow, Miss B. Five feet between the fifth and the fifteenth."

"Oh my goodness. It's only October!"

"Don't make no difference. Three years ago was even worse. That were pure hell. Us'n spent four days out in nothin' but sleet. Jest about froze to death. But we didn't lose a single heada livestock, did we, boss?"

"No we didn't. We were lucky. But we didn't have as many cows, and most of them calved later, in the spring. Calving this time of year is always a gamble."

She is going to be a ranch wife, Caleb thought. My wife, on my ranch. I'm not going to do what my father did and pretend ranching's all fun and games, and then have the whole agreement collapse when things don't go well. She should know the risks right from the start.

He leaned forward and talked directly to her. "I bought that bull in January. Looks like he got down to business right away and a lot of cows will be calving any day now. They had plenty of time to eat the best grass of the whole year while they were carrying, so they should drop healthy calves. But the weather could change at any minute. That's the risk with fall calving. Snow covering forage, calves being born onto icy ground, predators hanging around knowing the calves are helpless."

"So all the cows and calves will spend the winter in the barns and paddocks? I can't believe there's space for them all."

"There isn't. And we don't want to start feeding them stored hay yet. What we want to do is move them to areas where there's still good forage, let them eat that as long as they can get at it, and end up with the whole herd in fairly close so we don't have to ride all over god's creation bringing hay to them once winter sets in for good. Having them closer also makes it easier for us to ride herd on them and, uh, discourage coyotes and wolves."

"That makes sense. Thank you for explaining that."

"So, tomorrow—" Caleb's spoon clattered into his bowl and he looked around at his ranch hands, his friends. "We get started. Once you're finished with the tables and the pen, come and help me search for calves. I'll be starting east of the ranch buildings."

All four men pushed back their chairs and stood up.

"You all have a great deal of work in front of you. Why don't I take over fixing breakfasts?"

"We agreed that you would have time to do your own work, on the book."

"I have plenty of time now that I'm not taking the cart out every day."

Caleb could feel Hank and Bucky holding their breath, praying for Miss Barrington's breakfasts instead of oatmeal that somehow managed to be runny and lumpy at the same time. Miss Barrington's breakfast biscuits. Her hash-browned potatoes. Eggs fried the way each man liked them.

"That is a very kind offer, Miss Barrington. Arthur, are you comfortable giving up breakfast duty?"

The little man nodded several times in a row.

"Good. Very good."

"Thank you, Arthur." She dimpled at the little man. "And when I clean up in here each evening, I shall put up bags of lunch for you all."

"That would be most appreciated. Thank you."

"Toldja," Bucky said as he followed the older men out the door. "Toldja she was a honest-to-goodness ranch woman."

****

"Do you want lacy curtains?"

"What? Oh. Perhaps. I haven't given thought to any changes in your house."

"Our house, by next week."

"Our house. Yes. But I still have a great deal to do on the book, and that takes precedence."

"Understood." He looked around the bare living room. "My mother made the curtains in the log cabin, to keep in the heat from the stove and keep out the wind. I would say we could just move them here, but they're too small."

"Well then, Mr. Asher. Perhaps I will spend a few days this winter doing the wifely task of making curtains. When it is too cold to be outside looking for birds."

Perfect, Caleb thought. A perfect introduction to what I wanted to talk about with her. "I think I can arrange some help for you. The Tobin sisters belong to a group of women, a sewing circle or some such. They hold their meetings in different houses every month and help the homeowners sew curtains and what not. Why don't I suggest that the group meet here soon? It would give you a chance to meet some of the neighbors, and we would possibly end up with, er, lace curtains and frilly doodads. If that's what you want."

She looked at him for a few seconds, expressionless,

and then dimpled. "I am not much for frills, Mr. Asher. But warm wool curtains would be excellent."

\*\*\*\*

"Well now. That's good. That's very good." Caleb looked at the two pink and smiling faces. "This Wednesday it is. I'll let Miss Barrington know."

"And tell her that we are delighted to hear about your coming nuptials."

"Definitely." Now he had to look away from the two women sitting in front of him on their double porch swing. "And that brings up—Er—Um. There is something else I wanted to ask you ladies. It—It is a bit delicate but…"

"Oh come now, Mr. Asher. No need to be shy. We have known you since you were running around the ranch with your little behind naked to the sun, and your mother trying to catch you. Is it something to do with your upcoming wedding, perchance?"

"It is. Yes. Er. Yes." He fixed his gaze on their porch railings. "You may know that Miss Barrington, my bride-to-be, Miss Barrington, she was raised by her grandfather. The ornithologist."

"Yes?"

"She hasn't had a woman to talk to since she was six."

"Oh. I see." Mrs. or Miss Tobin sent a meaningful look toward her sister. "And you are thinking that perhaps your bride-to-be doesn't know what to expect of, of marriage? Am I right?"

"That is exactly right, Mrs. Tobin."

"I'm Miss Tobin. Elsie. Sophy here is the widow."

"I apologize."

"No need, dear boy. No need. And no need to say

another word. We understand completely. Sophy and I won't be part of the group on Wednesday, but we will leave a well-placed word in Helen Edgar's ear."

"She is a neighbor of ours—"

"And a member of the Choteau Area Women's Sewing Circle—"

"And a natural-born leader. She will—"

"Steer the conversation so that—"

"So that your bride gets the information she needs."

"And gets to ask any questions she might be having."

"I am indebted to you both. And to Missus Edgar."

"No need. No need at all."

Caleb stood up, looking from one smiling face to the other. "Just curious. Why won't you be part of the group?"

"We two are leaving early tomorrow for our annual expedition to Great Falls."

Two pairs of bright blue eyes positively sparkled.

"We stay in the grand hotel, we eat food we didn't have to cook—"

"Some of it we can't even pronounce!"

They both giggled.

"And we consume quite a lot of wine. From France!"

"Sophy!"

"Well, we do, Elsie."

"And we treat ourselves to a concert or a dramatic presentation."

"Sometimes both."

"And we do our Christmas shopping, mostly for Sophy's grandchildren—"

"I have five grandchildren, would you believe it?"

Caleb had no difficulty at all believing the little gray-haired woman was a grandmother five times over, but he thought it might be impolite to say so.

"I am astonished, Mrs. Tobin. Gobsmacked, in actuality." He grinned. "My daddy used to say that sometimes. He said Scottish people say that when they are so surprised it's like somebody hit them in the face for no reason at all. Gobsmacked."

He could hear them both tittering as he jumped down the porch steps.

"Well, I have to be heading back. Thank you, ladies. Thank you for arranging the sewing circle, and for your help and understanding."

**\*\*\*\***

He felt damn pleased with himself. He recognized a potential problem in his upcoming marriage, he faced up to that problem, and he took steps to solve it, even if it had been a bit embarrassing.

"Miss Barrington?"

She turned from the sink, drying her hands on one of Ku-Long's towels.

"Yes, Mr. Asher?"

"I took the liberty of talking with the Tobin sisters and making arrangements for the sewing circle to meet here at the ranch this coming Wednesday."

"Oh, my goodness. That's very soon."

"It is, but there's nothing you have to do to get ready. Well, maybe you could bake some cookies."

"Of course. And have tea or coffee, or both."

"Miss Tobin assured me that the ladies will come with all the materials and, er, equipment they need." His dark eyebrows furrowed. "They said they will bring bolts."

"Bolts of fabric?"

"Ah. Fabric. That makes more sense than what I was thinking."

"You were imagining them getting down from their wagons with armloads of metal?"

"I did wonder. I—I told them we are to be married."

Her dimple came and went. "Well. Knowing how fast gossip travels around here, I wouldn't be surprised if everybody in Teton County has heard the news by now. Do we have to do formal invitations at all?"

"No need. Everyone knows that everyone is invited. At least all the ranchers know."

"All right then."

"Back to the sewing circle."

Caleb felt his face heating up but he had to get through this conversation. It was difficult enough to broach the subject with the two sisters. This was going to be ten times trickier.

"And also. Uh. Miss Barrington. Have you ever— Uh. Have you ever talked with another woman about, er, marital relations? About what goes on, uh, between husband and wife? In the marriage bed?"

She flushed. "No. I have not."

"Good. No. I don't mean that. It's not good that you haven't talked about it. I don't think so anyway. But it is good that I figured out a way for you to get your questions answered. If you have any. Questions, that is." He took a deep breath. "I talked with the Tobin sisters and they assured me that the sewing circle women will be more than willing to advise you."

Her head went back, she lifted her chin and tightened her lips, and her blue eyes flashed. "Are you suggesting, Mr. Asher, that I sit around this very table with a group of women whom I don't know from Adam and ask them to, ask them if—Ask them to tell me about the marriage bed?"

"I am. Yes. I am suggesting that exact thing. Almost all those women are married, Miss Barrington. Or they're widows. It would be good for you to talk with them before our wedding. It would make things, er, easier for you."

"I see."

She looked past him, out the window, and he waited. When she turned to him, she was still scowling but not as fiercely.

"I will consider your suggestion. But I also maintain the right to avoid the topic completely. Or to ask that the sewing circle ladies not talk about it, if they should bring it up. Whatever I feel like doing at that moment."

"Understood. I hope, however, that you can find a way to have that conversation, Miss Barrington. I truly hope you can."

"Mr. Asher?"

"Yes, Miss Barrington?"

"I believe you could start calling me Teddy."

Chapter Seventeen

"I am grateful to all of you for coming. Thank you so much."

"Sweetie, we all been nosy eager to see the inside of this ranch house ever since it got built." The speaker was a large woman only a few years older than Teddy, with hair so blond it was almost white and a wide face that looked as if she was ready to burst out laughing.

"Speak for yourself, Gert. I have never felt that sort of snooping curiosity." The raw-boned widow at the far end of the table looked as if she never laughed in her entire life. Her name was Flora, but Teddy could not imagine a woman less like a flower. True, the long upright figure did resemble a stalk, and the graying blond hair was somewhat like goldenrod in late fall. But the woman's face was like the butternuts Teddy used to collect back in Boston: tight, brown, wrinkled and bitter.

"Well, any of you who do feel curious must feel free to look into the other downstairs rooms before you leave. Mr. Asher has—I mean we have—this large kitchen and a sitting room and his office and wash rooms on this level, with a pantry and root cellar below ground. There are four bedrooms upstairs."

"This is a good sizeable dwelling, Miss Barrington. You will be a fortunate woman indeed, part-owner of such a house."

Teddy had never even considered that possibility.

Part-owner of this big sturdy house, and the barns and paddocks and bunkhouse. Part-owner of Long Butte Ranch.

"Is that true?"

"Of course, pet. Comes with being a wife. If the husband passes on, there's someone to keep things going. And someone to pass it to the children."

"Oh."

"It's a fine spread. But the house has the look of a place that hasn't known a woman." That was Grace, a soft-spoken woman wearing a black dress, black stockings and shoes, a black shawl, black jet earrings, and a black velvet ribbon around her throat. She must be the one Caleb mentioned, the woman who had three stillborn babies in two years and always dressed in mourning.

"That isn't surprising, Grace." Flora again, her voice harsh. "It is common knowledge that Mr. Asher's mother ran off to Choteau and left her husband out here with the two little boys. And then she died. Purely selfish, I'd call it." She pursed her lips even tighter. "This house was completed after she was gone, so of course it has never known a woman."

"I didn't know that about the rancher's mother. How odd! Was there—Was there another man involved?"

Teddy leaned forward, somewhat surprised by her eagerness to protect Caleb's long-dead mother from gossip and speculation. "The house could use some prettiness, I agree. I had many items of clothing shipped to me from Boston, mostly winter dresses, coats, boots and hats, but just a few household items. It will be a treat to look around and see some of the beautiful work you all do."

"Well! Let's start with curtains!" That was Helen, the brisk gray-haired woman at Teddy's left. "We brought several fabric options. You choose what you want, and you or your new husband can reimburse the Sewing Circle later. Shall we start with white dimity, or chintz with little flowers of red, yellow, and green? We also brought two bolts of coarse wool woven right here in Choteau, one blue and one ivory."

"My goodness. What richness!" Teddy looked at the kitchen windows. "Flowery chintz would be ideal for this room since it can be somewhat gloomy. But perhaps wool would work better elsewhere. Blue wool. Closing heavy wool curtains on cold winter nights would make the living room and the—our bedroom wonderfully cozy!"

And that did it. Teddy didn't even have to bring up the delicate subject of the marriage bed. Blue wool curtains for their bedroom was the opening Helen had been waiting for, energetic Helen whom most of the others appeared to accept as leader.

"Cozy. Yes. Ahem. Teddy. I may sound as if I'm prying, but I have a reason. Am I correct that you were raised by your grandfather?"

"I was, yes."

"Was there ever a woman in the house, a cook or a housekeeper? An aunt?"

"Grund's housekeeper Mary was my nanny after my parents died, when I was three. She was very dear to me. I have many more memories of her than of my own mother, a sad thing to contemplate. I keenly remember how bereft I was when Mary met a wonderful man, a lobster fisherman, and moved to Maine."

"You were how old?"

"Six."

"Six years old, and you'd lost your mother and then your second mother. How very sad."

"It sounds that way, I know." Teddy looked around at five sympathetic faces and the one grim face at the end of the table. "But I had a mostly happy childhood. A bit unusual, to be sure, being raised by my grandfather. But happy."

Helen leaned a bit closer. "After Mary left, after you were six years old, was there ever another woman, a nanny or even a neighbor, to tell you important things about growing up a woman?"

"No."

"You must have been quite alarmed when you first got your monthlies."

Teddy flushed. "Oh. Yes. I was horrified, to tell the truth. I interrupted my grandfather in his study, and that was something that just wasn't done! I told him I was bleeding to death. The poor man was deeply embarrassed but I think even more he was upset with himself. *Angry* with himself. He kept saying he was a scientist, and a scientist should have prepared me. Scientifically!"

"So he explained what was happening. He calmed your fears."

"He did. Yes."

"And did he use that occasion to talk with you about men?"

"He muttered something about meeting a good man someday and living with that man as his wife. But my grandfather was teaching me to be a fellow ornithologist, a partner in his scientific endeavors. I think he believed marriage was far in the future."

"He never told you, scientifically or otherwise, what

a woman needs to know as she prepares for marriage?"

"No."

"Well, sweetie," Gert put down the fabric she had been cutting and looked around at the others. "It is high time you knew, with your wedding in only three days. Every one of us 'round this table has experience, and we can help."

There was a brief, awkward silence, and then Helen took a deep breath. "I guess I'll begin then. You know that men and women are made—Are built different."

Teddy felt her face getting even redder. "Of course I do. Of course."

"And you've seen male animals on this ranch."

"Of course."

"Well. Human beings mate somewhat like farm animals. The male puts his male organ into the female." She looked sharply at the blushing young woman beside her. "Between her legs. Where her monthlies come out."

This was what Teddy expected, and what Caleb wanted, but it was still hard to believe that these proper ladies were sitting around the ranch's kitchen table talking about—About *that*. She was sure nothing like this would happen back in Boston.

The sweet-faced woman on Teddy's right was large with child, her ninth if Teddy had heard correctly. "The wedding night, the first time, can be difficult for a young woman, pet. But—"

"Difficult is putting it mildly, Amelia." Flora smacked her scissors down on the table. "The wedding night is downright painful. Excruciating. The girl needs to be honestly forewarned."

Gert's broad face wrinkled with a warning scowl. "First time hurts. And 'specially with a big man like

Caleb Asher. You might even scream a little, sweetie, but don't you worry none. No one'll hear you, 'cept him, on account of the shivaree."

"I don't follow." Teddy was so focused on the possibility of hurting enough to scream that she missed the last word. "Shivery, like shuddering?"

"Lordy no. Shivaree's a celebration. Keeps the excitement of the wedding going. Whole town sticks around after the reception. Milling around the house, out in the yard, making all sorts of noise."

"That's—That sounds very odd. No one did anything like that in Boston." She gave a weak half smile. "Neighbors would complain."

"Things is different out here. Don't you worry, though. Everybody'll leave once they know you been properly bedded."

"How do they know that?"

Helen jumped back in to the conversation. "They just do. And, as I was saying before the interruption, it'll get better for you after that first time."

"For some women. Not always."

"Well, no, Flora. But often it does. It certainly did for me." She reached out and touched Teddy's hand. "Even though the wedding night might be uncomfortable—"

"Painful."

"It is likely to get better with time." She shot a quick look at the other woman as if daring her to disagree again. "And it will never hurt as much as that first time."

"Oh. That's good to know."

Flora gave a loud sniff.

The pregnant woman, Amelia, gently patted Teddy's other hand.

"My husband and I are both eager for our babe to appear, *both* of us, so we can resume our, our bedtime activities. We abstain for the last month, when I am so huge, and then for a month or so after the baby is born. By then we are both hungry for each other!"

"I remember that waiting, and that hunger." That was from a white-haired woman who had been silent so far. "It does indeed get better with time, Miss Barrington, and it becomes quite enjoyable for some fortunate women. I was one of them. My beloved husband passed on four years ago now, and I still miss what we used to do in the privacy of our bedroom." She looked around with lifted eyebrows and an unexpectedly mischievous smile. "And a few times in the barn. And on the living room couch. And once in the kitchen."

"The kitchen! On the floor?!"

"Good gracious no. My husband bent me over the kitchen table and rode me well and truly. He was like a stallion that afternoon." Margaret shook her head, her eyes a bit misty. "If we had started another little daughter that day, we were going to name her Kitty Tabitha." She looked around at the baffled faces. "For Kitchen Table."

There were a few gasps, a few giggles, a sharp hissing sound from Flora, and a surprisingly earthy chuckle from solemn Grace. Teddy thought every woman around the table was imagining white-haired Margaret bent over a table while her husband stood behind her, servicing her like a draft horse on a mare.

"Helen? Do you think we should tell her about how often? And how long it might last? So she knows what to expect?"

"A very good idea, Amelia." Helen again took the reins. "There is quite a range in how often different men want that service from their wives. Some men choose a particular day of the week, say Wednesday or Friday—"

"Or Wednesday *and* Friday." Another sniff.

Helen's suntanned brow wrinkled in a little frown. "Yes. Of course, Flora. Some men do require it twice a week. But whether it's once or twice, or more, if a wife knows ahead of time, she won't be caught by surprise and she can have a warm bath before, or perhaps a glass of sherry, to help her relax."

"Goes easier for some women if they can relax a bit."

"Exactly true, Gert. It can be helpful to know when one's husband is going to expect his rights."

"Some men want to use their wives primarily to get heirs." That was black-garbed Grace. "So they don't ride their spouses very often. They go into Choteau to satisfy their baser urges."

Teddy wondered if that was what Grace's husband did now, now that his wife had failed three times to give him a living child.

"You do know about the orange house in Choteau, Miss Barrington?"

"I—Yes. My grandfather mentioned it."

"And you must have had houses of ill repute in Boston."

Flora barked, "Whorehouses", and there were a few gasps.

"Oh. Yes. Of course we did. In certain parts of Boston anyway."

"Well now, Choteau's infamous house has bright orange paint on the outside of the second floor, as if proud to show the world what goes on up there." That was pregnant Amelia. "And lights on every minute of every night. They say the women serve food and drink on the first floor and then take the men upstairs to a dozen tiny bedrooms. Nothing but a bed in every single one, but that's all that's needed. Men pay good money to lie atop those women and hump to their heart's content."

Another round of gasps.

"Nothing to do with contenting their hearts." Helen looked down at her stitching, a wry little smile twisting her mouth. "More like lower on their torsos."

"Helen!"

Margaret shook her head. "The orange house meets male needs, Teddy, the same as the marriage bed does. But I wouldn't want you to think that every husband in these parts uses those services. Many men are faithful to their wives. They would never think of demeaning what should be sacred between two people joined in the sight of God. My husband was like that." She leaned back with the same reminiscent twinkle they'd seen earlier. "And I must say. *My* man would never have been satisfied with once a week, or even twice! For the first fifteen or sixteen years of our marriage, my husband and I physically celebrated our union three or sometimes four times a week. Even more, sometimes. The first time hurt, indeed it did, but after that I had no desire to refuse him, not ever."

"You poor dear."

"Not at all."

"Well." Flora's usually pursed mouth drew up even tighter. "Back to the issue at hand. It is well known that your husband-to-be, Theodora, does visit that house in Choteau. A few times each month, I understand. I think it is only fair to warn you. You can expect an active first year, at the very least."

"Flora is probably right on that account, Teddy. Your man Caleb is in the prime of his life. He's healthy and active. He can be expected to have powerful desires. And the more often you satisfy those desires, the less apt he is to head into Choteau."

"And the greater the bond will be between you and your husband."

Five women nodded. Flora scowled.

"Amelia mentioned, um, how long. How long it takes." Teddy knew she was now scarlet, but she didn't want to give up without knowing everything she should know.

"Well, pet. I know only my man, of course. But I understand from—" She looked around the table. "From other women that some men finish up in no time at all while others—"

Flora interrupted. "Others keep grunting and shoving and grabbing and holding on with their fingernails until their wives are ripped up and bruised and bloody."

"Oh, Flora." Kindly Margaret looked scandalized. "That is rare. Very rare. I am deeply sorry you had that kind of experience. But I wager that right around this table there are at least four women who never knew that kind of mating. Four out of six."

"Five," put in Grace.

"Five out of six then. I am deeply sorry you had such a dreadful time, but that's no reason to frighten this young woman who is probably a bit nervous as it is."

Flora snorted again, and Helen got up to measure a curtain against the kitchen window.

****

"Well, ladies. I am afraid I have to leave so I can get

home for my little ones. School's out soon." Amelia folded up her sewing. "Flora and Grace, will you be riding back with me? Thanks for the tea and cakes, pet. One of us will bring curtains out to you soon as they're hemmed."

There was a flurry of activity as three women rose and packed up their supplies. Teddy was sorry to see Amelia leave, but the atmosphere in the kitchen, the very air, changed the instant sour-faced Flora walked out the door.

"Would anyone like more tea? Or coffee perhaps?"

"Coffee! How wonderful!" Margaret leaned forward eagerly. "I gave up coffee after my Samuel passed on. It's just so dear and there are so many other places for my money to go. But I would love a cup!" Teddy started grinding the beans and Margaret tilted her head back and inhaled. "Ahhhh. I have missed that smell!"

"I have a question for you all. What do people wear for a wedding, around here?"

"Most wear their Sunday go-to-church clothes."

"But what about the bride?"

"Oh you poor thing." Gert looked up into Teddy's face, her eyes big and tragic. "You don't have a mother or sisters to fuss over you, or help you pick out a dress, or help you get ready on the day. Any one of us would be glad to help."

"Thank you, but that isn't what—I think I'll be fine. I just didn't know what kind of dress is appropriate. My trunks arrived yesterday, from Boston, and I have a long-sleeved dress of fine woolen fabric, in the color of—" She looked around at the three women. "Almost precisely the blue-green of your eyes, Gert."

Margaret and Helen turned and looked at the other woman and then back at Teddy.

"You will be lovely in that color, Teddy."

"Thank you. The dress isn't new but I like it. And Gru—My grandfather bought it for me, so wearing it will help me pretend that he is there, giving me away, the way he should have had the chance to do." She turned away, blinking away tears, and busied herself measuring the coffee into the pot and spooning more into the grinder. Once she had control over her voice, she said, "I am curious about Flora. Is she always so negative?"

"Oh. Poor Flora." Helen looked at the others. "She wasn't what you'd call cheery even as a child. Her family lived a few houses down from us. Big house, lots of money. There were eleven children, maybe twelve. Parents didn't spare the rod, I can tell you that. Flora was the last to leave home. She probably didn't *have* to go to work, but she got a job in the women and children section of the mercantile. Everyone thought she'd be a spinster and stay in that big house her whole life. There were shocked faces in town, I tell you, when the store owner up and married her and Flora moved from her parent's big rich house to his even bigger and richer house."

"And *that* house is right next to ours, me and my husband. Our little, tiny poor house, shadowed by his cold and scary mansion." Gert frowned. "I think the whole town believed Flora would have been better served if she had stayed single."

"Oh dear. What was he like? Was he cruel?"

"And cold. Cruel and cold. Flora went right on working in his store and he always treated her like she was a brand-new employee, not worth a bit of respect at all."

"So true!" Now all three women wanted to tell the story. "I remember one time she was feeling poorly and he yelled at her right in front of everyone in the store. Said he would dock her pay if she took time off to go to the doctor."

"And after a few years and no children, he would say right in front of people that Flora was worthless as a wife so she might as well be useful in some other way, and then he'd tell her to go sort out the backroom or some other menial task like that."

"That man was rich as Croesus, but he was always complaining about not having enough money. One day he put an announcement in the paper saying they was going to take in paying borders and fill the rooms that were supposed to be for their children. Said that right in the announcement, about the children."

"That is just awful!" Teddy placed a clean mug in front of Margaret and asked the others with a lift of her brow if they wanted coffee also. "Everybody? Good! Here's sugar and cream."

There was a brief pause in the story as everyone added to their coffee mugs and took the first sips and sighed with pleasure.

"And he told people, right out in public, that he didn't worry one bit about taking in male boarders because no man would look twice at his ugly skinny wife."

"So poor Flora had to run his boarding house and also work in his store?"

"Not for long. Their first boarder was a tidy little slip of a man. Shorter than me and not half as wide as Flora's husband. Worked as an ostler dawn to mid-morning, went back to lodgings to get some sleep, then dealt blackjack at the hotel in the evenings." Gert's face was suddenly split by a wide and toothy grin. "I'm telling you all! When that little man left for his evening job, he was a real dandy. Fresh polished shoes and pomade in his hair and a bright colored vest and a crease in his pants you could use to cut your bread."

Teddy sat down and pushed the plate of leftover cakes to the middle of the table.

"Flora's husband prob'ly didn't notice nothing different, but other folks in town sure did. That woman started looking, well, not all the way happy, but as if she thought happiness might just be a possibility."

"She even started pinning up her hair to make it curl a little. And one day I saw her with a cameo brooch and that woman *never* wore nothing fancy."

"Do you think the boarder gave it to her?"

"I doubt it. But maybe."

"No. It were her mom's, I think. Flora just wanted to look pretty."

"One afternoon I looked from our upstairs window into their yard and there they were, Flora and the blackjack dealer, having fancy afternoon tea! Flowers on the table and all! He poured her tea and he handed her a cup like she was a real lady, and he accepted a cookie and talked to her and smiled at her. And she almost smiled back!"

Gert heaved a long sigh before she continued. "It all went to hell in just one afternoon. Dunno what happened at the store, but Flora's husband started bellowing soon as he walked in the door. He bellowed often enough, that's for sure, but this time was just awful. I heard her crying, which she never did. I was wondering if maybe I should go next door and knock, to break things up don't you know, but then I heard another man yelling. He was saying 'Stop that Stop that, Stop that,' over and over, and Flora's husband was bellowing even louder." Gert's eyes got huge. "And then she screamed, and then there was silence."

"Then what? What happened?"

"Well, sweetie, I don't believe anyone will ever know for sure."

"But we can guess."

"That we can. About an hour later, right at his usual time, that neat little boarder left for his job dealing cards." Gert was coming to the climax of her story. "A short while after, Flora comes astaggering out of the house. Her apron's all covered with blood and she's screaming and saying her husband has injured himself and needs a doctor real quick."

Helen nodded. "The story the next day was that the husband was reaching up into a cabinet to get down a heavy stew pot for her and he fell off the chair and hit his head on the corner of the big iron cook stove."

"And died?"

"Well, sweetie, he died all right. But most folks don't believe Flora's story for one tiny minute. We all think he was beating on his wife and that little boarder man came to her rescue and shoved the big brute or pushed him or something and that's what made him fall over."

Margaret nodded. "He was a little fellow, but he was plenty strong. Had to be, to work with the big cart horses."

Helen's eyes looked troubled. "That boarder killed him and Flora covered for him. But the saddest thing is that the boarder moved out the very next day. Took the train to Bozeman."

"Oh, poor Flora!"

"Poor Flora indeed. But she was mighty lucky to be rid of that husband. And she got the big house."

"I haven't seen her at the mercantile."

"Oh gracious no. She quit before the funeral."

Teddy breathed in a long breath. "That is a very sad story. It goes far to explain that woman. Thank you for telling me."

****

*Some men keep grunting and shoving until their poor wives are ripped up and bruised and bloody.*

Surely Rancher Asher wouldn't be like Flora's husband.

But Teddy had no idea how powerful a man's urges could be, or what those urges might do to an otherwise decent person. Every man on the ranch had warned her that even an apparently gentle stallion or bull could be dangerous during mating season.

She marched to the door with the dishwater and tossed it out onto Ku-Long's little herb garden.

Well, if Caleb Asher started hurting her more than she thought was sensible, she would push him right off her and tell him to saddle up and head into Choteau. That's what she would do! And if that didn't work, she would take her bruised and bloodied body down the road to Margaret's ranch, and she would ask Margaret to get her to the bank and then the stagecoach, and she would just leave. Perhaps she would head for Boston and have Abigail put her up for a while, back in her grandfather's old home. Or perhaps she would go only as far as Wyoming and study birds there.

And she would thank her grandfather, again and

again, for making sure she had money that was hers. Private. Independent. Money she could use if her marriage to the rancher didn't work out. If he abused her. Or if he divorced her. She felt guilty that half of his house and half his ranch would be hers after they got married, while she would have a secret stash of money. But all the money from the Boston house, and more, would be Caleb's to do with as he wished, and that was probably more money than a Montana rancher could hope to see in a lifetime.

Chapter Eighteen

Judge Peterson wouldn't be out to Long Butte
Ranch until mid-afternoon, so the groom headed out to
do his regular morning chores and the bride went to her
cabin to look through the mail from the Kodak factory in
far-off Rochester, New York. Packets of her
grandfather's photos, pictures he took while the two of
them were at Freezout Lake, driving the pony cart along
the narrow ranch trails, sitting for hours in their blind.
Every single one brought back his words, his voice, his
beloved face. She knew she should save the photos for
another day so she wouldn't show up for her wedding
with her eyes red-rimmed from crying, but she wanted
so much to touch something of him.

"Grund," she said aloud. "You should be here today.
You should eat all the good food the Montana women
will bring, and you should dance with the wives and
daughters and spinsters, and you would charm every
single one of them. You should give me away, even
though we both believe that is an outdated and insulting
practice. Since you're not here, Grund, I am going to
give myself away. I am giving myself to Caleb Asher, as
one independent adult to another. There might be a few
disapproving frowns, but perhaps some of the women
will cheer, at least inwardly."

Her little laugh was mixed with a little sniffle. "This
will be vastly different from that wedding you hosted at

home, Grund, for the young couple from the BBA. Remember all the commotion? And all the flowers? The bridesmaids swarming around the poor bride, fussing with her veil and her hair and her dress and her bouquet? I was only eleven years old, but even then I thought that would drive me crazy. Today's wedding, I promise you, will be a lot simpler. More Montana. And more *me*. Oh!" One of the photos fell from a packet onto her lap. "Remember the avocets? You said you would love to put together a whole book about avocets. It would have been marvelous, Grund."

She sighed. "I am going to put your photos away for now. I shall find time tomorrow to come over here and look through them, and then I shall bring them across the yard to my new home." She looked out the window at the main house. "Rancher Asher—Caleb—cleared a desk in the living room and emptied the bookcase next to it. That will be my office, a place for me to sort through photos and work on the book. There's a window right there so I can look out at ridges and prairie and sky."

She stood up, restless and lonely and on edge, and wandered over to her bed, fingering the soft merino wool dress lying across it.

"The sky right now, Grund, is brilliant blue, with just a touch of green, too bright to look at without squinting. Winter is holding off, at least for today. People will want their wool pants and wool skirts and flannel shirts as the afternoon wears on, but we won't get rained on or snowed on or blown away. I shall be wearing this dress, one you gave me. You said it was an appropriate garment for an ornithologist because the color is robin's egg blue. It has long sleeves and a high neck, but I'm also going to wear the Metis shawl that Isabelle gave me the day she left." She looked over at the dark red, green, blue, and yellow shawl draped over the back of the bed, the long fringe hanging almost to the floor. "I will imagine you by my side, Grund. And I will imagine Isabelle standing on my other side as my friend."

She glanced at the top of the dresser. "The dark brown stockings that were part of my traveling outfit are clean and whole, and they go with the brown button-up traveling shoes. I will fasten my hair with two silver hair clips that were my mother's. And that's it. My bridal finery. The ladies in Boston would be scandalized."

**** 

The groom didn't get back until the yard was full of wedding guests. Women crowded around the long boards set up as tables, arranging platters of ham, whole roasted chickens, Dutch ovens of stew and chili and home-fried potatoes, baskets of rolls, plates of sausages and hard-boiled eggs, jars of pickles and jams, tins of pies and cakes and cookies, cider jugs and ale.

Caleb took one panicked look and hightailed it into one of the wash rooms. Twenty minutes later, he was standing in the yard, washed, shaved, and dressed in stiff new blue jeans, a crisp white shirt, and an emerald-colored vest that had been his father's and was a bit too loose around the waist.

"You look lovely, Miss—Teddy."

"As do you, Mr. Asher. Caleb."

He held out a small bunch of red hawkweed, goldenrod, and purple asters. "Most of the flowers around here are past their prime, but a bride should have a bouquet."

Oh dear, Teddy thought. I never understood why

people cry at weddings but I'm going to be crying before we even get started.

"They are beautiful. Thank you, Caleb."

"Are we ready?"

"I believe we are."

\*\*\*\*

Teddy was relieved to see some of the sewing circle women in the sea of unfamiliar faces. Sweet-faced Margaret hugged her, Helen gave her a businesslike nod, and large jolly Gert winked. And then she was standing next to the rancher, and the judge was addressing the crowd as *Dearly beloved*. She didn't hear anything else, not even the words that she and Caleb parroted in turn. She heard nothing at all until the stiff and important man in front of them pronounced them man and wife.

"You may now kiss the bride."

Caleb thought she looked startled. Didn't she know about the traditional wedding kiss? Her blue eyes widened and she took in a little gasp of air when he leaned closer. But just as his mouth touched hers, he was hit from behind by something small, hard, and fast. He lurched forward, grabbing her arms to avoid knocking her over, and they both turned to see a good-sized piglet racing away from them, pursued by a small person with tousled blond curls, pink overalls, and bare feet. The next several minutes were a chaos of laughter, hoots, people chasing the pig and trying to catch it, people shooing the animal away from the food tables, and repeated scolding from the two embarrassed parents. And all the while the child's voice, with increasing volume, explaining and cajoling and pleading.

"I just wanted to ride her! I been petting her and she likes it but when I opened the gate she ran out and she's so fast but I almost caught her 'cause I'm fast too, I really am, but she's even faster. But look!" The child squirmed around in her father's arms. "I took off my bootiful new black shiny shoes so I wouldn't step in poo and that was lucky, 'cause look!"

One little foot was covered to the ankle in soft brown gunk.

"It were warm and soft but my bootiful shiny black shoes are nice and clean still. And my white socks too. Ain't I your smart little girl?"

The moment for the wedding kiss had passed. The parents took their daughter off to wash her foot and find her shoes and socks, and the crowd, with much laughter and a constant murmur of conversation, turned its attention to the makeshift tables laden with food.

The next hour was a blur. Teddy stood with her new husband and smiled and nodded and gave up on trying to remember people's names. Men and women alike came to offer congratulations, and the men slapped Caleb's back and shook his hand and occasionally offered him something from small brown bottles. Everyone must have heard about her grandfather's death, because no one mentioned him at all. The main topics of conversation were the coming winter, the past haying season, the recent hanging of a man who robbed a bank in Great Falls, whether Montana's brand-new statehood would make any difference to any of them, and the price of cattle last fall.

"Weather's comin' in early," one gray-haired man said sagely. "Count on it. Wind pickin' up already."

"Mr. Williamson down at the mercantile sez he seen a pack a wolves outside a Choteau two days ago."

"Wolves, huh? They're not usually 'round here till

Thanksgiving. Gonna be a tough winter."

"How you doing for winter feed?'

"They get back the money from the robbery?"

"You got your cows in yet?"

"My Ed's promised me a new winter coat, on account a selling the forage."

"Come along, you two." It was Grace, the sewing circle member who wore black for her stillborn children. "Take some seats and have some grub. And then I do believe there might be some wedding gifts wanting your attention."

Teddy's throat was so dry that the first sip of cider tasted like heaven. She was a bit queasy at breakfast and ate almost nothing, but she had been smelling food for hours and realized with relief that she was hungry now. She knew the rest of the day was going to demand energy. And the night.

****

"You were right, Caleb." She felt self-conscious calling him by his first name. "This is an extraordinary amount of food. And it is all delicious."

Two glasses of cider and some food in her stomach made her feel almost normal.

"Are you ready for seconds? Uh, thirds?"

"I think I am stuffed."

"I'm not. Not yet."

He had spicy red sauce on one cheek. Feeling very much like a wife, Teddy reached up with her handkerchief and wiped it off. Then she sat back and watched the people. People she would get to know. People she might call friends. These people would be her community, much more than Grund's wealthy neighbors ever were.

A sudden loud noise like an out-of-tune organ drew her attention to a tall skinny man walking toward them, squeezing a red-and-gold accordion.

"Mr. and Mrs. Caleb Asher!" He bellowed. "It is time for you to receive your gifts!"

Caleb hurriedly shoveled in one last bite of ham, and then he stood up and held out his hand to her. The accordion player led them to two chairs at the front of the crowd, chairs she recognized from the front room of her log cabin, now decorated with streamers of bright fabric and bows of yarn.

"Caleb, can we ask for some paper and a pencil? I am going to want to write thank-you notes."

"Excellent idea, wife."

There were jars of elderberry jelly and jars of cucumber pickles and watermelon pickles and three kinds of relish. There were jars of something Teddy didn't recognize but Caleb said were pickled pigs' feet. There were several bottles of dandelion wine and two flasks labeled Montana Tornado Elixir. There were small bottles and cardboard boxes of powders, salves, and creams for various ailments. There was a burlap sack marked *Wild Rice from the Hawkins' Back Thirty*. And then white-haired Margaret from the Choteau Area Women's Sewing Circle handed Teddy the largest package.

"Oh my goodness. This is..." Her fingers were shaking as she worked with the knots holding what looked like a sheet around something soft and heavy. She finally got the package unwrapped and looked down, through tears, at a splendid white-on-white wedding quilt, with thousands of precise tiny stitches making swirls and fern shapes and spirals on the white fabric.

"This is—I am so touched. So awed. This is one of the most beautiful things I have ever seen. Thank you. Thank you all, every one of you."

Next to her, Caleb held up the quilt and echoed her thanks.

"And you already seen our gift." It was one of the vigilantes, Mr. Truchot. "You got beef and horses and chickens out here already. 'Bout time you had a pig." He held out a short piece of rope attached to the errant young animal.

"This is a mighty fine gift, sir." Caleb looked around. "Arthur here is the perfect man to take charge of it. He'll build a pen and maybe he can pick out a mate for this little one at next week's auction."

The wiry and silent man materialized out of the crowd, took the rope, and led the piglet away. The accordion player made another complicated loud sound, and then he was joined by a fiddler and a young boy holding two silver spoons.

"Have you ever square danced, wife?"

Wife. She was now a wife. His wife.

"No. I haven't."

He stood up and held out his hand. "Just listen to the caller and watch what everyone else is doing. I will try not to lead us into any real trouble."

"Caller?"

"See the man with the bright red vest?" He leaned closer and nodded toward a portly gentleman standing by the musicians. "He'll call out the steps. Like do-si-do. Or promenade or—" She was looking completely blank. "Don't worry. You'll catch on fast."

Teddy doubted that. She had tried ballroom dancing twice, once at a fund-raising gala for the Boston Birding

Alliance and once at the wedding hosted by her grandfather. Her feet never went where she wanted them to go, and she spent most of both evenings helping serve the punch and cookies. But she put her hand in Caleb's and he led her out into the space that had been cleared for dancing.

"Grab your partners and form your squares!" bellowed the man with the accordion.

\*\*\*\*

"This is such fun, Caleb! You told me it was easy but I didn't believe you! Can we do one more?"

She was flushed and breathless and happy, and he could hardly wait to take her indoors. Upstairs. To bed.

"One more. Of course. It'll be a few minutes before the fiddler replaces that broken string. Would you like to try Mrs. Unruh's mulled parsnip wine?"

"Par—That sounds odd, but yes."

Teddy felt cold as soon as he moved away. He had been close to her ever since the dancing began, his arm around her waist, his fingers close to her breasts, his hard thigh against hers. Now the sun was low on the horizon, and the wind was picking up, a cold wind from the north. With help from several teenage boys, Bucky and Hank piled sticks and logs into the pit that had been used to roast the beef, and then lit a bonfire so people could warm their hands during the shivaree. An iron pot hung over the fire, with a cloud of fragrant steam above it.

"This is pretty strong stuff." Caleb handed her a steaming mug.

"It smells wonderful." She took a sip. "And tastes wonderful." Another sip. One of the sewing circle women had recommended a glass of sherry to help her relax. Perhaps parsnip wine would serve the same purpose.

"ArkanSAW Traveler!" the caller bellowed, and three squares formed again. All around them, people were laughing, talking, flirting, going back to the food tables for one more cookie or that last savory bacon roll.

And then Gert was beside her, smiling and nodding and patting her shoulder. "Now you try and relax, sweetie. Think of peaceful things. And remember. It only hurts the first time."

****

From the yard outside the bedroom window, Teddy could hear hoots, laughter, long keening wails, spoons pounded against pots and pans, cowbells, harmonicas, and something that sounded like a military trumpet.

Caleb carefully closed the door and turned toward her.

"Do you have what you need? A nightgown?"

"Yes. Thank you for bringing my bag from the cabin."

"Tomorrow Hank and I will carry over your trunk and your grandfather's, and the dresser you've been using."

"Oh."

Her legs wouldn't support her much longer. There were two straight-back chairs in the room, one against each side wall, and she dropped into the closer one.

"Let me."

"What?"

Her new husband was on his knees, lifting one of her feet and starting to unfasten her shoe.

"Oh. Thank you. You don't—"

"You are trembling."

"I am fine. I will be fine."

He lifted the other foot, unfastening the buttons and then placing her shoes side-by-side against the wall.

"That first day," he murmured, "when I lifted you into the buckboard, I had a glimpse of your legs, in stockings just like these." He lifted her skirt and folded it back against her thighs.

"The same—The same ones. These are the ones I wore that—The ones I wore before."

She inhaled sharply when she felt his fingers sliding under the lace of her pantaloons, freeing the tops of her stockings, pushing them down her legs. She knew it was foolish, given what was coming, but she couldn't help clenching her knees together and stiffening all over.

He stood and draped her stockings across the top of the dresser.

"Goodness. That is an astonishing cacophony. Outside. That noise."

"Shivaree. They'll keep going until they see the bloody sheet."

"What?"

He knelt again, looking up into her face. "You know this first time might hurt."

"They told me. The sewing circle women."

"Good. That's good then." He ran a hand through his hair. "Well. There is usually a bit of blood the first time. For a woman. Not a lot. But a little. So when we're done, I'll hang the sheet out the window and they'll see it and they'll know I have made you my wife and then they'll all leave."

"Oh."

"It's just tonight, Teddy." He stood up. "After tonight, you'll know what to expect. Every married woman throughout history, all around the globe, has experienced this first night. All those women outside, eating and talking and dancing and laughing. They all went through the first time. And they're all fine. And happy."

"Yes."

"Here." He moved the Gladstone bag closer to her feet. "We should both get into, um, nightgowns. Your nightgown. My nightshirt." Even in the faint light of one candle, she could see his ears getting red. "Don't wear anything underneath. Just the shirt. Gown."

She stood on shaky legs, relieved when he turned his back to her. She pulled her wool dress up and over her head, fumbling in her haste to get rid of her chemise and put on her nightgown before he turned around. His vest and shirt were off now, and he took a long white garment from a peg on the wall and dropped it over his head before unfastening his pants. She couldn't find the top of her nightgown, and then she couldn't find one of the sleeves. She was shaking in earnest by the time she was finally covered and could reach up under and drop her petticoat and pantaloons.

"Are you ready?"

"Yes. What—What should I do?"

"Lie down. In the middle of the bed. Oh. Wait."

He grabbed the bedcovers, pulling them down and almost off. The bed was high, with two thick pads filled with corn husks and then several inches of down-filled feather beds, all topped with a white sheet. Teddy sat on the edge and nervously edged toward the middle.

"Lie down and hitch your, er, gown up your, er, up to your waist." He picked up a little glass jar from the side table. "I will put something on my, my male organ. To help it go in, er, go in—To make it easier for you."

He made a noise in his throat as she lifted her hips to free the thin fabric and she pulled her gown up and he looked down at her long bare legs and the cloud of dark hair. He wondered if it was red-gold, like the hair on her head, but it was too dark in the room to be sure. He wanted very much to see her in the light. He wanted to touch her there. He wanted—Oh god, he thought. What if I can't even wait until I'm in her?

"Spread your legs."

His voice wasn't steady, and Teddy had the unexpected understanding that he was nervous too. She heard a clink when he put the little jar back on the table. She felt the mattress dip as he knelt on the bed, and then he grabbed her ankles and pushed them further apart. She wanted to watch him, to look up at him, to be able to see what was coming next, but she couldn't see anything but his face because of the long white thing he was wearing. And she had to close her eyes when he touched her between her legs, one long finger barely skimming her cleft from top down, and then up, and then farther down. A bit of pressure, and she felt his finger inside her, moving a little, curling inside her.

Caleb was shaking almost as much as she was. Damn, she was tight. His only experience was with the women in the orange house. Were women her age usually this tight? Were virgins? What if he damaged her? Maybe he should go slowly and try to stretch her a bit. Could he get two fingers inside? Yes. Now he could make her just a little wider. The ointment for his cock was on his fingers too. He could smell that minty smell, and the soap in the wash rooms, and there was a spicy scent that was pure woman and that made him harder than he remembered ever being before.

"Your legs should be—" He was holding her ankles again, pushing them up toward her bottom. "Try to relax. Let me—"

A thicker part of him pushed against her, and his body was almost lying on her, and he was balanced on his elbows, and there was pressure and more pressure. And he was inside her. Part of him was inside her, thick and hard. It was unfamiliar and it was uncomfortable, but it wasn't painful. Perhaps she would be one of the lucky ones. He was moving in and out an inch or so at a time, and it still didn't hurt. She opened her eyes, and in the dim candlelight she could see his head tipped back, his face twisted, his teeth bared as if he was in intense pain.

"Now!" he said loudly, and he thrust hard. Her startled yelp of pain and protest was lost in the noise from outside. He was deep inside her now and rocking his hips faster and faster, breathing heavily and chanting the same words over and over.

"Sorry. Just a few minutes," he gasped. "Sorry. Won't last long. Sorry. Sorry it hurts. Over soon. Sorry."

Then he made a garbled noise like a smothered shout.

And then stillness. She could still feel him inside, but there was less of him now. And then he let out a long exhalation.

"I'll get the sheet, wife. And they'll go away. I'll wash up and I'll wash you." He lifted off her and helped her stand up beside the bed. "Don't move."

He grabbed the sheet with one fist, yanked it off the bed, and strode across the room. When he opened the window and slammed it shut again on a corner of the sheet, there was a huge upswelling of catcalls, whoops, cheers, whistles, cowbells, yelling, and drumming.

"The ladies put down a piece of rubber so the mattress and the sheet didn't get bloody. There's another sheet underneath."

"Oh. That was very—" She gulped. "That was very thoughtful of them."

"Stand with your feet apart."

She heard the trickle of water from the ewer into the basin, and then he was kneeling at her feet, a bit of flannel in his hand and the basin next to him on the floor. He washed the inside of her left thigh, where she could feel something thick and warm sliding toward her knee.

Was she bleeding that much?

No. The cloth he held was still white, and the water in the basin was clear. Of course. It must be what a man put inside a woman, whatever made a child. But it was all coming out, sliding down her leg. Did she do something wrong? Was she supposed to be able to hold it inside her? He didn't seem upset, though. Or angry.

She had to look away when he used two fingers to separate the folds of her sex, touching her gently with the warm wet cloth, rinsing it, returning, washing her again and again and again.

"Just a little blood. Not much."

"Oh," she gasped. "I'm glad."

"I am also, wife."

Like a wave receding, the various noises outside dropped out, one by one, until a single harmonica was left, playing an off-key version of "Red River Valley".

\*\*\*\*

Teddy had never slept with anyone else in the same room, much less in the same bed. Her nightgown was twisted under her. She knew she wouldn't be able to sleep until she straightened it out, but she didn't want to move for fear she might wake him. She lay rigid, almost on the very edge of the narrow bed. She hurt, between her legs, but it wasn't anything like what Flora said.

It was warm having another body in bed with her. Sometimes at night it took her a long time before she dared stretch out her legs and put her feet down into the cold pockets at the bottom of the bed. But now there was only warmth next to her, surrounding her, warm even near her feet.

She cautiously lifted her hips and pulled the nightgown straight. She heard distant owls and her husband's quiet breathing. And after a while, she closed her eyes and slept.

Chapter Nineteen

Teddy had given a great deal of thought to the wedding night. She had given no thought at all to the morning after. She hadn't thought about sitting down at the breakfast table with Hank and Bucky and Arthur, knowing they must have been outside the window the night before. They must have seen the sheet with her blood on it, blood from between her legs. They probably hooted and cheered along with everybody else. They were probably watching now to see if she winced when she sat down.

But they didn't even look in her direction, not even as she dished out sausage and scrambled eggs, handed around muffins, and refilled the huge coffee pot in the middle of the table. Not even her new husband was looking at her. He was all business on his first morning as a married man.

"Having this many cows ready to start calving at this time of the year is new to me. I've got some thoughts I want to run by you all, and I'd like to hear what you think."

He looked around at the three other men as he spoke. He didn't even glance at Teddy.

She plopped a spoonful of eggs on her plate with more force than necessary. She was a bit sore and a lot irritated. If these men were thinking that she was going to be a silent cook and serving maid, they were sadly mistaken. Her grandfather used to quote some preacher, that people should always start a new project the way they intended to go on. That was what she was going to do, right now on her first full day as part-owner of Long Butte Ranch. She was going to make it clear that Theodora Barrington Asher would be included every single time her husband used the words *you all*.

"We've got to start moving the part of the herd that's way out on the southwest grazing land," Caleb was saying. "We don't want to be winter feeding them way out there, and we'd have the devil's own time finding them after the winter wind starts."

"You'll have to explain to me."

All four men started. All eight eyes turned toward her end of the table.

"Explain what wind has to do with locating the cattle." She thought of jesting that the beasts were too heavy to blow away, even with the famed Montana winds, but it might not be wise to joke about losing livestock.

Caleb answered after a long moment of silence during which Teddy sat and gazed at her husband, waiting and unmoving.

"Cows don't like cold wind in their faces," he said finally, his eyes on the coffee mug in his hand. "They turn their backs to it and drift ahead of it, and they go wherever it takes them."

"Bogs," Hank put in gloomily. "Canyons. Upta the ridges where they can't hardly get down nohow."

"I see. So if they have their calves, *drop* their calves, in those places, you might not find them."

"You got it, Miss B. I mean Mrs. Asher, ma'am. You got it 'zactly."

"And every dead calf is lost income."

Caleb nodded curtly, and turned back to the men. "This week, and maybe next week as well, will be like fall roundup until we get the most distant part of the herd in closer."

"How long you 'spose, boss?"

"As long as it takes. Rushing cows could push them to calving early. We'll have to amble along at their speed, as long as the weather holds. Give them plenty of time to graze wherever there's good forage. It'll mean overnights out there, so we'll bring bedrolls and tarps and as much food as we can stuff in our saddlebags. We'll work it so no one is out there more than a few nights in a row. The four of us'll go out today and comb the cows out of the woods and work at getting the whole herd bunched together. Then Hank and Bucky stay put and Arthur and I head back in. After two nights, one of you come in and I'll go out for two nights. Then Arthur goes out. We'll keep trading off like that, one in and another one of us out, till the cattle are off the open range and at least down to that flat area Ike called Misty Pasture. That way, we'll have them all in close when snow flies and it'll be easy to bring bales to them. Sound good?"

Three men nodded. No one looked in Teddy's direction.

"You are going to stay out during the night," she asked, "to ensure that the cows don't wander off?"

Caleb gave one of Arthur's curt one-bob nods.

"Will you also have to protect them against predators?"

"Yes ma'am we will." Bucky leaned forward, eager for her to understand. "No tellin' what's out there.

265

Coyotes. Wolves. Mebbe a grizzly. But don't you worry none. The horses'll let us know if anything's close by, and we got shotguns and rifles and we all got pistols."

"Will you have to help with the calving itself?"

"No. In general, cows manage birth just fine by themselves."

Glory be, she thought. Her husband, the man who shoved his hard male organ inside her only hours ago, was meeting her eyes. He was sharing information with her, almost as if she were another thinking person living on the ranch.

"If a cow needs help, we know what to do. But most do it on their own. And you needn't worry about wolves, especially if calving holds off a few days. Wolves smell the blood, and they gather once calving begins, but they don't like being close to where humans live unless they're desperate, and they probably won't be desperate until later in the winter. And grizzlies never come close to the house."

"I see. Thank you all for explaining. Well then," she said brightly. "I will clean out the Lunch Box and put together some bacon sandwiches and wrap up the rest of the muffins."

****

Caleb and Arthur weren't back by sunset. Teddy waited two hours and then ate a solitary supper. After her few dishes were washed, and beans for the next day were soaking, she sat down at the living room desk that had become her workspace and returned to the endless task of making duplicate sketches and neater copies of her grandfather's notes.

She wasn't worried about her new husband. Not really. Those men were Montana born and bred. But the temperature was dropping, and the wind was picking up. She got up three times to stand by a window and look out into the night. Directly above the ranch yard, the sky was a giant black bowl turned upside down, with thousands of silvery pinpricks letting in bits of celestial splendor. But straight ahead, toward the open grazing land, clouds covered the stars, clouds that increased in size every time she looked out.

A particularly strong blast of wind sent her back to her chair near the living room woodstove. Icy wind found every space between windows and frames. The heavy wool curtains from the sewing circle should help, but she wondered if the rancher had considered solid wooden shutters for the coldest months. Once the cows were in, and once calving season was over, she might suggest it.

Of course, Caleb might be way ahead of her. There might be good heavy shutters in storage, and some morning he would ask Arthur to put them up and the living room would be cozy. She had married a man who knew and understood this wild land. And she was here, his partner on the ranch, looking ahead to the rest of her life on land she loved with all her soul. The wedding night was over, and Caleb wasn't at all like Flora's husband.

Yes. She had made the right decision.

It was almost midnight when she heard the two men ride into the yard and take their horses into the barn. They didn't say anything when they came into the kitchen, filthy from head to toe and stumbling from exhaustion. The unwritten rule was that no one came into the kitchen without washing up, but this time they both sat down and shoveled in food without saying a word and then disappeared into the two wash rooms.

Teddy finished cleaning the kitchen and headed upstairs to bed. She was still awake when Caleb finally pushed open the door, his damp hair standing on end and a flannel shirt tied around his waist.

"Fell asleep in the tub," he muttered. He stumbled past the foot of the bed, untied the shirt, and draped it over the back of a chair. He stood with his back to her, naked and shivering, patting the top of his dresser and peering around the floor. Teddy was about to tell him that his nightshirt was hanging up when he gave an exasperated grunt, tumbled onto his side of the bed, and was asleep in an instant.

She reached across and pulled up the sheet and wool blankets and the two heavy quilts, tucking them around his bare chest and arms. Then she blew out the candle on the bedside table and lay down, wide awake, staring up at the shadows on the ceiling made by clouds racing across the moon. In her mind's eye she was seeing her husband's long back, naked in the flickering candle light. His muscular arms and powerful neck. His legs and tight behind. She would like to see the front of him too, but for now she was glad he hadn't turned around. She would have been distracted by one part of him, and she wouldn't have recognized his beauty. She never knew that men could be as beautiful as wild horses or pronghorn antelopes. Her naked husband was an unexpected glimpse of elegant beauty, a statue carved in warm-colored flesh rather than cold white marble.

She felt an unfamiliar tickling sensation between her legs. That was probably natural, she thought. She was becoming a wife. She didn't know how often her husband would want to, to... She didn't think it was called rutting in humans, and she couldn't remember what the sewing circle ladies had called it. She thought they used phrases like "wanting his marital privilege". Whatever the term, she wasn't dreading the next time. She moved closer until her knee touched his warm thigh.

****

Arthur's rooster woke her as it had every morning since spring. She slid carefully out of bed, pulled pantaloons and petticoat up under her nightgown, and then quickly donned her chemise and dress before creeping out of the room with shoes and stockings in her hand.

Her husband was still sleeping when she returned a little later.

"Caleb," she whispered. She reached out and touched his shoulder. "Breakfast is ready." She shook him a little, and he groaned and turned toward her, his face creased from the sheet and his thick hair standing on end. "Wake up. Breakfast is ready, Caleb."

He sat up in a rush, waking as quickly and totally as he fell asleep. Then he made a noise deep in his throat and ducked back under the covers.

"Did I—I slept without a nightshirt?"

"You were exhausted. You just fell into bed."

"I apologize, wife. I had no intention of shocking you."

"I was not shocked, Caleb. Don't be silly." She felt a mischievous desire to giggle, looking down at her husband's red face and his hands holding the covers up around his neck. "You don't usually wear a nightshirt, do you?"

"No. But I thought—"

She looked at the garment hanging on one of the

269

wall pegs.

"That does not look like something you would wear, Caleb. Not with those lacy cuffs and that little bow."

He flushed even redder. "I found it. The morning of the wedding. It might have been my mother's. I thought I should—"

"You shouldn't." She turned to leave the room. "I have worn nightgowns since I was a little girl, so I will probably continue to do so. But you should sleep in what makes you comfortable. I'll see you downstairs."

****

"What happened yesterday, to make you both so late?"

Arthur made a sound that was like a snort and a groan combined.

"Brainless critters," Caleb muttered. He held out his cup for a refill. "A dozen cows got themselves mired down in the only patch of swamp in ten square miles. Hours and hours to wade in there, rope them, hitch them up to our horses, and drag them out."

"I sincerely hope Hank and Bucky have dry clothes with them."

She'll do, he thought. She is thinking like a rancher.

"It does me proud, wife, that you're worried about their comfort. But by the time we left, those two were in better shape than Arthur and me. By a long shot! They were sitting in warm dry clothes in front of a roaring fire, their bellies full of bacon sandwiches, and they were about to wrap up in heated blankets and sleep like lambs."

"Will today be as difficult as yesterday?"

"Worse in some ways. Listen to the wind."

It seemed impossible to Teddy that there had been

270

blue skies for their wedding day, high endless Montana blue skies with puffy white clouds and occasional gentle breezes that didn't become cold until sunset. Now the wind was howling and screaming, driving ice-tipped rain.

Caleb and Arthur left early and came back late, wet, chilled to the bone, and hungry. But when her husband came upstairs, she could see that he wanted her body before sleep. And she knew, seeing his front for the first time, that it was impossible. Her body could not hold him. He must not have been that large on their wedding night. She lay stiff as a board on her side of the bed, her arms to her side, her eyes huge. He could see the small movement of the covers over her shaking legs.

"The first time hurt, wife, but now it won't." He closed their bedroom door. "By a week from now, you'll be used to the whole thing. You try to relax and I will be quick."

She was prepared for the thickness, the pressure, the sensation of being impossibly stretched. His sudden deep thrust made her gasp and cry out, but it didn't hurt. Not at all. She unclenched her hands where they were knotting the sheet, and she tried to relax her legs. His voice was as harsh and breathless as that first night, but he was moving slowly, so very different from the first desperate mating.

"Oh holy god, wife," he groaned. "Oh glory. I hope you learn to like this. Or at least tolerate it. It is the best thing in the world for me. Slow or fast. Doesn't matter. Better than anything in the world."

She wondered if she could move her hands off the bed, if she could reach up and touch his hips, his bottom. She wished she had asked the sewing women.

"Not every night. At least not at first. Once you're used to it—" He gasped. "Once you're used to it, wife, then every night. Oh yes. Sometimes twice." He bared his teeth and pumped faster and faster and then threw back his head and gave the same oddly strangled yell that she heard on their wedding night.

When he slumped against her, his body quivering and heavy and damp with sweat, Teddy thought she could tolerate it easily. Even if it did happen every night. She was a wife now.

**\*\*\*\***

Bucky rode into the ranch yard before noon on the third day, and Caleb left. Two days later, Hank came in and Arthur left. At supper and breakfast, the men said only a few words at a time, if they talked at all, words that tallied the number of new calves and the number of cows already in from the range.

Four early calves born. Four cows in labor, all of them in the barn. Three dozen cows in the pens.

Ten calves, all healthy. Six more cows in labor. A hundred cows in the pens.

One calf lost to the weather.

More cows in labor.

Two hundred fifty brought in.

On the third afternoon, Teddy bundled up and went outside. The paddock where Bucky worked with mustangs, the other paddock, and the makeshift pen that Arthur had cobbled together between the buildings, were full of milling cattle. The horses had been moved into the smaller barn, and the big barn was full of bawling calves and their mamas. Even with the icy wind and the dark skies, the ranch yard was rich with life.

In Boston, Teddy thought, people would turn their

noses up at the smell and the noise. But it was warm and rich and alive.

Yes, she thought. I love it.

\*\*\*\*

Late on the sixth morning, the weather made another abrupt change. The wind died, and a weak sun reached down through thin clouds. Teddy looked up from her cluttered desk when the kitchen door slammed open.

"You're back early today!"

"We're just about done. We got 'em all down to Ike's meadow." His smile was faint but real. "Is that something you have to finish right now?"

"There is a ton to do. But there will be a ton to do tomorrow and a ton the day after. Do you need something?"

"You." He was unfastening his belt buckle. "I need you."

She twisted to look out the window. "It's still light—What if—"

"Hank and Bucky are up to their eyebrows with calving cattle. Arthur's staying with the herd."

He took her hand when she stood up, muttered something that might have been *thank you*, and almost dragged her up the stairs.

"Drawers off. Just your drawers." He pulled apart the front of his jeans. "Almost forgot." He reached for the little jar on the dresser. "You tell me if I forget this. Don't let me forget. I might hurt you if I forget."

He pushed her backward onto the bed, spread her legs with shaking hands, and thrust into her immediately.

"Oh gaudeamus," he gasped. "Couldn't think of anything but this all morning. All morning. Primed like a pump. Oh gaudeamus. Oh wife, this is pure glory." He was finished in minutes and pulled out of her and stood next to the bed, panting, his brown eyes shining. "I needed that, wife. I needed that more than plants need sunshine and water. Here." He took a clean bandana out of his pocket, bent, wiped at her and then wiped himself.

She stood up and pulled on her drawers.

"What was that word you used?"

"Glory?"

"No. Gow-something."

A slow grin spread over his face. "Gaudeamus. I read it in a book about the Holy Roman Empire. Latin. The noble language of Nero and Julius Caesar and those other ancient fellows. Gaudeamus means rejoicing." His grin widened. "I am rejoicing right now, wife. I am rejoicing indeed."

****

Shucky darn, to borrow one of Bucky's favorite phrases. Something else she wished she had asked the sewing circle ladies. What do married couples do at these times? Do men expect their wives to be available even during their monthly flow?

"Caleb?"

"Mmm?" His voice was muffled as he pulled his long underwear up over his head.

"Caleb." She was still fully dressed, standing by the door of their bedroom and looking tense and embarrassed. "I would like to sleep in one of the other rooms for the next few nights."

His head popped out of the shirt.

"Another room? Why?" His expression changed. "Oh. I see. I gather we have not yet started a small Asher."

"Not yet, no." She looked at the bed, with the covers

flipped back and the sheet glaring white. "I usually—Um. I usually sleep with a towel under me at these, these times. To avoid getting—Um. Staining a sheet."

"You could do that here, in our bed."

She didn't want to explain how uncomfortable she was about rinsing out her cloths in the morning, using the big white washbowl that they both used. Uncomfortable about hanging the cloths around the room to dry. And hanging them in the kitchen was out of the question.

"It will only be four nights, Caleb. Possibly five. Usually four."

He looked closely at her. Her usually pink cheeks and rosy mouth were pale, and she was bent slightly, her arms crossed on her belly. "I understand, wife. You should do what makes you most comfortable."

"I didn't know—What do—I have been wondering what men do at these times. Is this when they go into Choteau?"

She was surprised to see the wrinkles by his eyes tip up.

"Well," he drawled. "Some ranchers use their cows or their sheep."

"What?"

"Instead of their wives."

"Oh. Goodness. I never thought—"

"I have never done that, Teddy. And I'm not going to start now." He put his hands on her shoulders. "I won't go into Choteau either. We pledged that we would take no others. I intend to live up to that pledge."

"I have married an honorable man. I will try to hurry."

He bent, laughing, and touched his lips to the end of her nose.

"I can wait."

\*\*\*\*

One of the three unused upstairs rooms was empty. The others had two narrow beds each, with folded woolen blankets and quilts. Teddy chose the room right above the living room woodstove in the hope that it might be marginally warmer, but she still pulled on heavy stockings and wool socks and topped her nightgown with two sweaters.

"This should make up for Caleb's wondrous heat," she muttered. "I hope."

Yes. She was warm enough with all the extra clothes and extra blankets. And she drowsily looked forward to sleeping alone for a few nights every month. At least until they started a baby. She turned onto her side, reached up one hand to pull the quilts tight around her head, and fell heavily into sleep.

Chapter Twenty

"I have been a wife for a month now, Grund. You probably know that. I think it has been successful so far. Rancher Asher appears pleased with the arrangement. He is certainly smiling more, even joking from time to time. And he was whistling when he left the house yesterday morning.

"As for me, I have been doing pretty much what I was doing before. Except, of course, I live in the main house instead of our old log cabin. I bake bread and make suppers. And I took the breakfast duty from Arthur; I can't remember if I told you that. All the men go outdoors right after breakfast, but it's still almost dark so I work on the book for a few hours. Some days I take the wagon out once the sun is fully up. I won't today, though. Peek down, Grund, from wherever you are, and look at those clouds!"

The vast Montana sky was in motion, from ridges to valleys, from horizon to horizon. Towering gray clouds raced by like ships in full sail. Flat darker clouds hugged the ridges and buttes and mesas. Over to the east, a ray of brilliant sunlight streamed through an opening and bathed a distant ridge the exact color of the Italian lemon ices sold in summer back in Boston.

"I wonder if anyone in the whole state of Montana, except me, has ever tasted an Italian ice, Grund. Maybe I can make some for the men." She shook her head. "Silly me. Lemons are unheard of out here."

The wind shifted, and the hillside of lemon ice was gone.

"I don't see my husband very much, Grund. Breakfast and supper, of course, with the other men around. And then, of course—But that's private. I am going to sit here and think about that later, but I won't embarrass you by talking aloud."

She pulled her heavy coat closer around her. The sun still had some warmth, even in early November, but cloudy days always held the promise of bitter winter cold.

"You would have loved to have been with me yesterday, Grund. And it goes without saying that I would have loved to have you with me. Dang. I thought I was over crying for you, but I guess not." She dug out a handkerchief. "It keeps catching me when I'm not expecting it."

She wiped her eyes and her cheeks, and blew her nose.

"Where was I? Oh. Yesterday! Yesterday I went to Freezout Lake. For a full mile before I reached the turnoff, I could see shimmery, moving white. We haven't had any snow down in the valleys, and it hasn't been cold enough for sheets of ice. All that white was geese, Grund! Hundreds and hundreds of snow geese! And Canada geese of course. And several blue geese. Oh! And one little Ross's goose, like a snow goose magically reduced to the size of a mallard. I swear I forgot to draw a single line or take a photo for at least ten minutes. I just sat and stared. But then I had a half hour to document the beauty, the beauties, Grund, before a golden eagle flew overhead and the whole flock took flight. The noise was stupendous! I ended up laughing out loud. To use a word my new husband taught me, a word you probably know: Gaudeamus!"

She leaned forward and hugged the cold stone above the grave.

"I won't tell Caleb this next part because there's no point having him worry about me. But I will tell you, Grund, because you already know it turned out all right. For a few minutes on the way back to the road from the lake, I was afraid I had run into the kind of situation you both warned me about. Two rough-looking men on horses pulled up, one on either side of the wagon. I made sure my hand was around my little pocket Colt, and your gun was right under my skirt, against my leg. But the men turned out to be brothers who have neighboring ranches down near Great Falls, and they come every year to see the snow geese. It's their special holiday, just the two brothers. They see the geese and have a good meal at the hotel in Choteau and stay overnight. They buy gifts to give their wives and children for the holidays and then they head back home. I was pleased that I was prepared to defend myself, but I felt ashamed of my initial suspicions. I do believe, Grund, that the vast majority of humans are good." She straightened up, patting her grandfather's grave. "And now I'm going to have some private thoughts, Grund. I'll visit you again tomorrow if it isn't raining. Or snowing up a Montana blizzard."

Yes. Her daily life was pretty much the same as before, except for the five minutes before her husband fell asleep each night. The sewing circle women were right. It hurt the first time and after that it was just a hard thrust and a few minutes of shoving and grunting. Teddy couldn't imagine why any woman would refuse her husband those few minutes, when they obviously gave a man such intense pleasure. But she also couldn't imagine looking back on years and years of those few moments, and smiling like Margaret had. And Margaret used the word *we*. There was no "we" in what happened most nights in the upstairs bedroom. Teddy lay there, her hands to her side, and Caleb did what he wanted to do and then he fell asleep.

Maybe some men did it differently. Teddy had a mental image of Margaret bent over a kitchen table while her husband took her from behind. That sounded demeaning, but Margaret had smiled, laughed even.

The only women who would know if different men mated differently would be women who mated with many men. Teddy gave a snort of laughter as she imagined taking the cart and pony into Choteau, finding the orange house, boldly walking in, and asking the first woman she saw.

Maybe not all men were as quick as Caleb. Twice now, she thought it might be all right if he kept going, if it lasted just a bit longer. And a few times recently she felt an odd tingling low in her belly when she looked at him and remembered how he looked that night he stayed out on the range late and came home exhausted and stood for a moment naked in the candlelight. What would it feel like to touch his back? His shoulders? Had Margaret touched her husband's body?

The first set of finished curtains was hanging in the kitchen, but the wool drapes were still being finished. Perhaps Margaret would bring them out to the ranch and then Teddy could ask her questions she hadn't known enough to ask before.

****

Teddy took her usual perch on the edge of the extra chair in Caleb's office.

"Do you have a moment?"

"I believe I do."

"I have been a wife for a month now."

"Strange. I have been a *husband* for a month."

"Oh. Yes." Teddy was distracted by the teasing light in his eyes, and that new deeper, softer voice. "That's true. But I—I have never been kissed. Not once in my life."

"That's not true! I kissed you at our wedding. And I have a clear recollection of kissing your nose one day."

"The nose doesn't count."

"I did not realize that."

"And a runaway piglet interrupted our wedding day."

"Ah. Yes. How could I have forgotten the pig?"

"I don't want to go my whole life without being kissed." She looked over his head, out the window, her lips turning up at the corners in a mischievous smile. "And I don't believe it would be proper for me to go searching for kisses from someone else."

"I am relieved to hear that."

"So I would like it if you would." She met his eyes. "Kiss me, that is."

Caleb had thought of putting his lips to her full rosy mouth. He thought about that often. But he had the uncomfortable feeling that kissing might cause a female to jump to conclusions. To expect expressions of emotional attachment. He and Teddy had a sensible partnership. He was satisfied in bed. She was a good ranch wife. He liked the way things were.

Perhaps a few restrained kisses, and then she

wouldn't bring up the subject again.

"Well. I suppose I could. Should we—Uh, should we be standing up? Or sitting? I believe my father and mother often kissed while she was sitting on his lap."

Damnation. That was downright stupid. Mentioning his parents would remind her that his mother chose to leave her husband's home and go off and live by herself.

Caleb shifted uncomfortably in his chair. It also wasn't smart to think about his wife's soft bottom in his lap. He stood up abruptly, knowing his face was getting red and hoping she didn't look below his belt.

"Standing. Yes. Standing will be better." He came around his desk and put his hands on her arms. "I have never done this either."

"Surely you are teasing me!"

"Nope. I never courted anyone. And I understand that kissing is an integral part of courtship."

"But you…" She hesitated. "You go to Choteau. To that house. The orange one."

"Men do not kiss the women there."

"Really? You mean you just—"

"Jump on, hump, and pump."

"Caleb!"

"Then if we want another ride, we come up with another dollar."

"That sounds—It sounds very impersonal, for an activity that involves two people's, er, private parts."

"It is impersonal, Teddy. It is a job for those women. It's how they earn a living. Men pay for it just like we go into town and pay Mrs. Williamson at the mercantile for a new pair of denim jeans."

"Oh. That makes me sad."

"It speaks well of you, wife, that you think that.

Well." He bent his head toward her. "Let's do this."

She felt his firm mouth press hers briefly. And then once again.

There, he thought. That should be enough. She's been kissed.

"I believe we are supposed to, um, purse our lips."

He wanted to laugh at her solemn face tilted up toward his, her mouth pinched into a soft little cluster. But instead, he puckered up too. It was different this way. Softer. She was moving her lips. Tightening, then loosening. Pressing. Softening again. She was nibbling his mouth with her lips, nibbling without teeth, tasting and caressing. He tightened his hands on her arms and tried to keep her from getting close enough to feel what was happening to him. Kissing had never been a prelude to mating, not once in his life. So why was kissing his wife hardening him in an instant, making him ache to have her under him, ache to be inside her?

"There. We have both experienced kissing."

A slight frown appeared on her brow. "We have, that's true. But does that mean we can't do it some more?"

"I don't see any reason to do so."

"Not that it is enjoyable? Isn't that a reason? Oh dear! Perhaps you didn't enjoy it! I did. Very much." She reached up and caressed his mouth with fingers that were soft but not nearly as soft as her lips.

"All right then. Two more. Then I have to get back to work. And you—" He tried to scowl at her but ended up looking only at her mouth. "And you, er, you must have work to do also. Supper. The book."

When he touched his mouth to hers again, Teddy wanted very much to put her hands on him, to feel his warm chest under the flannel shirt, to touch the strong column of his neck. But he had her upper arms pinned to her sides. Frustrated, she reached out with only her fingers, needing to touch some part of him, and she fumbled at his shirt, just above his belt. He made a noise deep in his throat and jerked as if he'd been jabbed with something sharp. She opened her mouth to apologize, but his lips came down again and for a dizzying moment she felt his breath in her mouth, on her tongue.

Then he let her go. He pivoted on his heel and was sitting behind his desk before she opened her eyes.

"I…" She inhaled. "Thank you, Caleb. For the kisses."

**\*\*\*\***

Well, Teddy thought as she added more dried red pepper to the chili. That was both a success and not a success. She very much enjoyed kissing her husband, but he almost tripped over his own feet trying to get away from her.

And yet his body had responded, unmistakably.

She wanted more of her husband's kisses. Tonight, she decided. Tonight she would kiss him before they got into bed. His body would tell her if he liked it, even if he didn't say so in words.

**\*\*\*\***

"Caleb. Can we start with kissing?" She felt very bold as she took a step closer to him, put her hands on his bare chest as she had wanted to do earlier, and touched his mouth with hers, quickly, before he could say no.

Her lips were softer than before, held in a larger O, and anything he might have said was lost in the need to fit their mouths together so every part of hers was touched by every part of his. He had the passing thought that he was glad she was taller than most women, they fit together so well, but then he stopped thinking. They were both moving their mouths, caressing, learning. He didn't mean to taste her with the tip of his tongue, but once he started he couldn't stop. He had never felt like this, never. His whole body was hot and shivery with need, and the neediest part was straining, aching, throbbing, jutting against her soft belly.

He jerked his head back, away from hers, gasping.

"I need you, wife."

"Yes."

He grabbed her bottom with both hands, lifted her off the floor, took two steps to the bed and dropped her on it. Her nightgown was caught and he couldn't push it up far enough, but she lifted off the bed and grabbed the material in her two fists and pulled it to her waist as he fell on top of her. He grasped her thighs with his hands and pulled them up and apart and found her soft core, jerking his hips forward and ramming into her. He heard her gasp and then moan but he was pumping and thrusting and panting, and then he stiffened all over and let out a stifled roar.

And everything was still. She lay motionless, moonlight on her wide startled eyes. He slid out of her and pushed himself to a standing position.

"I should be shot."

His words made no sense to her.

"Hanged. I should be hanged. I will sleep in another room tonight."

Teddy scrambled into a sitting position. "What are you talking about?"

"No woman should have to sleep next to a man who

has abused her."

"You didn't—What do you mean?"

"I hurt you." In the flickering candlelight, his face looked tight and shuttered, his jaw set and his teeth clenched. "I forgot the salve. I manhandled you. I was too rough."

"You did not hurt me."

"I heard you, wife. You called out in pain."

"Caleb, I called out, but it wasn't pain. It was surprise." She held out one hand but he backed away. "Caleb, it was not pain. Not at all."

His brown eyes were still bleak, but now he was frowning, trying to understand, wanting to believe.

"I think I know you as honest, wife."

"I am. Yes."

"I hope to god you are being truthful now."

"I am."

"But all the other times, if I hadn't put salve on my male organ, I would not have been able to get into you without causing you pain. I know that's true. You were tight. Almost closed."

She had to tell him. She didn't know if it was normal for a woman, and she didn't know if it would disgust him, but she had to tell him.

"Look away, Caleb."

"What?"

"I want to say something and I don't want you looking at me when I do."

He turned slowly toward the door. He heard a long sigh. Then…

"This is another thing I wish I had asked the sewing circle women. But I didn't even know about it then, so I couldn't have asked them. I didn't even know it happened."

"Didn't know what happened?"

"I—I have been wet, between my legs, almost all afternoon and evening. Wet and, and open. I don't know if that happens to other women." Oh dear. Telling him was as embarrassing as she feared. But she had to finish. "I have been thinking that perhaps this is a way for a wife's body to prepare. For her husband. Do you know if it is? Do the women in the orange house get wet?"

He turned to face her. "The younger ones use various kinds of salves and ointments. The older ones are so stretched that they don't have to."

Teddy winced.

"I should have noticed, wife. You took me so easily. I should have noticed that. But I was—All I noticed was—Lightning. Yes, that's it." He gently traced the side of her face with his fingertips. "Lightning shooting through my entire body."

"This time felt different, for me too." She turned her flushed face and stared at a thin line of moonlight coming in the window. "You were, I thought you were—" The rest came out in a rush. "You felt bigger and you were deeper into me."

"I was deeper because of how I was holding your legs up. And that didn't hurt?"

"No."

"You weren't afraid? Alarmed?"

"I was startled. But not those other things." Teddy looked up at her husband's anxious face. The wetness between her legs was still there, more than a few minutes ago, and she felt as if her breasts were reaching up to him. "I have been thinking that perhaps it was the kissing that made me, made me wet."

His voice was almost a growl. "Kissing had an effect on me, that's for sure."

"I noticed."

A grin lifted one corner of his mouth.

"You noticed, did you?"

"I am noticing again now."

She watched, fascinated, as his organ lifted, straightened, swelled, and lengthened.

"Would you be willing to do it again?"

"Maybe I could put my legs around you. So you don't have to hold them."

"Oh glory yes."

He put his hands on her shoulders, pulled her over into the middle of the bed, pushed her legs apart and knelt between them. She held her breath as she slowly wrapped her legs around his hips and her arms around his back. She watched his face as her hands roamed over his back, feeling smooth skin stretched taut over muscle and bone. She saw him tilt his head back as he pushed into her, his face tight and intent.

"I think you are right, wife," he whispered. "I think this is what's supposed to happen. I think a wife is supposed to get wet so mating doesn't hurt her. She is supposed to hold her husband with her legs and her arms and her, her woman parts." His sudden grin gleamed white. "I think we just discovered something, wife. You and I."

He pushed farther in, very slowly.

"You are a wonder, wife. With your legs like this, you are letting me… Oh gaudeamus. You are letting me all the way in. You are holding my whole organ, for the first time. As far in as I want. You are truly a wonder."

He moved almost out and then pushed slowly in, and

Teddy raised her hips to meet him. She gasped again but this time he could see that she wasn't in pain. Her head was tilted back, her eyes were almost closed, and she was smiling. Moving up and down with him changed the feeling, made everything between her shoulders and her knees quiver and ache.

"This is good for you?"

She nodded, mute, lost in sensation.

He moved slowly for a few more minutes, and then faster, and it was much too soon when he groaned and stiffened and then he pulled out and Teddy knew he would be asleep within minutes. But she was wide awake. She wanted more of what just happened. Her body was thrumming with energy, alive with wanting. Alone in the dark, her husband sliding into sleep beside her, Teddy shivered and ached and throbbed. And then she smiled. Perhaps someday she would have what Margaret had. Perhaps soon.

****

By breakfast time, Teddy wasn't at all sure she liked what her body was doing. She knew her face and neck were flushed as she served up breakfast, as she sat in her place nearest the stove and poked at her food, as she listened to the men planning the day's ranch chores. Thinking about her husband's arms made her breasts ache. Thinking about his strong neck made her want to kiss it. She wanted to lie under him and feel him from head to toe and spend an hour or more kissing. She wanted him inside her the way he was last night. She felt jittery, waiting, and increasingly irritated.

But Caleb looked like an entirely different person from the man who touched her face so gently the night before, the man who cherished her mouth with his, the man who talked about lightning. He gave her a cool nod as he sat down to eat. He didn't say a word to her, not while he was eating corn fritters and bacon and hominy grits with Ku-Long's canned apple slices. She wouldn't know for sure until that night, but right now she thought her husband looked like a man who might be regretting everything that had happened with his wife the night before.

**\*\*\*\***

All that day, Caleb was focused more on memories than on chores. He could feel his wife holding him tight with her legs and her arms. He saw her smile, her pleasure at having him inside her. He relived the building sensation, so much stronger than he had ever felt before. He relived the explosion of ecstasy and relief.

And there was another memory, from when Ike was twelve and Caleb had just turned eight. Their father was sitting on the front steps, whittling, and Ike asked if men did the same thing to their wives that bulls did to cows. Ike had a crazy crush on little Lorna Williamson whose parents owned the mercantile, and he was thinking he might want to marry her, and he wanted to know what a man was supposed to do when he was a husband. Caleb was sitting cross-legged on the ground, trying to whittle like his father, trying to make a thick aspen branch into a sandhill crane. Their father glanced down at him, shrugged, and said he might as well hear this too because he would be coming of age soon and he should know.

Well, Pa said. Yes. Mating was pretty much the same for men and women as it was for farm animals. The male puts his male part into the woman, between her legs. Humans are usually lying down, though, and facing each other. That's one difference. And animals don't care about each other. They don't even have to know each other. A stallion can mount a mare and put a foal in her, and the two horses could be seeing each other for the first time that very minute. Women need to feel something. Affection, warmth, love.

Also, said Pa, cattle, and horses and pigs and sheep and other animals mate only a few times a year, but husbands and wives do it regularly. So god or nature or some such miracle fixed it that it hurts a woman only the first time, but not after that. Especially if she's real fond of the man she's lying with. If she loves him, then her body changes. It gets softer, and wetter, and it's real easy for a man to push himself inside, and it gives them both pleasure. Both of them.

Pa stopped gazing out at the distance and looked directly at his two sons. Now some men, he said, some right around here in Montana, they don't understand that. They force themselves on women who don't want them, and they hurt the women. Any man who does that is no better than a dumb animal, and my own belief is they should be treated like dumb animals and castrated.

He breathed deeply and his voice softened. But I look at you two, he said, and I know you for decent boys, decent boys who will be decent men. You will always treat girls and women with respect. And someday each of you will find a woman who loves you, and you will get married and have kids.

"Kids!" Ike snorted, twisting up his face like he just bit into a sour green apple. "I wasn't talking about kids! I was talking about Lorna being my wife!"

****

Caleb did not want Teddy to love him. He wanted her respect. That went without saying. He wanted her to

291

enjoy being a partner in the ranch. He wanted her to be a good mother for their children. But he would not wish on her, or on anyone, what his father had lived with. What his father had died from.

Women get soft and wet down there, Pa said, when they feel something for the man who's mating with them. When they love the man. If that was accurate, then Teddy might be thinking she loved him.

The horse tossed its head, sensing its rider's tension.

"I am going to have to be very cautions, Spike. I want my wife to enjoy what we do in bed. Of course. Last night was the—You being a gelding means you missed out on that experience, Spike. But I am telling you it is the most intense and powerful experience of a man's life. And knowing she was enjoying it too made it… It was… I want more of last night, again and again and again until we are too old to care. But, Spike." Caleb scowled down at the horse's cowlick. "I don't want her to love me."

## Chapter Twenty-One

The kitchen door slammed open, and Teddy looked up to see Hank with a mass of gray and white feathers over one shoulder.

"Here's yer goose."

He plunked the giant bird down on the table.

"It is a goose, I agree. Do I want a goose?"

"Acourse! For Thanksgiving!"

"Oh. Of course." She got up from her desk and walked into the kitchen. "That isn't a wild bird."

"Nope. The Whitcombs raise 'em. Call 'em tooloose or some such name. S'posed to be easy-goin', not like them ferocious guard geese some folks got."

"Well." Teddy stroked the soft feathers. "Easy-going isn't precisely what we need for a meal, but it certainly is a beautiful fowl. And big enough to feed a crowd. Is it traditional to have a big Thanksgiving dinner here on the ranch?"

"Ku-Long usually did somethin' special. Pie with nuts and syrup. Sweet taters."

"I see." She looked up. "Well then. Something special it will be. Thank you."

She stood staring down at the huge fowl long after Hank left. Maybe Arthur could help her pluck it. Grund's cook always bought turkeys that were plucked and ready to be stuffed and put in the oven. This bird was quite a challenge.

\*\*\*\*

"Wife, you have outdone yourself."

There was a chorus of agreement around the table, both male and female voices.

"Thank you, Caleb. And all of you. And thanks to Arthur who cleaned this fine goose for me, and to the Tobin sisters for bringing the dinner rolls and not one, but *two*, of their special black walnut pies."

The two guests dimpled, bobbed their heads in unison, and dabbed at their mouths with folded napkins before speaking.

"We are so fortunate Mr. Asher saw us, all bereft—"

"Almost weeping!"

"In the post office."

"Right after I opened a note from my dear daughter with the sad news that they wouldn't be joining us for Thanksgiving."

"Their youngest has measles and they knew the others would be getting it next."

"And my son is far, far away. In southern Texas, would you imagine?"

"It was going to be just the two of us!"

"And this is so much more festive!"

"It is indeed!"

"We are glad to have you here," Caleb said. "With or without your pie."

"Speak for yourself, boss." Bucky held out his plate for another piece. "This is the bestest taste I ever tasted."

\*\*\*\*

For more than two weeks now, Teddy's breasts had been sore, as if her chemise had shrunk. And there was a constant dull ache low in her belly. She wondered if she might be with child, but her monthly flow came right on schedule a week after the big Thanksgiving dinner. And when it ended right on schedule five days later, she was still uncomfortable, restless, unsettled. She hadn't been out with the pony cart in many days. Perhaps she just needed a little adventure.

"Today is positively beautiful, Caleb. I am going to take the pony and cart into Choteau, mail the latest batch of drawings and notes, and do some Christmas shopping."

He looked up from the breakfast table, his face a blank. "Christmas. Oh. Yes. I have never done anything about Christmas. But we should probably, er, give each other gifts. I hadn't thought of that."

"You don't have to do anything, Caleb. But I always enjoy the holiday, and I want to give gifts this year. The weather is splendid and I want an excursion."

"When you're in the post office, would you pick up the ranch mail, if there is any?"

"Of course. I'll be back in time to put the bread in the oven and stir the soup."

****

The mercantile first, she thought. And then she would explore Choteau's other retail establishments. And before heading home, perhaps she would stop at the bakery and get a few boxes of chocolate candies to surprise the men at supper. Or save them for Christmas dinner. Yes! Chocolate candies and perhaps peppermint candy canes.

Two hours later, Teddy had two canvas bags full of gifts. A blue cambric shirt for Caleb and a new leather strop for his straight razor. A bolo tie for young Bucky, to adorn the special shirt he always wore when he headed to the Truchot ranch with courtship on his mind. A snakeskin band for Hank's big black hat. And for Arthur, a thick rope of his favorite licorice and a jar of salve for his hands on those days when pain from arthritis made his lips tighten and his forehead crease. She also bought a pink silk blouse for Isabelle that might exactly match the flowers in her beaded sash, and a quilted jacket for Ku-Long from one of the Chinese laundrymen in Choteau. It was probably foolish to buy the jacket, when Ku-Long now lived in the midst of many Chinese businesses, but it looked so exactly like something he would wear that she couldn't resist.

She was coming out of the bakery, after adding three large boxes of sweets to her bags, when she heard someone call her name.

"Margaret! How nice to see you!"

"You look as if you're fixing to be the Long Butte Ranch Saint Nicholas this year."

"I feel triumphant, Margaret! I have just concluded a most satisfactory shopping expedition and I just received some excellent news from Boston. How about you?"

The older woman hefted the carpet bag she carried. "I too am finished with my shopping, and I am feeling famished. Would you like to come out to the ranch for lunch? It's on your way home."

"I would love to! That will make this already excellent day even better."

\*\*\*\*

"Oh my goodness, Margaret. That lunch was a treat."

"It's fun to eat someone else's cooking, isn't it?"

"Especially such tasty cooking. I think the men at

the ranch would make short work of that casserole. May I have your recipe?"

"Remind me before you leave." Margaret refilled their cups with steaming mint tea. "You mentioned some excellent news."

"Oh! Yes! You know that Mr. Asher, Caleb, hired the Boston Birding Alliance to do a bird survey, and that Grund, my grandfather, and I would then make the survey into a book."

The other woman nodded.

"I contacted the publishing company when I decided to stay here in Montana, even before Caleb and I were wed. Today I learned that they will delay publication of the book until summer so I can add information about winter and early spring birds. That means the book will be truly complete, instead of just covering birds from May through September!"

"Your grandfather would be delighted."

"I think he would, Margaret." Teddy looked away, out the window, and blinked away tears. There were a few moments of silence.

"So. How is married life treating you?"

"I am very happy at the ranch, Margaret, so much happier and more at home than I ever was in Boston." Teddy lifted her cup with both hands and breathed in the wonderful aroma. "I love the land, the wildness out here, the space. I am happy as a ranch woman. And this past week I have been unpacking some of the crates from Grund's Boston home and making the living room look more like mine."

"And between you and your husband?" The other woman touched Teddy's hand. "Forgive me for asking, but your list of what you enjoy didn't include your husband."

"That was not intentional, I assure you. Caleb is a wonderful man! He is serious and smart. He's a good rancher and an excellent manager of the ranch finances. The men look up to him and he is wonderful with them, and he's good with the animals."

"You respect him."

"I do. Immensely."

"And how is he with you?"

Teddy gave a little grin. "Getting better. Significantly better. When I first showed up with my grandfather, I think Rancher Asher had no doubt in his mind that a female on his ranch would bring floods, droughts, wildfire, tornados, plague, locusts, just about every disaster known to man."

"You were the first woman on the ranch since his mother left, and that was when he was, what? Three? Four?"

"Just a toddler, yes. But he did get to see her after that, whenever his dad went into Choteau and brought her out for a visit."

"A visit. How sad."

"It is. I believe that his mother's inability to live on the ranch colored Caleb's reaction to having any other woman around."

"But he saw right quick that you were made for ranching."

"It was *not* quick, Margaret. But he did see, finally. And he has apologized at least twice for his initial antipathy."

"He's a good man. An honest one."

"He is. He's still somewhat baffled, though. I think he's not entirely clear *yet* where I fit in his life. On his ranch. At first, he would talk with the men at meals and never even look in my direction." She looked at Margaret over the rim of her teacup. "I am afraid I was compelled to act in a most unladylike manner. I pushed myself into those oh-so-manly conversations. I am a member of the ranch and I intend to be treated as such."

"Good for you!" The other woman pulled a bright-colored napkin off a plate of sugar cookies. "And—Uh—Are things going well intimately? I wouldn't ask, normally, except we all talked about this."

"I don't mind at all. Well, it is a little embarrassing, of course. But you all helped me greatly before the wedding." She carefully placed her cup on its flowered saucer. "You were right, you and the other women. It did hurt the first time, and it doesn't hurt now. But—" Teddy leaned forward, determined to know what she needed to know. "Margaret, I simply cannot imagine looking back at that part of our life with the kind of pleasure you showed that day."

"I'm so sorry to hear that. Is your husband rough with you? Or abusive?"

"Oh heavens no. But it's—It's so short."

"Oh dear." The older woman's eyes were wide and sympathetic. "I never would have guessed. He's a good-sized man, and he looks so—I'm not sure what can be done to help. We raised a bull calf like that once. He looked healthy enough but when he reached maturity, he didn't—He wasn't—He simply wasn't equipped to get the job done." She shook her head dolefully. "We slaughtered him."

Teddy gazed blankly across the table, and then her face flooded with scarlet. "Oh! No! I didn't mean—No! Caleb is—I have nothing to compare him with, but his—

He is—He looks extremely—I know I wouldn't want him any bigger!" She wished they were drinking cider or icy spring water, anything but hot tea, so she would have a cold glass to press against her fiery cheeks. "But the, the whole process is over so quickly. He does it almost every night, and it never lasts more than a few minutes."

"Ah. Short that way."

"Yes."

"And you are thinking you might like it to last longer?"

"I am. But I cannot imagine saying that to Caleb."

Margaret leaned back in her chair. "Teddy," she said sternly. "You had to convince your husband to treat you as a partner on the ranch. Surely you can convince him that you are partners in the marriage bed as well." She reached out and touched her guest's hand. "You might have to convince yourself first. But if you don't say something, you are facing twenty years, or more, of exactly the same."

"That thought has occurred to me."

"Your young husband, Teddy, has known nothing but the orange house, where he's always aware that the clock is ticking and he'd better hurry."

"Oh. I hadn't thought of that."

"My Samuel heard there are two large clocks upstairs in that house, one at each end of the hall, and there's a slate fastened to the wall outside every door. Every time one of the women leads a man into a room, she marks the time on the slate. The owner, who calls herself Lady Vicky, walks back and forth checking the times. If a customer isn't out of the room by the end of fifteen minutes, she makes a note on a pad of paper that she carries in her pocket. And when that man finally leaves, he is met at the bottom of the stairs by a gigantic beast of a man called Axe or Bear or some such ridiculous name, a man whose only job is to remind men who take too long that they owe more money."

"Oh my gracious."

"And believe you me, those customers find a way to pay up, even if they have to borrow the money. I don't know if Lady Vicky's strong man has done any real physical damage yet, but most of the men around here believe he could. And would."

"But why—Oh. I was going to ask why the sheriff wouldn't get involved if there were violence, but there isn't a sheriff, is there?"

"There's only the vigilantes." Margaret snorted. "And most of them probably go to that orange house themselves. They surely wouldn't want that huge man to harbor a grudge against them." She poured the last of the tea into Teddy's cup. "Your Caleb has learned to be fast. It's time for him to learn something new."

****

"It is time for both of us to learn something new, patient pinto," she said aloud once Margaret's small ranch was behind them. "Not just Caleb. More accurately, it is time for me to put into practice what I already know. I am a modern woman. I have an education and a profession, two assets most women do not have. I was raised to believe I am equal to many men. But I have allowed myself, in bed anyway, to be a passive prop, rather than a living wife and partner."

She chirruped, encouraging a tad more speed than the placid pony preferred.

"There are two of us in that bed, pony, and from now on there will be two people satisfying their inclinations or desires. And I have a strong inclination to spend time touching my husband. I am done being passive. Being a doll. Huh. A doll. I wonder if there is such a thing, a doll for men to use. If not, pinto pony, that's something else for me to invent once my outdoor clothes for women have become famous throughout the world. Cows and sheep everywhere will thank me."

****

Teddy always undressed under her nightgown, as quickly as she could, before climbing onto her side of the bed. And Caleb always stood near his side of the bed, with his back to her, while he removed his shirt and took off his pants. He turned around only when he heard the rustling of the high mattress. But this night, as he dropped his jeans and underwear onto the chair by his side of the bed, he felt cool hands on his back.

His skin rippled, and Teddy immediately lifted her hands. Perhaps he was twitching like a horse that wants to rid itself of a pesky horsefly. Or perhaps he was merely startled. She had to find out if her husband liked being touched. She had to know. She placed both hands on the sides of his waist and moved slowly up his rib cage.

"What are you doing?"

"I am touching you, Caleb." Oh, glory, yes. She had wanted to touch this part of him for many weeks, to feel the taut skin stretched over his ribs, the softer valleys between that drew her fingertips into and along them. "I have wanted to touch you for a long time now. I hope you allow me to continue doing so."

He covered her hands with his and she thought No! Please don't make me stop! But he pushed down, pressing her hands against him, sandwiching her fingers between his warm strong hands and his warm sleek skin.

"Why—" He cleared his throat. "Why haven't you? Touched me?"

"I wasn't sure, Caleb. I had no way of knowing what was expected of me as a wife, other than what the sewing women told me about allowing you to, um, allowing you to exercise your marital rights. I didn't know if I was supposed to just—To just lie still while you—Or if I might, um, interrupt you. Distract you. If I touched you. I didn't know. I guess I still don't know."

He moved their hands down to his hips. "I have wanted you to touch me, wife."

"Why didn't you tell me? Ask me?"

His chuckle made her want to cheer. A normal chuckle. "Unlike you, I didn't even have the sewing women to advise me. I didn't know if you might be offended. Or alarmed."

She freed her hands so she could learn the shape of his hip bones from his waist to the top of his thighs and up again.

"I am very much enjoying touching you, Caleb."

There was a horizontal band of extra smooth skin where the top of his jeans and his leather belt fastened tight around him, and she followed it back and forth across his narrow waist, barely touching. He sucked in his breath, and she was fascinated at how his waist contracted, how she could feel the muscles of his belly.

Caleb was always hard as he got undressed, anticipating the pleasure and relief that waited for him in his wife's soft body. But now he was so hard that it hurt.

"You are turning me into a stallion in rut, wife."

"Not a stallion," she whispered. "A beautiful, beautiful man." She touched her lips to his back. "I would like you to kiss me, Caleb."

He turned in slow motion, dragging his aching organ against her hip and belly.

She had seen Hank without a shirt a few times, his massive torso covered with thick golden curls. She was pleased that her husband wasn't that hirsute. He had two small tufts surrounding tiny nipples, and a thin line of longer hairs pointing straight down until it disappeared into the thicker and much darker patch down... down there. She wanted very much to move her hands lower, to feel him there, but instead she slid her palms over his waist, up to his chest. She let the twin tufts tickle her palms and was startled when he twitched and groaned and then pressed her hands hard against his chest as he bent to take her mouth.

This time she opened for him, meeting his tongue with hers. She had no idea people did this, this dueling and caressing of tongues. Perhaps she and Caleb were the first people ever to think of it.

"You are still dressed, wife."

She looked down. "How very comical. I was undressing and then I—I was distracted by how you look, Caleb, without your clothes. I was so distracted that I forgot my skirt and petticoat and my drawers."

"Perhaps you left them for me to deal with."

He pulled her nightgown up and fumbled at her waist, searching for a button to loosen her skirt.

"It has a draw string."

"Oh. Yes."

"Isabelle..." The sensation of his fingers against her waist made her voice catch and raised goose bumps up and down her arms. "Isabelle's invention. She made this skirt from, from Grund's traveling coat."

The heavy garment dropped, followed by her petticoat. She felt his fingers along her thighs as he pulled her drawers down, and she felt herself getting wet, getting wetter. And then he was grasping her nightgown and pulling it up, and he moved her hands away when she tried to cover herself.

"You have seen me, wife. I am going to see you. Oh gaudeamus. Oh pure beauty."

He reached out and ran one long finger up her arm, over her shoulder, down to the side of her breast. When her nipple tightened, he made a low noise in his throat and touched the curve of her breast.

"Caleb. I—Oh!"

And then she was on the bed, on her back, and his thickness was inside her and she wanted him inside her, wanted him there for many minutes, and his hips were pumping and pushing and driving into her, and he was panting and groaning and making a whimpering noise. And then he gave a harsh almost-yell and lay heavily on top of her.

She moved her legs farther up his back and felt him begin to harden again.

"Wife," he gasped. "This might be one of those twice-a-nights."

"Oh. Yes. Yes please. And I—I have a request, husband."

"Anything."

"I don't know if this is possible for a man. But I have been wondering if it, if it can last a bit longer."

Drat. She planned to start with how much she had come to like what he did to her in the night. Now she was afraid he would hear a complaint rather than a compliment. She was surprised when he chuckled again.

"No problem there, wife. After an explosion like that, a second time always takes longer." He raised up and searched her face. "You truly want me in you for a longer time?"

"I do. I like—Caleb, I like what you do."

There. The compliment.

"I have heard that many women don't. Don't like this, I mean. If you do, I am even a luckier man than I thought." He moved inside her, an inch out, an inch back in. "If this goes on too long and you—If you start to hurt, or if you get bored—"

She looked up at him with eyes that sparkled with humor and need. "I guarantee that I will not get bored. And if I get sore, I will let you know."

"Well then. Oh gaudy, oh gaudy. You cannot possibly know how this feels, your body sheathing my organ, made to... made to hold me... perfect... Oh gaudy."

Teddy was in pain, of a sort, but there was no way she was going to ask him to stop. Her breasts ached. There was a deep dull throbbing in her belly. He kept moving, and she kept moving with him and she exulted in his organ stretching her, his organ touching places that hadn't been touched before, his organ like satiny steel, and her breasts reached up to him, hot and full, wanting his touch. The ache in her belly expanded and intensified.

She tightened her arms around his back and her legs around his waist. She wanted to pound on his back with her fists. She felt like biting his shoulder as hard as she could. She hurt and ached and wanted and she had no idea how to bring an end to it but she knew she didn't want him to stop. She lifted off the sheet, pushing up with her hips, trying to get him deeper and deeper, wanting him to go faster and harder and at the same time wanting him to push in as far as he could go and then stop, just stop, and let her feel him and let her move on him, let her feel his hard shaft inside her, stretching her as far as she could stretch. Let her feel him as part of her.

Without warning, her body vibrated with an extraordinary sensation, from her knees to her throat, down her shaking arms to her suddenly numb fingertips. She called out his name and dug her fingernails into his back and shuddered and shook and burst into tears.

"Teddy! Oh no. I'm sorry. Wife!"

She grabbed him with her hands and legs and wouldn't let him pull out.

"Are you hurt? Say something!"

She shook her head back and forth, back and forth, and then she startled both of them by laughing.

"Oh my husband! Oh, Caleb! You said you felt lightning. I did too! Lightning!"

"You are crying."

"Of course I am crying." She recovered enough to reach up and touch his face with shaking fingers. "I have just felt the most powerful sensation I have ever felt in my life." She laughed again. "I can't even say that. It compares to nothing. I have just felt something completely unknown to me. Don't leave me, Caleb. Stay inside me. Let me tighten around you, and feel you. Let me—"

"You got very wet. Something like I do when I feel lightning."

"How lovely. How perfectly lovely." She smoothed one of his dark eyebrows. "And now it is your turn. Move in me, my husband. Move in me until you feel the lightning too."

**\*\*\*\***

Dad always called it "the male organ" but his brother Ike called it a cock. Caleb liked that word. It sounded confident, strong. Male grouse were cocks. When they puffed up and put on all their colors and strutted and danced, the females following their every move.

Last night he had been a cock on his home territory, a cock watched by a female whose glowing eyes showed how much she admired what she was seeing, what she was experiencing. He was aware of his cock all that next day, while he was helping Hank take winter feed to the cows and calves, while he saddled Spike and rode out to check the water troughs and break the ice, while he paused on a high outcropping and looked down into the new enclosure out near the road for his bull and the two dozen heifers that the bull would soon be filling with calves.

He kept feeling her soft hands on his belly, on his chest, on his butt. Would she ever touch between his legs? He wasn't sure decent women did that. There were many things the women in the orange house would do, for extra money, that maybe wives didn't do. But he couldn't think of any reason a wife wouldn't touch her husband everywhere. He wanted to touch her everywhere. They were man and wife. Their bodies belonged to each other. Maybe she would touch more of him, in time. Just thinking of it made him hard again. Made sitting on his horse damned uncomfortable.

He would tell her he liked her hands on him. Maybe then… She said she liked touching him. She said she liked what they did together in bed. She said she liked his hard male organ inside of her. And he believed her. She got wet and her body reached up to his and she made sounds he didn't think she was aware of, sounds that went right to his cock and made his balls draw up so tight they almost disappeared.

And she didn't say anything about loving him. Perhaps a husband and wife could have what they had, every night, and not get trapped into thinking they loved each other. If that happened with him and Teddy, he would be the luckiest man alive.

Chapter Twenty-Two

Caleb stood in the kitchen doorway and watched his wife. She was thinner since her grandfather's death. He could see her shoulder blades under her blouse as she stood by the stoves, wrapped in one of Ku-Long's full-length white aprons, piling ham slices onto a chipped platter. Her curls were drawn back with a deep red bow, and wisps of damp hair curled around the back of her neck. She turned to put the platter on the table and saw him standing there, and her cheeks, flushed from the hot stove, got even rosier.

"Good morning, husband."

"Good morning, wife."

He knew the other men would notice the difference between this morning and all the other mornings. He knew they would hear that his voice was low, almost growling, and that she was breathless. He saw Hank and Bucky slide glances at each other. And as he settled into his chair at the end of the table, he saw silent Arthur's quick thumbs-up.

****

Teddy had a dim recollection of a Christmas Eve when she was five years old, after her parents died and while Mary was still a central part of her life. Much to Grund's dismay, Mary filled the little girl's head with stories of St. Nicholas, and stockings that would be miraculously filled with treats, and presents wrapped in bright paper and tied with immense bows and piled under a lighted evergreen tree. Teddy knew her grandfather didn't approve, so she was overcome with surprised delight when he ordered a tree for the front room. Mary and Teddy spent three whole days tying ribbon into bows and making paper chains and cutting stars and snowflakes from left-over wallpaper that Mary found in the attic. Even the cook and her husband took part, bringing bowl after bowl of popcorn and cranberries that Mary and Teddy made into strings for the tree. And then the long, long afternoon and evening, waiting until it was time to go to bed, wanting for night so St. Nicholas could come, and all the while wanting hours more to sit on the floor and stare at their beautiful tree.

Teddy felt exactly like that now. She wanted to sit by herself and hug her arms around her body and think about the night before, and at the same time the long wait until bedtime seemed unbearable. She tried working on the book but she couldn't concentrate. She didn't want to take the pony cart out because it was windy and spitting snow. She made three loaves of bread, set them on the back of one of the stoves to rise, and then filled a huge pot with chili for supper. She baked double batches of ginger snaps, sugar cookies, and molasses cookies— and there were still hours to go before bed.

She had never had another Christmas tree after that long-ago holiday. Never another excited Christmas Eve. What if she never had another night like last night?

\*\*\*\*

"That was a wonderful supper, wife, even when measured against your usual high standards. You must have been cooking all day."

The other men had cleaned their plates twice over,

then drained the last drops from their coffee mugs and headed for the bunkhouse, but Caleb was still sitting in his chair at the end of the table.

"Thank you, Caleb. Yes, to the all-day cooking. I was restless."

"Why were you restless, wife?"

She flushed. "Goodness. I have no idea. It must be the weather."

"Come join me for a few minutes. Then I'll help you with the washing up."

She started to move Arthur's chair closer to his, but he reached out and pulled her onto his lap.

"Come sit *with* me. Now, isn't this better?"

"Yes. Very."

It was. Very. Teddy hesitated and then slid her arms around him and leaned her head against his shoulder, smelling chili, coffee, horses, fresh air, and Caleb.

"Did you do anything else today, wife? Besides feeling restless and cooking for a herd of voracious male animals? Did you also think about anything?"

"I was remembering, Caleb."

"Remembering what, wife?" His voice was low and growly.

"I was… I was remembering a Christmas tree we had when I was five years old."

"Huh. That was all you were remembering?"

"Of course it was, Caleb. It was an extremely beautiful tree, and well worth remembering. It was twelve feet tall, as I recollect. Mary and I decorated it with hand-made bows and chains, and I thought it was the most astonishing sight in the world. Grund didn't approve, but even he said it was impressive."

She snuggled closer and felt him swell beneath her.

"Why—" He cleared his throat. "Why didn't your grandfather approve?"

"He was a scientist, and Christmas is highly unscientific. It started with pagan superstitions about bringing an end to the darkest time of the year, back when people knew nothing about the movement of the earth around the sun. Early Christians left many of the ancient superstitions intact but added what Grund called complete bunk, converting pagans by offering their old beliefs with a new twist."

New twist. That sounded good. She wiggled her bottom around as if trying to get more comfortable.

"And, Caleb, you would not have wanted to get Grund started about St. Nicholas!"

"What exactly are you doing, wife?"

"Right now?" She squirmed again.

"Right now."

"Right now I am enjoying the sensation of your— Your organ, um, increasing in size." She gasped when he tightened his arms around her and stood up. "What are *you* doing?"

"I would think that would be obvious, especially to the granddaughter of a scientist. I am carrying you. We are going upstairs."

"But—The dishes—"

"Will wait until morning. I'll help you clean up then. Pull your head in closer so you don't hit it on the wall."

\*\*\*\*

"I want to watch you get undressed, wife."

She had wanted to be naked with him all day long, from first cock crow all through breakfast, all through the long day, through baking bread and making cookies, through supper and trying to keep plates filled and coffee

313

mugs topped up and four hungry men filled and nourished. All those endless hours of waiting, waiting, wanting. But now she felt bashful when he removed only his shirt and his belt and then stood watching her.

"You are supposed to be taking off your clothes too, Caleb."

"Later."

Her hands shook as she loosened her drawers and let them drop and then lifted her chemise over her head.

"You should always be naked, wife." Her firm high breasts were pale in the moonlight, with deep rosy centers. He reached out one long finger and stroked up from her waist, up over the curve of her breast, up to her nipple.

"I don't—" Teddy couldn't catch her breath properly. "I do not think that would be practical. Being naked all day. On the—On the ranch."

He touched her other nipple and watched it tighten and pucker. "This part of you responds to my touch."

She couldn't answer. He smoothed his palms over her breasts and down her ribs to her belly, around her narrow waist, down the sides of her hips. He bent and touched his mouth to a swollen nipple but lifted his head immediately when she gasped and shuddered.

"I'm sorry. I didn't think. I didn't know that might be painful to you."

"Oh no. It is—I don't know what it is. It made me shuddery and aching and please do it again."

He didn't, not right then. He tightened his hands on her hips and pulled her close, pressing his swollen organ against her belly.

"Glory, wife. Why haven't we been touching each other all along?"

"It does not—" She gasped. "It doesn't matter, Caleb. We can do it now. All the time. Every night. We can—"

He leaned back just a bit and slowly ran his work-roughened hands up and down her arms, intent as if he had to memorize every softness, every bone, every curve. His whole body felt as hard as his cock, and his brown eyes were almost completely black with desire.

"I deeply regret all those nights lying under you, Caleb, with my arms stiff at my sides instead of holding you." She tilted her hips, wanting to get closer. "When you were asleep next to me, without a stitch on, the nearest I got to touching you was letting my knee nudge your leg."

"You touched me with your knee?"

"I d... d... did." Her hands, of their own accord, were sliding under his jeans in the back, tightening on his buttocks.

He bent and kissed her breasts again, this time with lips and tongue and teeth.

"Caleb!"

"Yes, my wife?"

"I don't—I don't know."

She felt his deep chuckle against her.

"Please undress, Caleb. Please take off your clothes. Please." Her legs were shaky. She lowered herself to the edge of the bed, her eyes huge in the candlelight. "I did not know men could be beautiful. Not until the first time I saw your back. You are beautiful, Caleb. Like a wild horse. Like a statue."

His pants dropped and then his underwear, and she stared right at him.

"Even after months, I—I am finding it hard to

believe that fits inside me."

"I too am finding it hard, wife. Extremely hard."

"Lie beside me. Let me touch you while we are lying down together. In our bed. While you are touching me."

He felt like Montana. Like their ranch. Strong and tough and ineffably beautiful. She had wasted all those hours when she could have been feeling skin stretched taut over muscles and bones. When she could have been relishing the contrasts of rough hair on the back of his wrists and satiny smoothness inside. When she could have learned the long silky hairs under his arms, and the soft short hairs on his chest that tickled her palms. When she could have been caressing his back, so much warmer than most of her body ever was, and his cool hard bottom with deep depressions on the cheeks that fit her hands perfectly.

Teddy had never imagined, not even after seeing Margaret's glowing face when she talked about being with her husband, that it was possible to feel so much, to feel with every part of her body, to be focused so wholly on touching and feeling and skin against skin. And she had never, ever in her life, imagined that she would delight in rubbing herself against her husband, that she would hold him close with her hands and wrap her legs around him and love his hard shaft against her belly, and hear him groan and know that he was feeling what she was feeling.

And all the while he was running his big warm hands over her and she wanted to feel those hands on her forever, all day, every day, even when she slept. When his hands traced the inside of her thighs from behind her knee to the softer, warmer, wetter place between her legs, her body jerked and melted toward him.

"I want—"

"I want too."

Even more than the night before. Almost frightening. Unstoppable. On and on, over and over, and she was reaching, needing, aching, and he was deep and deeper and she grabbed him with her hands and fingernails and legs and she knew he was feeling the lightning too, at the same time, jerking and throbbing and pouring his seed into her, and that made the lightning even more. And this time he yelled, not the muffled roar from all the other times but a deep-throated yell that mixed with the long moaning almost-scream coming from her own throat.

A long time later, Teddy moved her head and squinted up at him.

"Hank and Bucky and Arthur out in the bunkhouse might have heard us."

"Possible." He rolled off her, tucked her against his side, and pulled the covers up.

"I thought about reaching down and getting the blankets too, Caleb. But I have no working muscles."

His chuckle made the little hairs on his chest tickle her mouth and nose.

"Why did you always muffle it before? That noise you make?"

"Oh." His sheepish grin looked very white in the dark room. "Well, one, I have never felt what I felt these last two nights. And second, I was always, I don't know, not exactly shy. Private. I didn't want them to know I was, er… I was doing it alone, here in my bedroom."

Teddy had a sudden picture of her husband using one of those dolls she had imagined. "How did you— How do you do it alone?"

"My hand, Teddy. It's not anything as good as your body, but it suffices."

"Oh."

\*\*\*\*

They got out of bed at the first preparatory sounds from Arthur's rooster, pulled on their clothes, and headed for the doorway.

"Wife. Teddy. My wife. Before we go downstairs, I want you to know that I am one of the luckiest men on the planet. And I want to get back in bed with you right now."

She started to answer but he bent and covered her mouth with his and the kiss didn't end until they were both breathless and needing.

"The men—"

"I know. They'll be coming in soon and we have to be in the kitchen, with the supper things cleaned and breakfast on the table."

They stared into each other's faces. Then they sighed and headed downstairs.

Caleb added wood to the kitchen stove, ground the coffee, and tackled the dirty dishes while Teddy started the oatmeal and put molasses and raisins and quart jars of Ku-Long's applesauce in the middle of the table. Then she took the three loaves of bread she'd baked yesterday, sliced them all, spread the slices on cookie sheets, and slathered them with precious butter from the Whitcomb farm. She mixed brown sugar, white sugar and cinnamon in a bowl and sprinkled the mix onto the slices of bread.

"I am going for quick and easy this morning. Cinnamon toast instead of muffins or biscuits. These will go in the oven in a few minutes so they're hot and crisp and tasty when the men come through the door." She looked up. "This will be enough, won't it? More than five pieces each, plus the oatmeal and applesauce?"

"It's perfect, wife. Every single meal you feed us is perfect."

"I'll have to bake bread again today. I wasn't planning to use all three loaves this morning."

"After you get the bread started, I propose an expedition into Choteau. Just the two of us, and the buckboard, and one of the cart horses." He put his arms around her from behind and nuzzled her neck. "Arthur needs more chicken feed."

"He—" It was not easy to think with her husband's warm mouth moving along her neck and his arms tightening just below her breasts, lifting them. "He told you that?"

"He held up an empty bag and one finger. I deduced from that that there's only one bag left." His hands cupped her breasts. "I thought we might buy a Christmas tree too."

"Caleb!"

"What, wife? You don't want a Christmas tree?"

"I don't—" She removed his hands. "I don't want Hank busting in here and seeing your hands—Your hands there."

"Ah." He walked to his chair at the other end of the table. "Then I had better sit down. We probably don't want Hank noticing the fit of my jeans either."

She giggled. "No, we don't. We have to look like serious professional ranchers, starting a day of serious professional ranching, out here in the serious wilds of Montana."

"Yes to Choteau with me?"

"Yes. Yes." She looked up. "Good morning, Hank."

"It is, ma'am. Bit of blue sky. Best day in a week a Sundays." The big man plopped down in his favored chair and rested his fists on the table.

"Teddy and I are heading into Choteau to pick up chicken feed for Arthur. We'll pick up any ranch mail too, and I'm thinking we'll buy a Christmas tree from that black family."

"Cut one. Up to the ridge."

"I thought about our own trees, Hank. But that family's new to the area and I think they're barely getting by."

"Useta be slaves, you think?"

A side of Caleb's mouth curved up. "I think they came from upstate New York."

Teddy leaned over the table. "Coffee, Hank?"

"Ya have to ask??"

****

The black family's initial experience selling Christmas trees must have been a success. There were only three left in the lot: a behemoth that was fifteen feet tall and almost as big around, with a little boy standing awe-struck in front of it and begging his parents to buy it; another tree almost as tall but comically skinny; and a six-footer with a large empty spot on one side as if a gigantic moose had come along and taken a bite.

"If we put it in the corner of the living room away from the woodstove, and turn that side against the wall, I think it will be perfect."

"Perfect, huh?"

"Adequate then. Highly adequate."

Caleb caught the eye of the lanky teenager manning the lot, handed over the suggested price without quibbling, lifted the tree, and tied it down atop the bags of chicken feed in the buckboard.

"We are here in town, wife. Our errands are done and the weather is holding fine. What do you say to lunch at the hotel? Or at the bakery?"

"Lunch out, with you?" Her eyes sparkled. "That is truly a lovely idea!"

"We can leave the buckboard and horses here. Let's walk."

Two women were blocking the plank sidewalk ahead, one tall and spare, the other smaller and rounder with one gloved hand gently rocking an ornate wicker baby carriage.

"Amelia! Flora! How nice to see you!"

Flora gave a curt nod and Amelia's sweet face lit up.

"It's a treat to see you too, pet. And Mr. Asher! You are both looking as if wedded bliss is, well, bliss."

Flora snorted.

"And your beautiful drapes are just about finished, pet."

"Just in time for the most miserable days of winter." The dour widow's mouth was pursed and tight.

"My Ronald fixed up some rods and hooks to hang the drapes. If you stop by on your way home and pick them up, pet, it would save us a trip. We're the last house on the left on the way out of town, white with barn red trim."

"We will do just that." Teddy peered into the carriage, but the baby was so bundled up that she couldn't see anything but a curl of reddish hair. "What is your little one's name?"

Amelia laughed. "For three full days she was just Baby Girl. She's our ninth, you know. Five girls now and four boys. We had a boy's name picked out but we're running out of ideas for girls. We finally decided on Phoebe Agatha, Phoebe for one of Ron's great-aunts and Agatha for one of mine."

"That is a very elegant name."

"It is, isn't it? Our other daughters decided since their very first steps that they would be every bit as tough, as brave, as fast, and as—" She gave a spurt of laughter. "As dirt-covered as their brothers. Maybe Phoebe Agatha will be our one true lady."

"The west needs tough capable women, Amelia." Caleb glanced over at his wife. "I hope you encourage your daughters to go right on being brave and fast and, er, muddy."

Flora sniffed. "Amelia is greatly exaggerating. I have seen her children, and they are well-behaved youngsters. Every single one."

"Why, thank you, Flora. Ronald and I try." She twinkled at Teddy and Caleb. "We have made it clear that rowdiness is all right at home but there is a different standard in public."

"That sounds very sensible." Teddy looked up at her husband. "We're off to a late lunch. Would you recommend the hotel or the bakery?"

"For tasty and satisfying meals, the hotel. But don't order your dessert there. For sweets, nothing beats the bakery."

Caleb nodded. "Thank you. That's what we'll do. Ready, Mrs. Asher?"

****

When he was twelve or thirteen, and just beginning to notice girls, Caleb was very aware of the interested looks females of all ages gave to his broad-shouldered older brother, and he always felt puny and childish next to Ike. But since that year, he never gave a second thought to what other people saw when they looked at him. Until now. Until he was walking in Choteau with his wife by his side. He made himself stand straight, his shoulders back and his head up. He knew that every male in town was admiring his wife's glowing face, her chestnut curls peeking out from her bonnet, her tall slender beauty in the ankle-length blue wool coat that had come in her Boston trunks. He knew that every male was thinking about what he, Caleb Asher, got to do with her in their bedroom. And he was even more conscious of her and him and anyone who might be watching when she shed her coat and they were seated in the hotel dining room, she in the same wool dress she wore on their wedding day, and he had the sudden realization that there were two floors of bedrooms over their heads.

"What did you say, wife?"

"I said that I have eaten a lot of ocean fish but I know nothing about freshwater varieties. Do you like trout?'

He dragged his mind downstairs and looked at the menu.

"I apologize, wife. I was somewhere else."

"Where were you, husband?"

"I was—" He met her eyes. "I was in one of the bedrooms upstairs. With you."

She flushed. "Oh. Yes. I—I thought—I also thought about the bedrooms, as we walked in."

He raised his eyebrows. "You did?"

"I did."

"And what exactly did you think about them, wife? The bedrooms?"

She looked over his shoulder. "Here comes a waiter. We should focus our minds on ordering. Do you like trout, Caleb?"

"Ah. Yes." He picked up his menu. "Yes, I like trout very much, especially if it was caught this morning. We can ask."

"I might try that, then."

"And I'll have pork roast. I am willing to bet that our waiter can recommend a bottle of wine that goes well with both."

Wine. Eating out. Her handsome husband sharing a tiny table with her, his knees bumping hers. Both of them flushed from remembering the last two nights, upstairs in their own house, in their own bed, naked and entwined and panting and touching glory. Both of them anticipating the night to come.

Teddy had never guessed that married life could be so rich.

Chapter Twenty-three

Teddy stepped outside and sniffed. Cold clean wind. Dry sage. The sweetness of stored alfalfa. A whiff of manure. Not even a hint of the snow that all four men swore they could smell on the morning air. Hank predicted "slathers of snow", and Caleb said it would start overnight and wouldn't stop for weeks. If the men were right, she was running out of time to add to the winter bird list. She headed toward the barn, eager to harness up the pinto, hoping for a northern shrike or perhaps a flock of crossbills along the road to the next ranch. If she remembered her grandfather's notes correctly, crossbills weren't common in the area, but they weren't impossible. She could almost hear his voice. "Birds fly, Teddy my dear," he would say. "They could turn up anywhere."

She stopped, dismayed, when she saw a dark gray horse and dark gray chaise coming down the ranch road. She was even more dismayed when she recognized sour-faced Flora from the sewing circle.

Perhaps this could be a short visit. Very short. She managed a welcoming smile while the woman stopped her horse, climbed down, turned and pulled out a folded piece of wool.

"Good morning, Flora. May I help you with something?"

"You may take this. It is yours. You left it behind

when you picked up the rest at Amelia's."

"Oh, goodness! We haven't put the drapes upstairs yet so we didn't know one was missing. But you didn't have to come all this way to drop it off, especially not on Christmas Eve. One of the men could have picked it up when they went into town."

"I see no reason to celebrate Christmas." The older woman sniffed. "And snow will be starting tomorrow. You will all be stuck out here." She reached back into the chaise and lifted out a carved wooden chest three feet wide and two feet in depth and height. "This is my main purpose for coming out here. The drape was extra. I wish to go indoors."

"Oh. Yes. Of course."

Baffled, Teddy led the way back into the house and into the sitting room. She perched on the edge of a chair as Flora set the little chest on the horsehair couch and lowered herself beside it, her back straight, her knees together, her feet side by side on the floor. She removed her gloves, arranged the folds of her long skirt, took a deep breath, looked up and fixed Teddy with a fierce scowl.

"You know that I have no offspring."

"I—Yes."

"I expected to, Miss Barrington. Like most young girls." She laid one hand on the curved top of the little chest. "I am an accomplished seamstress and knitter. Have been since a very young age. I used to crochet also. I made booties and caps. Little dresses. Warm little sweaters for winter. Crib blankets." She snorted. "Lace, too. I made beautiful lace for me to wear if I ever wanted to catch a man. Never wore a bit of it. I learned early on that it is futile to try and gild an ugly lily."

Teddy opened her mouth but Flora was glaring at her with so much pain and defiance that there was nothing to say.

"I want you to have it all. The chest and everything inside."

"Flora, I—Flora, I can't. There must be someone closer to you, to whom you can give this. This is precious, Flora."

"It is precious. As I said, I am an accomplished craftswoman. And no, there is no one else. I have elected to give it to you. Your only polite response is to accept."

Teddy had an unexpected urge to bend forward in a deep bow, like she saw from the Chinese laundrymen in Choteau. There really was something regal about Flora, with her clipped speech and upright carriage and unsmiling demeanor.

"Then I thank you, Flora. From the bottom of my heart. I am deeply touched." She flushed. "I am not—To my knowledge, my husband and I are not yet expecting a child. We hope one comes to us, perhaps more than one, but of course that cannot be guaranteed."

"I am well aware of that fact, Miss Barrington. Well aware indeed. But you are young and healthy, and your husband is young and virile. And I saw you together. You enjoy each other." She fixed Teddy with a sharp look. "I am correct, am I not?"

"You—Yes, you are correct."

"Then you are going to need these. I am sure." She put both hands on her knees and stood up. "I will be going now."

"Won't you stay for a cup of tea? I made several kinds of cookies recently."

"No." Flora walked briskly across the room. "You

327

were heading out when I arrived. You have something to do."

"I was going to harness the pony cart, but that can wait."

"It can't. I imagine you were going to look for birds. You have very few days left in the calendar year to do so." She turned at the door. "What kinds of birds might you see today?"

"I am hoping to find crossbills. Or a shrike."

"Butcher bird."

"That is a common name for shrikes, yes. But they don't truly butcher anything, Flora, any more than a robin does when it's finding worms. When prey is plentiful, shrikes kill extra rodents or small birds and skewer them on thorns, to save them for later. More recently some shrikes use barbed wire."

"Dreadful stuff. Montana ranchers got by perfectly well without barbed wire for over fifty years." Her face changed and she met Teddy's eyes. "It is clever of the birds to use the barbs for their larder. Pantry."

"I agree. I have learned that birds are clever in many ways."

"Humph." The woman turned her back to Teddy. "You don't have to see me out. I know the way."

Teddy stayed in the living room, standing by her chair, staring after her surprising visitor. That was real interest in Flora's eyes, real appreciation for the idiosyncratic behavior of a shrike. Perhaps... Yes. Perhaps Flora would enjoy going out in the cart, in spring or early summer. Even spending time in the blind. Perhaps.

She looked down at the little chest. A hope chest, full of hopes that were never realized. I won't open it now, she thought. I am going to look for birds and hear their sounds. I am going to delight in the richness of life. I will set Flora's tragedy aside for a while.

**\*\*\*\***

Teddy had heard the men talking about horses that were uncannily attuned to the weather, becoming agitated and anxious hours before their riders realized that a storm was coming. Apparently, the patient pinto was not of that ilk. It kept plodding along at its usual steady pace, even when the vast sky, now almost uniformly gray, seemed barely an arm's length above its pointed ears. Even when the chickadees and crows and magpies stopped making noises and everything around them was eerily silent.

She had seen a shrike, silhouetted against the sky, its characteristic hooked bill easily identifiable and, she hoped, clearly visible in the photos she took. She had seen a small flock of redpolls and one surprise western evening grosbeak, a species she thought might show up only during migration. If she kept going along the dirt track past the ranch, she might be fortunate and find crossbills, but there were still several things to do that day and she was eager to be home. Baked beans were already in the oven, and jars of sauerkraut waited to be opened and heated. Bread was ready, but she had to make some kind of dessert.

And if Hank was back from Choteau, she would have a lot of putting away and neatening up to do, in the kitchen, pantry, and root cellar. She spent hours the previous afternoon inventorying their food supplies, figuring out how much of everything she used in a week, multiplying by the number of weeks until the end of May, adding a fourth more of everything, and then drawing up a shopping list. Hank eyeballed it, raised one curly eyebrow, and tucked the sheet of paper in his vest pocket. It made her feel deliciously rich to know that they wouldn't run out of rice, beans, or flour, yeast, sugar, or coffee if they got snowbound.

*When*, not if. She had been assured of that.

The food supplies were her responsibility. The men were responsible for everything else, and Teddy could not have predicted how much work there was to get the ranch ready for winter. Every day there were chickens, ducks, geese, horses, and the pig to feed, and stalls to muck out, and calving mothers to check on. And the evening before, Arthur and Bucky put up solid winter shutters while she and Caleb hung the new woolen drapes. All the downstairs windows were covered now, except one in the kitchen and the one over her work area, so she could have natural light.

The cattle needed special attention in the winter. Caleb told her that windbreaks were almost as important as food and water, so a few years ago Arthur made large, lightweight movable walls of willow twigs and leftover burlap feed sacks. The things were stored up above in the big barn during the summer and then brought down and fastened to fence posts or trees, so every paddock and pen had a somewhat sheltered area where the cattle could get out of the wind and wouldn't be belly-deep in snow.

Every pen also had to have a water trough and one of the triangular alfalfa feeders designed by the ever-creative Arthur. Caleb said the ranch used to waste a lot of alfalfa hay by tossing it on the ground where it got trampled into snow and mud. The new wooden feeders kept winter feed dry, and the cattle quickly learned how to pull out a mouthful at a time.

"Grund," she said aloud, "I know so much more than I did last spring, and there is still so much I don't know yet. And tomorrow is my first Montana Christmas. My first Christmas on the ranch. Our ranch. My first Christmas as a married woman. I am a happily married woman, much more so than I ever imagined. Do you remember, Grund, when I said I might come to love him, perhaps?" She gave a joyous little whoop. "Well, he is not here now to be frightened by the word. I will say it aloud for the very first time. I love him. It is true. I love my husband."

\*\*\*\*

Christmas dawned the same as the many days before, with low gray clouds and a heavy, waiting feeling in the air. Teddy made a special breakfast of eggs, bacon, and ham, potatoes fried with onions and garlic, and cinnamon buns warm from the oven. As soon as the men finished their second servings, she ushered them into the living room.

"Bucky will be leaving soon to spend the day at the Truchot ranch, so I would like us all to gather together now. I have a few gifts for everyone."

No one but Caleb had seen the tree yet.

"Lawsy, Miz Asher. That's purty as a pitsher."

"Yup," Hank growled. "Purty."

"Thank you, both."

The oddly shaped tree was now decorated with pinecones, paper stars and hearts and leaves, and "icicles" made of braided fescue and bluestem grass.

Arthur touched one of the paper stars and looked up with a question in his eyes.

"Ku-Long left a stack of seed catalogues, Arthur. The covers are in color so I cut them up for decorations."

331

The wizened man lifted both eyebrows, nodded, and then touched another of the improvised ornaments.

"That is a true frontier creation, wife."

"I think so too, Caleb. Sit, everyone, please sit."

But Hank met Bucky's eyes, jerked his head toward the door, and the two men abruptly left.

"Goodness. I was hoping they would sit a while."

"They'll be right back, wife. You're not the only person on Long Butte Ranch with Christmas secrets." He sat on the couch and patted the cushion beside him.

"Oh. Goodness."

"I have something for you too, but it might not arrive until full spring."

The boughs of the Christmas tree tossed in a gust of frigid wind as the two ranch hands came back into the house, carrying between them a perfect replica of the main barn, almost two yards long and one yard wide, with open sides, painted the same red as the original. They bent and laid their gift in front of the tree.

Teddy stood up slowly.

"It's a feeder, Miz Asher. A bird feeder."

"Bucky sunk posts yestiddy. Set this on top and you kin sit right atcher desk and count the birds."

"Hank. Bucky. This is—I cannot think of a suitable word. This is magnificent. It is truly magnificent."

The younger man darted around her, ducked behind the couch, and lifted out two feed bags.

"These go with it, miss. Ma'am. Miz Asher. Jason down at the feed store says folks in town use chicken feed for jays and such." He hefted the smaller bag. "And this here's for the smaller birds."

"Thank you both so, so much." She knelt on the rug and patted the red painted roof of the magnificent gift. "I can hardly wait to see what birds come to feast here. I shall take photos with Grund's camera, and this wonderful feeder will be included in the book. With credit given to the two men who made it!"

They both turned red, and Hank muttered "no need fer that".

Something nudged her shoulder and she turned to see Arthur holding out a loosely wrapped package of newsprint. He pushed it against her again and she reached up and took it from his hands. There were hard shapes inside, but she couldn't guess what they were. The first shape she pulled out was rounded, about the size of a chestnut. Puzzled, she held it in her palm and turned it over.

"Oh my goodness, Arthur! This is absolutely beautiful!"

She held up an intricately carved chickadee, snuggled into her hand as if sitting on eggs in a cozy little nesting cavity, perfect right down to its tiny bill.

"This is extraordinary!"

He gestured toward the package and Teddy pulled out the other shape. This one was larger, reaching from her wrist past her fingertips.

"It's—Oh. A nutcracker. A Clark's nutcracker." Tears filled her eyes as she looked at the shy and solemn old man. "My Grund, my grandfather, wanted very much to see one before he—We were looking for a nutcracker on the day he—My grandfather would love this, Arthur. I love it." She set both birds down on the wrapping paper, lurched to her feet, and put her hands on his skinny shoulders. "I thank you, Arthur, for my grandfather and me both." He looked alarmed but she tightened her hands, leaned forward, and kissed his weathered cheek.

"Well." She blew her nose. "It's time for me to hand out my gifts for you all."

Caleb handed her a clean bandana, and as Teddy wiped her eyes, she felt one of Arthur's calloused hands patting her shoulder.

**** 

The heavy snow that the Montana sky had been promising, had been threatening, finally arrived mid-afternoon. When Teddy stepped outside to ring the dinner bell, a blanket four inches deep covered the ground, and there was so much snow in the air that she could barely see the light in the bunkhouse.

"Ma'am?"

A man-shaped patch of white a few yards away moved closer.

"Wouldja save some supper for me? Gotta take care a Beauty first."

"My goodness, Bucky! You're almost invisible. Did you roll around in the snow?"

"It were comin' right at me the whole way home. Proper packed onto my front side."

"You tend to your horse and get some dry clothes on. I'll keep a couple of plates warm in the stove for you."

"'Preciate it."

When the young man turned to go, Teddy saw that the back of his big sheepskin-lined coat was completely dry. She would describe it for Caleb later, how the young horse trainer was completely white in the front and completely dark in the back. How if he turned round and round, he would flicker in and out of visibility. The image would make Caleb laugh.

****

The other men were finishing up their second servings when Bucky slid into his seat. Hank reached out a huge paw and cuffed the younger man on the side of the head.

"Thought we'd lost ya, Buck. Thought you was buried in the snow and we'd dig up yer bony carcass come spring thaw."

"Glad you're back, Bucky."

"Thanks, boss." He was staring toward the heaping plate of food Teddy was just removing from the warming oven. "Can't see a damn—'scuse me, ma'am—a durn thing out there. Had to get off Beauty and walk the whole way jest so's I could tell I was still on the road." He reached up both hands and took the plate. "Half hour gettin' to Jeannine's place, more'n three hours gettin' back home."

"You eat, Bucky. Meanwhile, are the rest of you ready for cobbler?"

\*\*\*\*

"Thought you was goin' to the Truchot place for Christmas dinner. Didn't they feedja none?"

Bucky had polished off two plates of food with three thick slices of bread and was making short work of his second bowl of cobbler.

"You ever tried eatin' while yer bein' watched by a gal's daddy and mommy and a mean-faced spinster aunt and a toothless old grandma?"

"Can't say I have."

"Well, Hank, you are a lucky man. Everything smelled so good and I was jest about starving, but they was all eatin' real dainty-like. Cuttin' their turkey into little teeny bits and touchin' their lips with fancy white napkins jest about after every bite. I wanted seconds so bad but I tell you I was plumb scared."

"No wonder you were hungry when you got home, Bucky."

"Yes'm. Stomach knockin' round my innards like a pebble inside a pickle jar, and that's the honest truth." He beamed up at her. "But now, ma'am, my stomach's right purrin'. Happy as it ever was." The spoon clattered into his empty dessert bowl, and he looked around the table. "Happy fer another reason too. Jeannine 'n me had a half hour to ourselves, in the sittin' room, and I done did it. I asked her to marry me."

"I'm guessing by that wide grin that she didn't smack your face and run out of the room."

"She said yes, boss! Jeannine agreed to be my bride! My wife!"

Arthur grabbed Bucky's shoulder and shook it, while Caleb reached a hand across the table and Teddy smiled and twinkled at him.

But big Hank groaned. "Trapped for life, Buck. Young feller like you, and trapped for life."

"I know it! My whole life with that lovely gal! I tell you all, I can't wait!"

Caleb leaned back in his chair, still smiling widely. "Did you two lovestruck youngsters talk about future plans, while you were alone there in the sitting room?"

"Well, boss. I'm a horse trainer to my soul. That's what I gotta be, and Jeannine knows that. So she's not expectin' us to move into town or nothing. It'll prob'ly be a year or so before we get married, and by then I hope to have a horse training business up and running. And a little house, mebbe."

Caleb met his wife's eyes. He raised his eyebrows and made a slight movement of his head and right shoulder, and she nodded.

"Why not grow your business right here at Long Butte, Bucky? People around here know you, and they're already recommending you to their neighbors. Maybe you and I and—" He looked at Teddy again. "And Mrs. Asher here can sit down and work up a deal to give you more time for breaking horses. Once you get busier, we'd have to hire another ranch hand, but that's not a big problem."

He again looked a question at Teddy, and she again nodded.

"Perhaps," she said, "you and your wife might want to move into the cabin that Grund and I used, at least for a few years. You'd have to talk it over with her, of course."

"Criminy. I'm jest—Criminy. That'd be— Criminy."

"You think it over, Bucky. And talk with Jeannine. We'd like having you sticking around."

Before the emotion-laded silence got awkward, Teddy stood up briskly.

"Hand your bowls this way, if you would."

\*\*\*\*

"Thank you, Caleb."

He paused in unbuttoning his flannel shirt.

"You're welcome, wife. But I haven't done anything yet. Give me a minute and I'll try my best to do something that merits your thanks."

Teddy flushed. "Thank you for including me when you were talking with Bucky. And checking in with me about the cabin. That is what you were doing, isn't it? When you raised your eyebrows and did that thing with your shoulder?"

337

"That is exactly what I was doing. I was hoping you'd get my message."

He finished unbuttoning, hung the shirt on a peg and pulled off his warm undershirt.

"There is something else I want to talk with you about, Teddy. Without the other men around."

She watched his torso stretch, beginning to feel the prickling sensation low in her belly, and the softness between her legs, that she now felt every single night.

"We have never heated two buildings all winter long. We close the bunkhouse when it gets this cold."

"So where—Oh. I see. The men come here, don't they? To the main house?"

"Yes."

She didn't want him to see how dismayed she was. Hank sleeping in the next room. The three men undressing, the men using chamber pots, only a yard from where she was getting ready for bed. The men listening to every noise that she and Caleb made.

"Well!" she said brightly. "If they are here, there will be no need to keep shoveling from this building to the bunkhouse, and from the bunkhouse to that privy. That's an additional benefit."

"That is true." He sat on the edge of the bed. "They don't have to stay in the upstairs bedrooms this year, Teddy. We can move beds downstairs, into the sitting room. You and I will still have to be fairly quiet in bed, but the others don't have to be upstairs with us."

"Oh. That is good, Caleb. Thank you, thank you!" She moved closer and put her hands on his warm chest. "You ask them to move the beds downstairs tomorrow, at breakfast. But tonight, I believe, we should make good use of our last opportunity to make some noise."

"I very much like that idea, wife."

Chapter Twenty-Four

Hank started it. On the fifteenth morning after the men moved into the main house, everyone was startled out of sleep by explosive and gargantuan sneezes interspersed with grumbled expletives. The big man spent the next several days stumbling through his chores in slow motion, with a neckerchief hanging out of every pocket to catch the almost constant sneezing.

Bucky was next. He looked a bit pale at breakfast, and when he sat down for supper he said he wasn't hungry. Teddy felt his forehead, made him some willow tea, and he slept most of one day and one night. Then he sat up, cautiously stood, stretched, and declared himself fit as a fiddle.

On the third morning, Arthur and Teddy were the only ones who wanted breakfast. Bucky was in the midst of his marathon nap, and Caleb and Hank, both looking drawn and pale, said they might eat something later.

"It's just the two of us, Arthur. I can make an omelet."

The little man watched solemnly as Teddy plopped some bacon fat into a skillet and added diced onions and garlic. She separated ten eggs, beat the yolks and whites in different bowls, and then carefully folded them together. She added two big handfuls of diced ham to the pan and stirred until it was hot. The eggs went in next, and after a few minutes, she added a hefty grating of the cloth-wrapped cheese that was always stored in a wooden box in the root cellar.

"This is the tricky part, Arthur. Wish me luck."

She bit her lower lip as she made a valley down the middle, ran a spatula under the eggs on one side of pan, and flipped one half of the huge omelet over the other half.

"Ah! It worked!" She glanced at the silent little man. "We are going to have an exceptional breakfast!"

Another few minutes and it was done, golden on top and bottom, tender and fluffy and cheesy in the middle, dotted with tasty bits of vegetables and ham. She cut a quarter of the omelet off one end for herself, carefully unloaded the rest onto a warmed plate for Arthur, and pushed a basket of hot cornmeal molasses muffins to his end of the table.

"Thankee."

They exchanged solemn nods.

"You are welcome, Arthur."

She wanted to giggle. What a picture they made! The two of them sitting in their regular places at the big table, separated by several feet of empty space, both looking down at their food and eating in silence. But he had said a word again.

\*\*\*\*

Caleb came in a few hours later with a sore throat and a fever. He slept downstairs for the next few nights so he wouldn't infect his wife, but she got it anyway. By the fifth morning of the February flu, Teddy ached all over, her throat hurt, the glands in her neck were swollen, she couldn't swallow properly, and her nose wouldn't stop dripping. When her monthly flow didn't happen, she decided the flu was affecting her body's regular rhythms.

Worse, much worse, than the physical discomfort, Teddy felt betrayed. Her beautiful Montana had betrayed her. Winter ailments were part of life back in soggy cold Boston where people were crowded together on busy streets; in tenements, shops and eateries; in windowless factories and fish canneries; in churches that held hundreds at a time. Winter in Boston always came with drippy noses, coughs and catarrh, grippe, quinsy, even lung fever. But her chosen state of Montana had wide open spaces, endless fresh air, and miles of emptiness between human beings. No one should get winter sick in Montana. She was sure Hank had contaminated them all with some evil miasma brought back from that cursed orange house.

Only wizened little Arthur stayed healthy. He harnessed up the big black horses, filled a cart with hay, fed all the cattle in the distant pens, and made sure there was water, helped by the pale and silent wraiths of whatever men were out of their beds. Then he unharnessed the wagon, brushed down the horses, checked their hooves, and fed the fowl and the pig. He never seemed to be in a rush, never seemed flustered, just kept moving at his own comfortable pace, but whatever he set out to do got done.

****

If it hadn't been for the wolves, Caleb would have noticed when his wife didn't move into the smaller bedroom to sleep alone toward the end of February. And Teddy didn't mention that her monthlies hadn't come for the second month in a row. Worrying about wolves was all her husband had time for, and she decided that the same worry was affecting her body.

The wild beasts had learned how easy it was to

travel on the main road, now rolled and packed every few days by the Amish farmer and his team of huge oxen. Before dawn one frigid morning, Arthur heard panicked bellowing in the far distance. When the four men got to the pen closest to the road, the massive bull had his head down and shoulders hunched, pawing the frozen ground, snorting and bellowing. Two silver-gray wolves were inside the pen, crouched and snarling, while six more raced back and forth outside the fence, their complete silence more threatening than howls or barks. The heifers were huddled together in one corner of the pen, the whites of their eyes gleaming in the dim light. Bucky picked off one of the wolves with his pistol, and Arthur scattered the rest by firing his ancient shotgun, but the men knew the pack would return.

The next two weeks differed from any others Teddy had experienced at Long Butte Ranch. Two of the men patrolled the cattle pens every minute, all day and all night, armed with pistols, rifles, and shotguns. The wolves patrolled as well, ghostly gray and black shapes haunting the cattle pens, the pack increasing to over two dozen hungry predators. Sharp-eyed Bucky killed two more, but one large animal left the pack and climbed a wind-formed drift to drop silently into the pen closest to the house, and took one of the youngest calves.

The cold was too bitter for men or horses to be outside long, especially at night, so they worked in shifts. Caleb slept downstairs, fully dressed, ready to leave immediately whenever one of the others came in and tapped his shoulder. Teddy knew he took double shifts at least twice, once to let Bucky sleep longer and once because Arthur was moving as if every bit of his skinny old body hurt.

Teddy brought a box of writing material into the kitchen instead of working at her desk, so she wouldn't interrupt the men who were catching a few hours of sleep between shifts. But she had almost no time for writing. She hauled wood from the shed beside the house, kept the stoves going, and shoveled the walkways. There were no real mealtimes; large pots of hot soup, stew, or chili waited for the men day and night. The coffee pot was always full, as were the metal bread box and the three cookie tins. One morning Teddy peeled every one of the remaining potatoes from the root cellar, added sliced onions, ham, and some milk from the cow whose calf was killed, and filled three long pans. She cooked them separately, one in the morning, one at noon, and the other when it was already dark, so that every one of the men got a chance to eat scalloped potatoes hot from the oven, crisp on the top, and bubbling all around the edges.

Every night when she headed up to bed alone, Teddy was deeply grateful that the ranch hands had brought their bedrolls over from the bunkhouse. Without Caleb's warm body next to her, she needed the extra quilts, even with a pair of his long underwear, her thick wool stockings, his wool socks, a flannel nightgown, and a heavy knitted sweater.

****

"Spike, I can't remember the last time I kissed my wife."

One long ear flicked but the horse kept munching hay.

Maybe it was sometime last week. Or the week before. Caleb felt muddle-headed from too many days without enough sleep, too many hours in the saddle taking hay to the cattle and fighting off wolves. He was

344

pretty sure he touched his wife just yesterday as she was heading upstairs to bed. She was tiptoeing through the living room when he stumbled in to wake up Bucky, and she turned and moved to him so quickly he thought she must be floating, and she whispered his name and folded him in her arms. He almost fell asleep right there, standing against her warm body. But she led him to the bed he'd been using, pushed him down, and tucked the covers around him.

As for being alone with her, upstairs in their bed, feeling her long legs wrapped around him, knowing that she was as eager as he was, pushing inside her tight silken warmth... That was a memory from another lifetime.

"But not dead yet, Spike," he muttered to the horse when he felt a prickle of interest behind the front of his jeans. "Not gonna happen today 'cause I gotta get up in four hours and feed the cattle." He finished rubbing the horse down and started checking hooves for hardened ice. "Not tonight either. I gotta sleep tonight, Spike. I think they're gone. The wolves. I think it'll be safe to sleep. I need a solid twelve hours. There. Hooves look good." He opened a metal barrel and scooped out two handfuls of oats mixed with molasses. "You deserve this."

Dawn was a faint promise as Caleb walked to the house. Yellow lantern light made a wavy rectangle in the snow outside the kitchen window. He dropped his heavy coat and boots in the mudroom, hung up his hat, and pushed open the door into his blessedly warm home.

"The wolves are gone."

"Oh, Caleb." She turned with the glorious wide smile he had missed for so many days. "I am more than relieved."

"Too many guns, maybe. Went looking for easier prey than our cattle. Not hide nor hair, more'n forty hours now."

He sounded, and looked, so different from the man she married. From the man she met back in May. He was even dirtier than on that first day, when he had been coated in mud. His voice was low and raspy and he spoke in partial sentences. He had purple circles under red-rimmed eyes, his mustache was longer and fuller, his face looked leaner, and he had almost two weeks of dark beard.

"Do you want something to eat? Or drink? I just heated up some mulled cider."

"Cider."

"You're dead on your feet, Caleb."

"I am."

"Do you want to sleep upstairs, where you won't be disturbed?"

"Not before a bath." He took the mug of cider. "Hits the spot. Thank you."

"Go and sleep then, my—" She caught herself. "Go to sleep now, Caleb."

She watched him weave through the crowded living room, and she ached for him. She wanted to hold him and miraculously make him less tired. She wanted to arrange reality so he would never have to work himself to exhaustion again. And she wanted, very much, to tell him she loved him. She had almost used that word, almost called him *my love*. She wanted to use that word.

****

For the first time in two weeks, all four men were around the table for supper that night, hollow-eyed, hairy, and monosyllabic. The mingled smells of garlic, beef, and cabbage almost, but not quite, canceled out the smell from bodies that hadn't known soap or water for two weeks. Teddy made one of Ku-Long's meals: a huge bowl of rice mixed with onions and garlic fried in bacon fat, and more onions cooked with the last cabbage of the summer and then mixed with four quarts of the seasoned chopped beef she had helped to preserve way back in the summer. She opened a jar of big head pickles and another of sweet pickled carrots and put them in the middle of the table, with two loaves of bread, pitchers of water, and the big coffee jug. There was no conversation, just the clink of cutlery, until the plates had been emptied twice. Then Caleb looked over at his foreman.

"Been thinkin' about roo dogs."

"Like Yoder gots?"

Caleb nodded. "Keep wolves away."

"What're roo dogs?"

Caleb slowly turned his head toward Bucky. "Greyhound and some sorta sighthound. Scottish deerhound maybe. Fight kangaroos."

"Why'd anyone want to fight a kangaroo?"

But now all eyes were fixed on the plates of still-hot gingerbread that Teddy was passing around, and no one answered the young man. Caleb spoke again only after the dessert was gone.

"Yoder's got puppies."

"You getting' some?"

"Pricey." Caleb stared into space, frowning. Then he nodded. "Think so. Two females."

After supper, Bucky and Arthur headed back out to break ice in the watering troughs and ride one more time around the cattle pens, and Hank picked up a canvas bag from under his chair and disappeared into one of the two bathing rooms.

"Clean clothes." Caleb put both hands flat on the table and pushed himself up.

"I'll get them for you."

When Teddy came back downstairs, the door was open to the second bathing room. The small space held a long narrow metal tub, a table with a lantern on it, a four-legged stool, a shelf, a row of pegs on the wall, jugs of cold water along one wall, and an old wooden apple crate for clothes in need of washing. Liquid trickling noise filled the little room, and she blessed Arthur yet again for the clever arrangement that let hot water flow from the tank next to the kitchen stove, through pipes in the wall, and into the tubs.

Caleb's jeans, the bottom half of his long underwear, his socks and his belt were in a pile near his feet, and the lantern light was soft on his bare legs and the dark area above. He looked up and met her eyes and she ached, knowing again how tired he was, how close he was to complete exhaustion. She laid clean underwear and wool socks on the shelf and hung up her grandfather's heavy brocade robe.

"Stand in the tub, Caleb. Stand just for a moment."

She scooped a pitcher of warm water and poured it over his shoulders, and then another pitcher down his back, and quickly rubbed his arms and chest with a square of flannel and Ku-Long's sage-scented soap. More water to rinse him, and then she pulled the plug.

"That got rid of some of the dirt." She bent to put the plug back in. "Now you can lie down in clean water and soak your tired muscles and get warm."

Caleb lowered himself slowly into the bath,

stretching his legs, resting his head against the back of the tub. She had never had a good look at his male organ when it was soft. He was always ready for mating when he came to bed, and he got dressed in the morning with his back to her. She was astonished that a part of his body could change so much, and so often. Where did the extra length come from? The extra bulk? It was like magic.

"Keep your eyes closed while I wash your hair."

Through the wall, they could hear Hank's rumbling off-key rendition of "Fanny Power", a tune Teddy remembered from outdoor concerts in Boston. Caleb didn't make a sound as she massaged soap into his scalp and rinsed. He didn't move when she lifted first one foot and then the other, washing the high arches, between the toes, the calloused soles. She rubbed on more soap and slowly scrubbed his calves, watching the dark hair lift and drift as the water rose in the tub. But when she ran the washcloth behind one bony knee, he twitched and made a little noise.

"Ticklish?"

"Hmm."

She would never tire of looking at her husband's chest and shoulders and arms. They defined masculine beauty for her. She soaped and rinsed and rubbed and caressed, again and again, and then ran her soapy hands down his arms, delighting in the smooth underneath and the mat of hair on top.

"Skipped something."

"I'm getting there."

When she picked up his hand, she was appalled to feel a tremor. Oh sweetheart, she thought. Oh my love. She held his hand in both of hers, rubbing with her thumbs, trying to erase the dark oily mark his leather gloves left on his wrist. After she washed his other hand, she brought it to her lips.

They heard the door to the other bathing room open, followed by the familiar creak of the kitchen pump.

"Hank. Refilling the water tank."

"He's a good man, Caleb."

"They all are." His eyes were open now, half-mast. "You missed something else."

"Oh. Yes. I…"

She had never touched him there. Now she watched, fascinated, as he stirred, lifted, grew. She rinsed the cloth again and gently, so gently, ran it along the twin creases at the top of his thighs. He made a low noise and moved his legs apart. Suddenly she didn't want the flannel between her hands and her husband. She dropped the cloth into the water and soaped her hands, watching him watch. Then she touched the soft but tightening flesh low between his legs, cupping him in both hands, feeling the two hard nuts roll under her fingers, feeling the smooth flat part behind his balls. His cock was hard now, jutting out from a nest of wiry hairs that were a shade darker than on his head or beard. She touched him, first with her fingertips and then with her palms. The looser, folded skin at the top pulled down with her palms and she looked at the head, glistening with water and soap and something silkier. His whole body twitched when she caressed the velvety steel hardness and slid the foreskin up and down.

"This loose part—" she whispered. "It pushes down when you come into me. So this sensitive part of you gets stroked by your own skin and also stroked by me, by inside of me." Her hands caressed him from top to base, again and again, watching him grow still larger and harder. "That sounds like a most excellent system."

His deep chuckle was a surprise. "A most excellent system." He put both hands on the sides of the tub and stood up. "I am afraid I will fall asleep if we go upstairs. I want you here, wife."

"But—" She looked around the tiny room and then toward the door.

"Hank is already snoring." He moved to the bench, holding her hands and pulling her with him. "May I take your drawers off?"

"Yes, my—Yes, my husband."

He reached up under her long skirt and fumbled for the drawstring, and the ache between her legs was painful, wanting.

"Straddle me," he whispered.

"Oh, yes."

She stepped out of her underwear and kicked it to one side, and he lifted her skirts around her so she could kneel on the bench.

"I won't last long, my wife. I will try to hold on. But I have needed you for days. Weeks."

She wiggled forward a bit, the wooden stool hard beneath her knees, his face warm and hard between her breasts. She felt his hands on her bottom, pulling her even closer, and then oh glory she felt the thickness of him pressing against her and entering her and stretching her and she pushed down on him and they both groaned and then they were moving, striving, wanting, loving. He held on, lasted, waited, until he felt her bury her face against his shoulder and shudder and spasm around him. Then he pulled her down hard and pushed up hard and shattered inside her, pulsing and pulsing until he thought he might black out.

And then there was quiet and tight closeness and their arms holding each other as if they would never let go.

After an infinity of sweet time, he shivered. She opened her eyes. "You're cold again." Her little laugh was ineffably dear to him. "You need another bath to warm up."

He carefully lifted her off him. "You will warm me, wife. In our bed."

She handed him the underwear and held her grandfather's robe out and he pushed his arms in the sleeves and tied the belt. Then he gave her the lantern.

"You carry this. I might need my hands—" His crooked smile showed white in the dim room. "To help me crawl up the stairs. But tonight I will sleep in your arms."

"Oh yes, my—Oh yes, Caleb, my husband."

## Chapter Twenty-Five

Teddy was painfully cold, even wearing every warm garment she owned. But it took so long to get dressed that she was reluctant to turn around and return to the house. She sat on the top stair to the outhouse, her back against the door, looking out at the white world.

She was ready for her first Montana winter to end. Winters in Boston were cold and wet, with massive blizzards that left mountains of snow that reached second-story windowsills. But Bostonians knew they could wait a week or so, and then a warmer day would melt the snow and there would be a brief respite before the next storm. Winter in Montana was nonstop. The Christmas storm had not let up, not even for one full day, and it was almost April.

She had imagined winter as a time of relative relaxation for ranch workers. The men would spend a few hours outside each day taking winter feed to the cattle, and then Arthur would be in the barn repairing tack and whittling and building whatever he felt needed to be built, Bucky would work with a few mustangs, and Caleb would bring the ranch books up to date. And then he would sit by the woodstove with his wife, each with a book, enjoying their cozy home and each other's company.

But even before the wolves, she didn't see her husband any more than she had during the fall. Twice a day, the men took food to the cows and calves, and the bull and his harem. They checked the cattle for sores or signs of disease. They carried short heavy hatchets and broke holes in the ice that formed overnight in the watering troughs. They rode the fence lines and did any necessary repairs. Arthur fed his chickens, ducks, geese, and the lone pig. Bucky mucked out stalls and fed the horses. And whenever any one of the men had a free minute, he hefted an axe and split more firewood.

The new stock had to be branded, and the bull calves castrated. Teddy watched some of the process, but the bawling of the animals, the blood, and the smell of burning hair and flesh made her queasy. She lost her breakfast that morning, and the next three mornings, and then she was fine. Morning sickness was supposed to last for weeks, she thought. Perhaps she wasn't expecting their first child after all. Perhaps she missed two months because of the flu and then anxiety about the wolves. Her monthly flow was due any day now. She would wait another week before talking with Caleb.

She thought women were fatigued when they were carrying a child, but she had abundant energy. Mr. Yoder and his oxen kept open the main ranch road and the side path to the two distant cattle pens, but the paths connecting barns and house and bunkhouse and privies were shoveled by hand.

Way back on New Year's Day, after the first week of snow, Teddy said she would be responsible for shoveling the short path from the main house to their privy. She was sure the men expected her to last only a day or two, but she was still doing that task and she shoveled *all* the paths during the wolf invasion. For the first week, her whole body complained every time she lifted another shovel of heavy white stuff, every time she kneaded bread or stirred cookie dough. Now she could feel her arms and back getting stronger, and she was proud of the narrow paths lined on both sides with mounds of snow almost as tall as she was.

Her new sense of strength and abundant health made it difficult to spend hours and hours at her desk. Earlier that morning, in a sudden burst of high spirits, she ran along every one of the shoveled paths, returning to the house flushed and rosy and ready to go back to writing an article for the spring newsletter of the Boston Birding Alliance. It was about dominance patterns in northern finches, inspired by hours of watching evening grosbeaks at the beautiful new feeder.

Almost everything was white from where she sat. She could see a thin strip of red near the bunkhouse roof, above the top of the snow, and a wider red strip on the barn. The tallest evergreens on the far side of the big barn were dark green where the wind had shaken the heavy boughs. But everything else was white. She wanted the snow gone. She wanted to feel warmth. She wanted to walk out the door wearing only a few layers.

And she wanted a return to nighttime privacy. She and her husband still held each other tight, they touched and kissed and shuddered with desire, they mated, but they were always aware of the three men downstairs. Even though it was Caleb's office below their bed and not the living room, they could hear occasional bits of conversation, a laugh, the characteristic rattle of dominoes, Hank's snoring. They no longer rolled around on the bed, tickling and whispering and laughing. Caleb no longer roared at the end, not even the muted roar from the early days of their marriage. Teddy never moaned and certainly never screamed, and she didn't always feel the lightning.

**** 

On March twenty-sixth, central Montana saw a full day of sun for the first time since Christmas. It was still bitterly cold, but there was almost no wind. When Mr. Yoder came with his huge oxen to roll the ranch roads, Teddy ran out to give him a bag of ginger cookies and a mug of hot chocolate, and to take the mail bag and a heavy box addressed to her. She was shivering in her indoor clothing, but she stood in the ranch yard and tore open the brown paper.

*Birds of Central Montana—By Professor Theodore E. Barrington and Miss Theodora Barrington.*

Teddy wanted to yell, holler, whoop, bellow with all the power in her newly strengthened body. Nobody from the ranch was nearby, but Mr. Yoder was turning his team around, and she ran to the big cart, waving the package in the air.

"Look, Mr. Yoder! Our book! My grandfather's and mine!"

The Amish farmer reached down a huge, weathered hand and took the title page from her.

"This here's a mighty wonder, Mizz Asher. You wrote all those pages?"

"My grandfather wrote a lot of it. I added some text after he died. The photos are his, and the drawings are mine."

She held up two more pages and the man examined them solemnly, reading a few lines here and there, holding a photo up to the sun, making little chirping noises with his lips.

"Well, Mizz Asher, this is reason to crow for sure. I

could learn a plentitude if'n I were to spend some time with this book. All of us should know about the creatures of God that share this world with us."

"I will make sure you get a copy for at least a few days, Mr. Yoder. This is just the first hundred pages. It's a proof, for me to check for errors. I will have final copies by summer, and I shall loan you one."

"We would 'preciate that. Well, lot to do, Mizz Asher. That English gent Jeffy Chaucer said it. Time and tide wait for no man. Well, time and Montana winters don't wait neither. C'mon, Babe. C'mon, Beau. You folks stay healthy, hear? Lotta flu in town still."

A handwritten note from the publisher asked her to read the pages carefully and notify him by telegram if she found any errors. He went on to say that the volume would be the first book printed on their brand-new linotype machine, a wonder that allowed an experienced user to turn out many thousands of words per hour instead of typesetting one letter at a time. That was pleasing, of course, but even one letter at a time was fine with Teddy. This was their book!

**** 

"Oh goodness!" Teddy got up out of her chair. "I was so excited about the book I forgot the other mail!"

Plates had been cleared twice and dessert bowls scraped, and Teddy ran to get the bag from the living room. There were letters to Bucky from his mother, grandmother, and two sisters; an envelope for Hank that caused him to turn scarlet and immediately stuff the thing in his vest pocket; a seed catalog addressed to Head Gardener at The Long Butte; a small parcel for Caleb; and an envelope addressed to *C and T Ashr, Long Byoot near Shoto MT.*

Puzzled, Teddy opened the envelope and pulled out a single piece of lined paper.

"It's from the newlyweds! In Boston!" She looked up. "Don't leave yet! This is for all of us! *I cousin,*" she read. "*I write for Koolong Izbelle. They learn read write but not good now. They say hello all persons at ranch. Ashr. Miss Teddy. Hayink. Rthr. Bukkee.*"

She wondered if she should pass the letter around so the others could see how their names were spelled. But she had no idea if any of the ranch hands could read, and she didn't want to risk embarrassing them. Besides, she scolded herself, she had no right to make fun of a Chinese person writing in English, a language that didn't even share an alphabet with Chinese, while she couldn't learn French from her own grandfather. Or mischief from Isabelle.

Michif. At least she remembered the name!

"*They say thank Teddy for closes. Ver prett. Thank.*" She looked up. "I don't believe either Ku-Long or Isabelle celebrates Christmas, but I sent a blouse and a shirt anyway."

"Gift-giving is often more a treat for the giver than the receiver."

"How very wise, Caleb!" She looked down again. "*Do well NY. Home. Frends. No guns. No hate Chinaman. Safe. Bizzee. He cook she make closes in room. Sell store down street. Good munnee.* I can believe that! Isabelle is amazing with needles and thread. She could make a dress out of a used burlap sack and women would pay to wear it!"

"Smart little lady."

"You are right, Hank. Isabelle is quick to learn anything, and she is very, very smart." Teddy turned the letter over. "Oh! *Baybee come summer. Ver happee.* A baby! How excellent!"

"And their baby will be born in a place that is safe for them all."

"That makes me happy, Caleb." She looked down the table at her husband, at the man she loved with all her heart. Tonight, she would tell him that a baby might be coming for them too. And she would tell him she loved him.

But not with the others around.

\*\*\*\*

The three ranch hands went out to do evening chores. Caleb disappeared into his office but was back within minutes.

"Leave the dishes for a few minutes, wife." He took her by the shoulders, turned her around, and gently pushed her down into her chair. "I hoped to have this for the holidays but I had to send all the way to Bannack City. A German man there, name of Keppler, has the only jewelry store in the whole state, far as I can tell."

He held out the small box that had come in the mail.

"Caleb, I assured you that you didn't have to get me a gift." She looked up at him earnestly. "You have given me a life here on the ranch. Where I want to be."

"Remember what I said at supper? Gift-giving is not only for the person who gets the gift."

"Oh. Yes."

"It is important for me to give you this." He nudged her hand with his. "Open it."

The first thing she saw was a small irregular rectangle of deep glassy blue.

"Oh! This looks like—It looks like ice. Dark blue ice. No, it looks like the Montana sky just before sundown in full summer. But even clearer."

"It's a Montana sapphire. Dad called it Caleb's Pebble. I found it up on the ridge when I was seven or eight. All three of us searched for more but never found any."

When she picked up the stone with two fingers, she saw it was attached to a thin gold chain.

"Oh! It's a necklace!"

He was grinning now, his dark eyes sparkling. "It is indeed. I asked the jeweler to polish my pebble up a bit and make it into a necklace for my wife." He touched the stone with one long finger. "The whole thing used to be this paler color, sort of milky, but the jeweler tumbled it around with an abrasive to let the glassy rock underneath show. His note said he could do more polishing but there's a danger of breakage. I think I like the contrast, the milky edge and the clear gemstone."

"So do I, Caleb! It is absolutely—It is gorgeous. That's the word! Gorgeous." She held the gem up to the lantern light. "I've never even heard of a Montana sapphire. Another surprise from my chosen home!"

"Hank told me gold miners used to toss these things aside as junk. But now they're in demand for jewelry as far away as Europe. They're almost as hard as diamonds, and they're usually found in rivers or streams so you don't even have to dig. Turn around, wife. Let me put this on you."

He lifted her hair, his fingers caressing her neck.

"There. Let me see."

The brilliant blue gem gleamed against her wool dress.

"I have never had anything this beautiful, Caleb. Thank you. Thank you."

She got up from the chair so she could kiss him.

"When it's warmer upstairs, Teddy, and when we are alone in the house…" His voice trailed off, suddenly deeper and raspy. "I would like you to wear that."

"Of course I will, Caleb! I'm never going to take it off."

He reached up and touched her lips with two fingers. "And nothing else."

"Oh." She knew she was blushing from her knees to the top of her head, and she was suddenly wet between her legs. "Yes. I will do that, Caleb."

"Kiss me again."

"Yes. I will do that, Caleb."

They were both breathing hard when he lifted his head and looked down at her flushed face and swollen lips. "We should stop. Unless—We could try my office. Maybe atop my desk."

"I think that sounds—" She wondered briefly if she should mention Margaret and her husband and their kitchen table. It wasn't a secret. Margaret had told all the women seated around this very kitchen table. But she might not want a man to know. "The others will be back in a few minutes."

He groaned. "I am very much looking forward to spring, wife."

"I am too." She took a deep breath. "Now. It's your turn to sit down, Caleb. I have a gift for you, too." She took his hands and pressed them against her belly. "I believe we have started a child."

She had wondered what his reaction might be. Would he grab her and lift her toward the ceiling and yell his delight? Would his mouth drop open? Would he merely nod and say it was about time?

She had not expected that his whole body would go completely still, or that he would stop breathing.

"Caleb?"

He slowly lifted his head and met her eyes.

"Wife. I am delighted. Overwhelmed." His hands moved over her belly. "Can the baby feel me, do you think?"

"I don't think so. Not yet. I think he or she is only this big." She held up two fingers a half-inch apart. "But your hands are so warm. Maybe our baby can feel your warmth."

His brown eyes were somber. "There are risks in having a child, Teddy."

"I know that. But I'm young and healthy. We will be fine, both me and the babe." Her dimple made a brief appearance. "Even the proud father will be fine."

He didn't smile. "I'm worried about last night. And all the other nights these past few weeks. Is it safe, what we've been doing upstairs?"

"Amelia, the woman in the sewing circle who just had her ninth child, said she and her husband don't— Um. They don't have marital relations for the month before the baby is born, or the month after."

"But surely the baby gets, er, bounced around."

"Maybe it is like being rocked in a cradle." She smoothed back the lock of hair that always fell over his forehead. "There's a lot I don't know, Caleb. I should take the pony cart soon and sit down with Margaret or Amelia and learn what I need to know about the next months. Tomorrow, if the weather holds. You can write down questions too, for me to ask."

"Fine idea." He moved his hands to her hips and pulled her closer, bending so he could put his face against her. "Hello, little one," he murmured. "I will be talking with you often. You will know your mother's voice and mine long before you are born." He looked up. "When, do you think?"

"I didn't—My flow didn't come in January or February—"

He started to speak, but she put her thumb on his mouth.

"You didn't notice because we all had flu in January, and then because of the wolves. I think we made this babe in the first weeks of the year. So he or she will be born in September."

"Are you anxious? Or worried?"

"I keep remembering Bucky's mare, when she gave birth for the first time. Her body knew what to do. I believe my body will know what to do too, when the time comes." Now her eyes were sparkling. "I am excited, Caleb. I want to hold our baby, cuddle him or her, look down at that tiny face. I love this babe already. Our babe."

She moved her hands to his weathered face, which had become so dear to her. His strong jaw and straight nose, the hollows under his cheekbones, the dark mustache, the firm mobile mouth that she loved to kiss, loved to feel on her breasts and neck. With one finger, she traced his eyebrows and then his lips.

"I love you also, Caleb. I know that word makes you uncomfortable, and you don't have to say it. But I have been wanting to tell you for many weeks now. If it will make you more comfortable, perhaps we can find a substitute word." She looked around the kitchen and her eyes fell on the row of potted plants she had brought in from Ku-Long's greenhouse when temperatures began plummeting. "We could say *herb*. Herbs add flavor to life. I herb you, Caleb Asher. Or, no! Ranch! We could say *ranch*. The ranch is huge. And varied. And uniquely beautiful. I ranch you, my husband. I really do."

She couldn't read the expression on his face. Amused? Bemused? Wary?

"Herbs, huh? I—"

"Boss, we needja out in the barn."

Caleb pulled his hands away from his wife's belly.

"That black bull calf took a mind to jump the barb wire fence. Cut up pretty bad. Gonna take two stitchers workin' fast if we're gonna save 'im."

"I'm right behind you."

\*\*\*\*

Caleb could feel the word *love* hanging in the air the next morning. In their bedroom as they quickly pulled on their clothes. Drifting with them down the stairs. Around their heads as they greeted the ranch hands. It even began forming itself in the elderberry syrup he poured on his flapjacks.

"Caleb?"

She must have tried to get his attention more than once, because the other men were all staring at him.

"I asked if you think the calf will survive."

"Oh. Sorry. My mind was elsewhere." He stared down at his plate. Where the hell did half his breakfast go? "That's the biggest Angus bull calf of the year. I hoped to breed him with longhorn heifers, and the longhorn bull with Angus heifers, and that would give us a good start on the hybrid herd." He glanced at his foreman. "Hank and I talked about putting the animal down, but we decided to try and save it."

"Took me and Hank both to hold it," Bucky broke

in. "Betcha Boss and Arthur put two hunnerd stitches into that black hide. Cut up all over, it were."

"The poor thing!"

"Most of the cuts were superficial. If infection doesn't set in, the animal has a good chance of growing into an adult bull." He raised one eyebrow at her. "He will look pretty impressive, strutting around all covered with scars."

"Boss tried that new carbolin stuff."

"Carbolic. Last summer I read an article about treating wounds with carbolic acid to stop infection. Hank picked some up in town."

"Won't the calf worry at the stitches? Try to bite them out?"

Damn, she was pretty. Her cheeks were flushed, and her blue eyes were wide and worried, and he wished he could grab her and kiss her and feel her tongue flirting with his and hold her strong soft body as close to him as they could possibly get with clothes on. The Montana sapphire gleamed against her pale green wool dress, and the soft fabric molded the shape of her breasts, her waist, the flare of her hips and curve of her thighs.

"Arthur fixed up a collar so the animal can't turn its head. We'll take it off to let him nurse."

"Ma's in another stall. Jest step outside and you kin hear her bawlin'. Don't much like being kept away from her baby!"

"I don't imagine any mother would, Bucky."

Caleb wiped up the syrup with the last piece of flapjack, his face a mask, and Hank met Teddy's eyes with a somber frown.

"Caleb. I wanted to ask you. I've never driven a sled. Should I harness up the pony or use one of the bigger horses to go into town?"

A change of subject. And she wanted to talk with another woman, to ask if it was all right for the baby if they mated every night.

"Arthur?"

The little man looked up.

"You're going into town this morning, right? Would you take Teddy as far as—Where?"

"I'd like to stop at Margaret's first. Margaret Pope. If she's not there, I could go a bit farther to Amelia Hazlett's place."

Arthur nodded once.

"It'll be better if Arthur takes you, wife. Packed snow or ice can be tricky." Caleb stood up. "Thank you for an excellent breakfast. Time to get to work."

****

Twelve hours ago, Caleb was happy. He was delighted that she liked his gift. He was excited about their baby. Awed to think the tiny thing was only inches from his hands when he touched her belly. Horny as hell thinking about her wearing the necklace and nothing else.

Now he was just plain confused. His wife loved him. Hell, he probably loved her too. If he thought about the most important people in his life, she was right up there along with Ike and Dad. She was way ahead of his mother, because no matter what excuses Dad made, that woman left her husband and two little boys because she hated ranching and she wanted to walk to the store to buy sugar.

But he didn't want to follow in his father's footsteps. He didn't want to be so much in love with his wife that the emotion destroyed him. He could still see Ike's face

366

the time he got back from a barn dance and punched a fence post and just about broke his hand. While Caleb held his brother's hand under icy spring water, Ike told him that men were talking about their parents and one said their dad wasn't man enough to hold onto a wife and the others laughed. He could still hear the pain in his older brother's voice. He could still see the light die in their father's eyes every single time she asked him to drive her back into Choteau. Loving that woman ate away at their father, stripped him of his dignity. Caleb didn't want to end up a laughingstock. And he sure as hell didn't want to end up so broken by a woman that he looked forward to nothing but death.

That damnable word *love* hung in the air while he and Hank harnessed the black horses to the big sled, loaded winter feed, went around to all the cattle pens, filled the alfalfa feeders, and broke ice on the watering troughs.

"Looks like your new bull's earnin' his keep, boss."

The bull's giant head was raised, lips pulled back, smelling and tasting the air. As Caleb and Hank drew closer, the animal reared on its hind legs, front legs awkwardly straight ahead on both sides of the nearest heifer. Three quick thrusts, a bellow from the heifer, and the bull pulled out and dropped its front feet to the ground.

"Gotta feel good."

"Well, sure, Hank. If that bull could grin, he'd be grinning right now."

"I mean fer you. Gotta feel good to take a chance buyin' that animal and have it pay off."

"It does, Hank. It surely does."

The bull was now butting his head against another

heifer, pushing her toward the fence, smelling her.

"Good crop of calves last fall, 'nother good one this year, mebbe the year after, and that beast'll pay for itself six times over."

"By then the Angus bull calf will be ready to take over, if it lives. And maybe a half dozen or so of this bull's calves."

Hank distracted the longhorn so Caleb could go inside the pen, fill the alfalfa crib and break the ice on the watering trough. By the time the two men had turned the wagon, the huge animal was mounting a third heifer.

"Yes indeed. That risk is going to pay off."

Hank snorted. "Whole thing's a risk. Wouldn't own a ranch if somebody up and give me one!"

Caleb twitched the reins and the team of big horses started the slow trip back.

"Long Butte has benefited greatly from your decision to stay here, Hank, instead of working your own ranch." He went on quickly, before either man could feel uncomfortable. "You're right. There's never a dull day with ranching. Every decision a rancher makes could turn out to be disastrous."

"Not jest decisions, neither. Hard freeze at the wrong time, you start losin' calves. Too much snow all to once, cattle can't move and lay down and die. No rain and you git no winter feed."

"Grass fires."

"Heavy rain jest when the alfalfa's beginnin' to look good."

"Tornadoes."

"Wind like to blow down the windmills."

"Locusts. Not since '74, though."

"Could happen agin."

"It could, Hank."

"Cows git sick. Break a leg."

"Wolves."

"Coyotes. Grizzlies."

Caleb grinned. "It's true, Hank. Ranching is speculation, pure and simple. But every time I stop and look around me, it does my soul good."

"Yup."

****

Yup. Ranching was one risk after another. Caleb was one of the lucky ones. He inherited good acreage, he had excellent men working for him, some of his decisions turned out right, and he'd been pretty fortunate with the weather.

And he had a perfect rancher's wife.

Theodora Barrington had taken risks too, when she decided to stay in Montana instead of going back to Boston where she knew every street, where there were libraries, concert halls, museums, and fancy eateries where girls her age met up with friends for lunch. When she agreed to marry a man she had known less than a year. When she agreed to share his bed, be his mate, bear his children.

Her grandfather took a risk too, coming out here at his age, knowing his heart was failing. They both showed courage, an elderly professor-banker from Boston, and a girl ornithologist. But he, Caleb Asher, Montana rancher, still had one eye on escape. If he never said he loved her, if he kept himself from loving her, then he wouldn't fall apart if she left.

What did that make him?

A coward, he guessed.

He *knew* his wife wasn't like his mother. Teddy was

a fine ranch wife. The men just about worshipped her. She was making the house look like a home. She pitched in and did what had to be done, even while she was working hard to get that book finished. And their time together in bed was better than anything Caleb had ever dreamed.

Now she was carrying his baby.

He would tell her.

Damn if he was going to say he *ranched* her, though. Or *herbed* her, for Pete's sake. He would just come right out and say he loved her. He would tell their children how much he loved them. He would tell them all every single day, more than once.

If he kept on being scared, so be it. His feelings for Teddy weren't likely to change. If she suddenly decided she couldn't stand living on the ranch, if she grew tired of the constant work, if she wanted to be closer to other women, then so be it. They would have had days, months, maybe years of loving first.

Epilogue

Drawing humans was trickier than drawing birds. Dimples appeared for a moment, then they were gone. Eyebrows were fiercely knitted, or one was up and one was down, or both were climbing up a forehead. Eyes squinted against the sun, then opened wide in surprise. Mobile mouths twisted in thought or stretched in laughter, or pouted, or were tight with determination.

Teddy held out her tenth sketch of the morning and eyed it critically. Would she be able to look at her drawing twenty years from now and remember the energy and youth in front of her?

The ranch yard was full of children: the two little ones belonging to Bucky and his Jeannine; the somber lad who came with their quietest ranch hand, newly widowed when he arrived; and the three she shared with Caleb. Their oldest was leading the three youngest of the group in a game involving skipping, marching, hopping, and singing, with occasional bursts of straight-out running, little legs pumping and little arms flailing. Two skinny lads stood apart from the chaos, leaning on the fence like serious old men, deep in conversation. Caleb called their middle child The Thinker, and both parents rejoiced that their Thinker had a companion in the quiet ranch hand's son. The two were always talking, studying, planning, and inventing. They approached Arthur's shop as if it were a shrine, and they were the old man's hands when arthritis prevented him from picking up a nail or using a screwdriver. They started many of their sentences with "Arthur says", although Teddy hadn't heard a word from the man in over a decade.

The second little Thinker and his father showed up

just when Buck's Horse Taming began demanding more and more of his time. Teddy went out to ring the first bell for supper and looked up to see a wagon approaching, driven by a long skinny man with a long sad face. She walked out to greet him, met his sleepy toddler, and invited them in. Over supper, Jed said he'd been a ranch hand in Wyoming since he was a teenager. When asked why they left, the man's face grew even longer and the little boy's eyes filled with tears.

"Boy's mam died," the man mumbled. "Baby daughter too. Figured Eliot and me, we needed a change."

Teddy always thought of that afternoon as the beginning of years of change. And almost all the changes were good.

****

One crisp morning in early fall, a handsome black and gold sign appeared on Main Street: *Flora's Long-term Lodging—Clean and Decent Men Only.* The dour woman told the other seamstresses she knew it was more proper to use a *last* name on the sign but she couldn't bring herself to do her late husband that honor. After a few months, the dapper little ostler and card dealer got off the stagecoach and moved right back into Flora's house, and the general feeling was that Flora deserved whatever happiness she could find.

Flora had been birding with Teddy, often, especially during spring migration when new birds were arriving every day. The older woman said that seeing orioles and hummingbirds and thrushes return, every single year, gave her faith in the kindness of nature.

****

And on one hot day in July, three youngsters

heading for their favorite fishing hole came upon the astonishing sight of the Long Butte Ranch foreman rolling around on the ground with the almost-as-big woman who was principal of the Choteau school and also the eighth-grade teacher. By afternoon, the story was all over town, and by the next morning every rancher and rancher's wife and ranch hand in the whole county knew about the very improper behavior of Miz Wye, the very proper schoolmarm. There was no choice. Hank and his unexpected sweetheart stood up and were married. The new Mrs. Hank, now returned to the semblance of propriety, remained in her position as no-nonsense principal and strict teacher of the occasionally rowdy eighth graders, and the erstwhile foreman of Long Butte Ranch moved his horse and saddle, his duffle bag of clothes, and his favorite coffee mug and settled down to working the twenty acres his bride had inherited from her parents.

The couple wasn't blessed with offspring of their own, although Hank told Bucky it sure weren't for lack of trying. But one evening Miz Wye, as much of the town still called her, came home with two filthy and half-starved children, a three-year-old girl and her five-year-old brother.

"Their father took off," she announced. "Their mother's been trying to make it on her own taking in washing and mending, but the children say she's been sickly for a long time. This morning neighbors took her down to that new hospital run by the holy sisters, in Great Falls. She probably—" She glanced down at the children. "The prognosis is not good, Hank. You and I are taking them in."

So they did. And the town got used to seeing the big

curly-haired man walking around town with a chatty carrot top on his shoulders and a somber tow-headed little boy holding his hand.

****

After Hank's departure, Arthur had the bunkhouse to himself until Caleb and Teddy hired two of the Yoder boys, beefy young men who agreed to stay at least three years while they saved up to buy a ranch down south, near the brand-new town of Billings. When the three years were up, only one of the brothers left and was immediately replaced with yet another Yoder son. Now both young ranch hands spent every free moment courting Amelia Hazlett's two oldest daughters.

"I'm telling you, pets," Amelia laughed as she looked around at the other seamstresses around the Long Butte Ranch kitchen table. "Those boys may be big and they may be strong, but they're gonna have their big strong hands full with *my* girls. My oldest has her heart set on being a *mid*wife, not a ranch wife."

"She could be both, you know," Helen said.

"I know. But I'm jest afraid she'll fall for that Yoder boy even harder than she already has and she'll up and join him on some ranch out in the middle of nowhere afore she finishes training with that traveling nurse from Great Falls."

"We surely need more midwives."

There was a moment of quiet after Jeannine spoke up, and everyone around the table remembered how the young woman might have lost their second child if Bucky hadn't ridden into town in the middle of a howling blizzard, and then even farther up into the hills, and brought back a Metis midwife.

"Amen to that."

\*\*\*\*

Quiet Grace lost her husband to pneumonia after one particularly hard winter. She wore her usual black for five months after his death, and then one brisk June morning she was seen taking a stroll with the new Methodist minister, the man beaming all over his face and Grace decked out in a fluffy pink dress with matching bonnet and parasol. The two were married by Christmas. Grace gave birth to a healthy daughter the following Yule, and the couple turned out a child every December for the next four years and named their brood Noel, Holly, Ivy, Angela, and Joseph.

\*\*\*\*

A year after Jed and his boy moved into Ku-Long's cabin, the solemn man headed into town with the other men to indulge in the pleasures of the orange house. But instead of going inside, Jed crossed the muddy road to help a skinny woman, a girl really, who was wrestling to put storm shutters on a building that looked like it would fall down with the next gust of wind. She glared fiercely and told him she was perfectly capable of managing by herself, thank you *very* much, and she wished men who were interested in *that* house would stay away from *her* yard.

He picked up a shutter anyway, and he spent an afternoon every week for the next month trying to weatherproof her ramshackle house before he threw up his hands and asked her to marry him instead. Now he, his son, and his skinny and sharp-tongued little wife had a new frame house on Long Butte Ranch, around the corner of the ridge where they had some privacy.

\*\*\*\*

Teddy put down her sketchbook and leaned back

against the top step of the porch, hugging her knees. Long Butte Ranch had looked prosperous when she first saw it. It looked even better now. Glossy Angus-Longhorn cattle grazed in the distant fields. A new red barn glowed in the afternoon sun, with a large indoor area where Bucky trained horses in the winter. All the older buildings had been repainted. The log cabin where Teddy had stayed with her grandfather was double its original size now, to fit the young horse trainer's growing family. Ku-Long's gardens had increased every year, and his glass house for growing vegetables was going to be enlarged as soon as Caleb and Jed returned from Choteau with the necessary supplies.

A wide porch now stretched across three-fourths of the house, with three rocking chairs and a wooden chest full of toys. The other one-fourth of the front was Teddy's square little office, warmed by the cooking stoves, with a built-in desk and bookshelves, a window facing the front yard and another facing the side yard, and a clever pocket door to close when she needed uninterrupted time to work. Her shelves now held copies of five books: the heavy tome with her grandfather's name and hers on the cover, and four more recent books with her name only. On the desk was a high pile of paper, waiting for her to complete organizing her notes about courtship patterns of Montana's migratory waterfowl.

"Papa! Papa!"

"Dad!"

The two Thinkers bolted from the fence and pelted along the ranch road toward the Long Butte sign. Now the other children saw the buckboard and the two big horses, the pile of lumber and wooden boxes, and Caleb and Jed in the front. Teddy stood up, sketching forgotten, and watched as Caleb stopped the horses and all the children piled in, some on the men's laps, some between them on the front seat, the rest in the back. As the wagon drew up to the main house, her husband slowed the horses and stopped and there was a brief reshuffling of children. Then he jumped to the ground and Jed slid over and took the reins.

"It's gonna take Jed twice as long as usual to take care of the horse and wagon," he put an arm around her shoulder and winked at her. "I told the kids he would have a special job for every one of them."

"He will, too. He's very good with children."

"He is indeed." He pulled her closer. "And you and I have a few minutes to ourselves."

He lifted his head a few blissful moments later, and Teddy slowly opened her eyes.

"Thirteen years married," she murmured, "and we have never kissed like that out in the open, where anyone could see us."

"Past time then." He tightened his arms until she felt the unmistakable surge of his maleness against her belly. "Thirteen years married and you still have this effect on me."

"And you—And I—You still make me wet and soft, Caleb."

"A wonderful system."

"Indeed it is."

"I was thinking about that wonderful system all the way back from town. I didn't hear a word Jed said."

"I'd be surprised if he said much anyway."

"True. Now..." He took her arms and held her away from him. "We have been given a gift, thanks to Hank and his Ellie. A whole day and a whole night for kissing and…" He raised both eyebrows. "And whatever we might want to do."

"I am mystified. What do Hank and Ellie have to do with, um, our kissing?"

"There's a traveling rodeo show coming to Choteau day after tomorrow. Hank and Ellie are taking their two, and they suggested we all come in for the ten in the morning show. And then you and I head home and they'll take the whole kit and caboodle to the town barbecue in the afternoon, keep 'em overnight, take 'em to the morning rodeo if they're interested, and then drive out and deliver to us what is ours."

"Kit and caboodle?"

"Just heard that, in town. It means the whole thing, every single piece."

"And what did you tell them? Hank and Ellie?"

"Is there any doubt? I almost grabbed Hank and kissed his furry face." His eyes darkened until they were almost all black. "If we have a night alone, Teddy, we could make noise."

"We could, couldn't we? You might even roar, like you used to."

"I might," he agreed solemnly. "And I will do everything in my power to ensure that you do some noise-making as well. All the way home I was thinking up ways to make you howl. I even thought of a couple of moves that might have you yipping like a coyote."

"Caleb! Proper Bostonian ladies do *not* yip!"

"You have never been a proper Bostonian lady, Teddy Barrington Asher."

She tilted her head back, her eyes sparkling with mischief, and sent several authentic-sounding coyote sounds into the air while he laughed, picked her up, and twirled her around.

"We'll have to close the windows, Caleb," she said breathlessly. "The ranch hands will still be here."

"Nope. We'll do morning chores and then give everyone the day off to go to the rodeo and the barbecue."

"That is a splendid idea. Truly splendid."

"Hank and his wife have an anniversary coming up next month, and he wants to take her out for a fine meal at the hotel and then a leisurely stroll back to their house and then…"

"So we could take their two kids for the night."

"We could, and we should."

"Maybe trading off like that will become a tradition."

"A fine idea, wife."

"Would you ring the first supper bell?"

They climbed the porch stairs together, arms around each other's waists.

"Wife?'

"Yes, Caleb?"

"I deeply love you."

"I deeply love you too."

# APPENDIX

Teddy and her grandfather saw many birds that now have different names than they did in the 1800s. The Latin, or scientific, names rarely change, but common English names can be changed by the American Ornithological Union for various reasons. These include: new or more extensive information about a species' range; consistency with the same species' name elsewhere in its range; changing cultural sensitivities; DNA testing that shows that one species is actually more than one or that two species are actually one.

## Old Name...Current Name

Blue Goose...morph of Snow Goose
Baldpate...American Wigeon
Carolina Rail...Sora
Western Nighthawk...Common Nighthawk
Upland Plover...Upland Sandpiper
Holboell's Grebe...Red-necked Grebe
Buzzard...Turkey Vulture
Ferruginous Rough-legged Hawk...Ferruginous Hawk
Batchelder's Woodpecker...Downy Woodpecker
Wright's Flycatcher...Gray Flycatcher
White-rumped Shrike...Loggerhead Shrike
Black-headed Jay or Rocky Mountain Jay...Steller's Jay
Long-tailed Chickadee...Black-capped Chickadee
Pallid Horned Lark...Horned Lark
Willow Thrush...Veery
Western Vesper Sparrow...Vesper Sparrow
Pileolated Warbler ...Wilson's Warbler
Rocky Mountain Grosbeak...Pine Grosbeak

**A word about the author...**

Maeve Kim is a teacher, nature guide, gardener, musician and writer. She lives in Vermont with her sweetheart, living a romance and writing about romance. She has visited central Montana twice and fell in love with the wind-sculpted scenery and the smell of wild sage.

Thank you for purchasing
this publication of The Wild Rose Press, Inc.

For questions or more information
contact us at
info@thewildrosepress.com.

The Wild Rose Press, Inc.
www.thewildrosepress.com